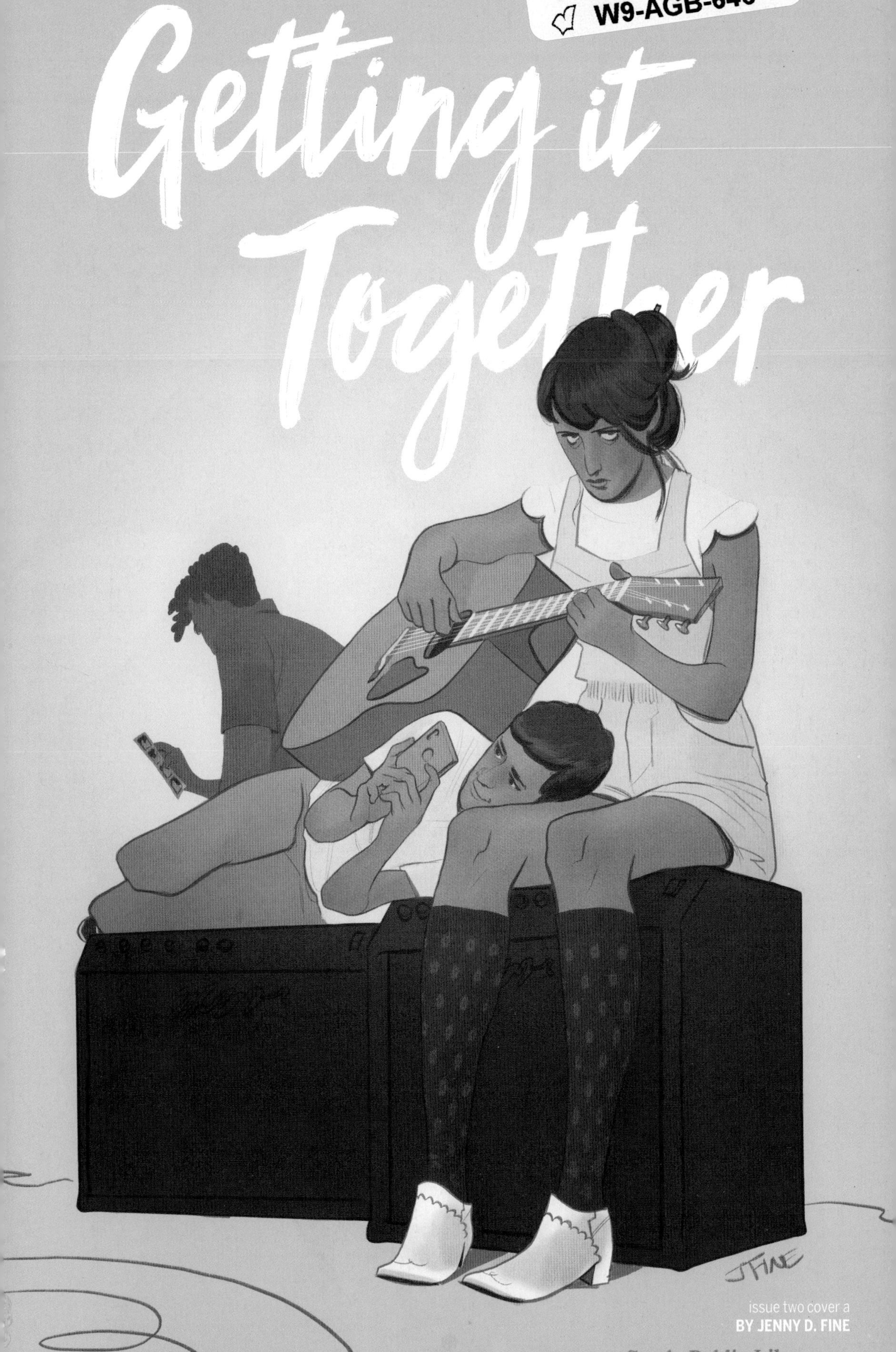
Getting it Together
JFINE
issue two cover a
BY JENNY D. FINE

issue one
knowhere games & comics retailer exclusive
BY SINA GRACE & MX. STRUBLE

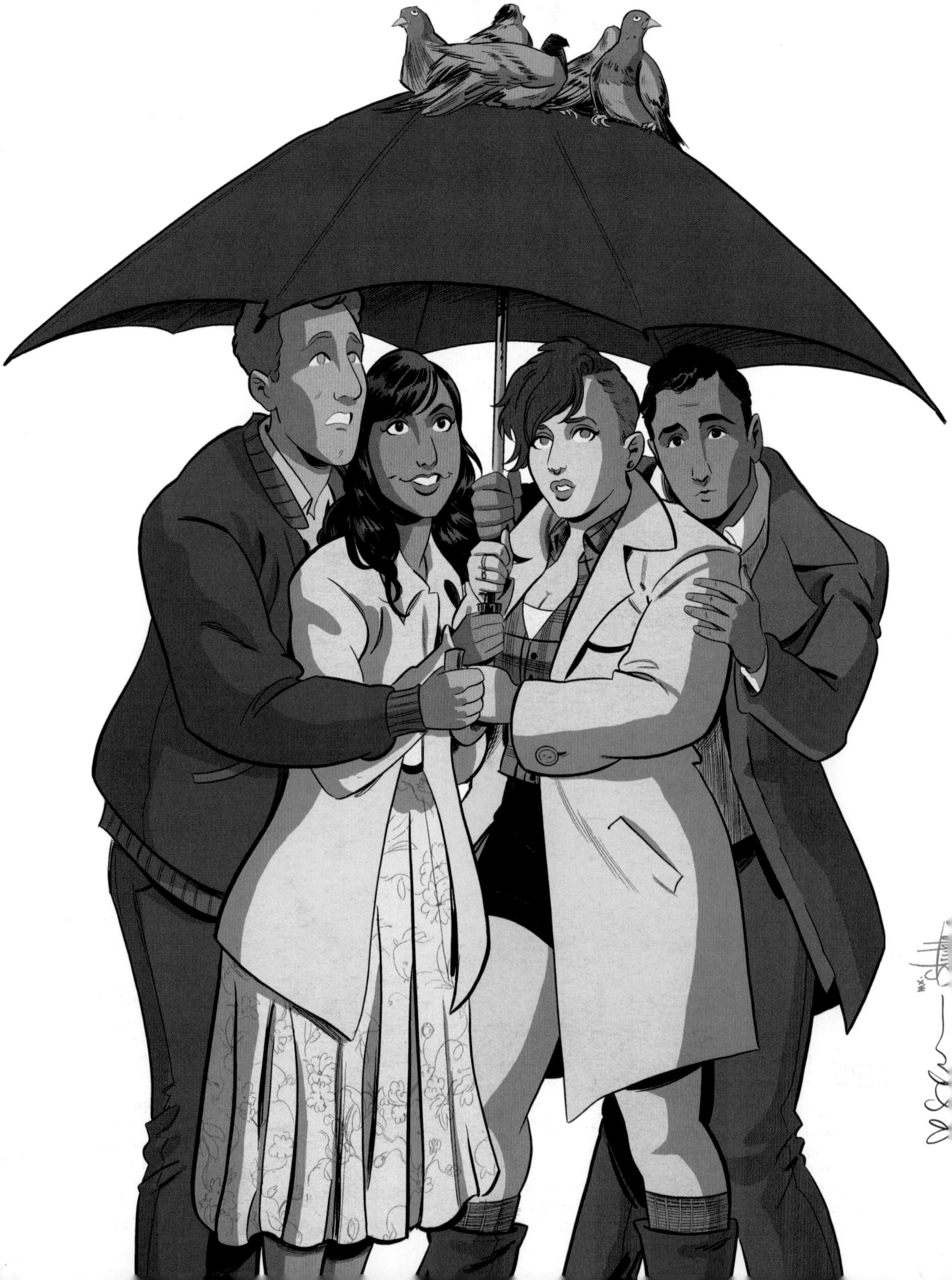

Getting it Together

CO-CREATORS/CO-WRITERS
SINA GRACE & OMAR SPAHI

ARTISTS
JENNY D. FINE (pretty much everything)
SINA GRACE (flashbacks & Lauren's chapter)

COLORIST
MX. STRUBLE

BACK-UP STORIES ARTIST
ERIKA SCHNATZ

LETTERER
SEAN KONOT

EDITOR
SHANNA MATUSZAK

COVER ARTIST
JENNY D. FINE

PRODUCTION DESIGN
ERIKA SCHNATZ

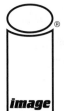

IMAGE COMICS, INC. • **Todd McFarlane**: President • **Jim Valentino**: Vice President • **Marc Silvestri**: Chief Executive Officer • **Erik Larsen**: Chief Financial Officer • **Robert Kirkman**: Chief Operating Officer • **Eric Stephenson**: Publisher / Chief Creative Officer • **Nicole Lapalme**: Controller • **Leanna Caunter**: Accounting Analyst • **Sue Korpela**: Accounting & HR Manager • **Marla Eizik**: Talent Liaison • **Jeff Boison**: Director of Sales & Publishing Planning • **Dirk Wood**: Director of International Sales & Licensing • **Alex Cox**: Director of Direct Market Sales • **Chloe Ramos**: Book Market & Library Sales Manager • **Emilio Bautista**: Digital Sales Coordinator • **Jon Schlaffman**: Specialty Sales Coordinator • **Kat Salazar**: Director of PR & Marketing • **Drew Fitzgerald**: Marketing Content Associate • **Heather Doornink**: Production Director • **Drew Gill**: Art Director • **Hilary DiLoreto**: Print Manager • **Tricia Ramos**: Traffic Manager • **Melissa Gifford**: Content Manager • **Erika Schnatz**: Senior Production Artist • **Ryan Brewer**: Production Artist • **Deanna Phelps**: Production Artist • **IMAGECOMICS.COM**

GETTING IT TOGETHER, VOL. 1. First printing. March 2021. Published by Image Comics, Inc. Office of publication: PO BOX 14457, Portland, OR 97293. Copyright © 2021 Sina Grace & Omar Spahi. All rights reserved. Contains material originally published in single magazine form as GETTING IT TOGETHER #1-4. "Getting It Together," its logos, and the likenesses of all characters herein are trademarks of Sina Grace & Omar Spahi, unless otherwise noted. "Image" and the Image Comics logos are registered trademarks of Image Comics, Inc. No part of this publication may be reproduced or transmitted, in any form or by any means (except for short excerpts for journalistic or review purposes), without the express written permission of Sina Grace & Omar Spahi, or Image Comics, Inc. All names, characters, events, and locales in this publication are entirely fictional. Any resemblance to actual persons (living or dead), events, or places, without satirical intent, is coincidental. Printed in the USA. Representation: Law Offices of Harris M. Miller II, P.C. (rightsinquiries@gmail.com). ISBN: 978-1-5343-1776-5.

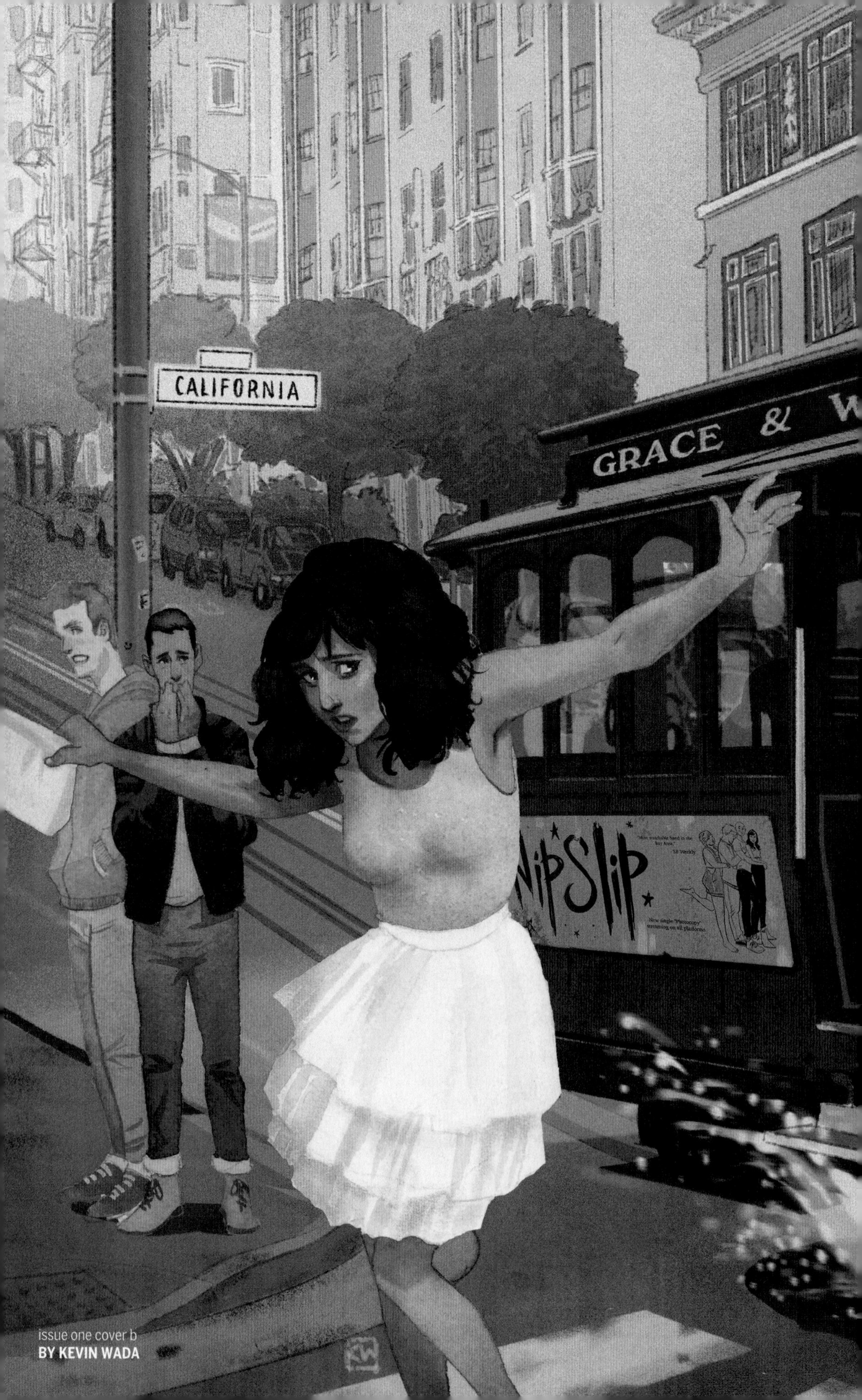

issue one cover b
BY KEVIN WADA

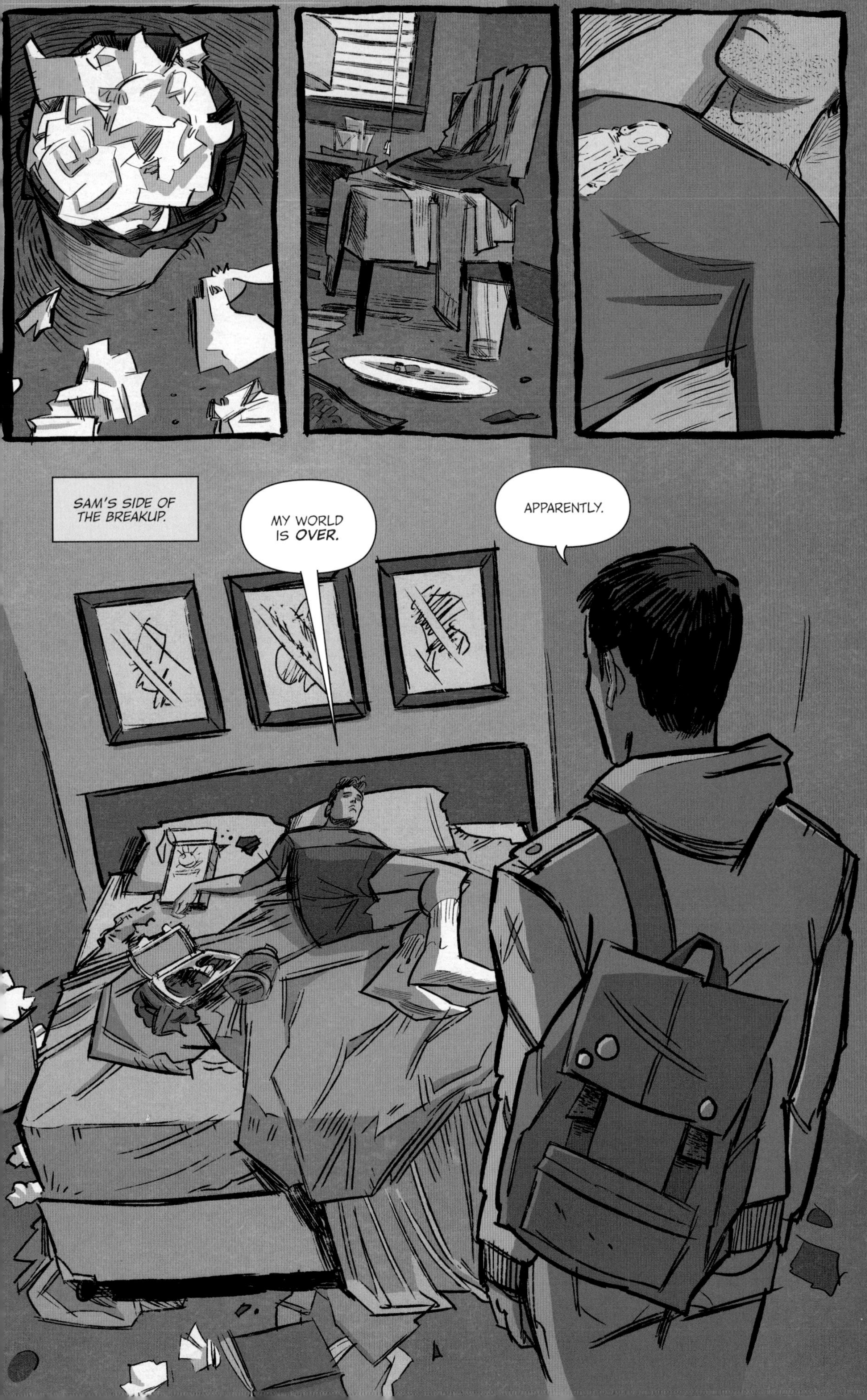
SAM'S SIDE OF THE BREAKUP.
MY WORLD IS OVER.
APPARENTLY.

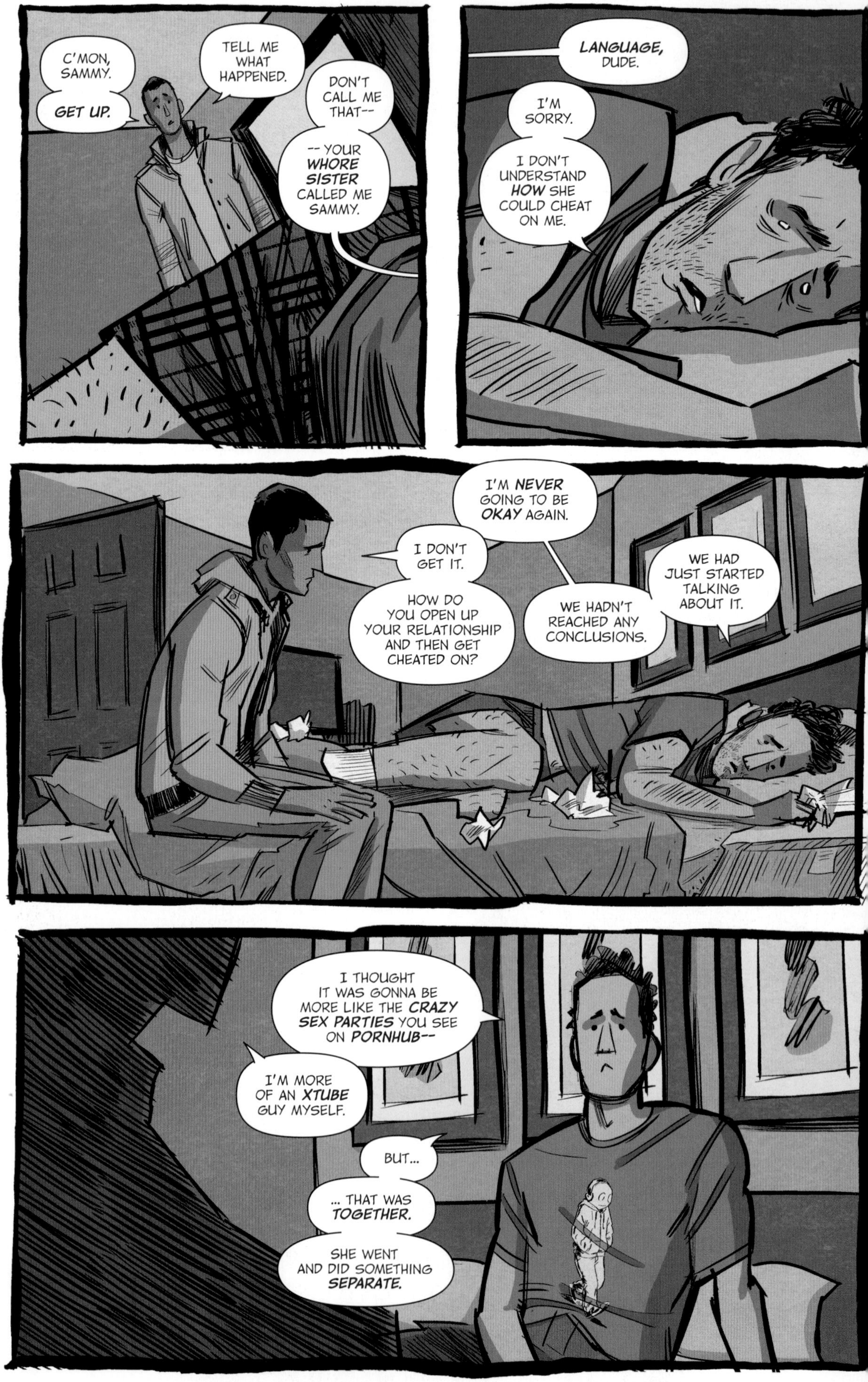
C'MON, SAMMY.
GET UP.
TELL ME WHAT HAPPENED.
DON'T CALL ME THAT--
-- YOUR WHORE SISTER CALLED ME SAMMY.
LANGUAGE, DUDE.
I'M SORRY.
I DON'T UNDERSTAND HOW SHE COULD CHEAT ON ME.
I'M NEVER GOING TO BE OKAY AGAIN.
I DON'T GET IT.
HOW DO YOU OPEN UP YOUR RELATIONSHIP AND THEN GET CHEATED ON?
WE HADN'T REACHED ANY CONCLUSIONS.
WE HAD JUST STARTED TALKING ABOUT IT.
I THOUGHT IT WAS GONNA BE MORE LIKE THE CRAZY SEX PARTIES YOU SEE ON PORNHUB--
I'M MORE OF AN XTUBE GUY MYSELF.
BUT...
... THAT WAS TOGETHER.
SHE WENT AND DID SOMETHING SEPARATE.

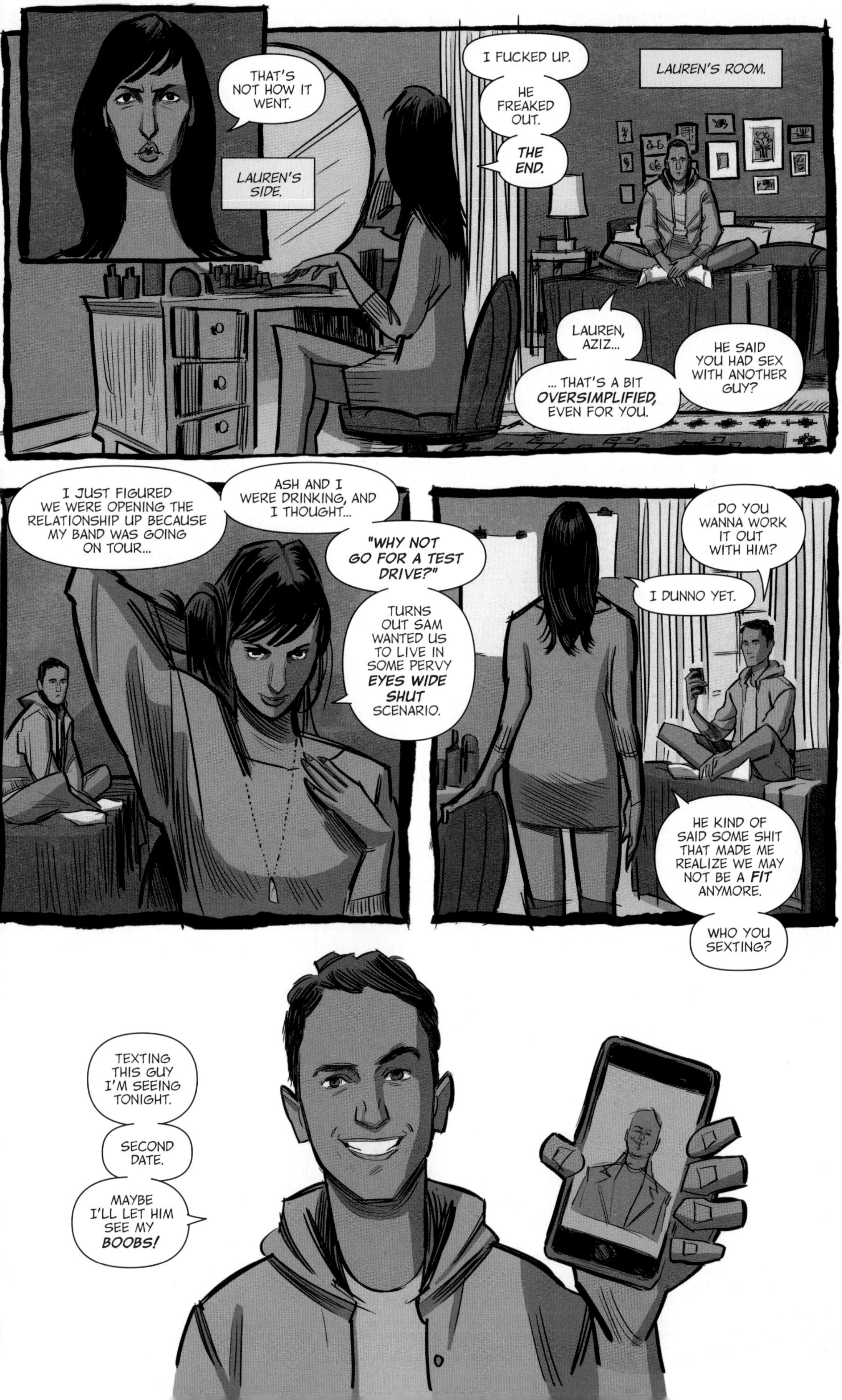
THAT'S NOT HOW IT WENT.
LAUREN'S SIDE.
I FUCKED UP.
HE FREAKED OUT.
THE END.
LAUREN'S ROOM.
LAUREN, AZIZ...
... THAT'S A BIT OVERSIMPLIFIED, EVEN FOR YOU.
HE SAID YOU HAD SEX WITH ANOTHER GUY?
I JUST FIGURED WE WERE OPENING THE RELATIONSHIP UP BECAUSE MY BAND WAS GOING ON TOUR...
ASH AND I WERE DRINKING, AND I THOUGHT...
"WHY NOT GO FOR A TEST DRIVE?"
TURNS OUT SAM WANTED US TO LIVE IN SOME PERVY EYES WIDE SHUT SCENARIO.
DO YOU WANNA WORK IT OUT WITH HIM?
I DUNNO YET.
HE KIND OF SAID SOME SHIT THAT MADE ME REALIZE WE MAY NOT BE A FIT ANYMORE.
WHO YOU SEXTING?
TEXTING THIS GUY I'M SEEING TONIGHT.
SECOND DATE.
MAYBE I'LL LET HIM SEE MY BOOBS!

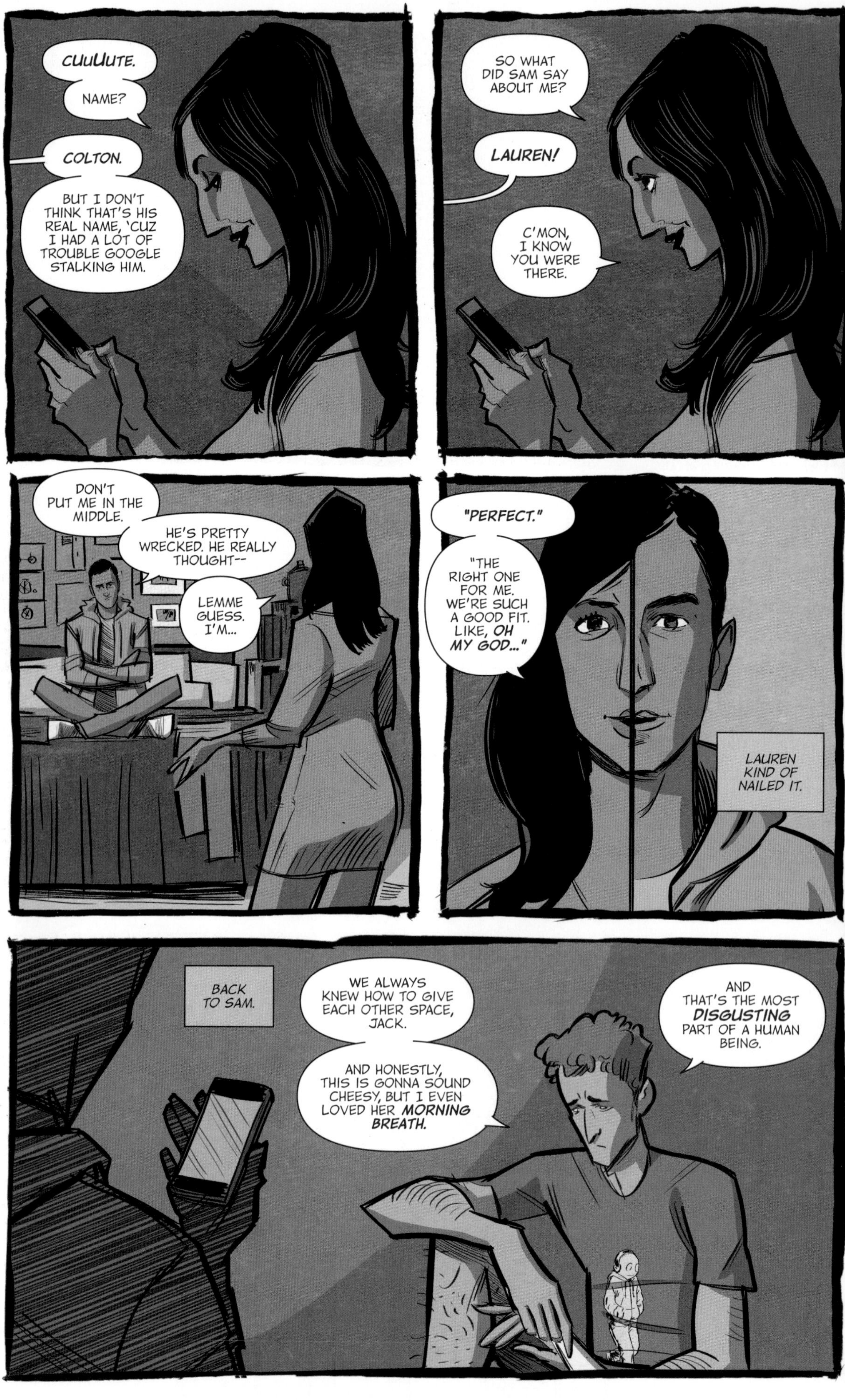
CUUUUTE.
NAME?
COLTON.
BUT I DON'T THINK THAT'S HIS REAL NAME, 'CUZ I HAD A LOT OF TROUBLE GOOGLE STALKING HIM.
SO WHAT DID SAM SAY ABOUT ME?
LAUREN!
C'MON, I KNOW YOU WERE THERE.
DON'T PUT ME IN THE MIDDLE.
HE'S PRETTY WRECKED. HE REALLY THOUGHT--
LEMME GUESS. I'M...
"PERFECT."
"THE RIGHT ONE FOR ME. WE'RE SUCH A GOOD FIT. LIKE, OH MY GOD..."
LAUREN KIND OF NAILED IT.
BACK TO SAM.
WE ALWAYS KNEW HOW TO GIVE EACH OTHER SPACE, JACK.
AND HONESTLY, THIS IS GONNA SOUND CHEESY, BUT I EVEN LOVED HER MORNING BREATH.
AND THAT'S THE MOST DISGUSTING PART OF A HUMAN BEING.

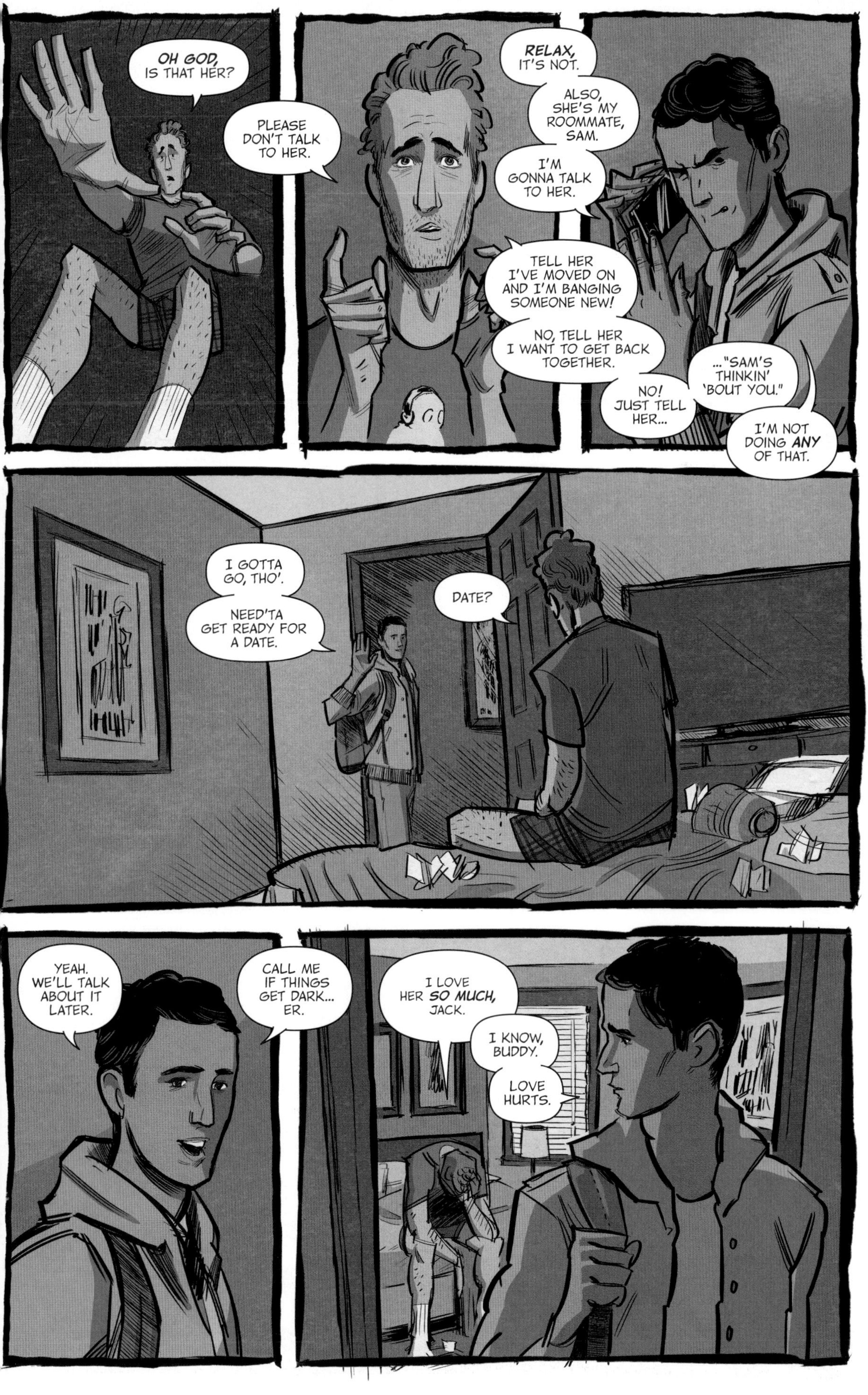
OH GOD, IS THAT HER?
PLEASE DON'T TALK TO HER.
RELAX, IT'S NOT.
ALSO, SHE'S MY ROOMMATE, SAM.
I'M GONNA TALK TO HER.
TELL HER I'VE MOVED ON AND I'M BANGING SOMEONE NEW!
NO, TELL HER I WANT TO GET BACK TOGETHER.
NO! JUST TELL HER...
..."SAM'S THINKIN' 'BOUT YOU."
I'M NOT DOING ANY OF THAT.
I GOTTA GO, THO'.
NEED'TA GET READY FOR A DATE.
DATE?
YEAH. WE'LL TALK ABOUT IT LATER.
CALL ME IF THINGS GET DARK... ER.
I LOVE HER SO MUCH, JACK.
I KNOW, BUDDY.
LOVE HURTS.

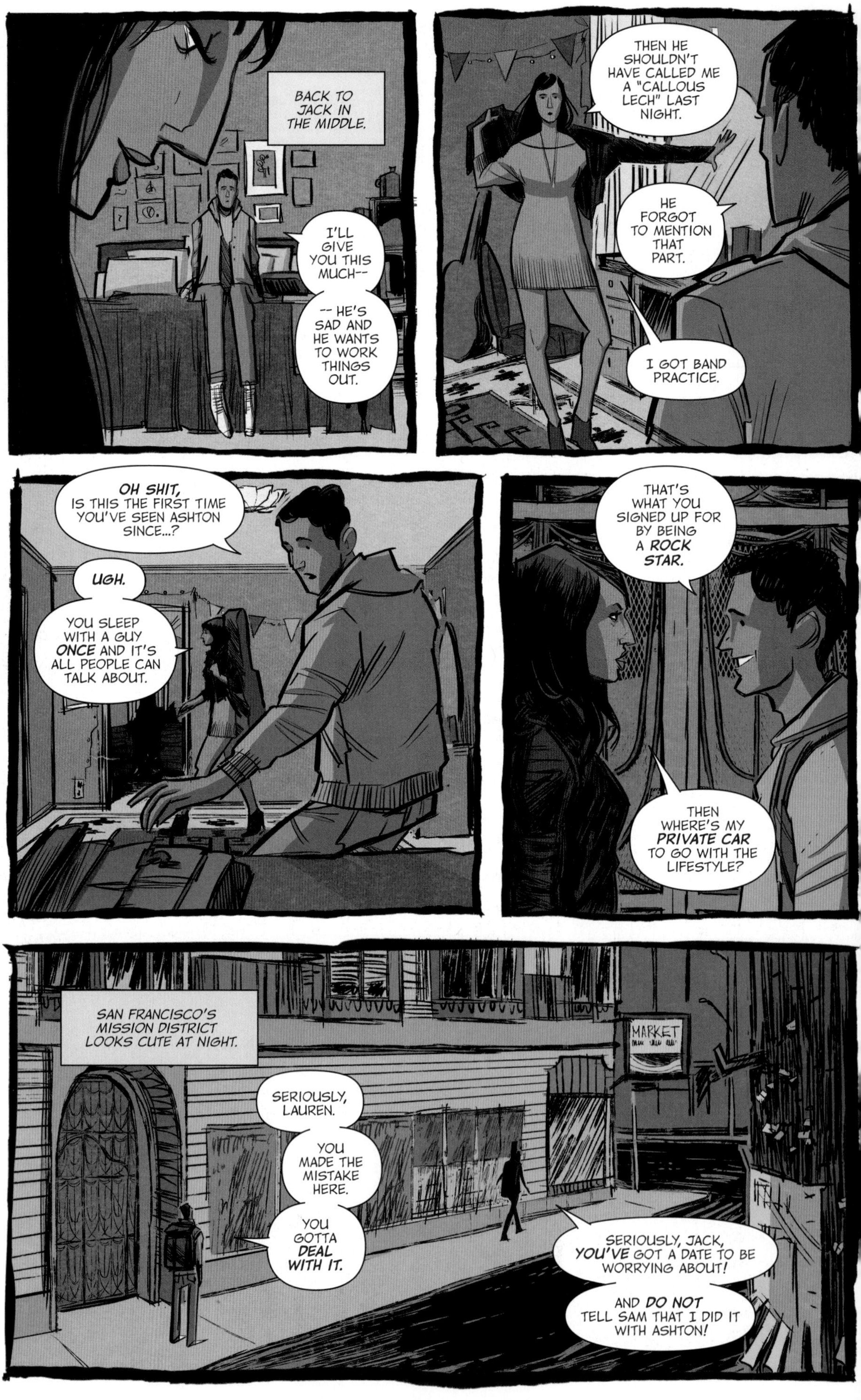
BACK TO JACK IN THE MIDDLE.
I'LL GIVE YOU THIS MUCH--
-- HE'S SAD AND HE WANTS TO WORK THINGS OUT.
THEN HE SHOULDN'T HAVE CALLED ME A "CALLOUS LECH" LAST NIGHT.
HE FORGOT TO MENTION THAT PART.
I GOT BAND PRACTICE.
OH SHIT, IS THIS THE FIRST TIME YOU'VE SEEN ASHTON SINCE...?
UGH.
YOU SLEEP WITH A GUY ONCE AND IT'S ALL PEOPLE CAN TALK ABOUT.
THAT'S WHAT YOU SIGNED UP FOR BY BEING A ROCK STAR.
THEN WHERE'S MY PRIVATE CAR TO GO WITH THE LIFESTYLE?
SAN FRANCISCO'S MISSION DISTRICT LOOKS CUTE AT NIGHT.
MARKET
SERIOUSLY, LAUREN.
YOU MADE THE MISTAKE HERE.
YOU GOTTA DEAL WITH IT.
SERIOUSLY, JACK, YOU'VE GOT A DATE TO BE WORRYING ABOUT!
AND DO NOT TELL SAM THAT I DID IT WITH ASHTON!

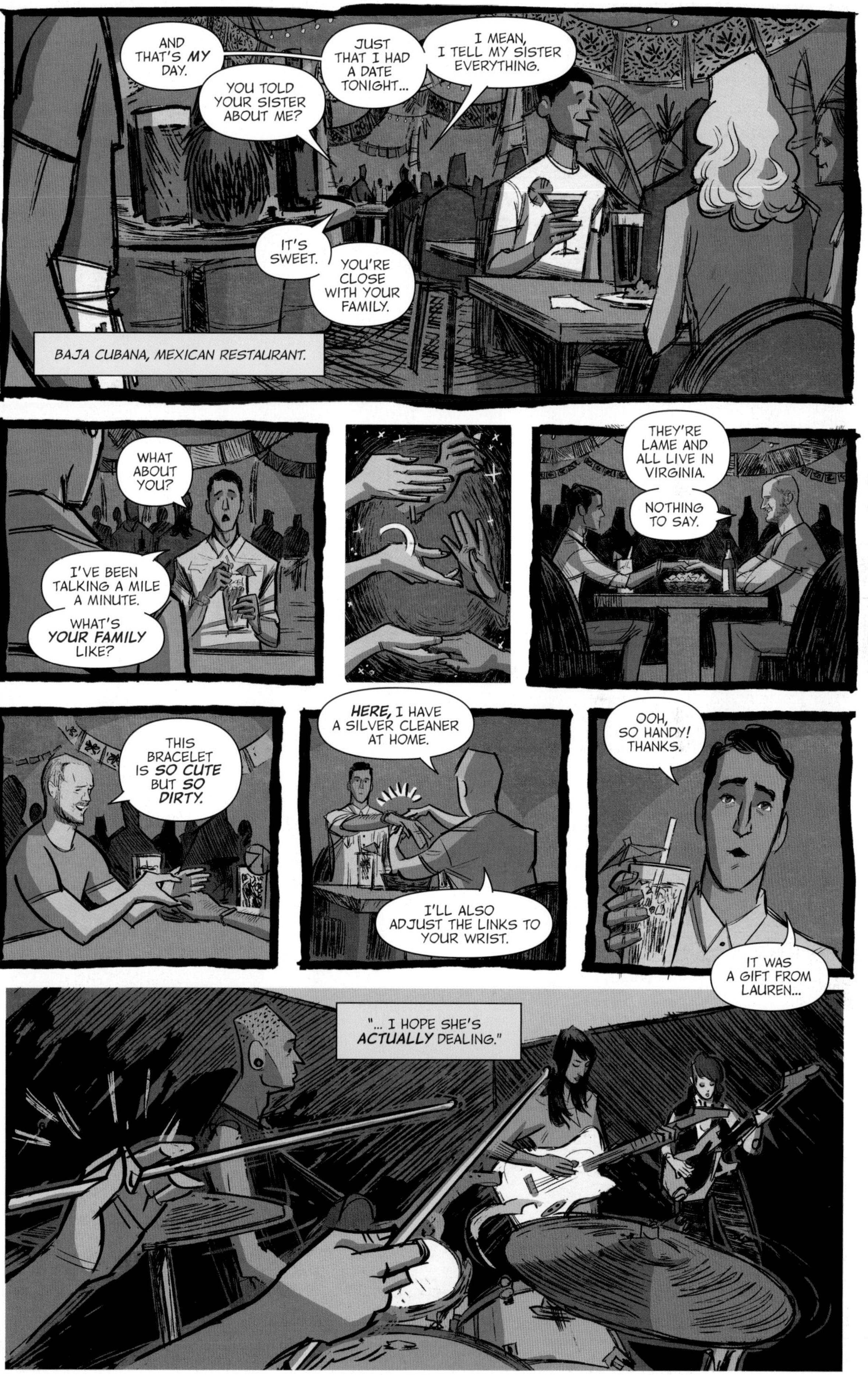
AND THAT'S MY DAY.
JUST THAT I HAD A DATE TONIGHT...
I MEAN, I TELL MY SISTER EVERYTHING.
YOU TOLD YOUR SISTER ABOUT ME?
IT'S SWEET.
YOU'RE CLOSE WITH YOUR FAMILY.
BAJA CUBANA, MEXICAN RESTAURANT.
WHAT ABOUT YOU?
I'VE BEEN TALKING A MILE A MINUTE.
WHAT'S YOUR FAMILY LIKE?
THEY'RE LAME AND ALL LIVE IN VIRGINIA.
NOTHING TO SAY.
THIS BRACELET IS SO CUTE BUT SO DIRTY.
HERE, I HAVE A SILVER CLEANER AT HOME.
I'LL ALSO ADJUST THE LINKS TO YOUR WRIST.
OOH, SO HANDY! THANKS.
IT WAS A GIFT FROM LAUREN...
"... I HOPE SHE'S ACTUALLY DEALING."

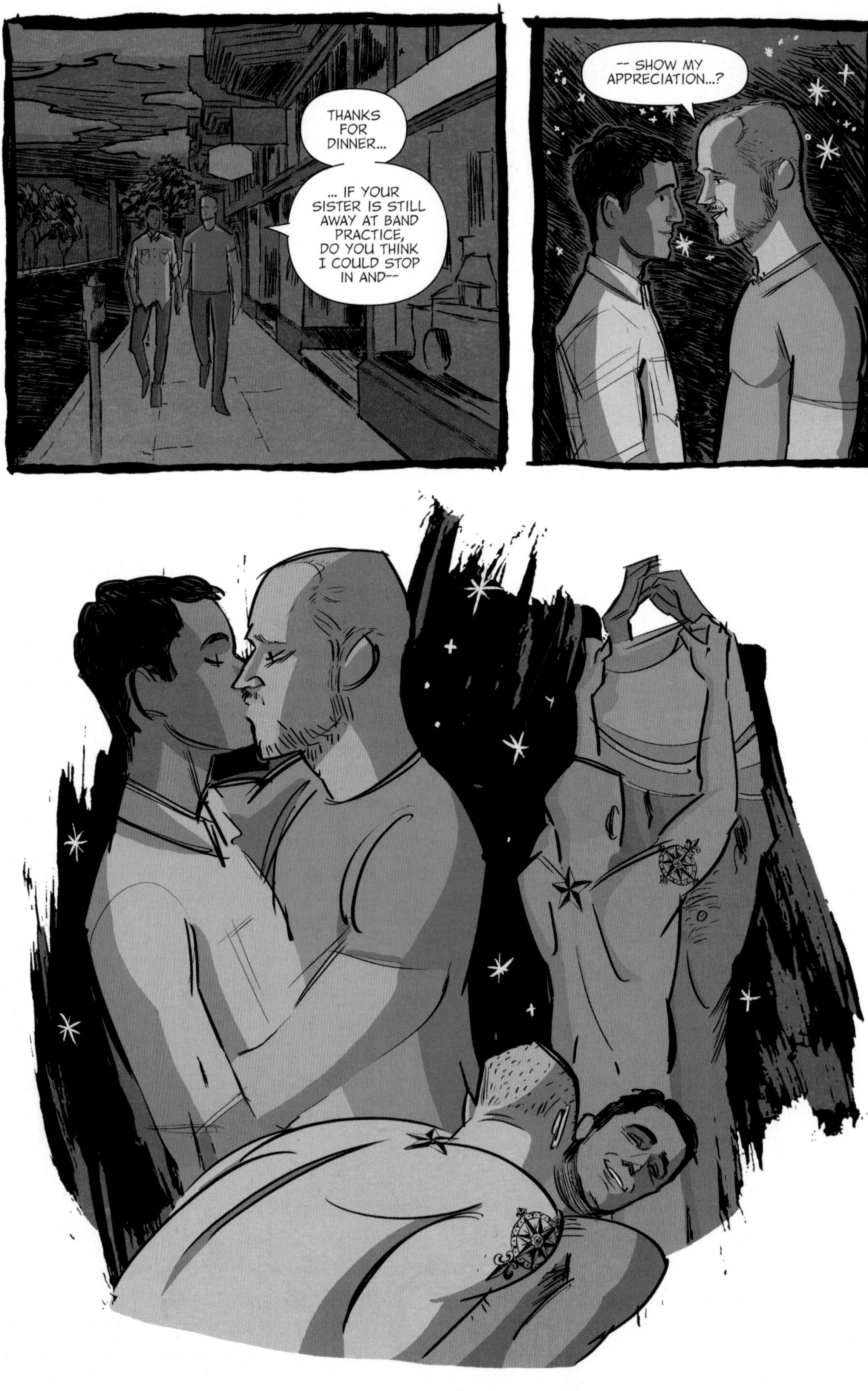
THANKS FOR DINNER...
... IF YOUR SISTER IS STILL AWAY AT BAND PRACTICE, DO YOU THINK I COULD STOP IN AND--
-- SHOW MY APPRECIATION...?

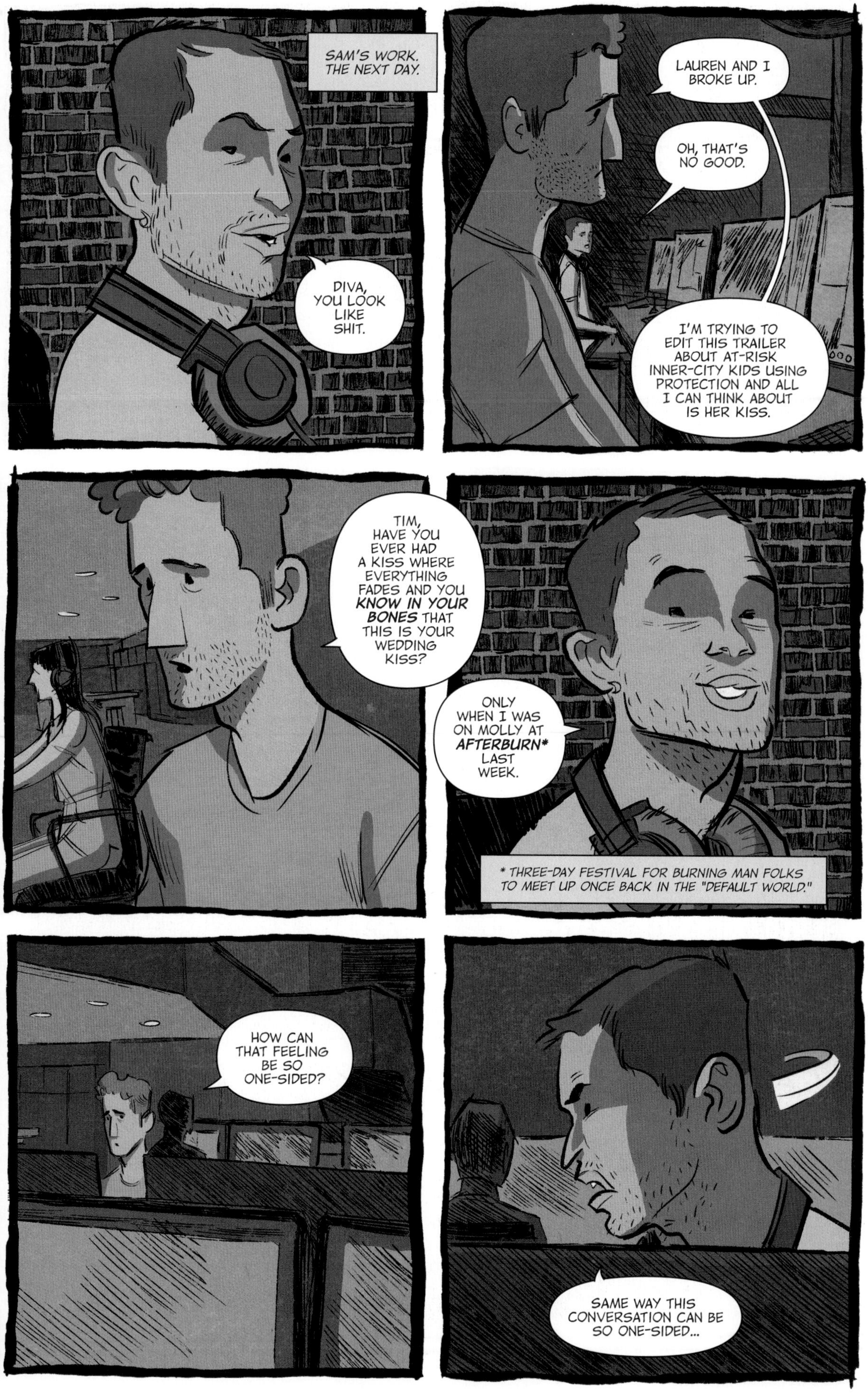
SAM'S WORK. THE NEXT DAY.
DIVA, YOU LOOK LIKE SHIT.
LAUREN AND I BROKE UP.
OH, THAT'S NO GOOD.
I'M TRYING TO EDIT THIS TRAILER ABOUT AT-RISK INNER-CITY KIDS USING PROTECTION AND ALL I CAN THINK ABOUT IS HER KISS.
TIM, HAVE YOU EVER HAD A KISS WHERE EVERYTHING FADES AND YOU KNOW IN YOUR BONES THAT THIS IS YOUR WEDDING KISS?
ONLY WHEN I WAS ON MOLLY AT AFTERBURN* LAST WEEK.
* THREE-DAY FESTIVAL FOR BURNING MAN FOLKS TO MEET UP ONCE BACK IN THE "DEFAULT WORLD."
HOW CAN THAT FEELING BE SO ONE-SIDED?
SAME WAY THIS CONVERSATION CAN BE SO ONE-SIDED...

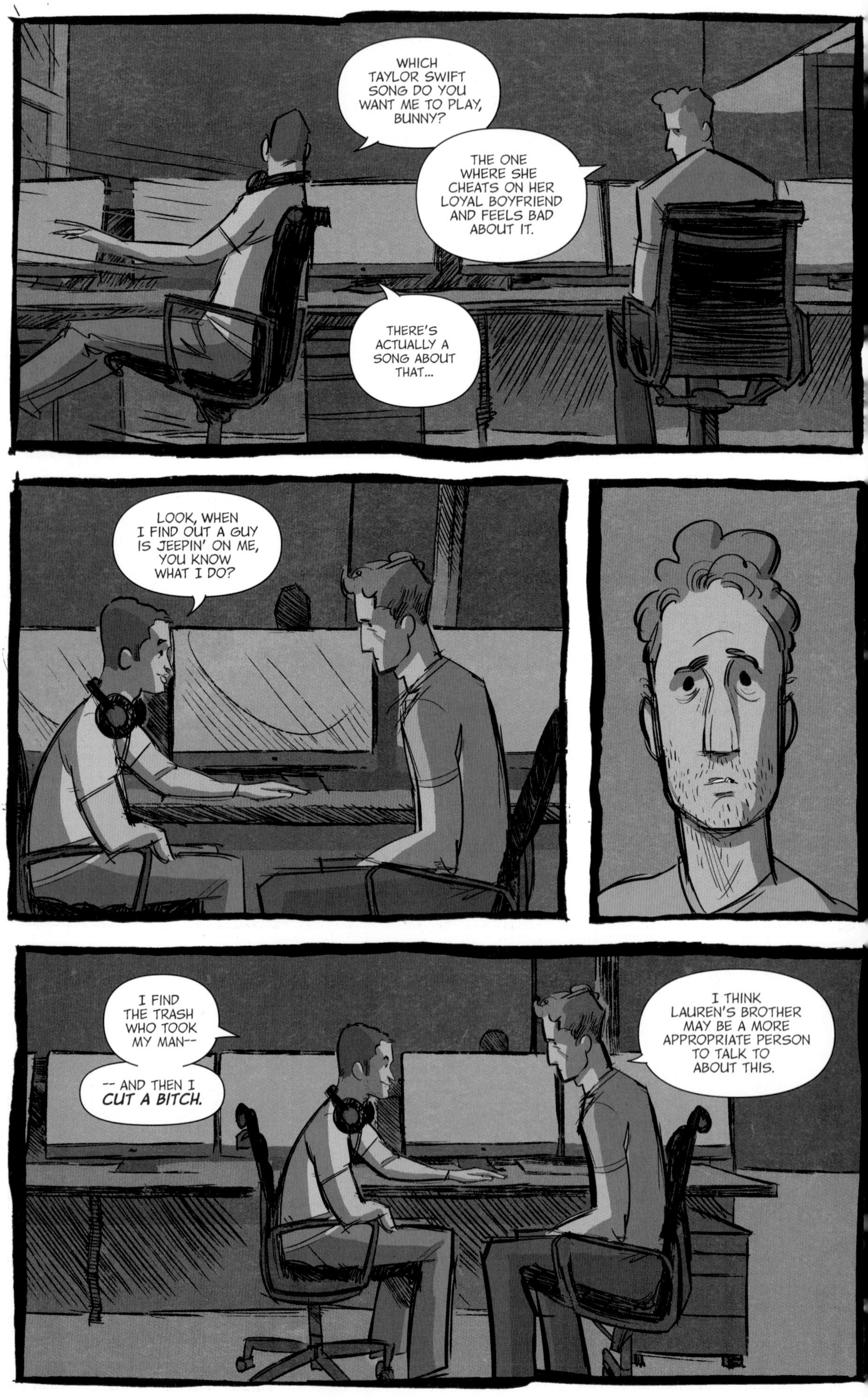
WHICH TAYLOR SWIFT SONG DO YOU WANT ME TO PLAY, BUNNY?
THE ONE WHERE SHE CHEATS ON HER LOYAL BOYFRIEND AND FEELS BAD ABOUT IT.
THERE'S ACTUALLY A SONG ABOUT THAT...
LOOK, WHEN I FIND OUT A GUY IS JEEPIN' ON ME, YOU KNOW WHAT I DO?
I FIND THE TRASH WHO TOOK MY MAN--
-- AND THEN I *CUT A BITCH.*
I THINK LAUREN'S BROTHER MAY BE A MORE APPROPRIATE PERSON TO TALK TO ABOUT THIS.

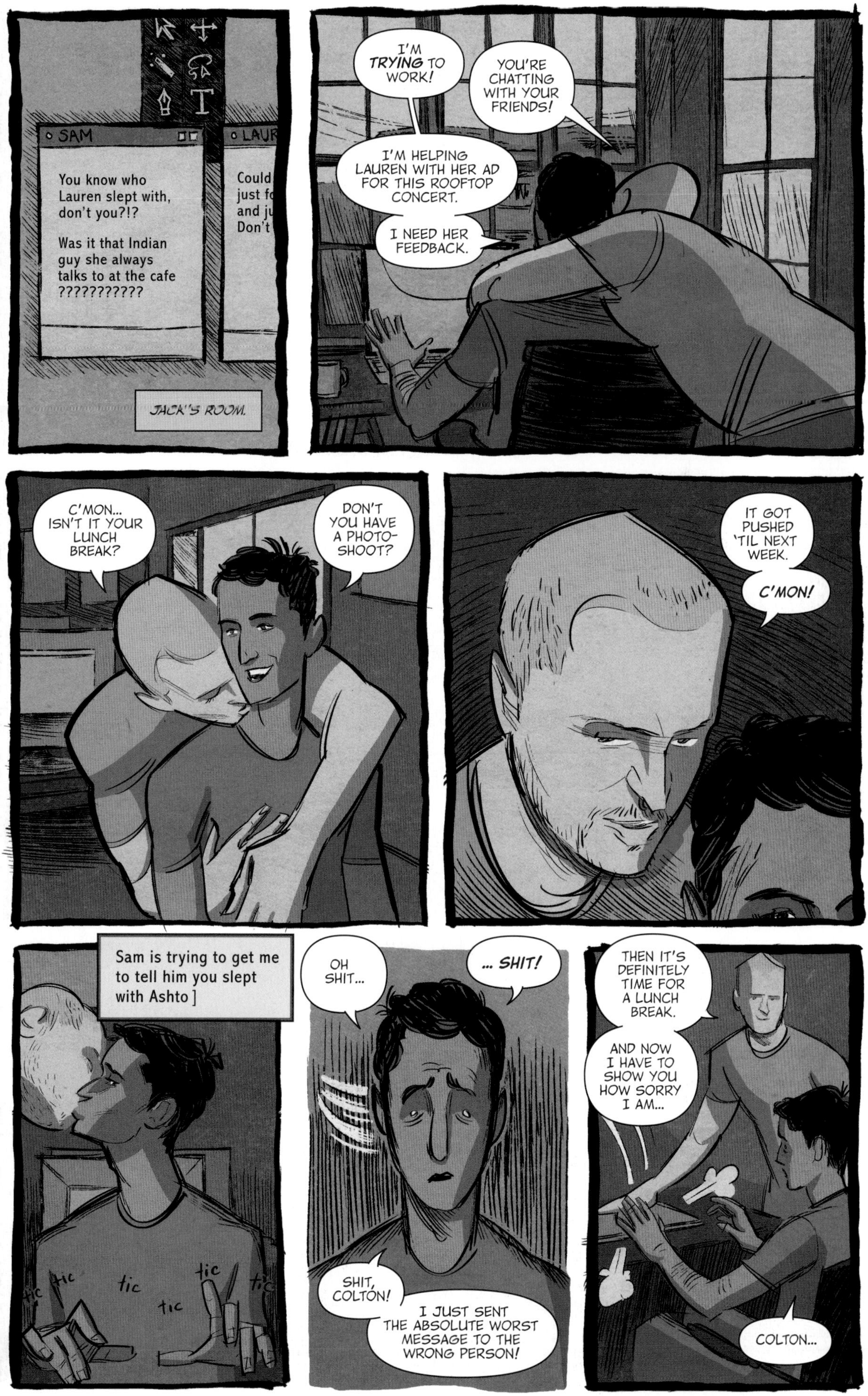
SAM
You know who Lauren slept with, don't you?!?
Was it that Indian guy she always talks to at the cafe ???????????
LAUR
Could
just f
and j
Don't
JACK'S ROOM.
I'M TRYING TO WORK!
YOU'RE CHATTING WITH YOUR FRIENDS!
I'M HELPING LAUREN WITH HER AD FOR THIS ROOFTOP CONCERT.
I NEED HER FEEDBACK.
C'MON... ISN'T IT YOUR LUNCH BREAK?
DON'T YOU HAVE A PHOTO-SHOOT?
IT GOT PUSHED 'TIL NEXT WEEK.
C'MON!
Sam is trying to get me to tell him you slept with Ashto]
tic tic tic tic tic tic
OH SHIT...
... SHIT!
SHIT, COLTON!
I JUST SENT THE ABSOLUTE WORST MESSAGE TO THE WRONG PERSON!
THEN IT'S DEFINITELY TIME FOR A LUNCH BREAK.
AND NOW I HAVE TO SHOW YOU HOW SORRY I AM...
COLTON...

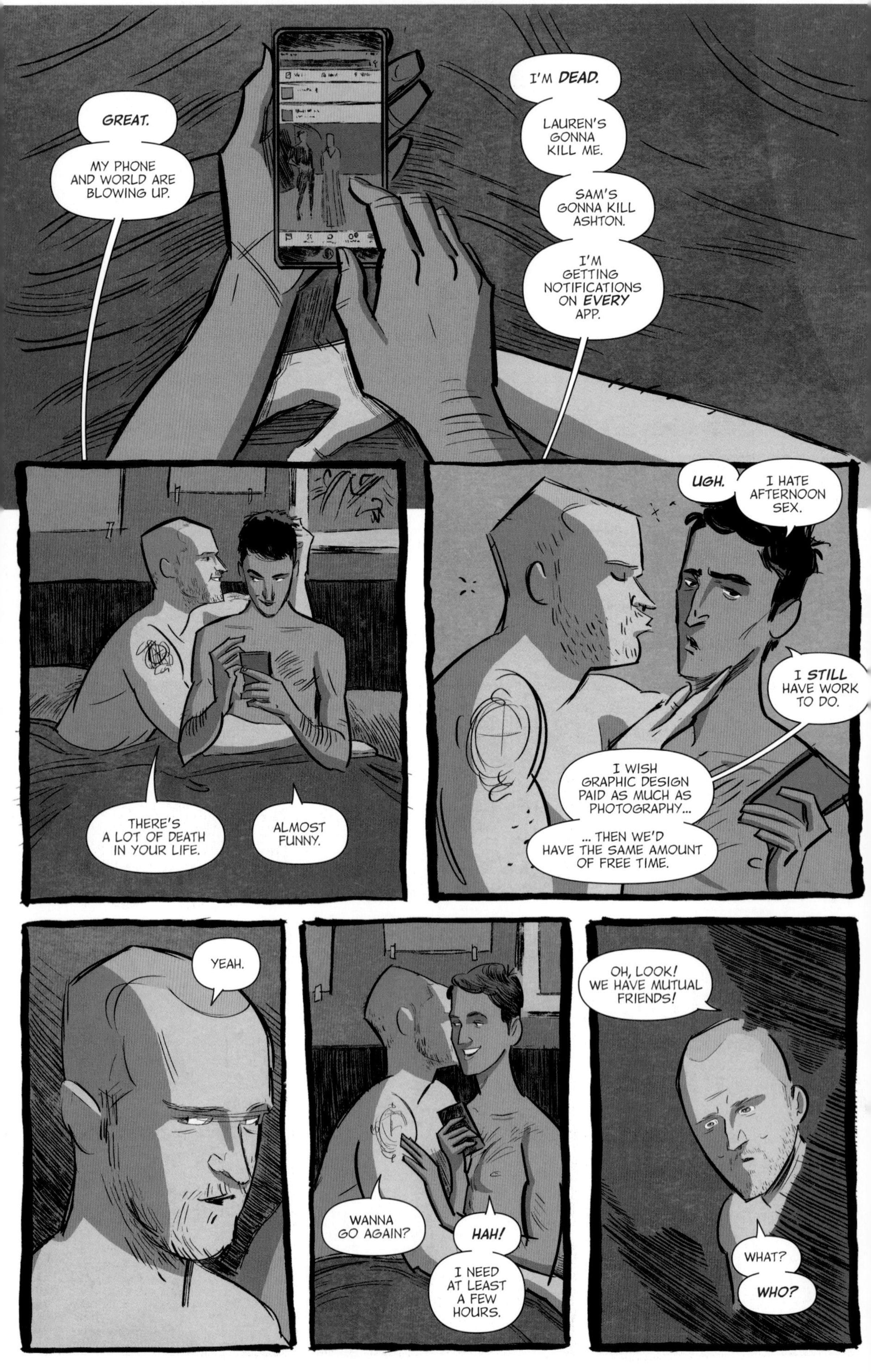
GREAT.
MY PHONE AND WORLD ARE BLOWING UP.
I'M DEAD.
LAUREN'S GONNA KILL ME.
SAM'S GONNA KILL ASHTON.
I'M GETTING NOTIFICATIONS ON EVERY APP.
THERE'S A LOT OF DEATH IN YOUR LIFE.
ALMOST FUNNY.
UGH.
I HATE AFTERNOON SEX.
I STILL HAVE WORK TO DO.
I WISH GRAPHIC DESIGN PAID AS MUCH AS PHOTOGRAPHY...
... THEN WE'D HAVE THE SAME AMOUNT OF FREE TIME.
YEAH.
WANNA GO AGAIN?
HAH!
I NEED AT LEAST A FEW HOURS.
OH, LOOK! WE HAVE MUTUAL FRIENDS!
WHAT?
WHO?

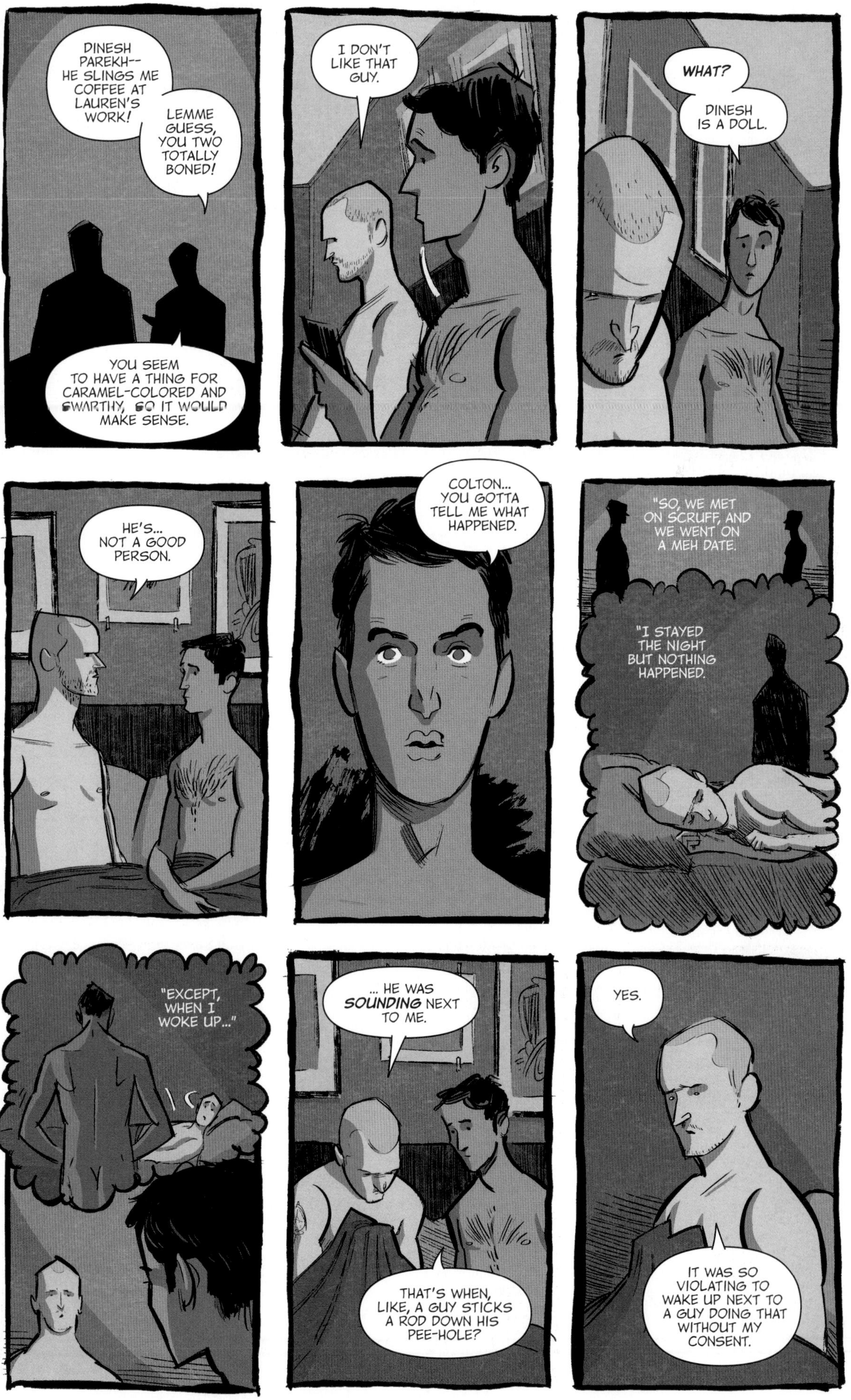
DINESH PAREKH-- HE SLINGS ME COFFEE AT LAUREN'S WORK!
LEMME GUESS, YOU TWO TOTALLY BONED!
YOU SEEM TO HAVE A THING FOR CARAMEL-COLORED AND SWARTHY, SO IT WOULD MAKE SENSE.
I DON'T LIKE THAT GUY.
WHAT?
DINESH IS A DOLL.
HE'S... NOT A GOOD PERSON.
COLTON... YOU GOTTA TELL ME WHAT HAPPENED.
"SO, WE MET ON SCRUFF, AND WE WENT ON A MEH DATE.
"I STAYED THE NIGHT BUT NOTHING HAPPENED.
"EXCEPT, WHEN I WOKE UP..."
... HE WAS SOUNDING NEXT TO ME.
THAT'S WHEN, LIKE, A GUY STICKS A ROD DOWN HIS PEE-HOLE?
YES.
IT WAS SO VIOLATING TO WAKE UP NEXT TO A GUY DOING THAT WITHOUT MY CONSENT.

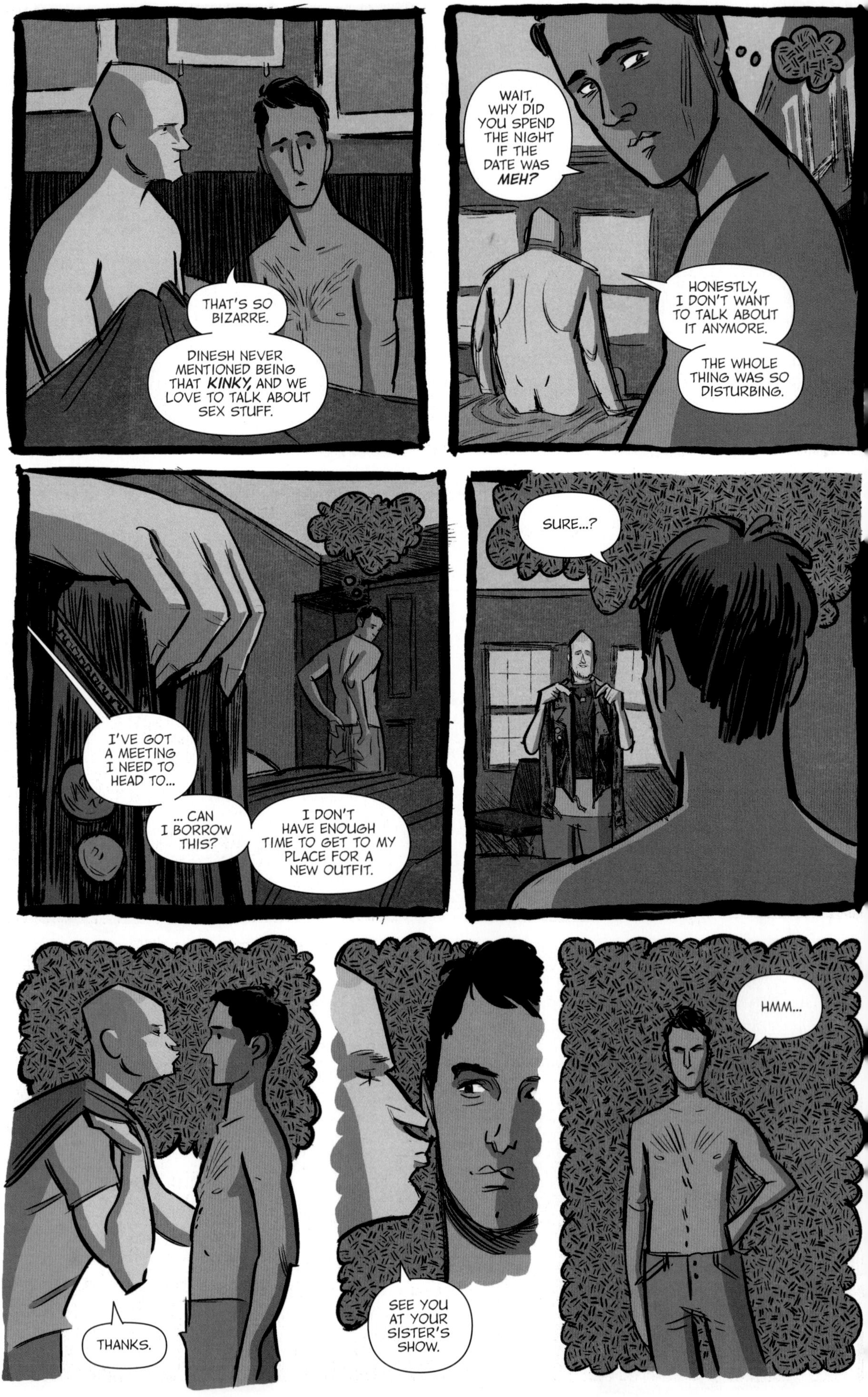
THAT'S SO BIZARRE.
DINESH NEVER MENTIONED BEING THAT **KINKY,** AND WE LOVE TO TALK ABOUT SEX STUFF.
WAIT, WHY DID YOU SPEND THE NIGHT IF THE DATE WAS ***MEH?***
HONESTLY, I DON'T WANT TO TALK ABOUT IT ANYMORE.
THE WHOLE THING WAS SO DISTURBING.
I'VE GOT A MEETING I NEED TO HEAD TO...
... CAN I BORROW THIS?
I DON'T HAVE ENOUGH TIME TO GET TO MY PLACE FOR A NEW OUTFIT.
SURE...?
THANKS.
SEE YOU AT YOUR SISTER'S SHOW.
HMM...

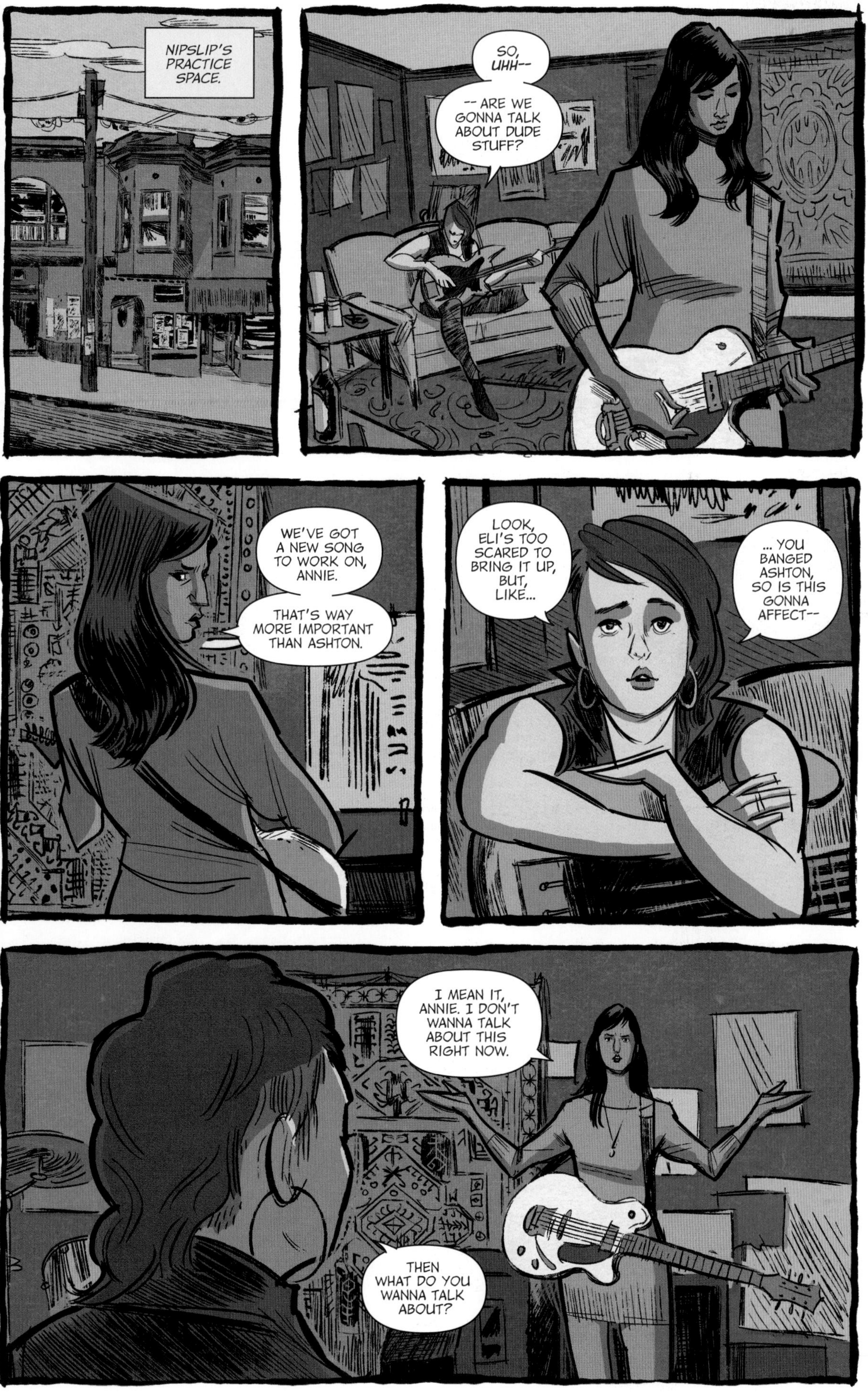
NIPSLIP'S PRACTICE SPACE.
SO, UHH--
-- ARE WE GONNA TALK ABOUT DUDE STUFF?
WE'VE GOT A NEW SONG TO WORK ON, ANNIE.
THAT'S WAY MORE IMPORTANT THAN ASHTON.
LOOK, ELI'S TOO SCARED TO BRING IT UP, BUT, LIKE...
... YOU BANGED ASHTON, SO IS THIS GONNA AFFECT--
I MEAN IT, ANNIE. I DON'T WANNA TALK ABOUT THIS RIGHT NOW.
THEN WHAT DO YOU WANNA TALK ABOUT?

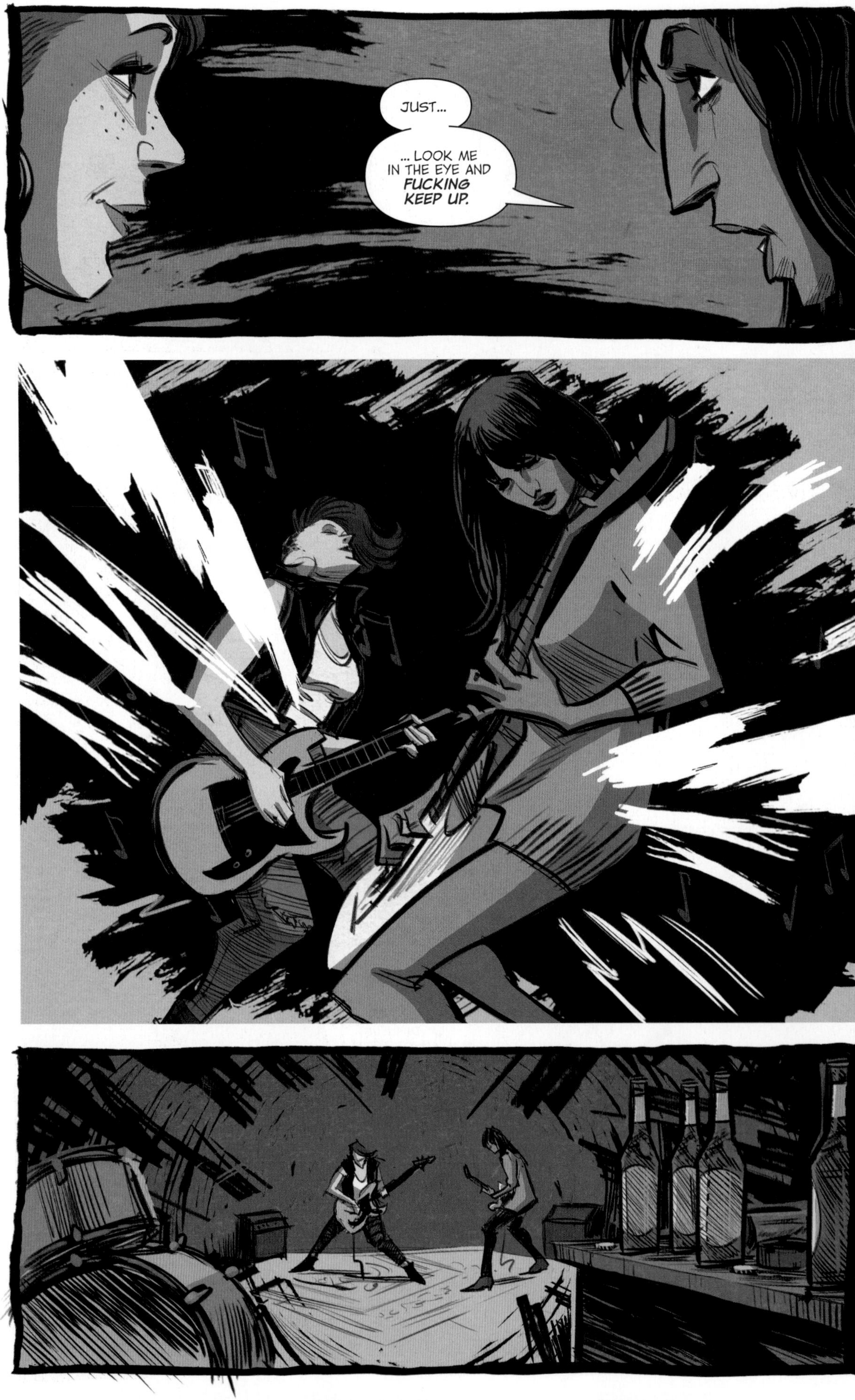
JUST...
... LOOK ME IN THE EYE AND FUCKING KEEP UP.

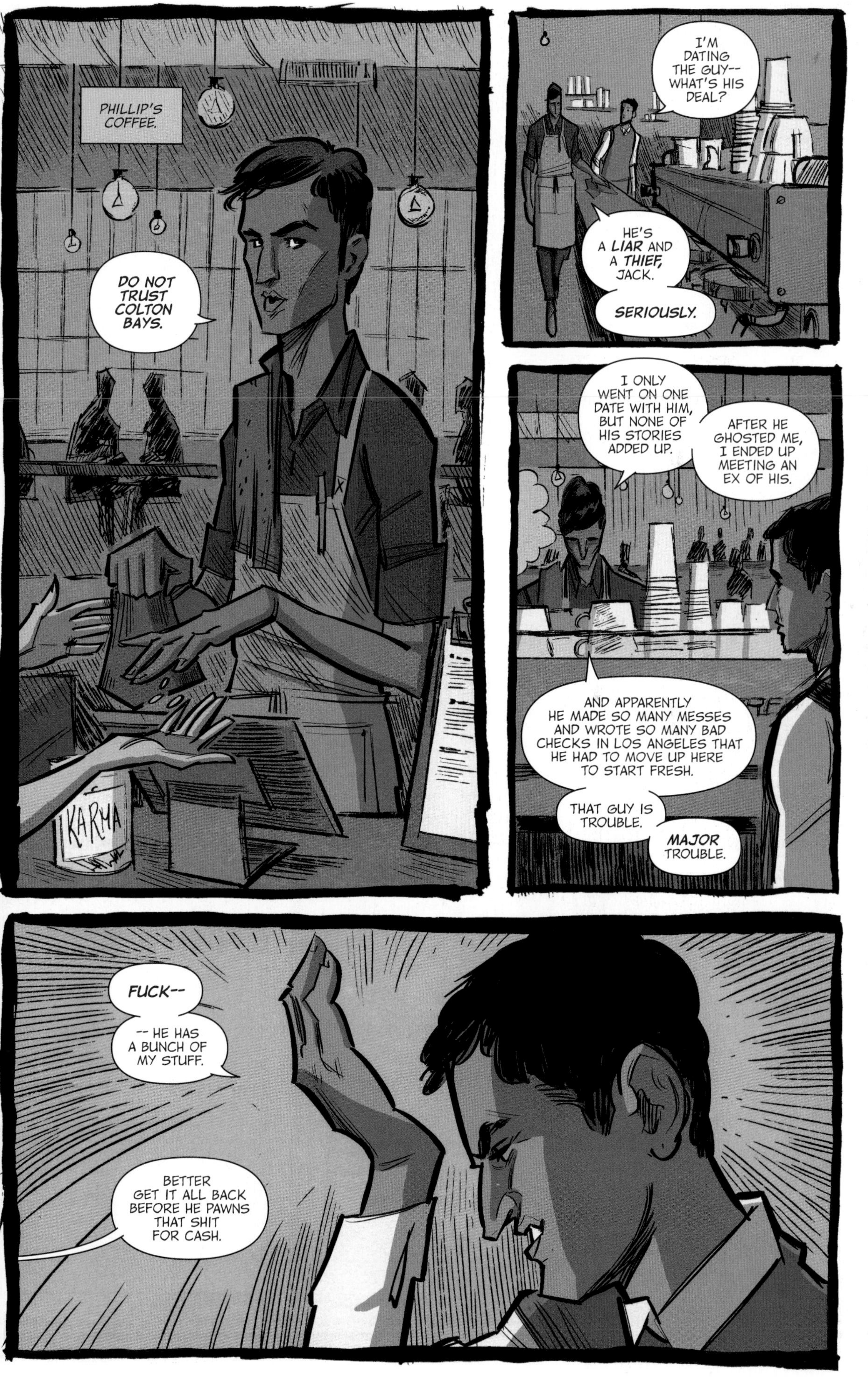
PHILLIP'S COFFEE.
DO NOT TRUST COLTON BAYS.
I'M DATING THE GUY-- WHAT'S HIS DEAL?
HE'S A LIAR AND A THIEF, JACK.
SERIOUSLY.
I ONLY WENT ON ONE DATE WITH HIM, BUT NONE OF HIS STORIES ADDED UP.
AFTER HE GHOSTED ME, I ENDED UP MEETING AN EX OF HIS.
AND APPARENTLY HE MADE SO MANY MESSES AND WROTE SO MANY BAD CHECKS IN LOS ANGELES THAT HE HAD TO MOVE UP HERE TO START FRESH.
THAT GUY IS TROUBLE.
MAJOR TROUBLE.
KARMA
FUCK--
-- HE HAS A BUNCH OF MY STUFF.
BETTER GET IT ALL BACK BEFORE HE PAWNS THAT SHIT FOR CASH.

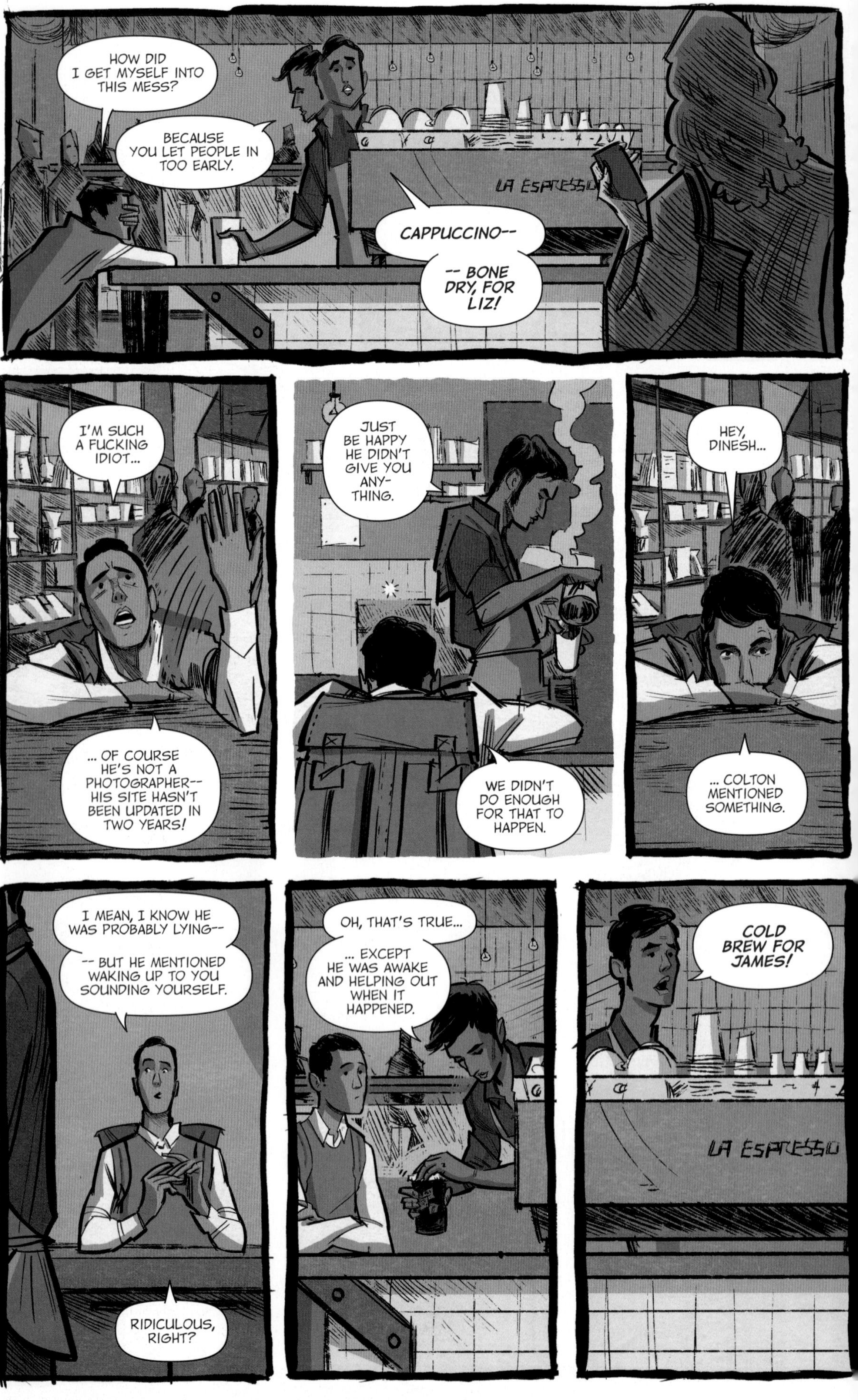
HOW DID I GET MYSELF INTO THIS MESS?
BECAUSE YOU LET PEOPLE IN TOO EARLY.
LA ESPRESSO
CAPPUCCINO--
-- BONE DRY, FOR LIZ!
I'M SUCH A FUCKING IDIOT...
... OF COURSE HE'S NOT A PHOTOGRAPHER-- HIS SITE HASN'T BEEN UPDATED IN TWO YEARS!
JUST BE HAPPY HE DIDN'T GIVE YOU ANY-THING.
WE DIDN'T DO ENOUGH FOR THAT TO HAPPEN.
HEY, DINESH...
... COLTON MENTIONED SOMETHING.
I MEAN, I KNOW HE WAS PROBABLY LYING--
-- BUT HE MENTIONED WAKING UP TO YOU SOUNDING YOURSELF.
RIDICULOUS, RIGHT?
OH, THAT'S TRUE...
... EXCEPT HE WAS AWAKE AND HELPING OUT WHEN IT HAPPENED.
COLD BREW FOR JAMES!
LA ESPRESSO

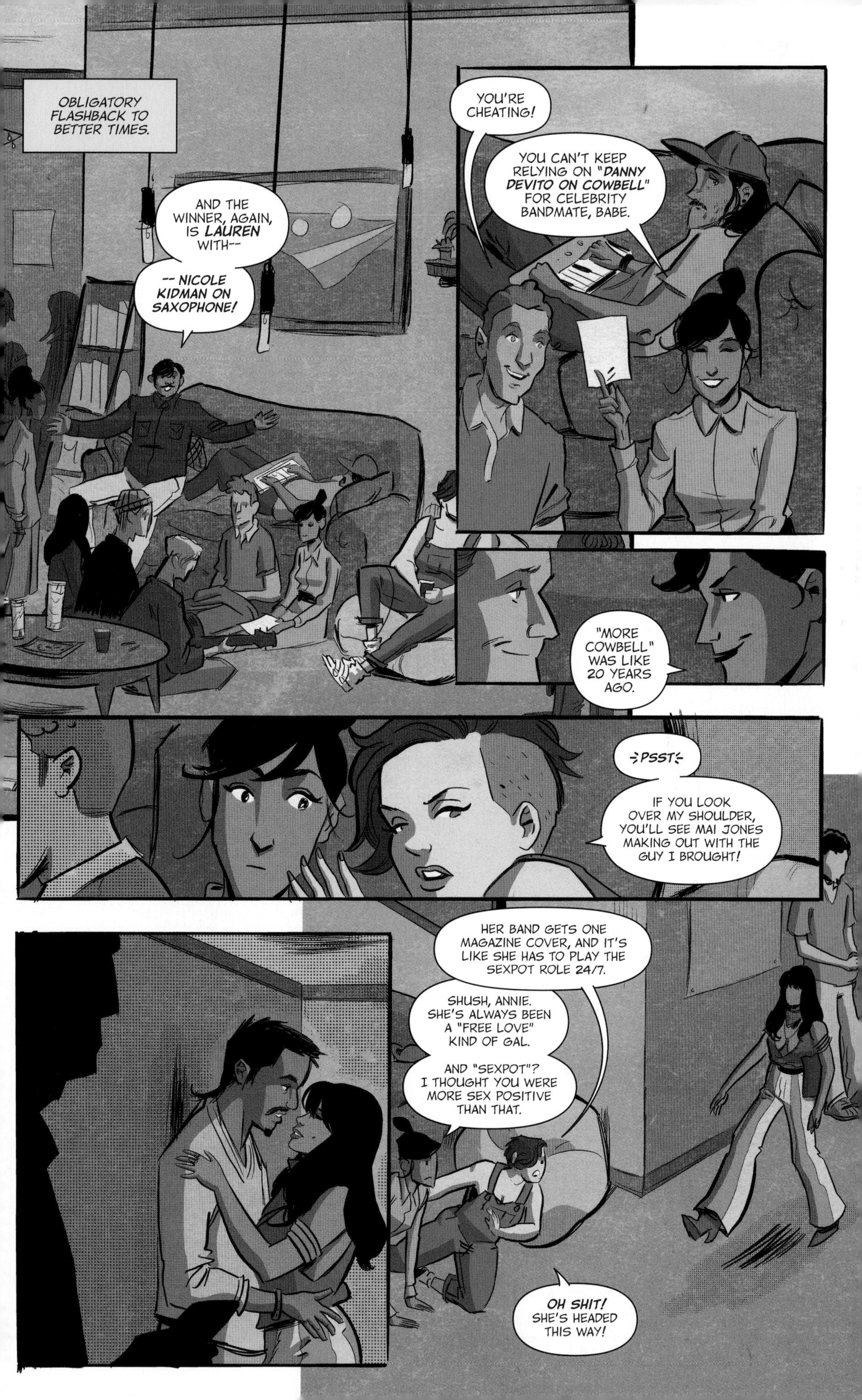

OBLIGATORY FLASHBACK TO BETTER TIMES.
AND THE WINNER, AGAIN, IS LAUREN WITH--
-- NICOLE KIDMAN ON SAXOPHONE!
YOU'RE CHEATING!
YOU CAN'T KEEP RELYING ON "DANNY DEVITO ON COWBELL" FOR CELEBRITY BANDMATE, BABE.
"MORE COWBELL" WAS LIKE 20 YEARS AGO.
PSST
IF YOU LOOK OVER MY SHOULDER, YOU'LL SEE MAI JONES MAKING OUT WITH THE GUY I BROUGHT!
HER BAND GETS ONE MAGAZINE COVER, AND IT'S LIKE SHE HAS TO PLAY THE SEXPOT ROLE 24/7.
SHUSH, ANNIE. SHE'S ALWAYS BEEN A "FREE LOVE" KIND OF GAL.
AND "SEXPOT"? I THOUGHT YOU WERE MORE SEX POSITIVE THAN THAT.
OH SHIT! SHE'S HEADED THIS WAY!

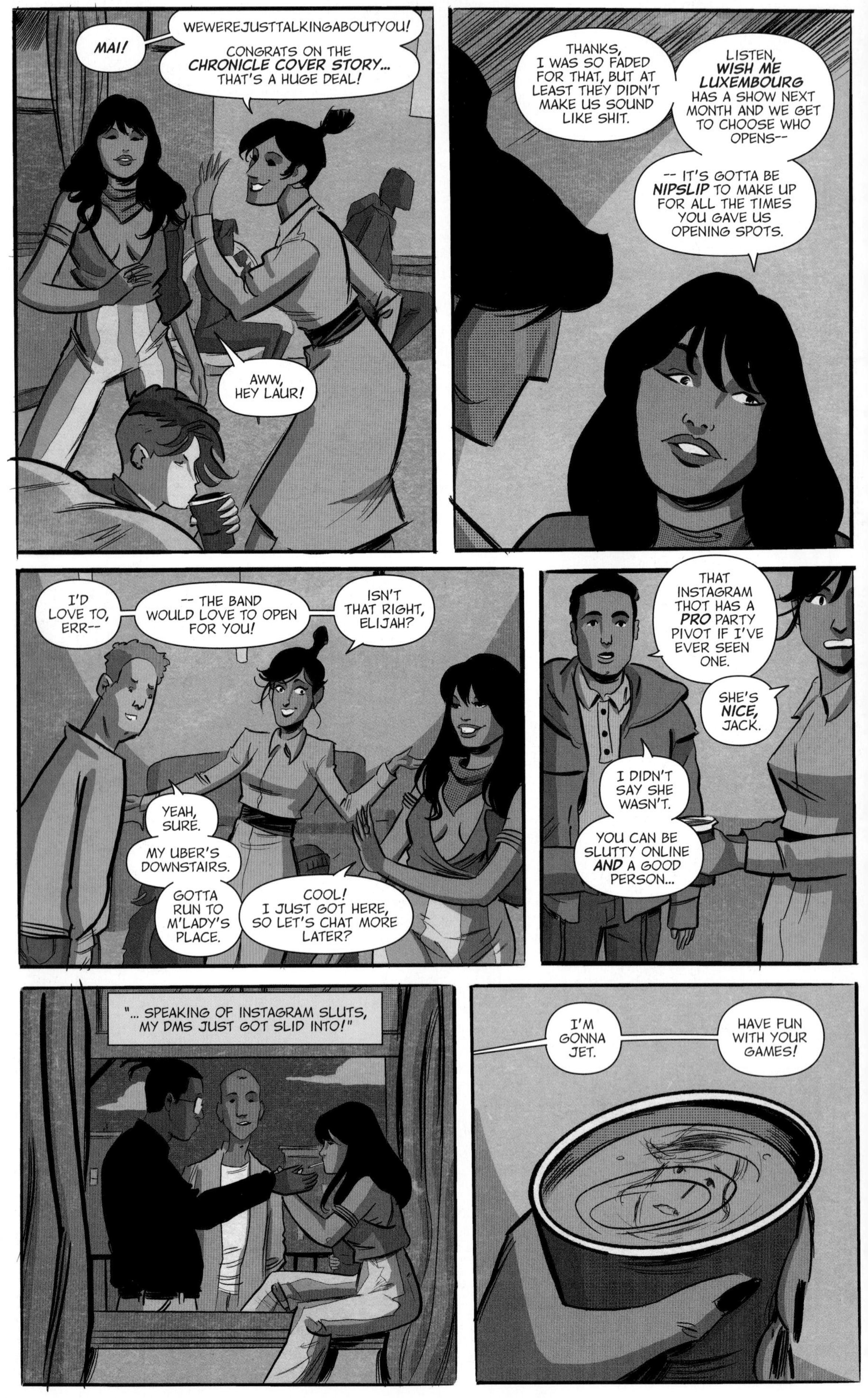
MAI!
WEWEREJUSTTALKINGABOUTYOU!
CONGRATS ON THE CHRONICLE COVER STORY... THAT'S A HUGE DEAL!
AWW, HEY LAUR!
THANKS, I WAS SO FADED FOR THAT, BUT AT LEAST THEY DIDN'T MAKE US SOUND LIKE SHIT.
LISTEN, WISH ME LUXEMBOURG HAS A SHOW NEXT MONTH AND WE GET TO CHOOSE WHO OPENS--
-- IT'S GOTTA BE NIPSLIP TO MAKE UP FOR ALL THE TIMES YOU GAVE US OPENING SPOTS.
I'D LOVE TO, ERR--
-- THE BAND WOULD LOVE TO OPEN FOR YOU!
ISN'T THAT RIGHT, ELIJAH?
YEAH, SURE.
MY UBER'S DOWNSTAIRS.
GOTTA RUN TO M'LADY'S PLACE.
COOL! I JUST GOT HERE, SO LET'S CHAT MORE LATER?
THAT INSTAGRAM THOT HAS A PRO PARTY PIVOT IF I'VE EVER SEEN ONE.
SHE'S NICE, JACK.
I DIDN'T SAY SHE WASN'T.
YOU CAN BE SLUTTY ONLINE AND A GOOD PERSON...
"... SPEAKING OF INSTAGRAM SLUTS, MY DMS JUST GOT SLID INTO!"
I'M GONNA JET.
HAVE FUN WITH YOUR GAMES!

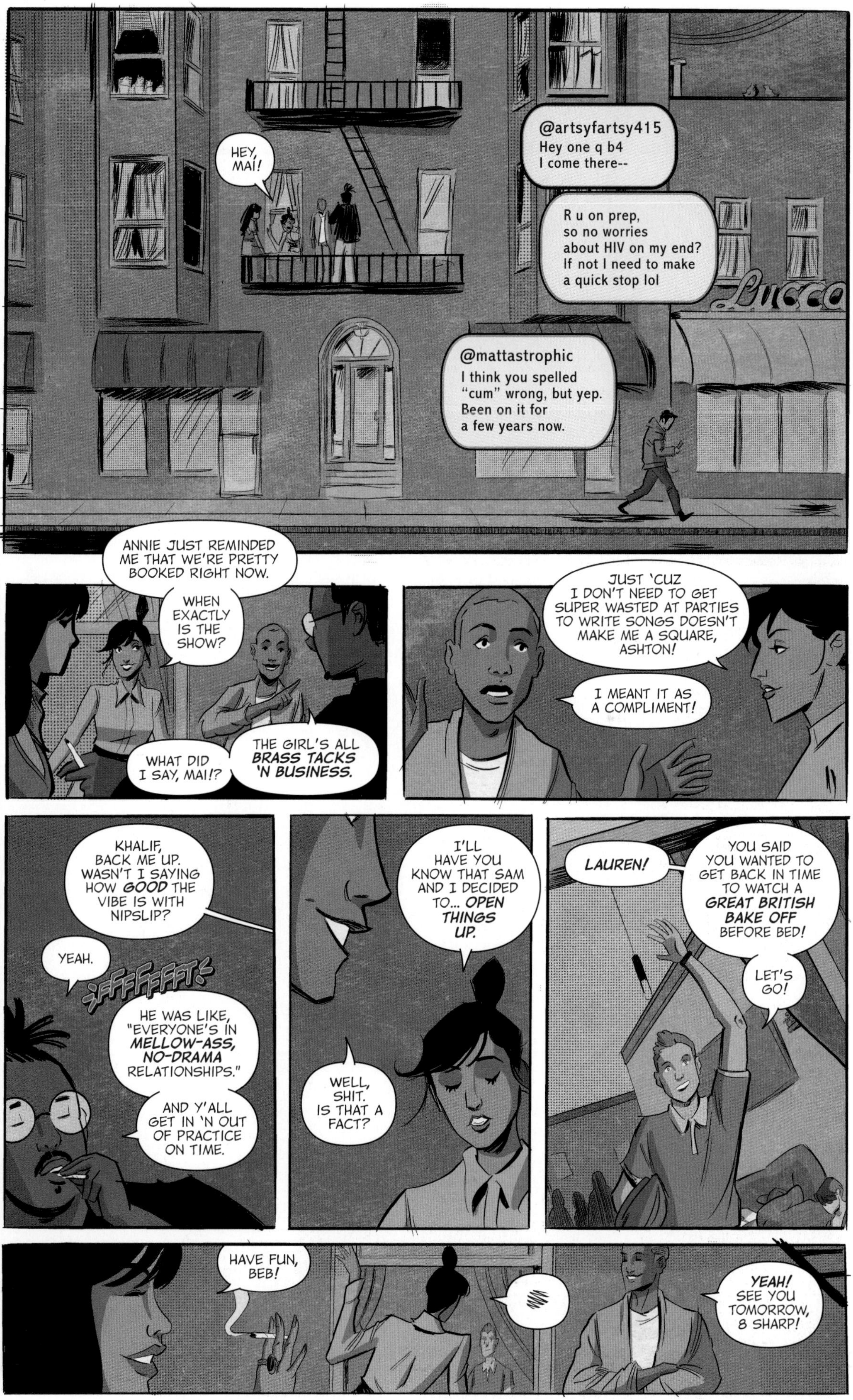
HEY, MAI!
@artsyfartsy415
Hey one q b4 I come there--
R u on prep, so no worries about HIV on my end? If not I need to make a quick stop lol
@mattastrophic
I think you spelled "cum" wrong, but yep. Been on it for a few years now.
Lucca
ANNIE JUST REMINDED ME THAT WE'RE PRETTY BOOKED RIGHT NOW.
WHEN EXACTLY IS THE SHOW?
THE GIRL'S ALL BRASS TACKS 'N BUSINESS.
WHAT DID I SAY, MAI!?
JUST 'CUZ I DON'T NEED TO GET SUPER WASTED AT PARTIES TO WRITE SONGS DOESN'T MAKE ME A SQUARE, ASHTON!
I MEANT IT AS A COMPLIMENT!
KHALIF, BACK ME UP. WASN'T I SAYING HOW GOOD THE VIBE IS WITH NIPSLIP?
YEAH.
FFFFFFFT
HE WAS LIKE, "EVERYONE'S IN MELLOW-ASS, NO-DRAMA RELATIONSHIPS."
AND Y'ALL GET IN 'N OUT OF PRACTICE ON TIME.
I'LL HAVE YOU KNOW THAT SAM AND I DECIDED TO... OPEN THINGS UP.
WELL, SHIT. IS THAT A FACT?
LAUREN!
YOU SAID YOU WANTED TO GET BACK IN TIME TO WATCH A GREAT BRITISH BAKE OFF BEFORE BED!
LET'S GO!
HAVE FUN, BEB!
YEAH! SEE YOU TOMORROW, 8 SHARP!

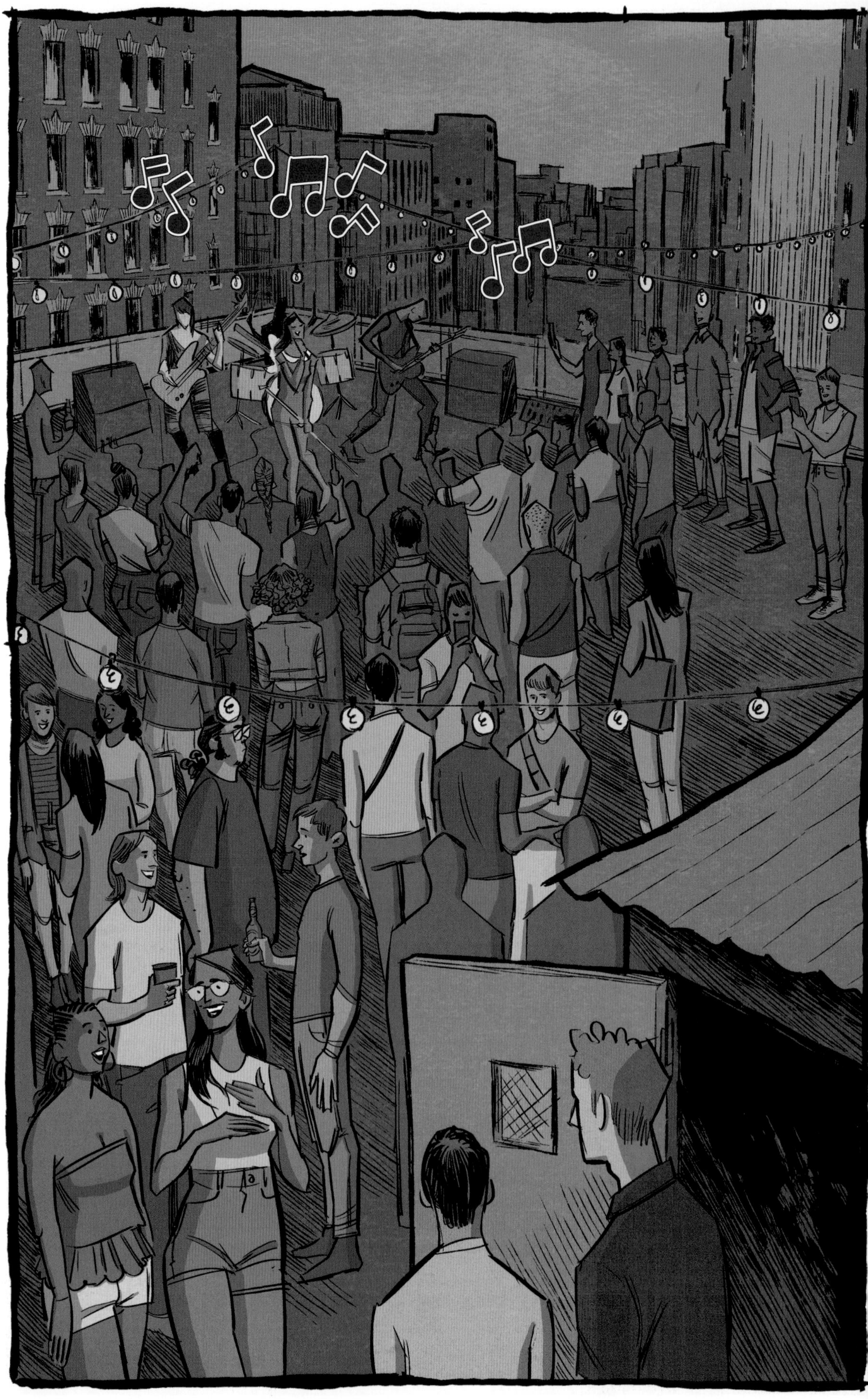

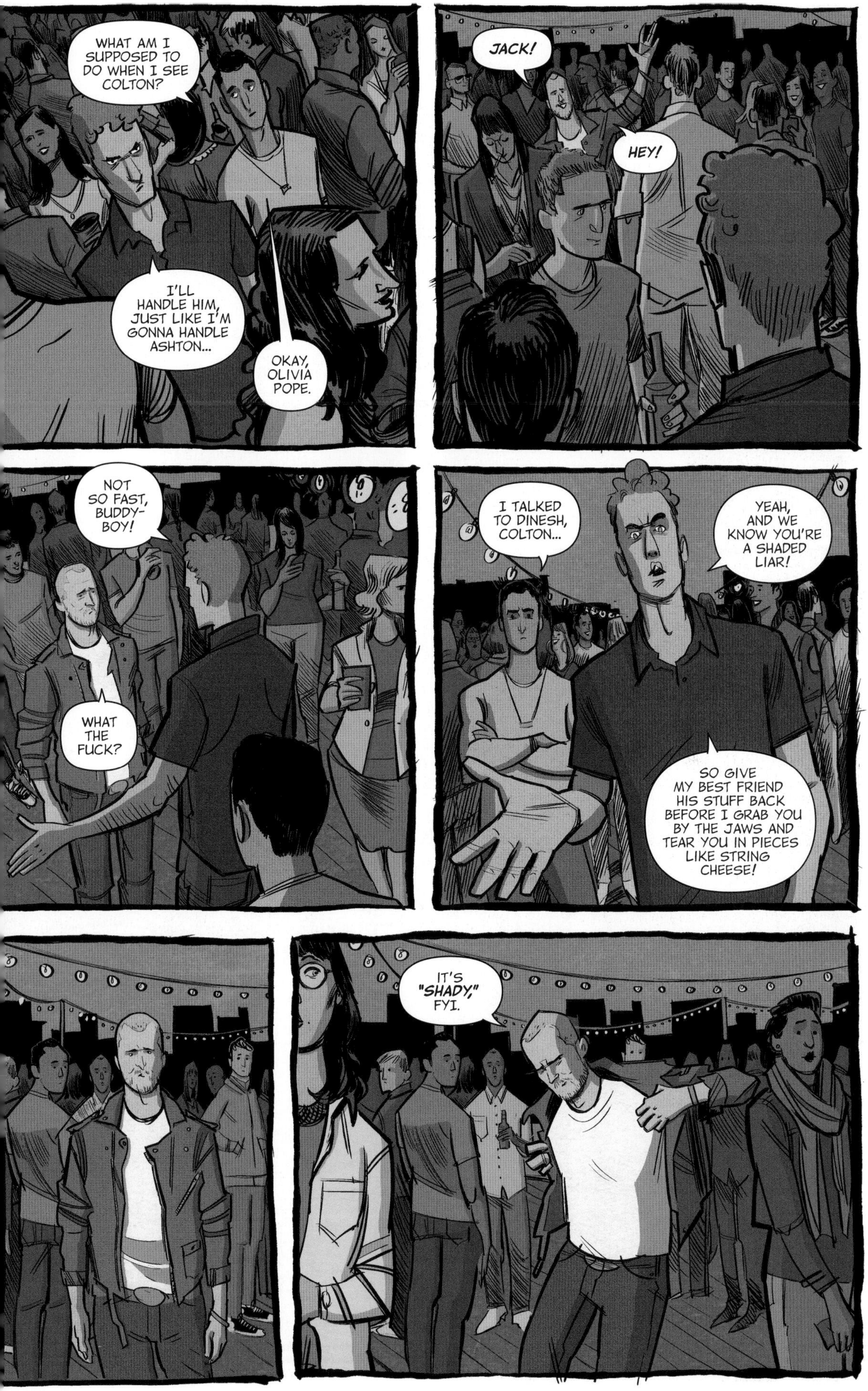
WHAT AM I SUPPOSED TO DO WHEN I SEE COLTON?
I'LL HANDLE HIM, JUST LIKE I'M GONNA HANDLE ASHTON...
OKAY, OLIVIA POPE.
JACK!
HEY!
NOT SO FAST, BUDDY-BOY!
WHAT THE FUCK?
I TALKED TO DINESH, COLTON...
YEAH, AND WE KNOW YOU'RE A SHADED LIAR!
SO GIVE MY BEST FRIEND HIS STUFF BACK BEFORE I GRAB YOU BY THE JAWS AND TEAR YOU IN PIECES LIKE STRING CHEESE!
IT'S "SHADY," FYI.

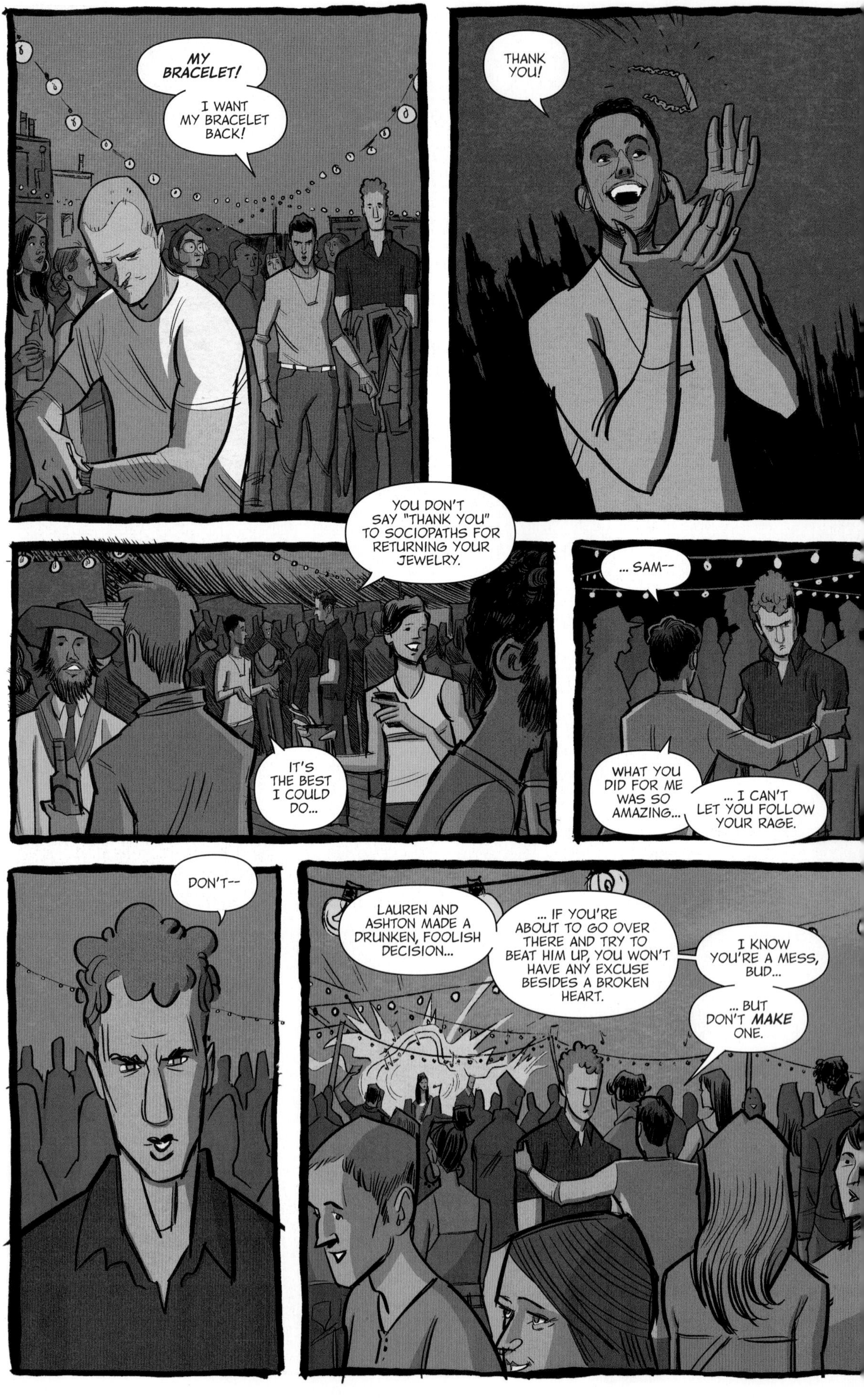
MY BRACELET!
I WANT MY BRACELET BACK!
THANK YOU!
YOU DON'T SAY "THANK YOU" TO SOCIOPATHS FOR RETURNING YOUR JEWELRY.
IT'S THE BEST I COULD DO...
... SAM--
WHAT YOU DID FOR ME WAS SO AMAZING...
... I CAN'T LET YOU FOLLOW YOUR RAGE.
DON'T--
LAUREN AND ASHTON MADE A DRUNKEN, FOOLISH DECISION...
... IF YOU'RE ABOUT TO GO OVER THERE AND TRY TO BEAT HIM UP, YOU WON'T HAVE ANY EXCUSE BESIDES A BROKEN HEART.
I KNOW YOU'RE A MESS, BUD...
... BUT DON'T MAKE ONE.

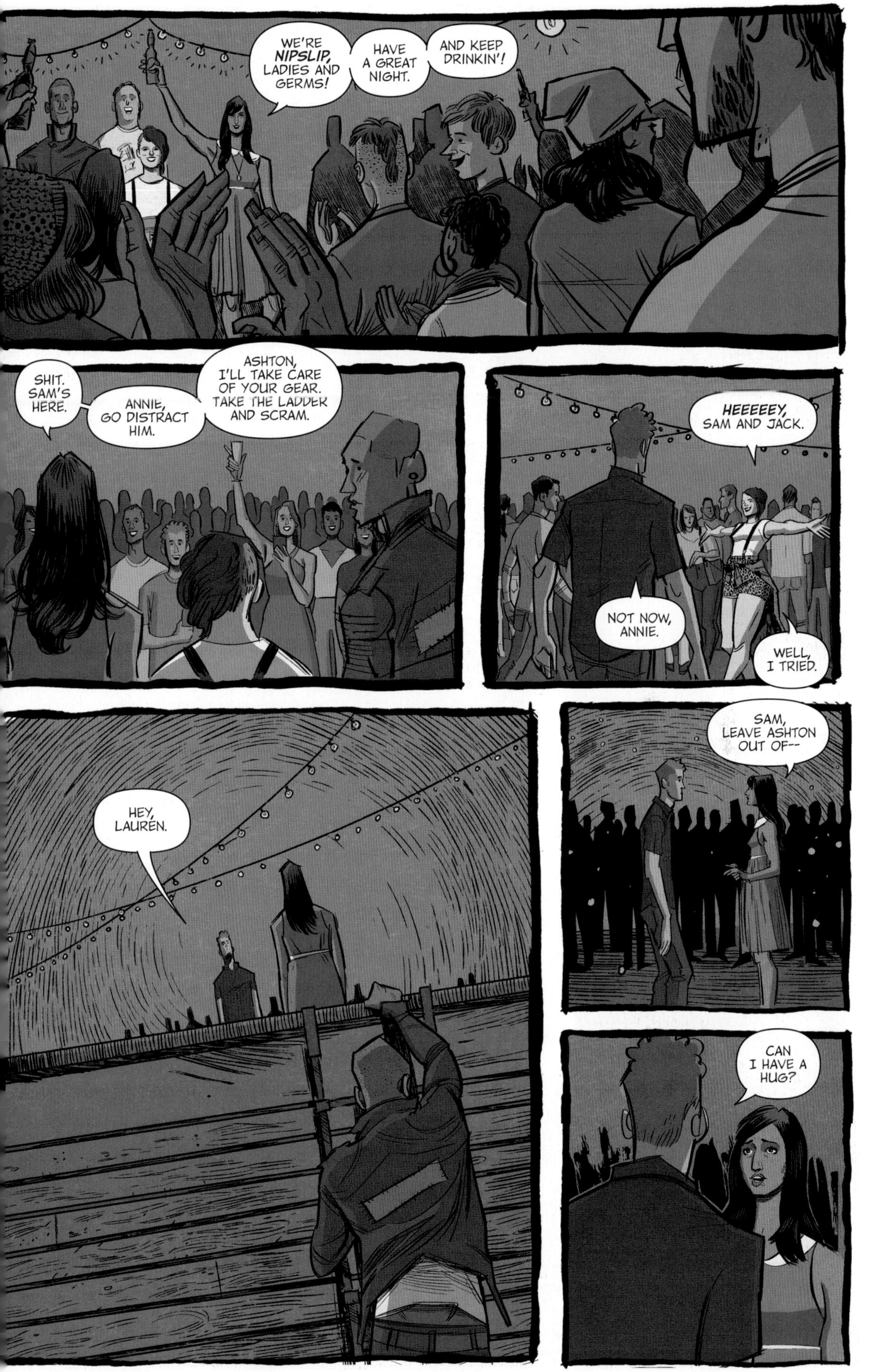

WE'RE NIPSLIP, LADIES AND GERMS!
HAVE A GREAT NIGHT.
AND KEEP DRINKIN'!
SHIT. SAM'S HERE.
ANNIE, GO DISTRACT HIM.
ASHTON, I'LL TAKE CARE OF YOUR GEAR. TAKE THE LADDER AND SCRAM.
HEEEEEY, SAM AND JACK.
NOT NOW, ANNIE.
WELL, I TRIED.
HEY, LAUREN.
SAM, LEAVE ASHTON OUT OF--
CAN I HAVE A HUG?

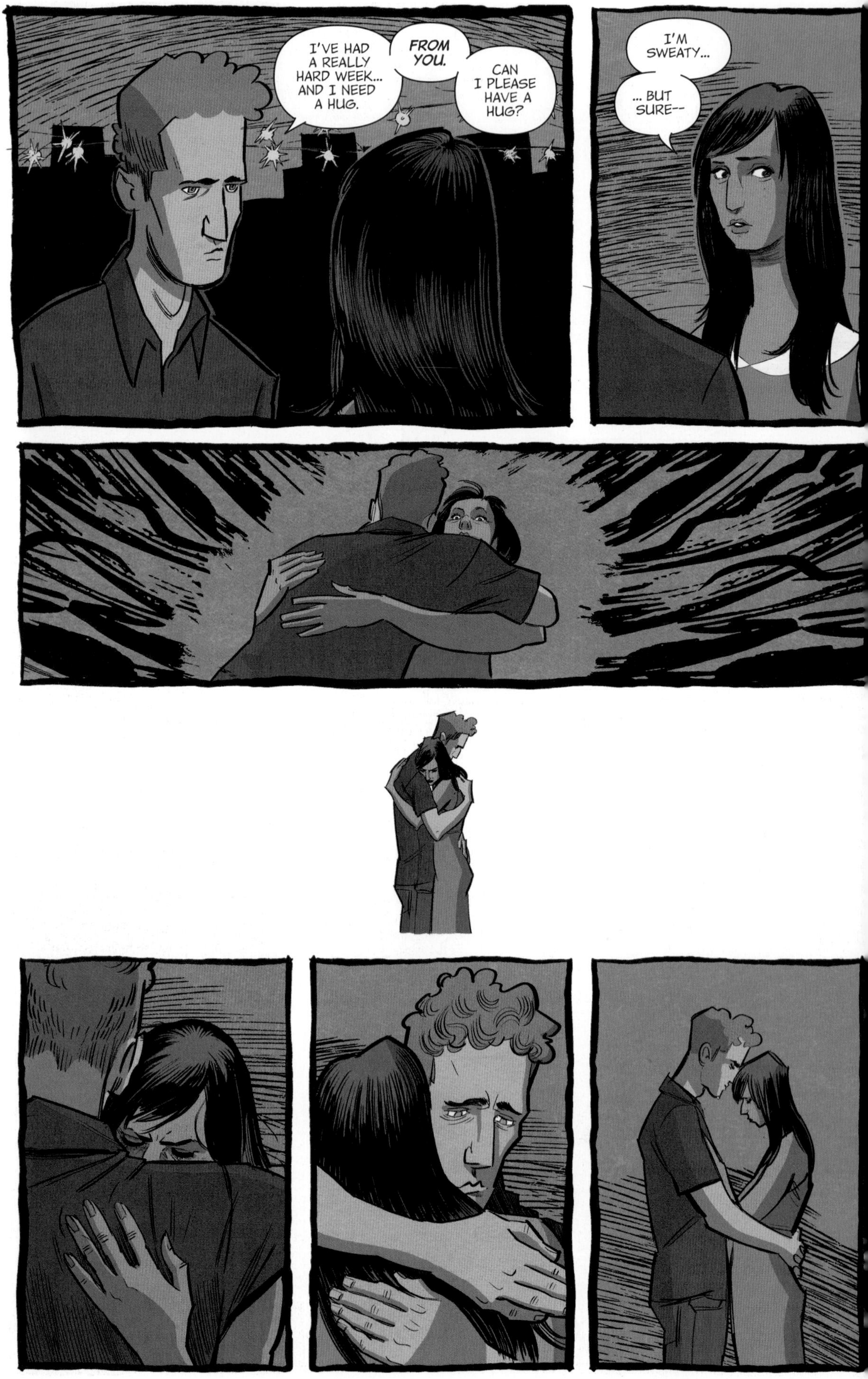
I'VE HAD A REALLY HARD WEEK... AND I NEED A HUG.
FROM YOU.
CAN I PLEASE HAVE A HUG?
I'M SWEATY...
... BUT SURE--

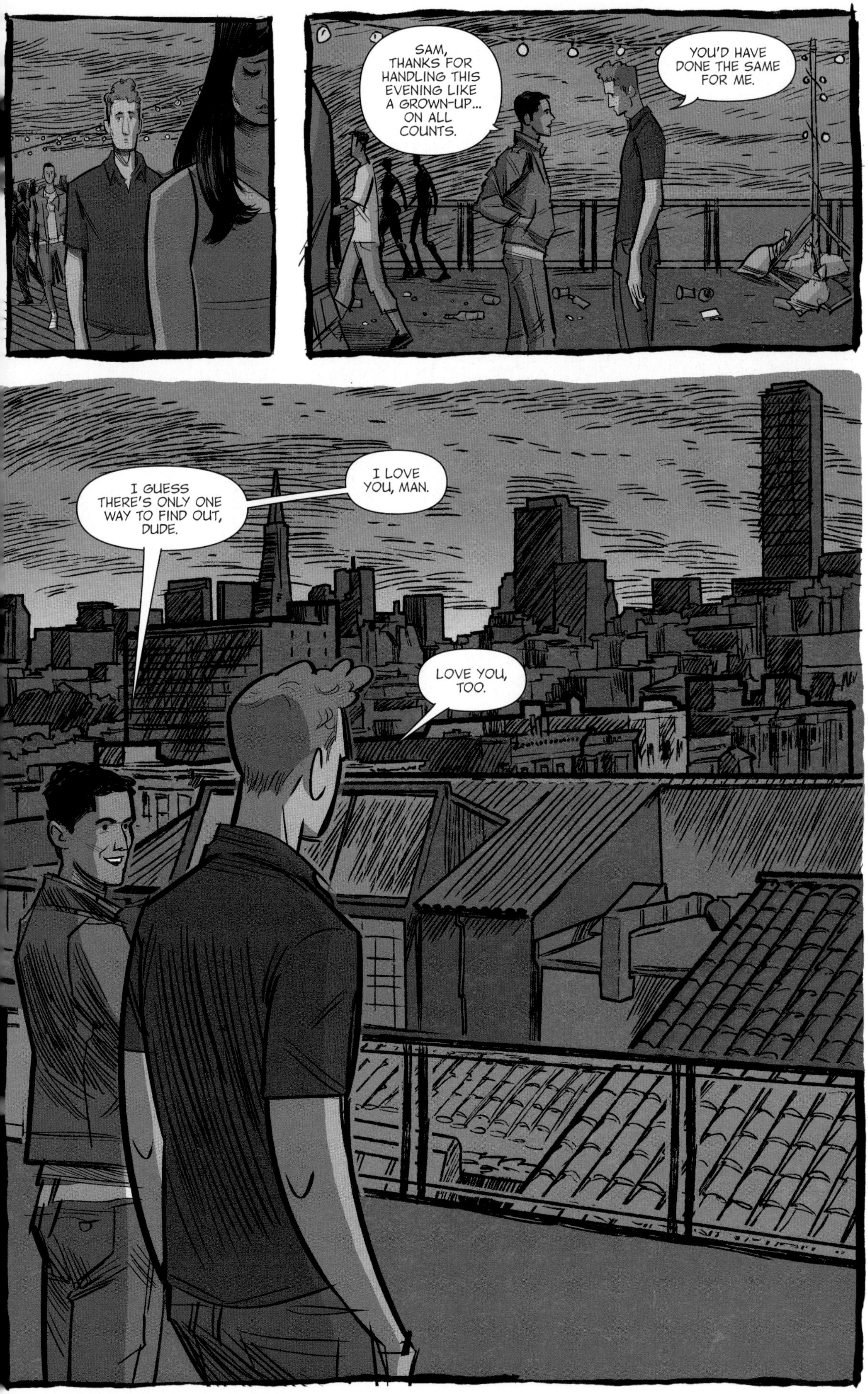

SAM, THANKS FOR HANDLING THIS EVENING LIKE A GROWN-UP... ON ALL COUNTS.
YOU'D HAVE DONE THE SAME FOR ME.
I GUESS THERE'S ONLY ONE WAY TO FIND OUT, DUDE.
I LOVE YOU, MAN.
LOVE YOU, TOO.

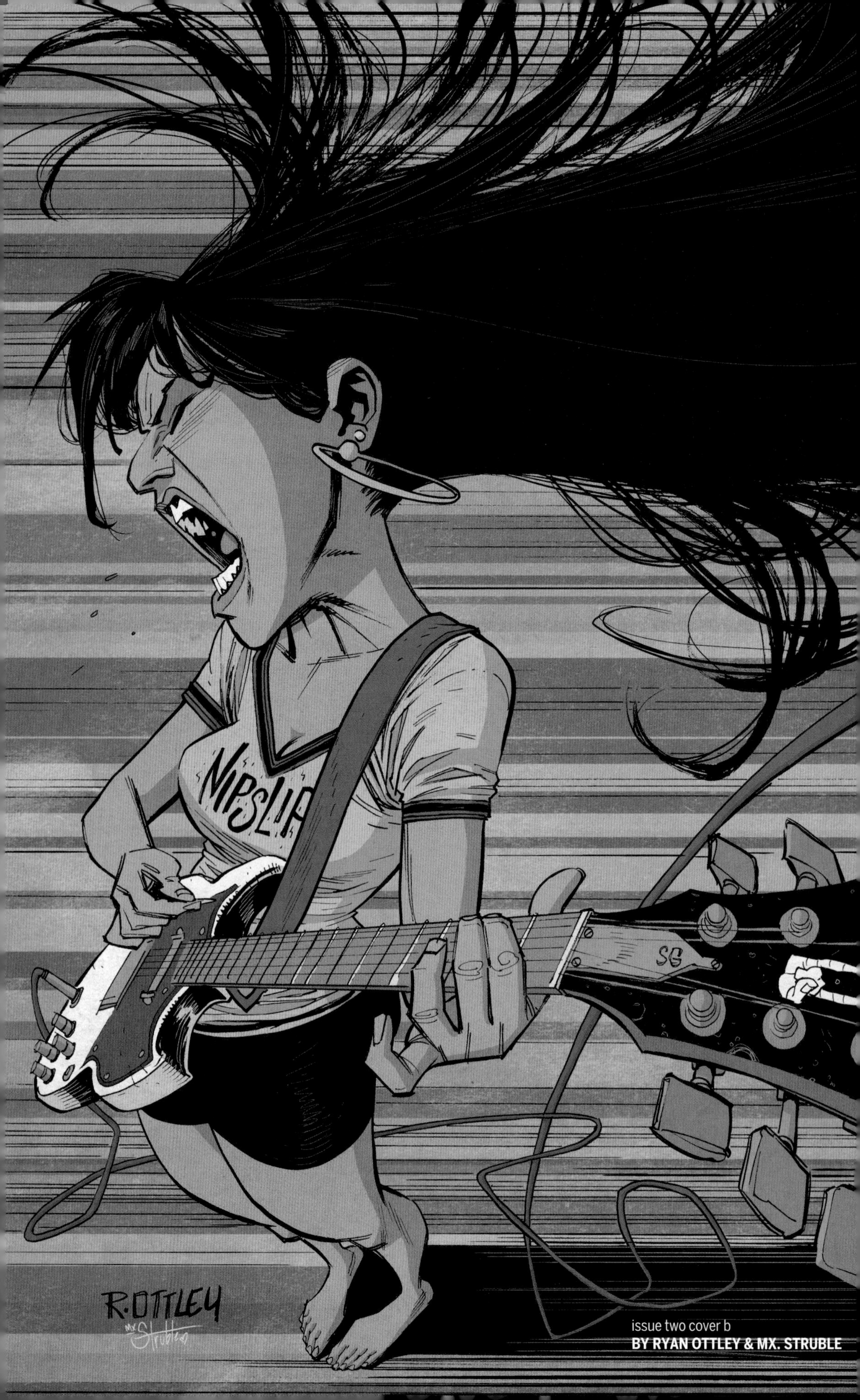
SG
R.OTTLEY

issue two cover b
BY RYAN OTTLEY & MX. STRUBLE

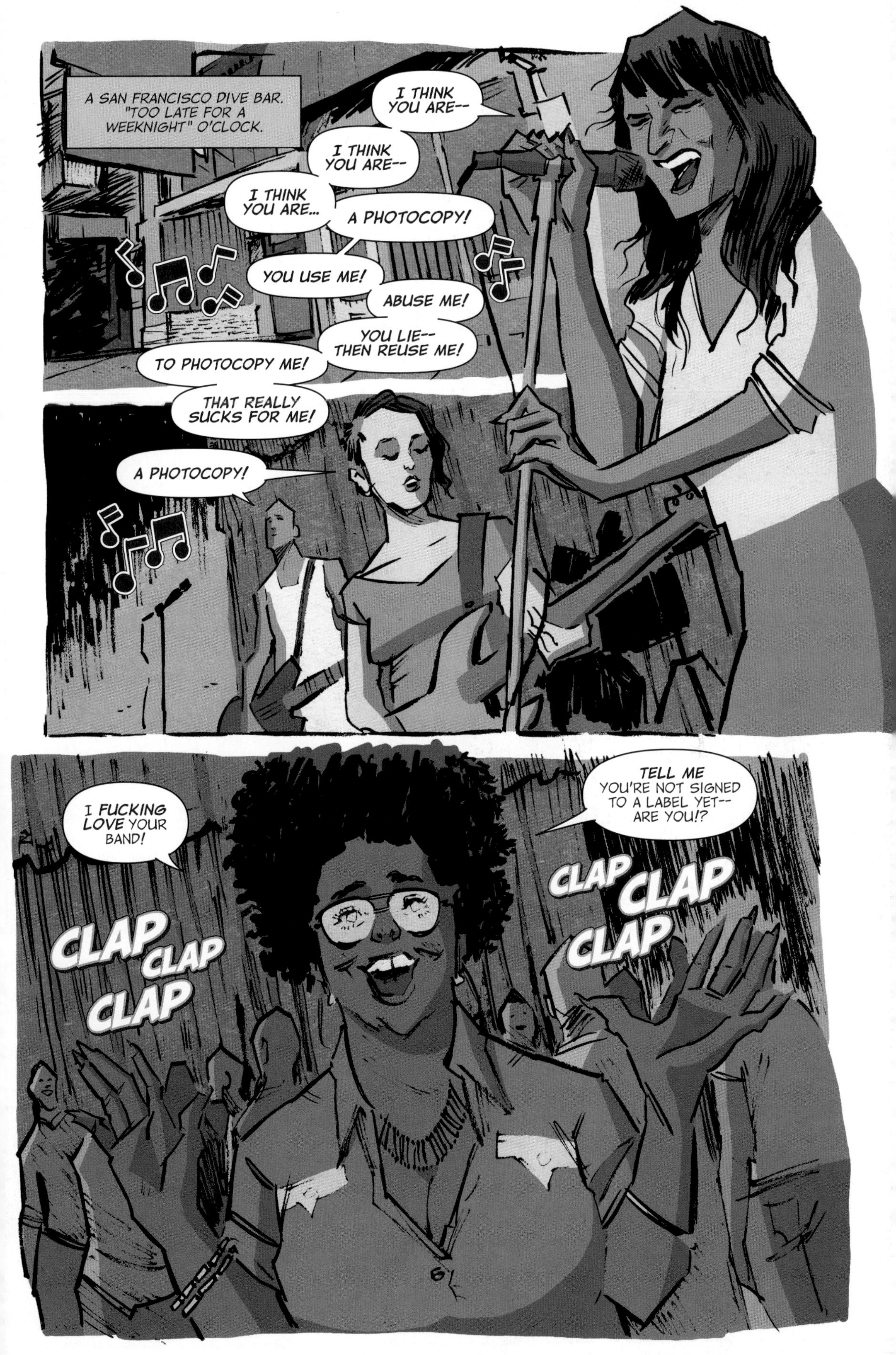
A SAN FRANCISCO DIVE BAR. "TOO LATE FOR A WEEKNIGHT" O'CLOCK.
I THINK YOU ARE--
I THINK YOU ARE--
I THINK YOU ARE...
A PHOTOCOPY!
YOU USE ME!
ABUSE ME!
YOU LIE-- THEN REUSE ME!
TO PHOTOCOPY ME!
THAT REALLY SUCKS FOR ME!
A PHOTOCOPY!
I FUCKING LOVE YOUR BAND!
TELL ME YOU'RE NOT SIGNED TO A LABEL YET-- ARE YOU!?
CLAP CLAP CLAP
CLAP CLAP CLAP

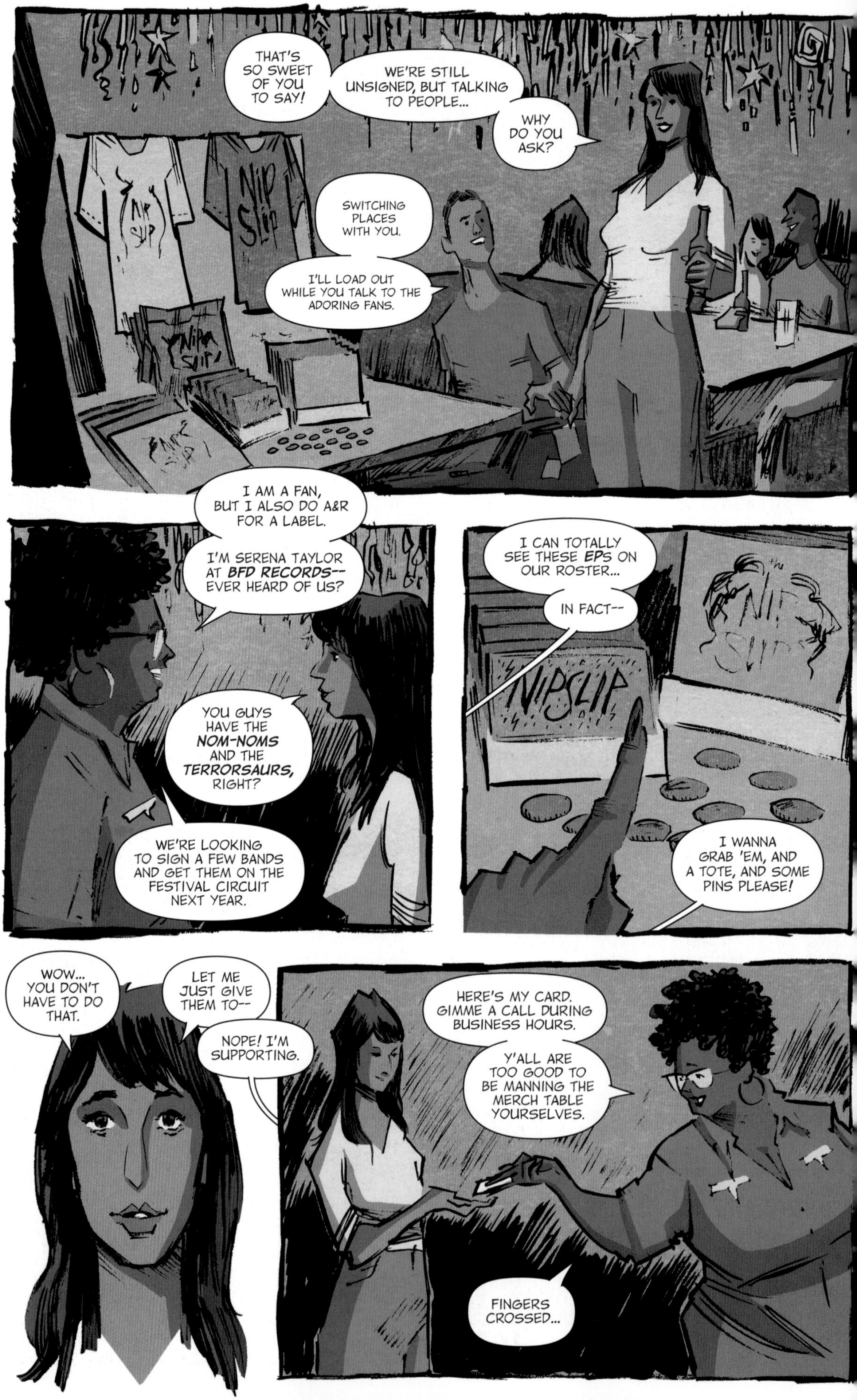
THAT'S SO SWEET OF YOU TO SAY!
WE'RE STILL UNSIGNED, BUT TALKING TO PEOPLE...
WHY DO YOU ASK?
SWITCHING PLACES WITH YOU.
I'LL LOAD OUT WHILE YOU TALK TO THE ADORING FANS.
I AM A FAN, BUT I ALSO DO A&R FOR A LABEL.
I'M SERENA TAYLOR AT BFD RECORDS-- EVER HEARD OF US?
YOU GUYS HAVE THE NOM-NOMS AND THE TERRORSAURS, RIGHT?
WE'RE LOOKING TO SIGN A FEW BANDS AND GET THEM ON THE FESTIVAL CIRCUIT NEXT YEAR.
I CAN TOTALLY SEE THESE EPs ON OUR ROSTER...
IN FACT--
I WANNA GRAB 'EM, AND A TOTE, AND SOME PINS PLEASE!
WOW... YOU DON'T HAVE TO DO THAT.
LET ME JUST GIVE THEM TO--
NOPE! I'M SUPPORTING.
HERE'S MY CARD. GIMME A CALL DURING BUSINESS HOURS.
Y'ALL ARE TOO GOOD TO BE MANNING THE MERCH TABLE YOURSELVES.
FINGERS CROSSED...

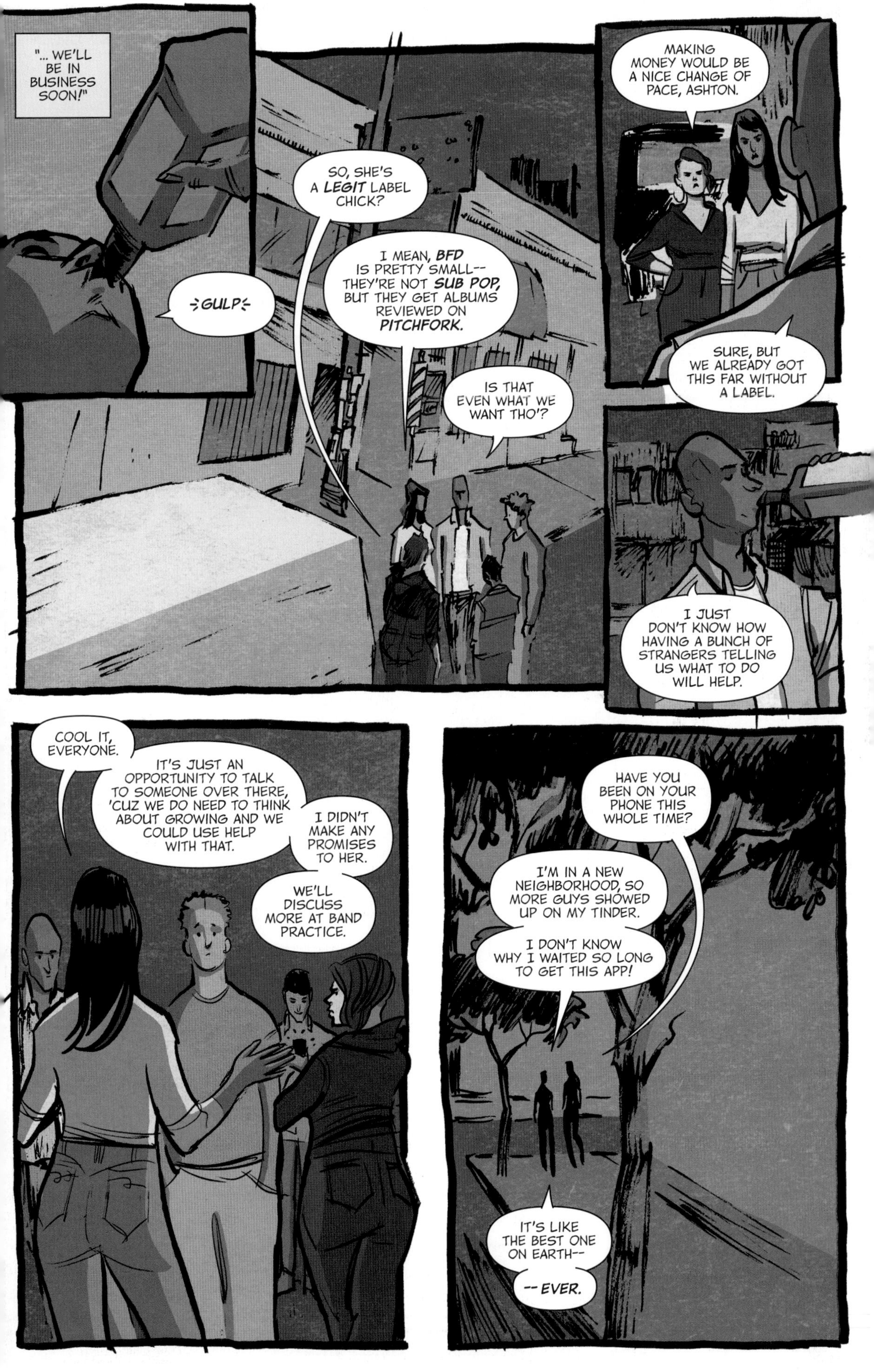
"... WE'LL BE IN BUSINESS SOON!"
GULP
SO, SHE'S A LEGIT LABEL CHICK?
I MEAN, BFD IS PRETTY SMALL-- THEY'RE NOT SUB POP, BUT THEY GET ALBUMS REVIEWED ON PITCHFORK.
IS THAT EVEN WHAT WE WANT THO'?
MAKING MONEY WOULD BE A NICE CHANGE OF PACE, ASHTON.
SURE, BUT WE ALREADY GOT THIS FAR WITHOUT A LABEL.
I JUST DON'T KNOW HOW HAVING A BUNCH OF STRANGERS TELLING US WHAT TO DO WILL HELP.
COOL IT, EVERYONE.
IT'S JUST AN OPPORTUNITY TO TALK TO SOMEONE OVER THERE, 'CUZ WE DO NEED TO THINK ABOUT GROWING AND WE COULD USE HELP WITH THAT.
I DIDN'T MAKE ANY PROMISES TO HER.
WE'LL DISCUSS MORE AT BAND PRACTICE.
HAVE YOU BEEN ON YOUR PHONE THIS WHOLE TIME?
I'M IN A NEW NEIGHBORHOOD, SO MORE GUYS SHOWED UP ON MY TINDER.
I DON'T KNOW WHY I WAITED SO LONG TO GET THIS APP!
IT'S LIKE THE BEST ONE ON EARTH--
--EVER.

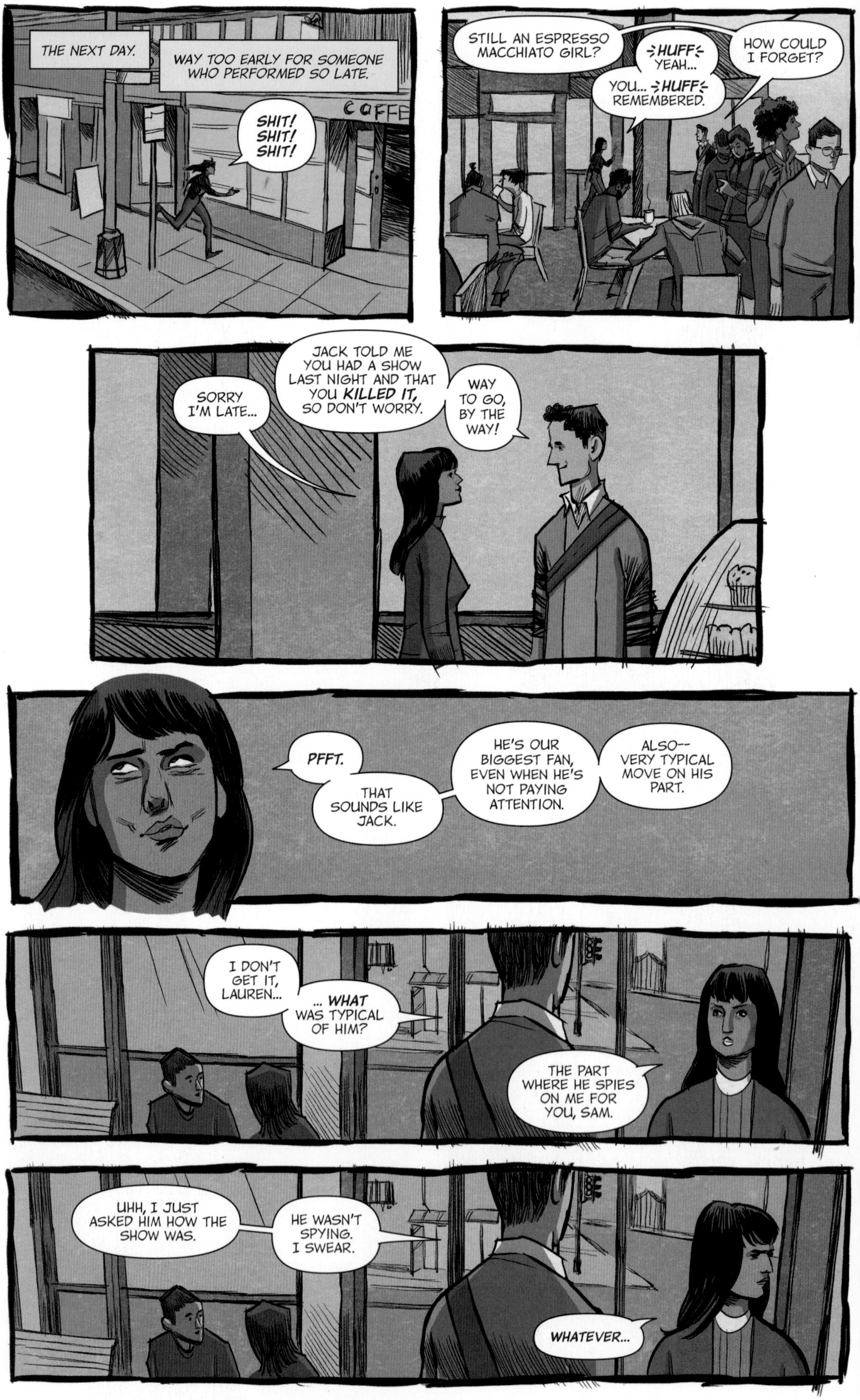
THE NEXT DAY.
WAY TOO EARLY FOR SOMEONE WHO PERFORMED SO LATE.
SHIT! SHIT! SHIT!
STILL AN ESPRESSO MACCHIATO GIRL?
HUFF YEAH...
YOU... HUFF REMEMBERED.
HOW COULD I FORGET?
SORRY I'M LATE...
JACK TOLD ME YOU HAD A SHOW LAST NIGHT AND THAT YOU KILLED IT, SO DON'T WORRY.
WAY TO GO, BY THE WAY!
PFFT.
THAT SOUNDS LIKE JACK.
HE'S OUR BIGGEST FAN, EVEN WHEN HE'S NOT PAYING ATTENTION.
ALSO-- VERY TYPICAL MOVE ON HIS PART.
I DON'T GET IT, LAUREN...
... WHAT WAS TYPICAL OF HIM?
THE PART WHERE HE SPIES ON ME FOR YOU, SAM.
UHH, I JUST ASKED HIM HOW THE SHOW WAS.
HE WASN'T SPYING. I SWEAR.
WHATEVER...

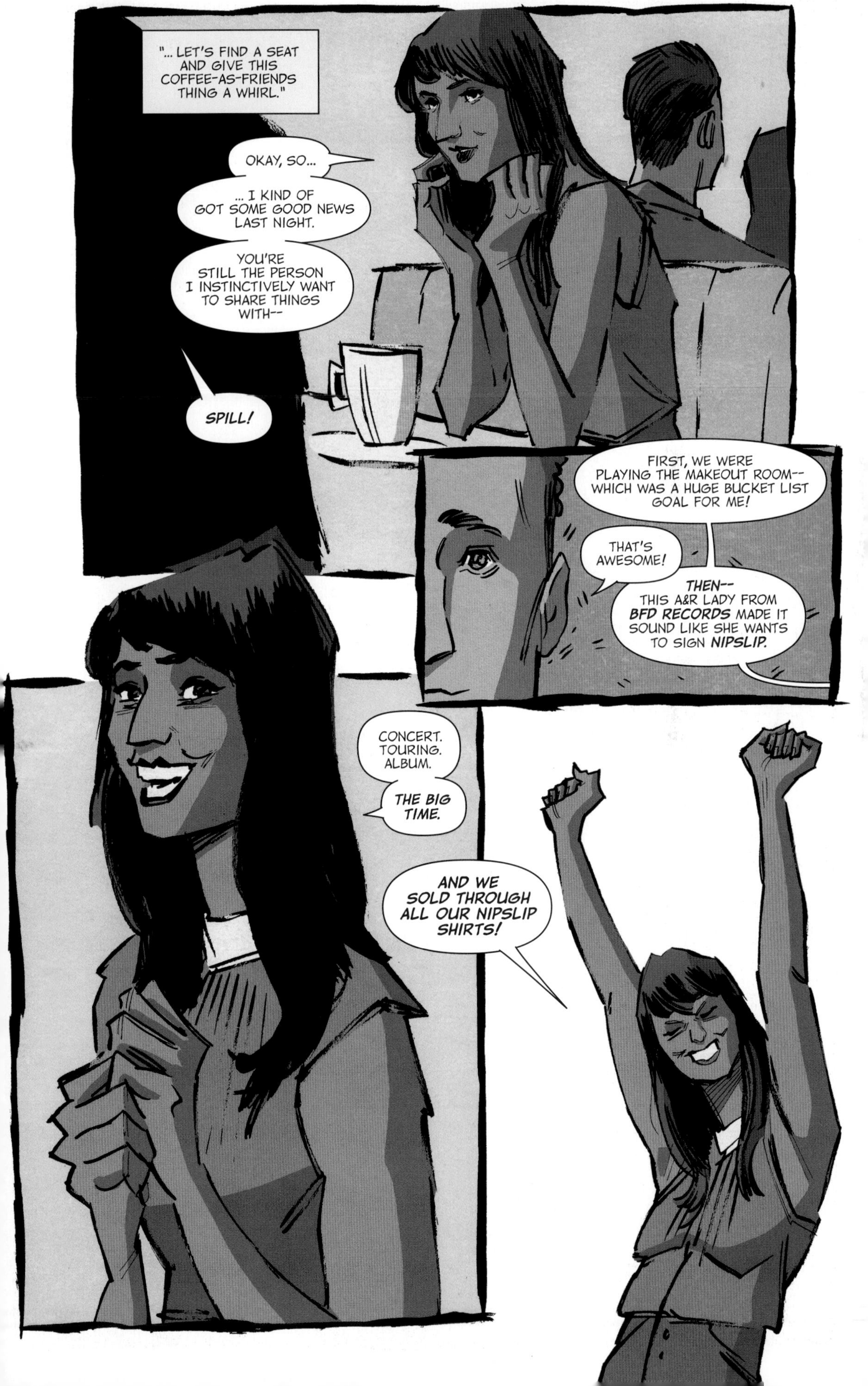
"... LET'S FIND A SEAT AND GIVE THIS COFFEE-AS-FRIENDS THING A WHIRL."
OKAY, SO...
... I KIND OF GOT SOME GOOD NEWS LAST NIGHT.
YOU'RE STILL THE PERSON I INSTINCTIVELY WANT TO SHARE THINGS WITH--
SPILL!
FIRST, WE WERE PLAYING THE MAKEOUT ROOM-- WHICH WAS A HUGE BUCKET LIST GOAL FOR ME!
THAT'S AWESOME!
THEN-- THIS A&R LADY FROM BFD RECORDS MADE IT SOUND LIKE SHE WANTS TO SIGN NIPSLIP.
CONCERT. TOURING. ALBUM.
THE BIG TIME.
AND WE SOLD THROUGH ALL OUR NIPSLIP SHIRTS!

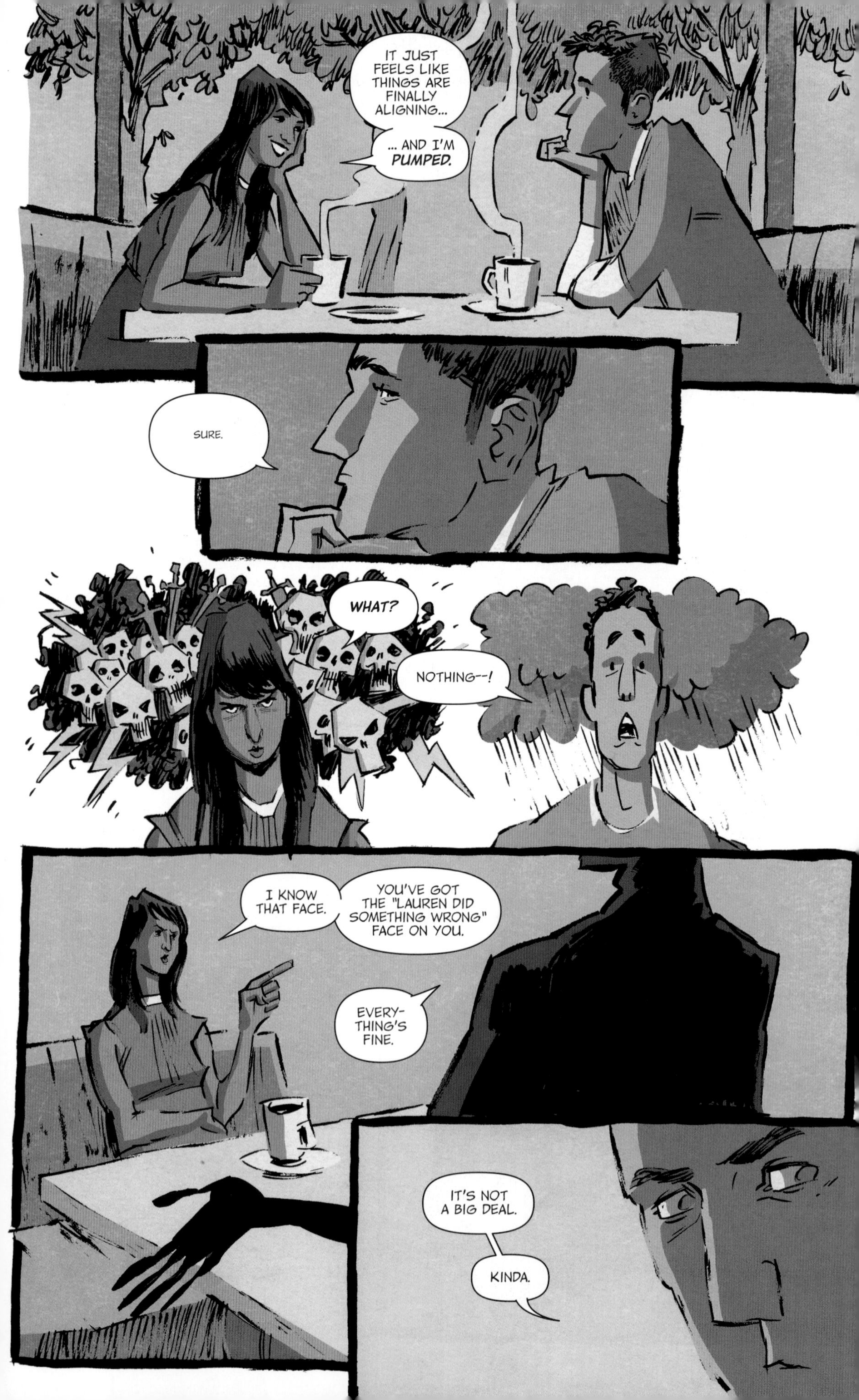
IT JUST FEELS LIKE THINGS ARE FINALLY ALIGNING...
... AND I'M PUMPED.
SURE.
WHAT?
NOTHING--!
I KNOW THAT FACE.
YOU'VE GOT THE "LAUREN DID SOMETHING WRONG" FACE ON YOU.
EVERY-THING'S FINE.
IT'S NOT A BIG DEAL.
KINDA.

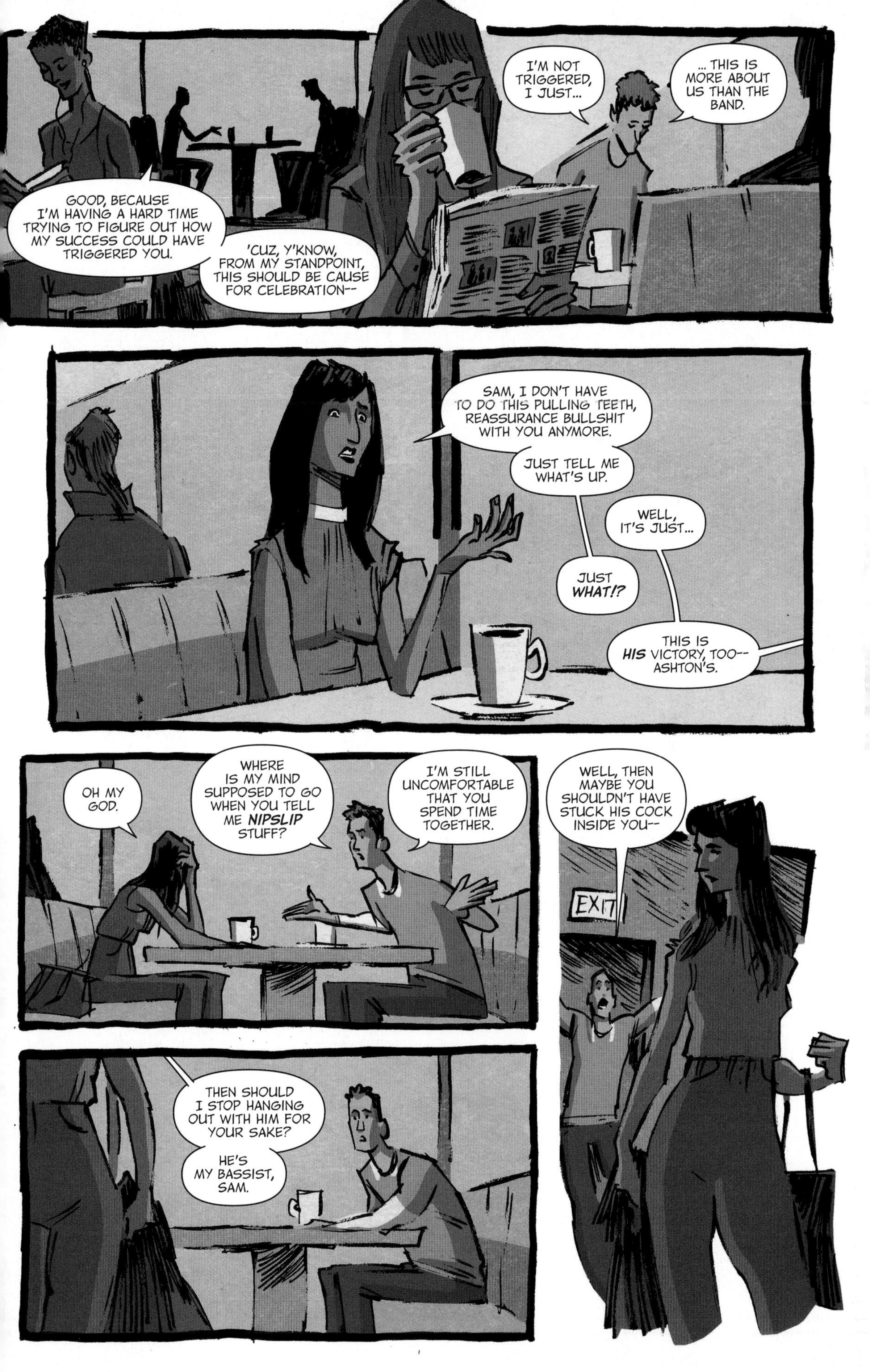
I'M NOT TRIGGERED, I JUST...
... THIS IS MORE ABOUT US THAN THE BAND.
GOOD, BECAUSE I'M HAVING A HARD TIME TRYING TO FIGURE OUT HOW MY SUCCESS COULD HAVE TRIGGERED YOU.
'CUZ, Y'KNOW, FROM MY STANDPOINT, THIS SHOULD BE CAUSE FOR CELEBRATION--
SAM, I DON'T HAVE TO DO THIS PULLING TEETH, REASSURANCE BULLSHIT WITH YOU ANYMORE.
JUST TELL ME WHAT'S UP.
WELL, IT'S JUST...
JUST WHAT!?
THIS IS HIS VICTORY, TOO-- ASHTON'S.
OH MY GOD.
WHERE IS MY MIND SUPPOSED TO GO WHEN YOU TELL ME NIPSLIP STUFF?
I'M STILL UNCOMFORTABLE THAT YOU SPEND TIME TOGETHER.
THEN SHOULD I STOP HANGING OUT WITH HIM FOR YOUR SAKE?
HE'S MY BASSIST, SAM.
WELL, THEN MAYBE YOU SHOULDN'T HAVE STUCK HIS COCK INSIDE YOU--
EXIT

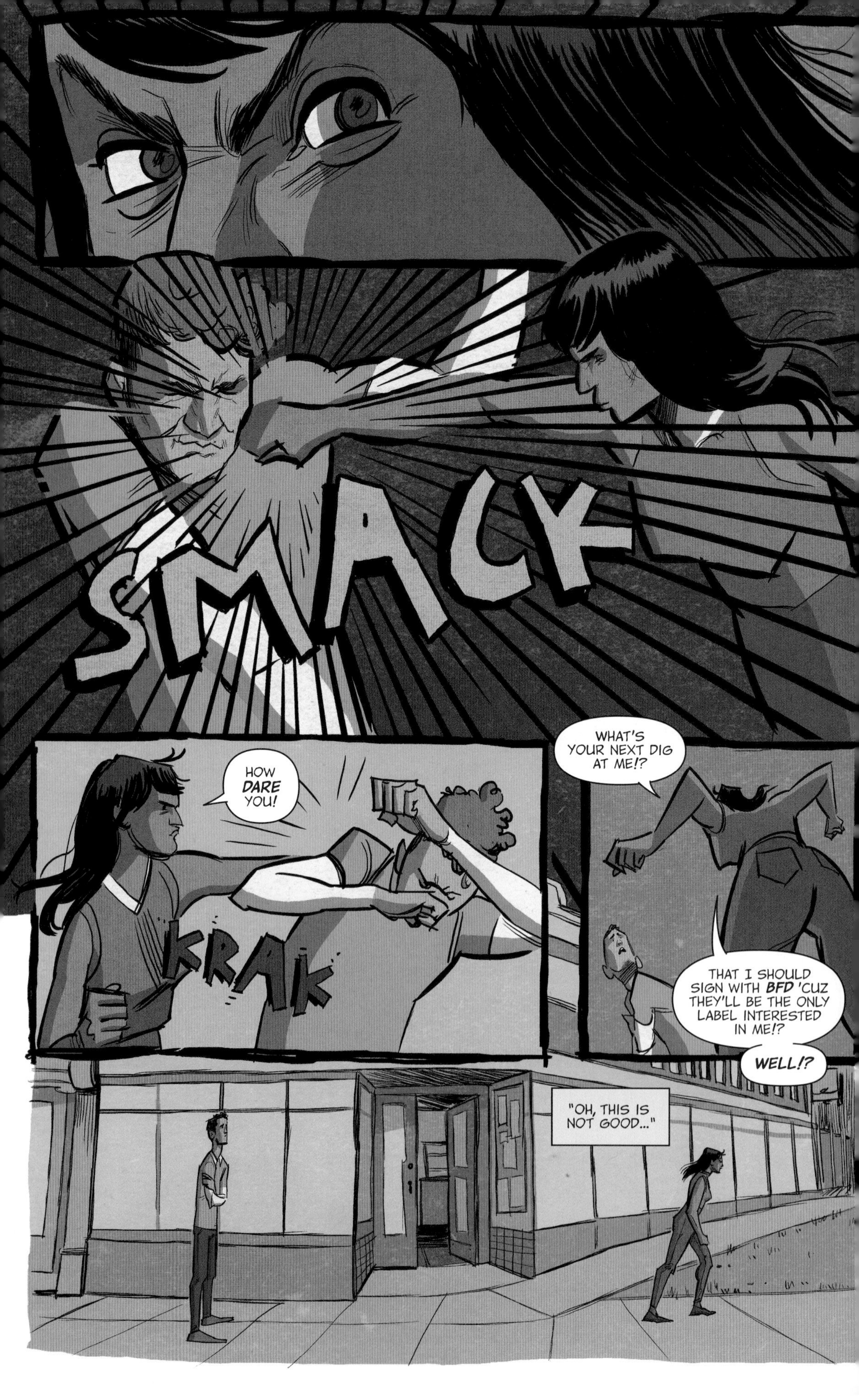
SMACK
HOW DARE YOU!
KRAK
WHAT'S YOUR NEXT DIG AT ME!?
THAT I SHOULD SIGN WITH BFD 'CUZ THEY'LL BE THE ONLY LABEL INTERESTED IN ME!?
WELL!?
"OH, THIS IS NOT GOOD..."

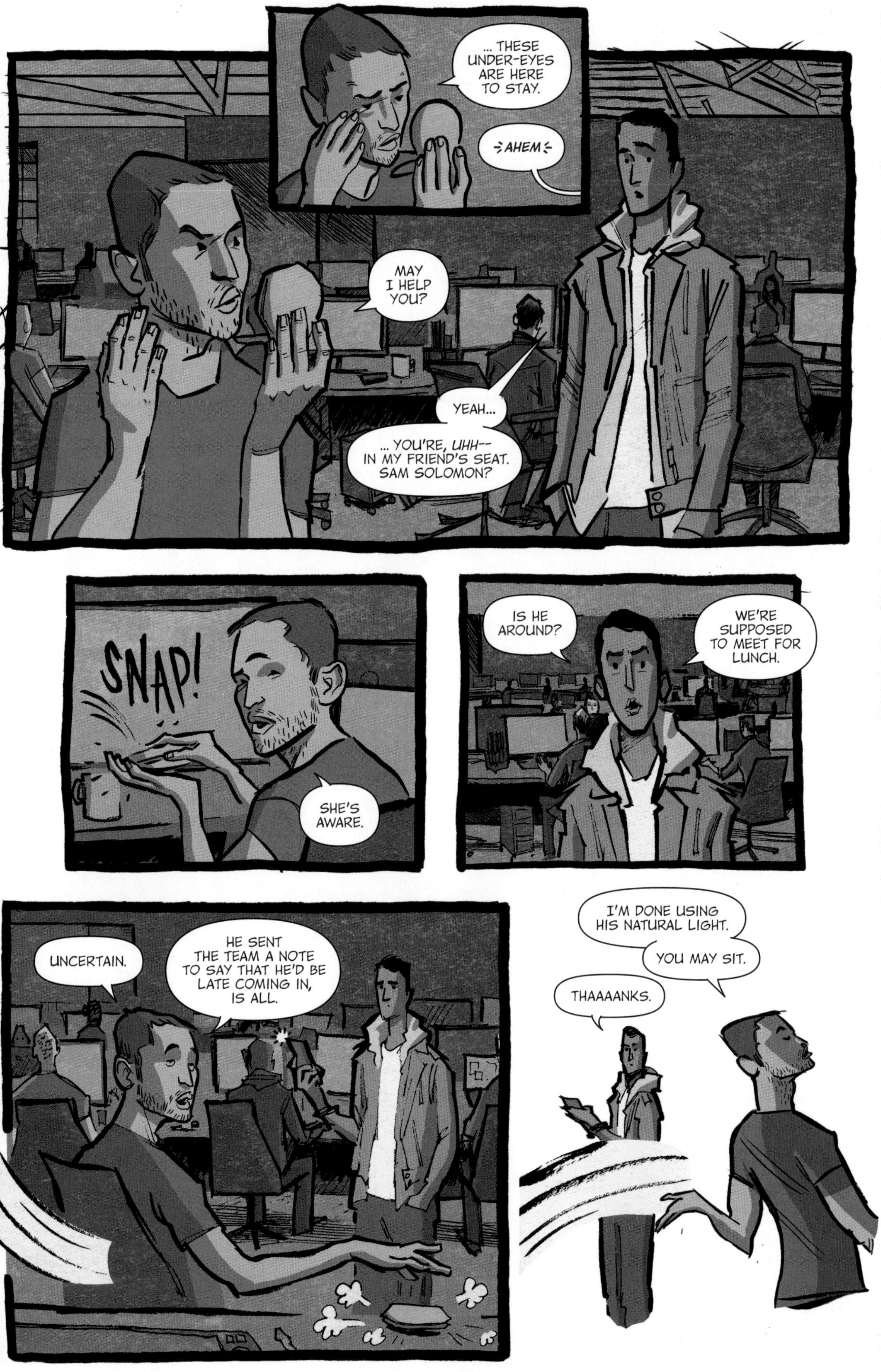
... THESE UNDER-EYES ARE HERE TO STAY.
AHEM
MAY I HELP YOU?
YEAH...
... YOU'RE, UHH-- IN MY FRIEND'S SEAT. SAM SOLOMON?
SNAP!
SHE'S AWARE.
IS HE AROUND?
WE'RE SUPPOSED TO MEET FOR LUNCH.
UNCERTAIN.
HE SENT THE TEAM A NOTE TO SAY THAT HE'D BE LATE COMING IN, IS ALL.
I'M DONE USING HIS NATURAL LIGHT.
YOU MAY SIT.
THAAAANKS.

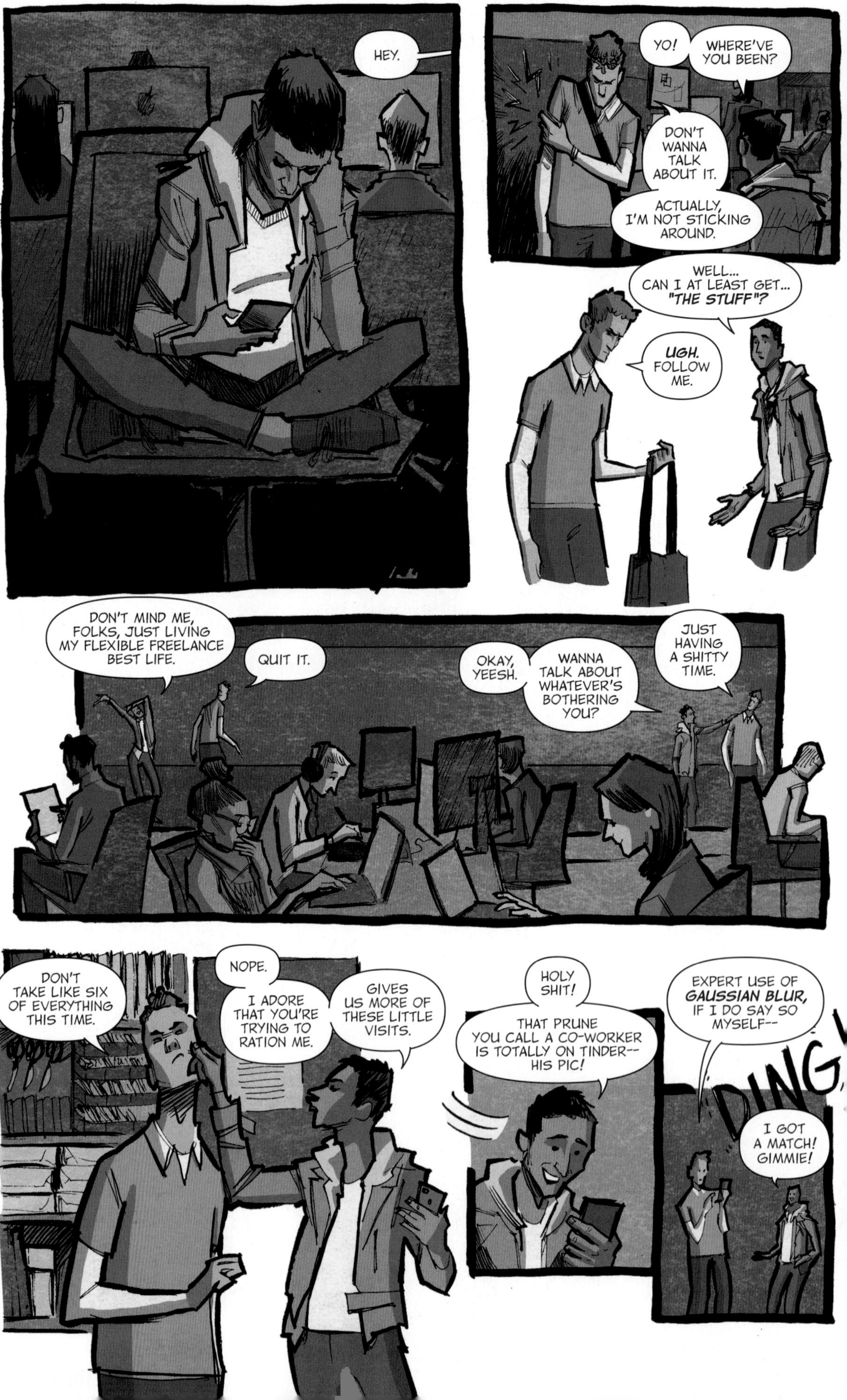
HEY.
YO!
WHERE'VE YOU BEEN?
DON'T WANNA TALK ABOUT IT.
ACTUALLY, I'M NOT STICKING AROUND.
WELL... CAN I AT LEAST GET... *"THE STUFF"?*
UGH. FOLLOW ME.
DON'T MIND ME, FOLKS, JUST LIVING MY FLEXIBLE FREELANCE BEST LIFE.
QUIT IT.
OKAY, YEESH.
WANNA TALK ABOUT WHATEVER'S BOTHERING YOU?
JUST HAVING A SHITTY TIME.
DON'T TAKE LIKE SIX OF EVERYTHING THIS TIME.
NOPE.
I ADORE THAT YOU'RE TRYING TO RATION ME.
GIVES US MORE OF THESE LITTLE VISITS.
HOLY SHIT!
THAT PRUNE YOU CALL A CO-WORKER IS TOTALLY ON TINDER-- HIS PIC!
EXPERT USE OF ***GAUSSIAN BLUR,*** IF I DO SAY SO MYSELF--
DING!
I GOT A MATCH! GIMMIE!

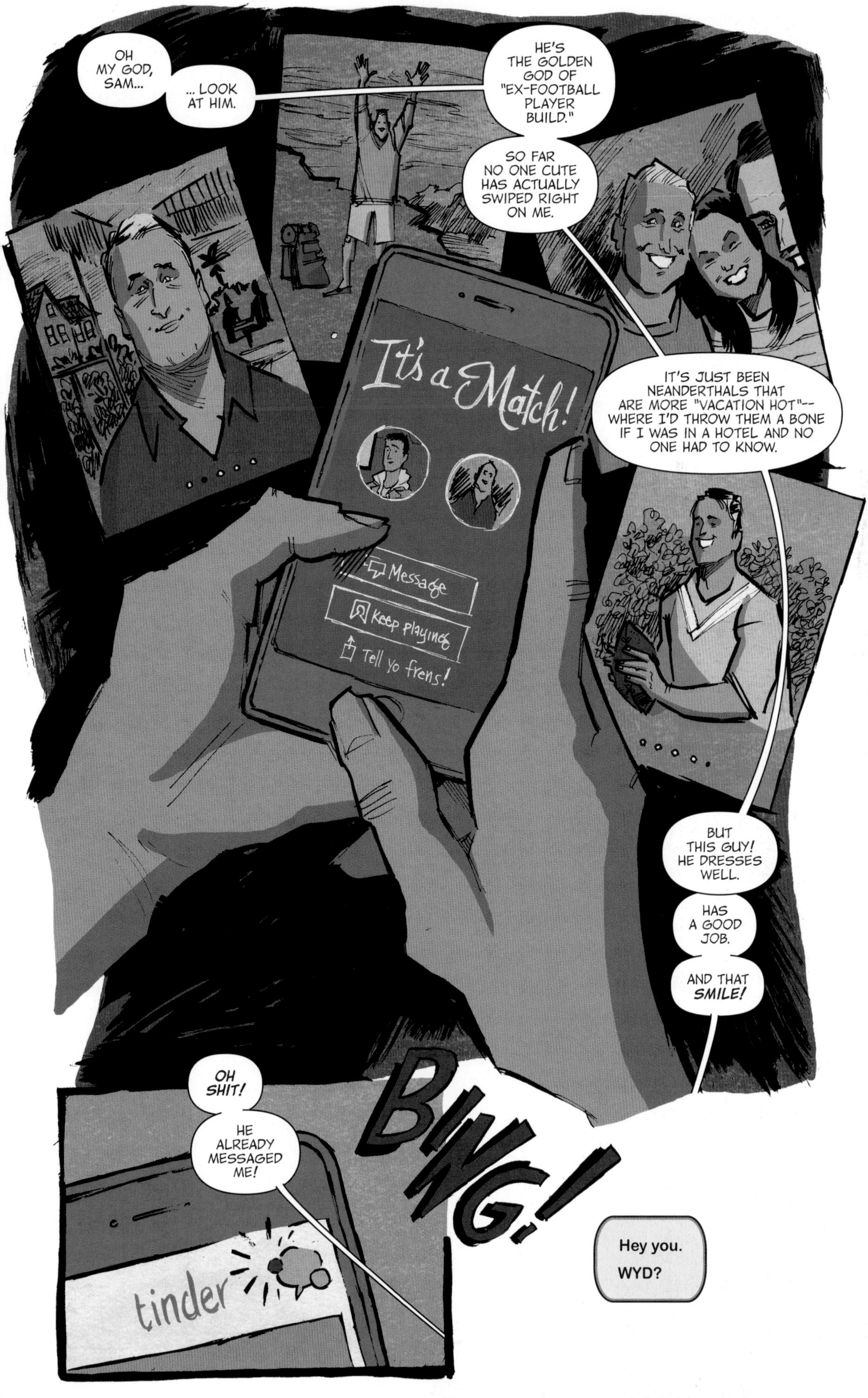
OH MY GOD, SAM...
... LOOK AT HIM.
HE'S THE GOLDEN GOD OF "EX-FOOTBALL PLAYER BUILD."
SO FAR NO ONE CUTE HAS ACTUALLY SWIPED RIGHT ON ME.
It's a Match!
Message
Keep playing
Tell yo frens!
IT'S JUST BEEN NEANDERTHALS THAT ARE MORE "VACATION HOT"-- WHERE I'D THROW THEM A BONE IF I WAS IN A HOTEL AND NO ONE HAD TO KNOW.
BUT THIS GUY! HE DRESSES WELL.
HAS A GOOD JOB.
AND THAT SMILE!
OH SHIT!
HE ALREADY MESSAGED ME!
BING!
tinder
Hey you. WYD?

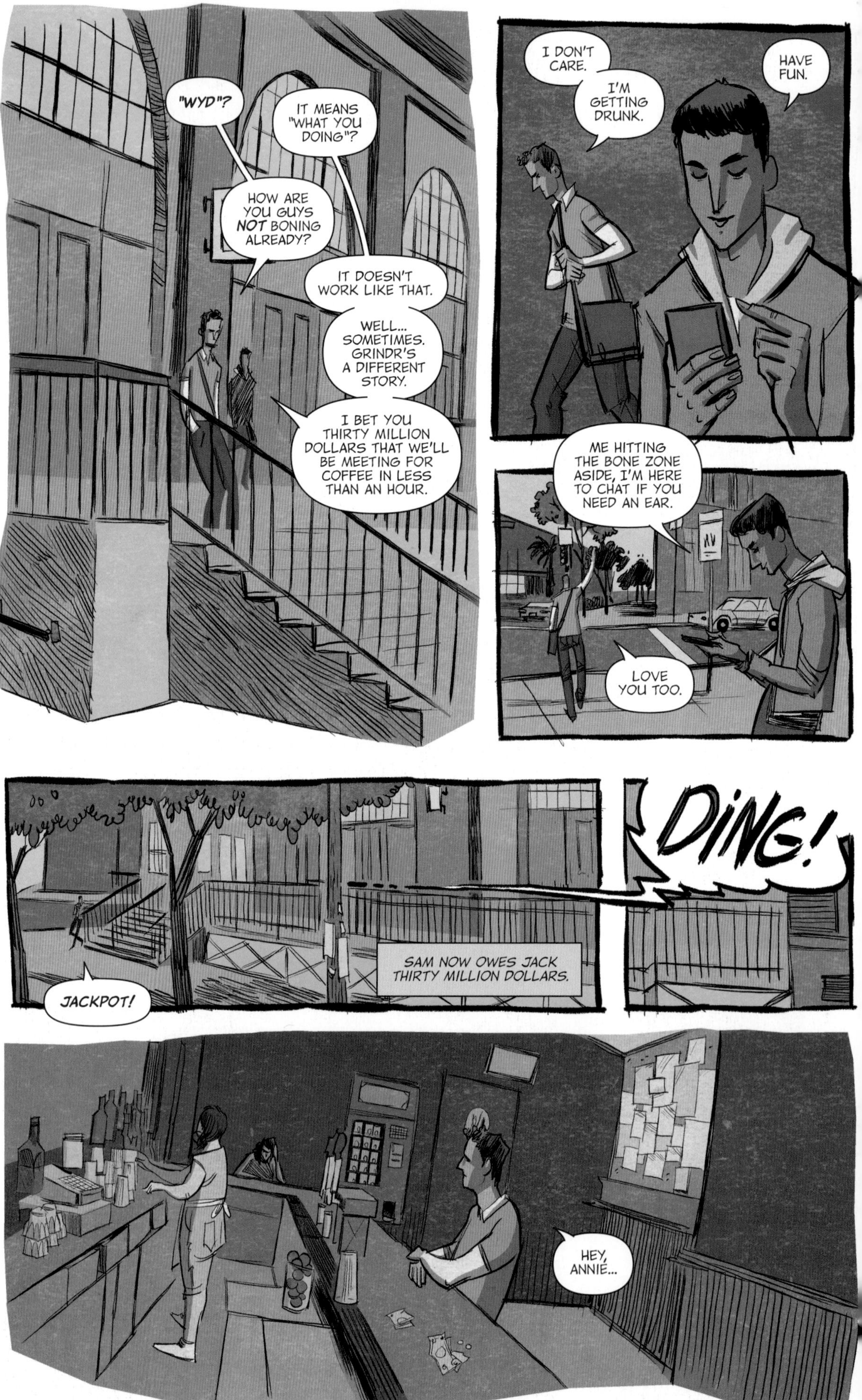
"WYD"?
IT MEANS "WHAT YOU DOING"?
HOW ARE YOU GUYS NOT BONING ALREADY?
IT DOESN'T WORK LIKE THAT.
WELL... SOMETIMES. GRINDR'S A DIFFERENT STORY.
I BET YOU THIRTY MILLION DOLLARS THAT WE'LL BE MEETING FOR COFFEE IN LESS THAN AN HOUR.
I DON'T CARE.
I'M GETTING DRUNK.
HAVE FUN.
ME HITTING THE BONE ZONE ASIDE, I'M HERE TO CHAT IF YOU NEED AN EAR.
LOVE YOU TOO.
JACKPOT!
SAM NOW OWES JACK THIRTY MILLION DOLLARS.
DING!
HEY, ANNIE...

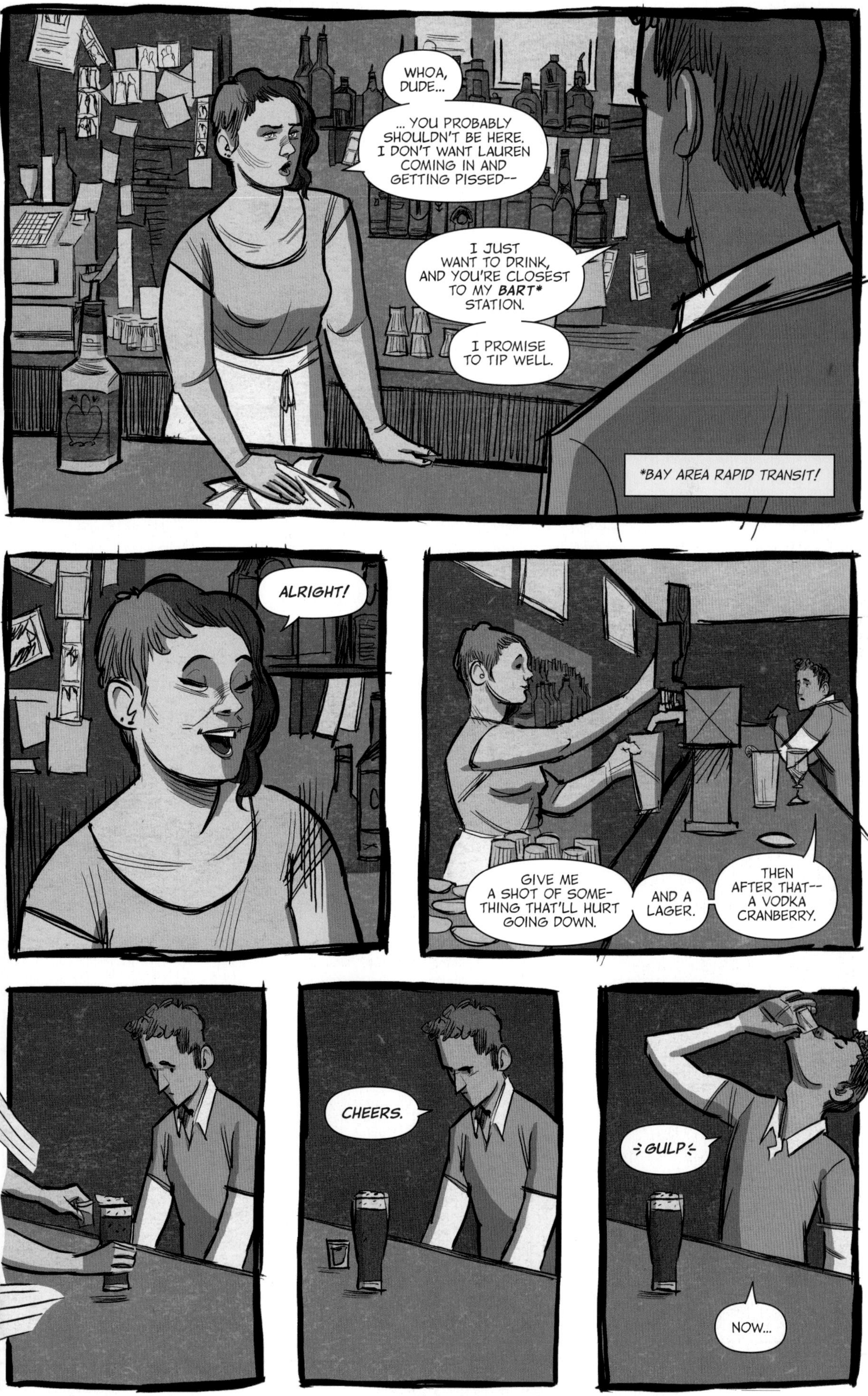
WHOA, DUDE...
... YOU PROBABLY SHOULDN'T BE HERE. I DON'T WANT LAUREN COMING IN AND GETTING PISSED--
I JUST WANT TO DRINK, AND YOU'RE CLOSEST TO MY BART* STATION.
I PROMISE TO TIP WELL.
*BAY AREA RAPID TRANSIT!
ALRIGHT!
GIVE ME A SHOT OF SOMETHING THAT'LL HURT GOING DOWN.
AND A LAGER.
THEN AFTER THAT-- A VODKA CRANBERRY.
CHEERS.
GULP
NOW...

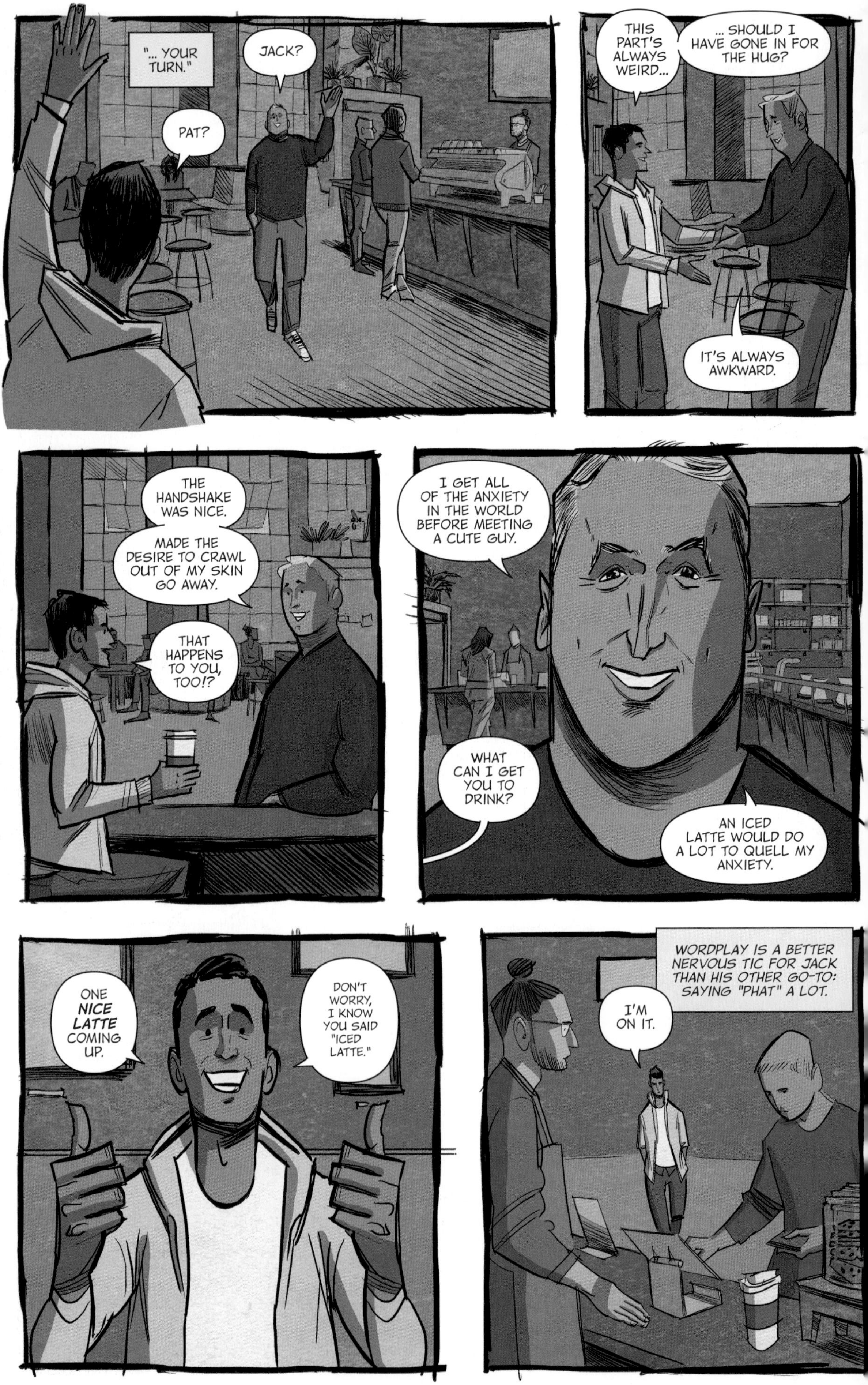

"... YOUR TURN."
JACK?
PAT?
THIS PART'S ALWAYS WEIRD...
... SHOULD I HAVE GONE IN FOR THE HUG?
IT'S ALWAYS AWKWARD.
THE HANDSHAKE WAS NICE.
MADE THE DESIRE TO CRAWL OUT OF MY SKIN GO AWAY.
THAT HAPPENS TO YOU, TOO!?
I GET ALL OF THE ANXIETY IN THE WORLD BEFORE MEETING A CUTE GUY.
WHAT CAN I GET YOU TO DRINK?
AN ICED LATTE WOULD DO A LOT TO QUELL MY ANXIETY.
ONE **NICE LATTE** COMING UP.
DON'T WORRY, I KNOW YOU SAID "ICED LATTE."
WORDPLAY IS A BETTER NERVOUS TIC FOR JACK THAN HIS OTHER GO-TO: SAYING "PHAT" A LOT.
I'M ON IT.

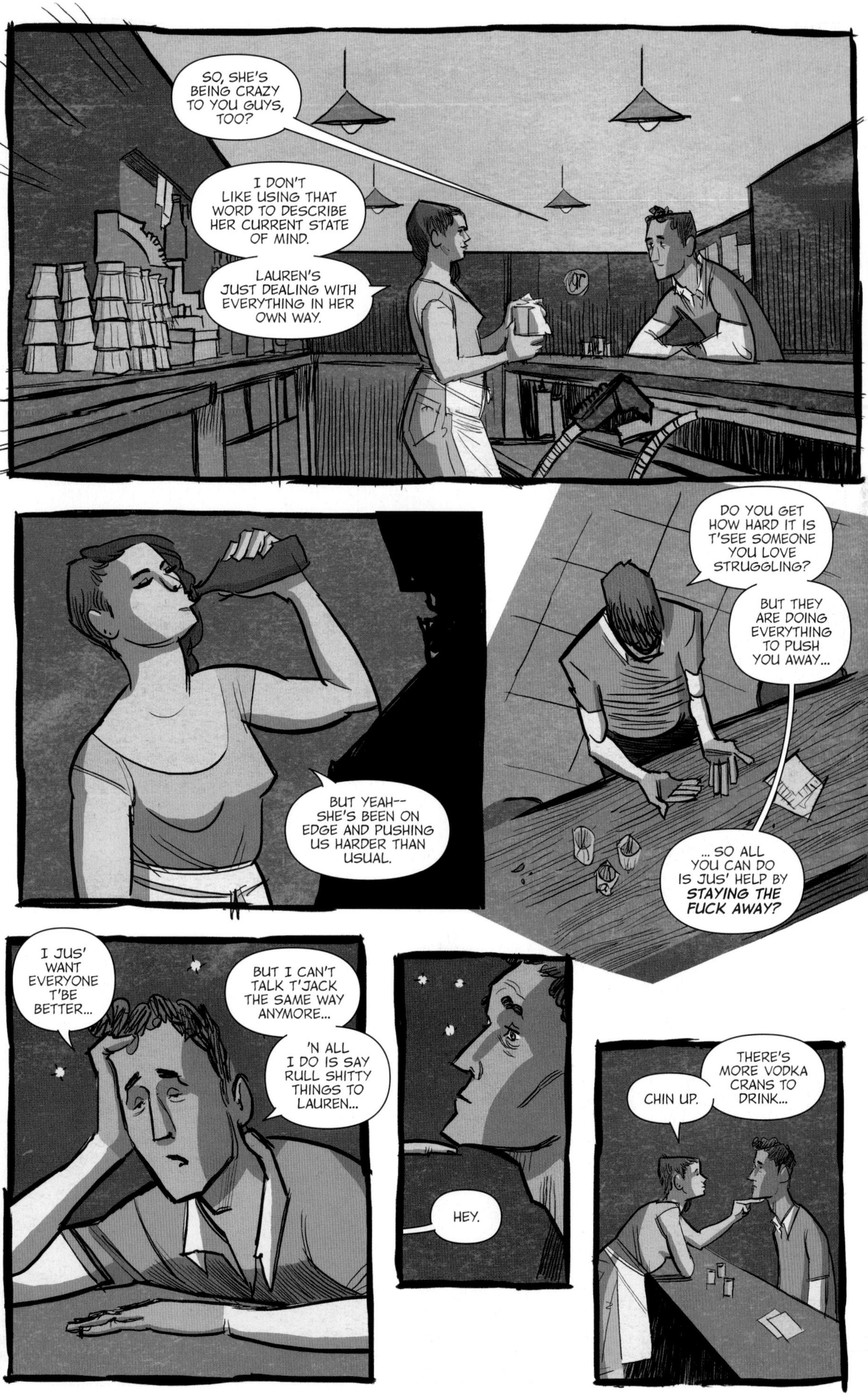
SO, SHE'S BEING CRAZY TO YOU GUYS, TOO?
I DON'T LIKE USING THAT WORD TO DESCRIBE HER CURRENT STATE OF MIND.
LAUREN'S JUST DEALING WITH EVERYTHING IN HER OWN WAY.
BUT YEAH-- SHE'S BEEN ON EDGE AND PUSHING US HARDER THAN USUAL.
DO YOU GET HOW HARD IT IS T'SEE SOMEONE YOU LOVE STRUGGLING?
BUT THEY ARE DOING EVERYTHING TO PUSH YOU AWAY...
... SO ALL YOU CAN DO IS JUS' HELP BY **STAYING THE FUCK AWAY?**
I JUS' WANT EVERYONE T'BE BETTER...
BUT I CAN'T TALK T'JACK THE SAME WAY ANYMORE...
'N ALL I DO IS SAY RULL SHITTY THINGS TO LAUREN...
HEY.
CHIN UP.
THERE'S MORE VODKA CRANS TO DRINK...

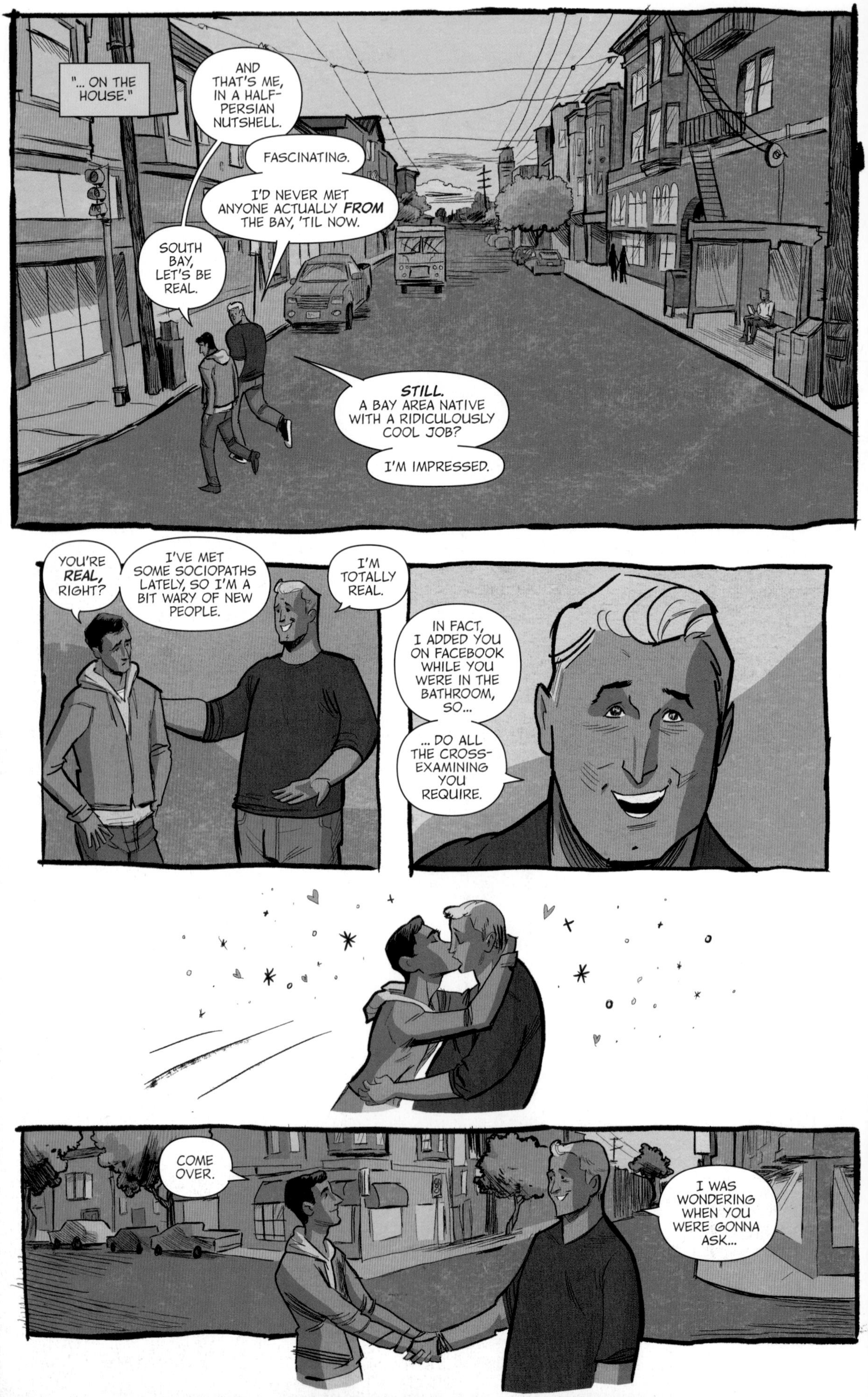
"... ON THE HOUSE."
AND THAT'S ME, IN A HALF-PERSIAN NUTSHELL.
FASCINATING.
I'D NEVER MET ANYONE ACTUALLY **FROM** THE BAY, 'TIL NOW.
SOUTH BAY, LET'S BE REAL.
STILL. A BAY AREA NATIVE WITH A RIDICULOUSLY COOL JOB?
I'M IMPRESSED.
YOU'RE **REAL,** RIGHT?
I'VE MET SOME SOCIOPATHS LATELY, SO I'M A BIT WARY OF NEW PEOPLE.
I'M TOTALLY REAL.
IN FACT, I ADDED YOU ON FACEBOOK WHILE YOU WERE IN THE BATHROOM, SO...
... DO ALL THE CROSS-EXAMINING YOU REQUIRE.
COME OVER.
I WAS WONDERING WHEN YOU WERE GONNA ASK...

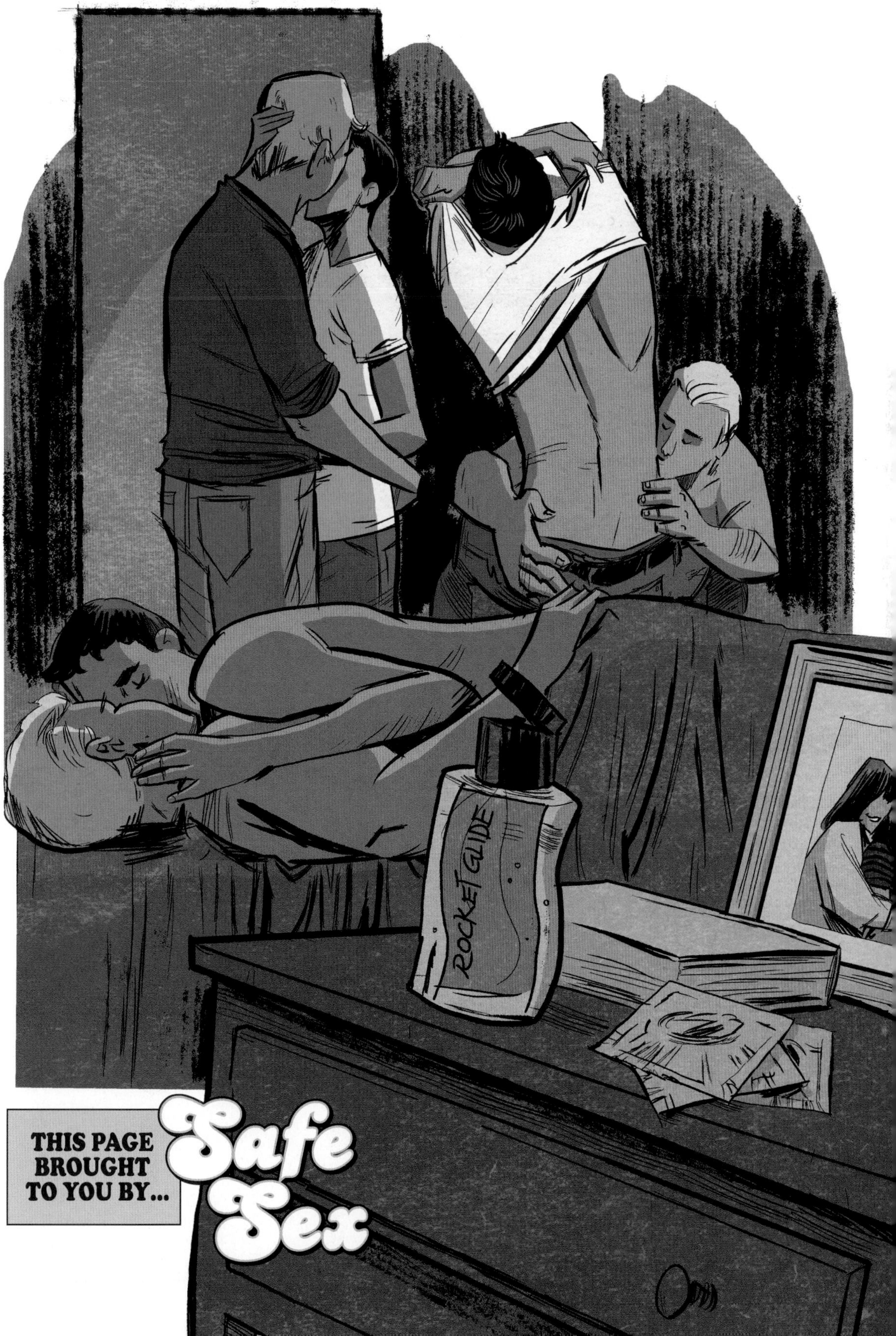
ROCKET GLIDE
THIS PAGE BROUGHT TO YOU BY...
Safe Sex

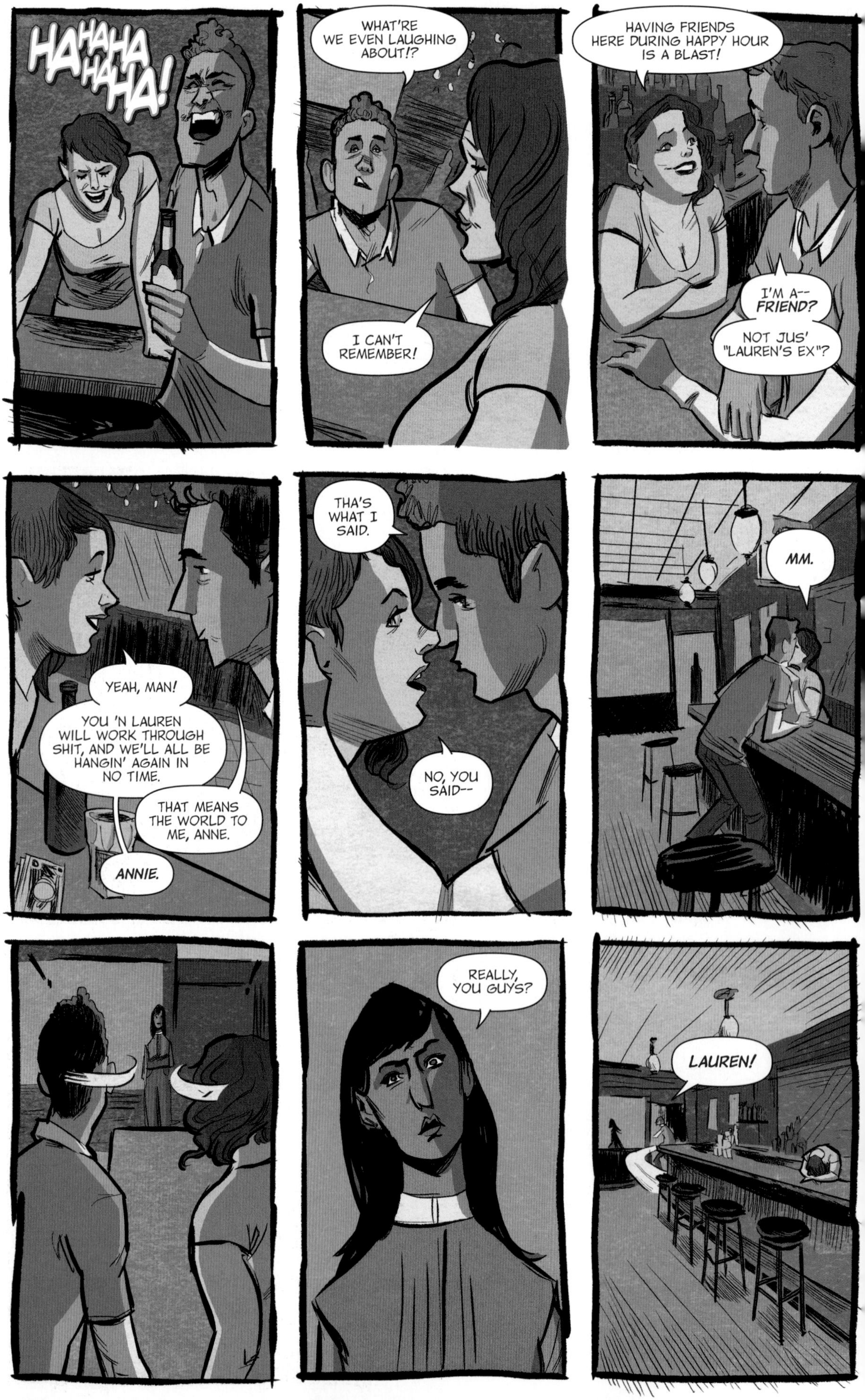
HAHAHA HAHAHA!
WHAT'RE WE EVEN LAUGHING ABOUT!?
I CAN'T REMEMBER!
HAVING FRIENDS HERE DURING HAPPY HOUR IS A BLAST!
I'M A-- FRIEND?
NOT JUS' "LAUREN'S EX"?
YEAH, MAN!
YOU 'N LAUREN WILL WORK THROUGH SHIT, AND WE'LL ALL BE HANGIN' AGAIN IN NO TIME.
THAT MEANS THE WORLD TO ME, ANNE.
ANNIE.
THA'S WHAT I SAID.
NO, YOU SAID--
MM.
REALLY, YOU GUYS?
LAUREN!

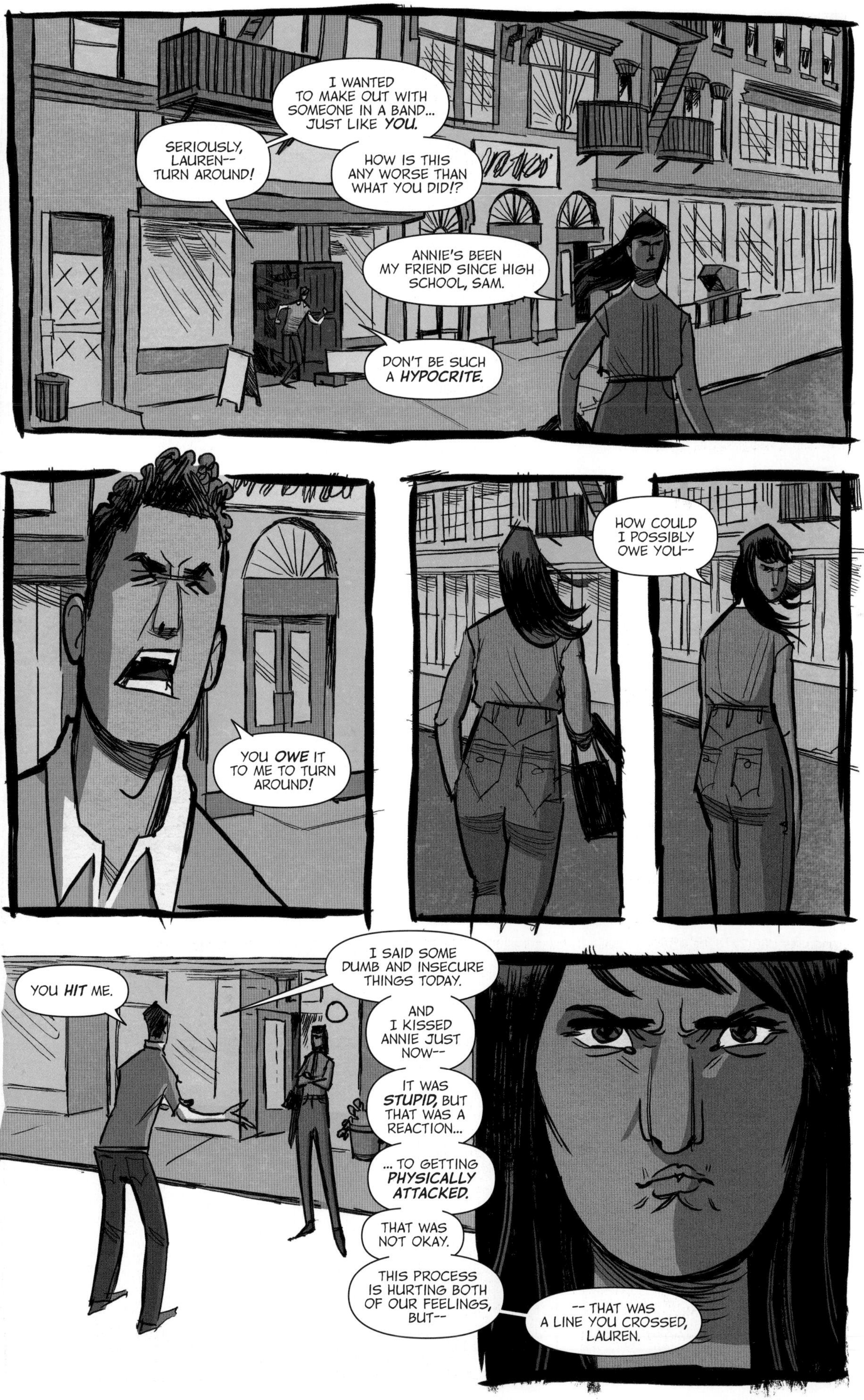
I WANTED TO MAKE OUT WITH SOMEONE IN A BAND... JUST LIKE YOU.
SERIOUSLY, LAUREN-- TURN AROUND!
HOW IS THIS ANY WORSE THAN WHAT YOU DID!?
ANNIE'S BEEN MY FRIEND SINCE HIGH SCHOOL, SAM.
DON'T BE SUCH A HYPOCRITE.
YOU OWE IT TO ME TO TURN AROUND!
HOW COULD I POSSIBLY OWE YOU--
YOU HIT ME.
I SAID SOME DUMB AND INSECURE THINGS TODAY.
AND I KISSED ANNIE JUST NOW--
IT WAS STUPID, BUT THAT WAS A REACTION...
... TO GETTING PHYSICALLY ATTACKED.
THAT WAS NOT OKAY.
THIS PROCESS IS HURTING BOTH OF OUR FEELINGS, BUT--
-- THAT WAS A LINE YOU CROSSED, LAUREN.

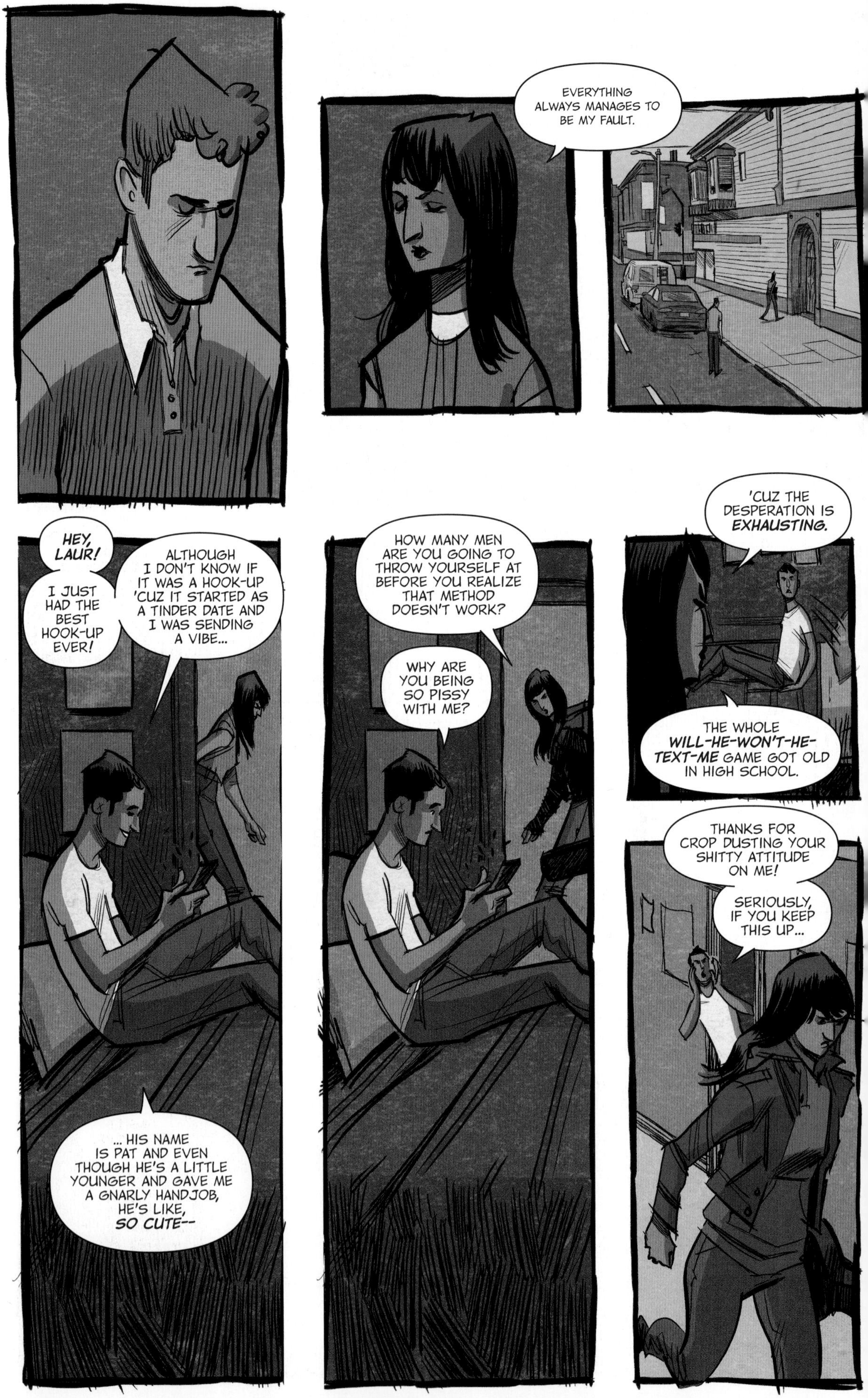
EVERYTHING ALWAYS MANAGES TO BE MY FAULT.
HEY, LAUR!
I JUST HAD THE BEST HOOK-UP EVER!
ALTHOUGH I DON'T KNOW IF IT WAS A HOOK-UP 'CUZ IT STARTED AS A TINDER DATE AND I WAS SENDING A VIBE...
... HIS NAME IS PAT AND EVEN THOUGH HE'S A LITTLE YOUNGER AND GAVE ME A GNARLY HANDJOB, HE'S LIKE, SO CUTE--
HOW MANY MEN ARE YOU GOING TO THROW YOURSELF AT BEFORE YOU REALIZE THAT METHOD DOESN'T WORK?
WHY ARE YOU BEING SO PISSY WITH ME?
'CUZ THE DESPERATION IS EXHAUSTING.
THE WHOLE WILL-HE-WON'T-HE-TEXT-ME GAME GOT OLD IN HIGH SCHOOL.
THANKS FOR CROP DUSTING YOUR SHITTY ATTITUDE ON ME!
SERIOUSLY, IF YOU KEEP THIS UP...

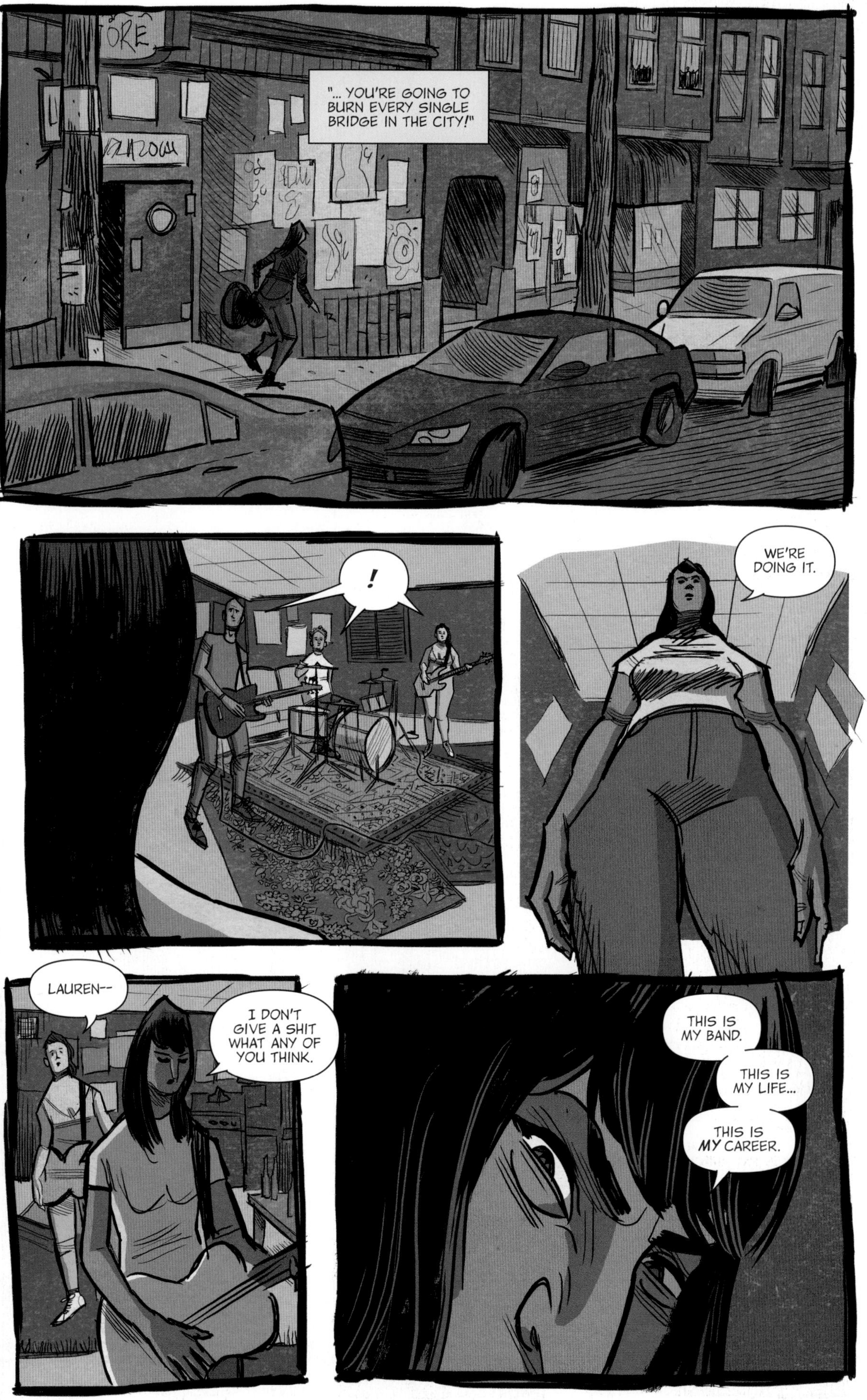
"... YOU'RE GOING TO BURN EVERY SINGLE BRIDGE IN THE CITY!"
!
WE'RE DOING IT.
LAUREN--
I DON'T GIVE A SHIT WHAT ANY OF YOU THINK.
THIS IS MY BAND.
THIS IS MY LIFE...
THIS IS MY CAREER.

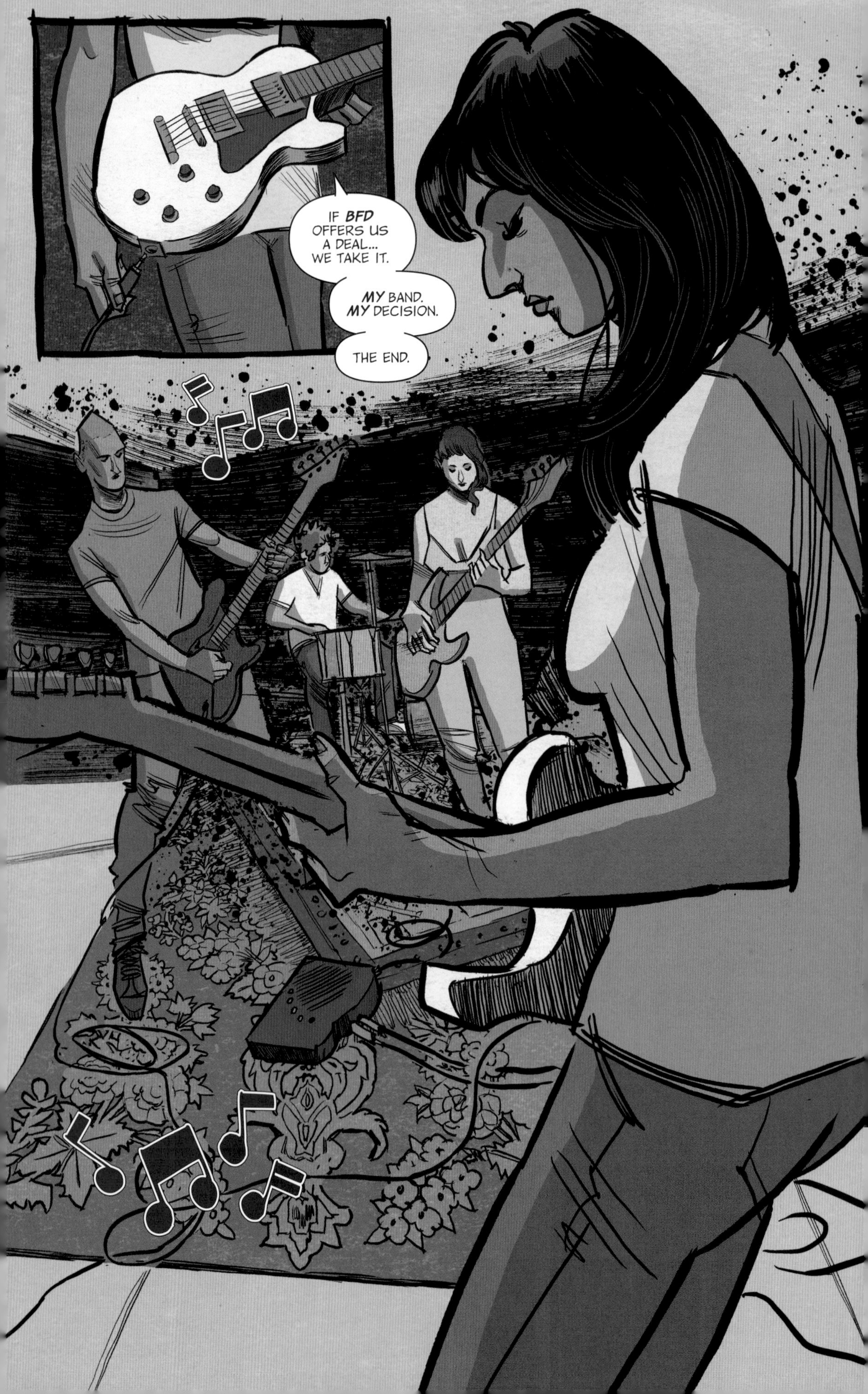
IF **BFD** OFFERS US A DEAL... WE TAKE IT.
MY BAND. **MY** DECISION.
THE END.

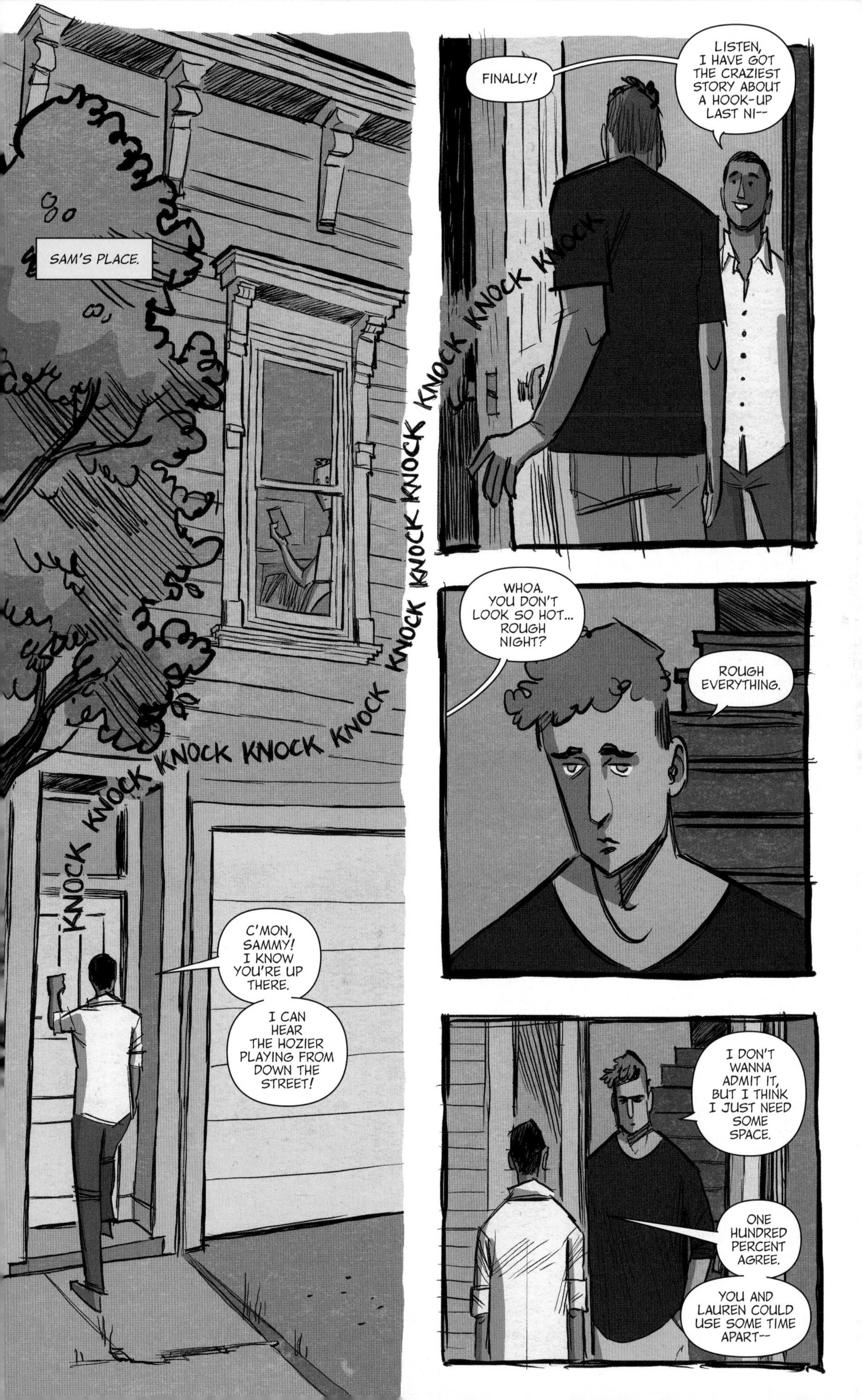
SAM'S PLACE.
KNOCK KNOCK KNOCK KNOCK KNOCK KNOCK KNOCK KNOCK KNOCK KNOCK
C'MON, SAMMY! I KNOW YOU'RE UP THERE.
I CAN HEAR THE HOZIER PLAYING FROM DOWN THE STREET!
FINALLY!
LISTEN, I HAVE GOT THE CRAZIEST STORY ABOUT A HOOK-UP LAST NI--
WHOA. YOU DON'T LOOK SO HOT... ROUGH NIGHT?
ROUGH EVERYTHING.
I DON'T WANNA ADMIT IT, BUT I THINK I JUST NEED SOME SPACE.
ONE HUNDRED PERCENT AGREE.
YOU AND LAUREN COULD USE SOME TIME APART--

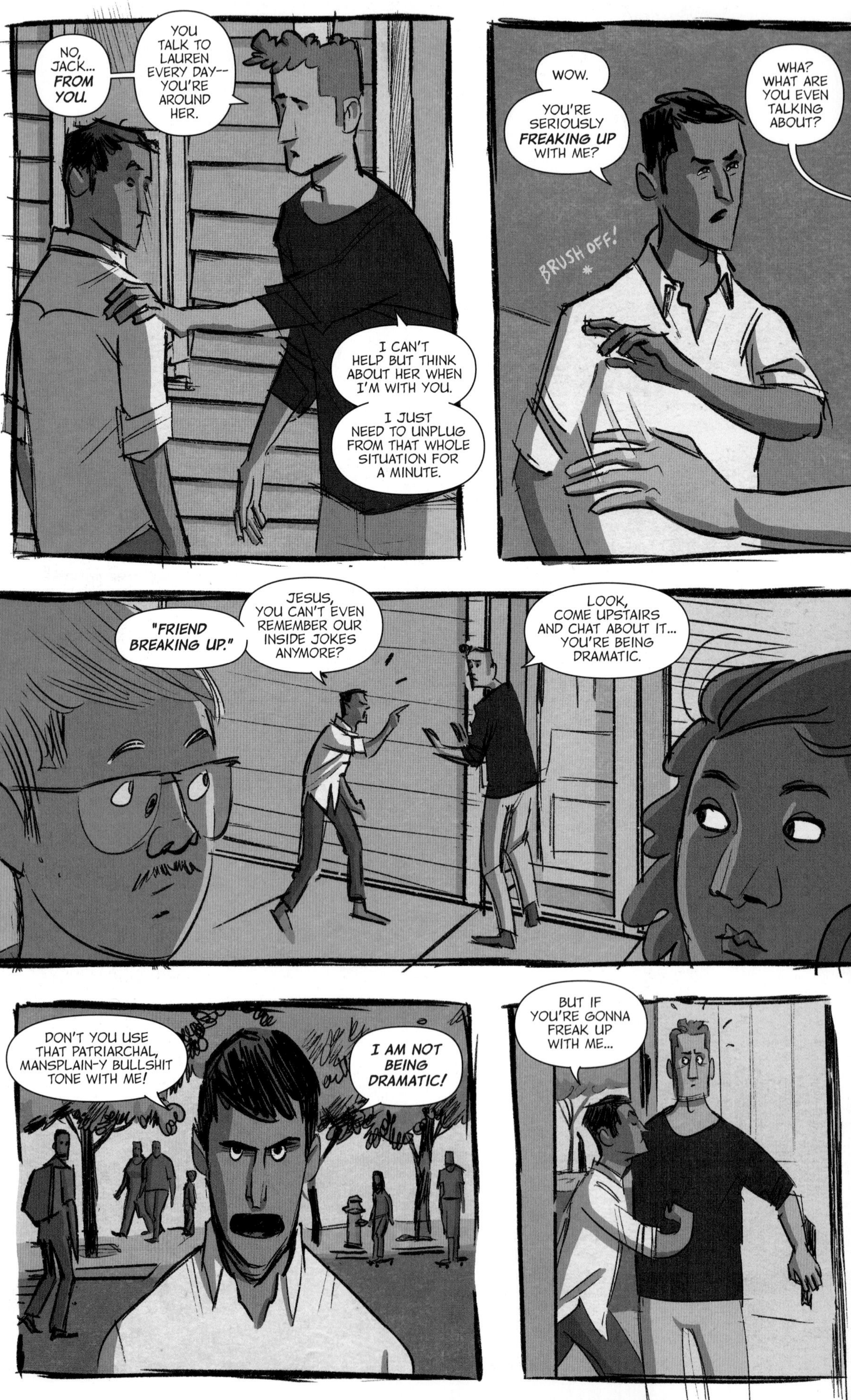
NO, JACK... **FROM YOU.**
YOU TALK TO LAUREN EVERY DAY-- YOU'RE AROUND HER.
I CAN'T HELP BUT THINK ABOUT HER WHEN I'M WITH YOU.
I JUST NEED TO UNPLUG FROM THAT WHOLE SITUATION FOR A MINUTE.
WOW.
YOU'RE SERIOUSLY **FREAKING UP** WITH ME?
WHA? WHAT ARE YOU EVEN TALKING ABOUT?
BRUSH OFF!
"FRIEND BREAKING UP."
JESUS, YOU CAN'T EVEN REMEMBER OUR INSIDE JOKES ANYMORE?
LOOK, COME UPSTAIRS AND CHAT ABOUT IT... YOU'RE BEING DRAMATIC.
DON'T YOU USE THAT PATRIARCHAL, MANSPLAIN-Y BULLSHIT TONE WITH ME!
I AM NOT BEING DRAMATIC!
BUT IF YOU'RE GONNA FREAK UP WITH ME...

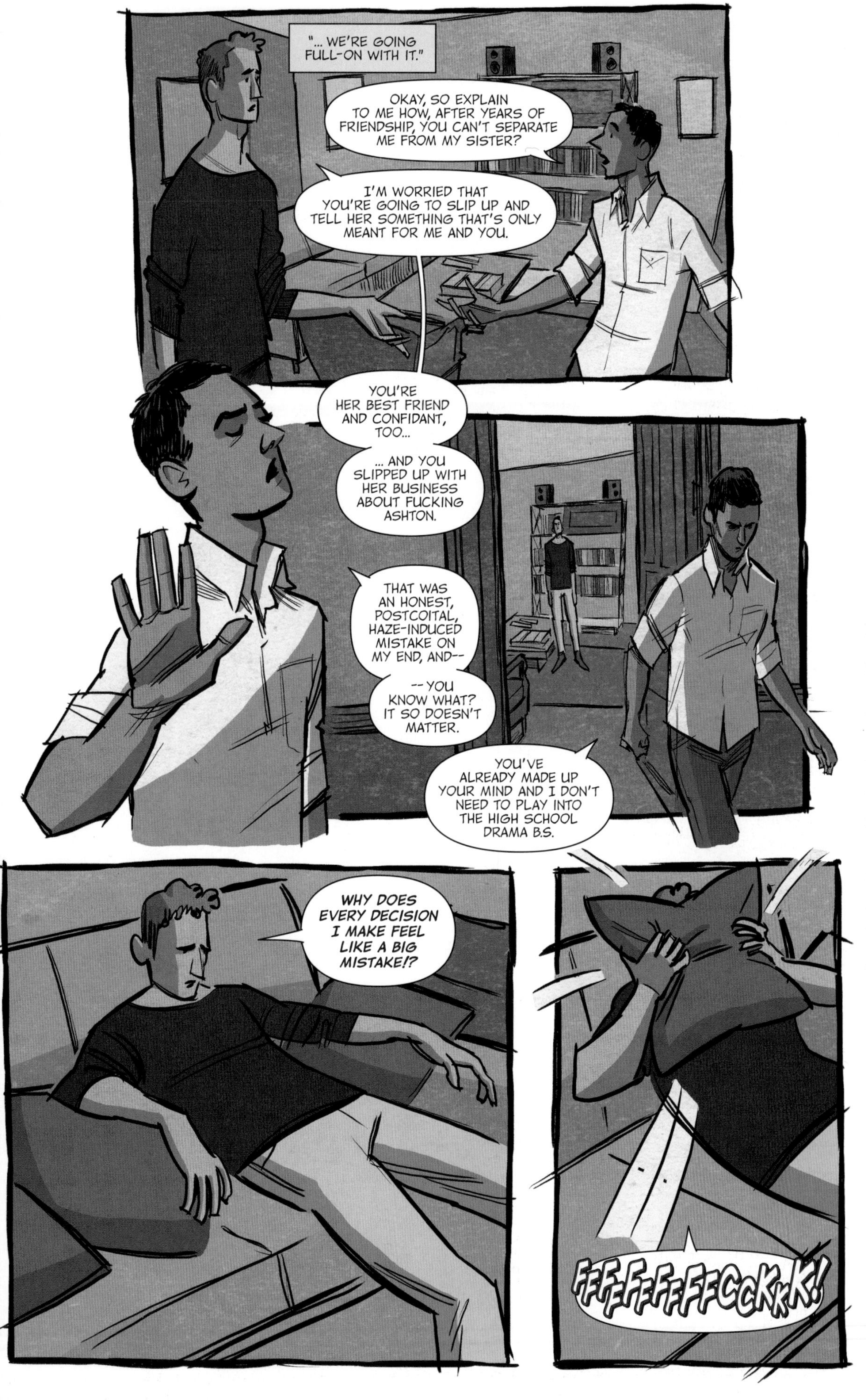
"... WE'RE GOING FULL-ON WITH IT."
OKAY, SO EXPLAIN TO ME HOW, AFTER YEARS OF FRIENDSHIP, YOU CAN'T SEPARATE ME FROM MY SISTER?
I'M WORRIED THAT YOU'RE GOING TO SLIP UP AND TELL HER SOMETHING THAT'S ONLY MEANT FOR ME AND YOU.
YOU'RE HER BEST FRIEND AND CONFIDANT, TOO...
... AND YOU SLIPPED UP WITH HER BUSINESS ABOUT FUCKING ASHTON.
THAT WAS AN HONEST, POSTCOITAL, HAZE-INDUCED MISTAKE ON MY END, AND--
--YOU KNOW WHAT? IT SO DOESN'T MATTER.
YOU'VE ALREADY MADE UP YOUR MIND AND I DON'T NEED TO PLAY INTO THE HIGH SCHOOL DRAMA B.S.
WHY DOES EVERY DECISION I MAKE FEEL LIKE A BIG MISTAKE!?
FFFFFFFFFFCCKKK!

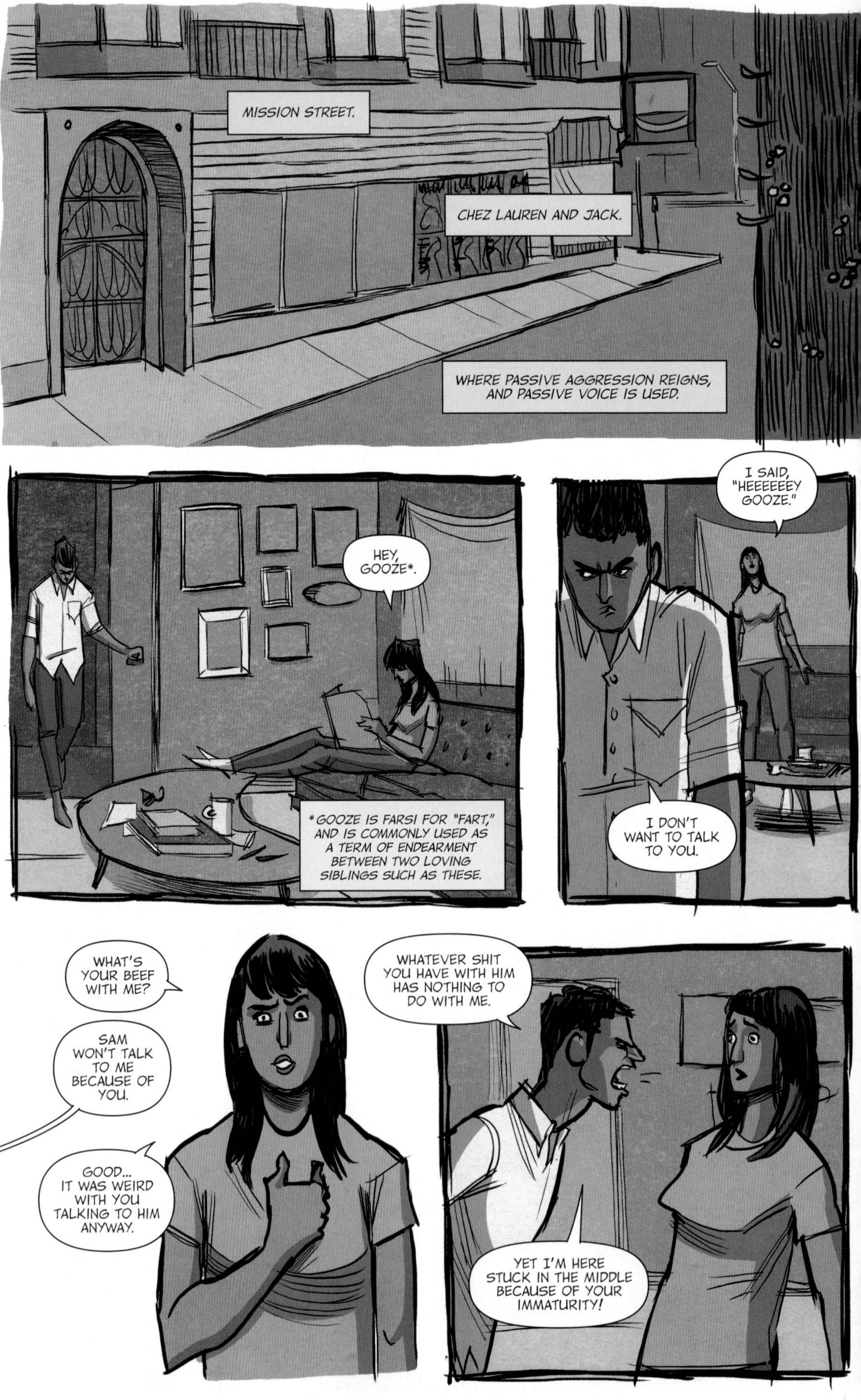
MISSION STREET.
CHEZ LAUREN AND JACK.
WHERE PASSIVE AGGRESSION REIGNS, AND PASSIVE VOICE IS USED.
HEY, GOOZE*.
*GOOZE IS FARSI FOR "FART," AND IS COMMONLY USED AS A TERM OF ENDEARMENT BETWEEN TWO LOVING SIBLINGS SUCH AS THESE.
I SAID, "HEEEEEEY GOOZE."
I DON'T WANT TO TALK TO YOU.
WHAT'S YOUR BEEF WITH ME?
SAM WON'T TALK TO ME BECAUSE OF YOU.
GOOD... IT WAS WEIRD WITH YOU TALKING TO HIM ANYWAY.
WHATEVER SHIT YOU HAVE WITH HIM HAS NOTHING TO DO WITH ME.
YET I'M HERE STUCK IN THE MIDDLE BECAUSE OF YOUR IMMATURITY!

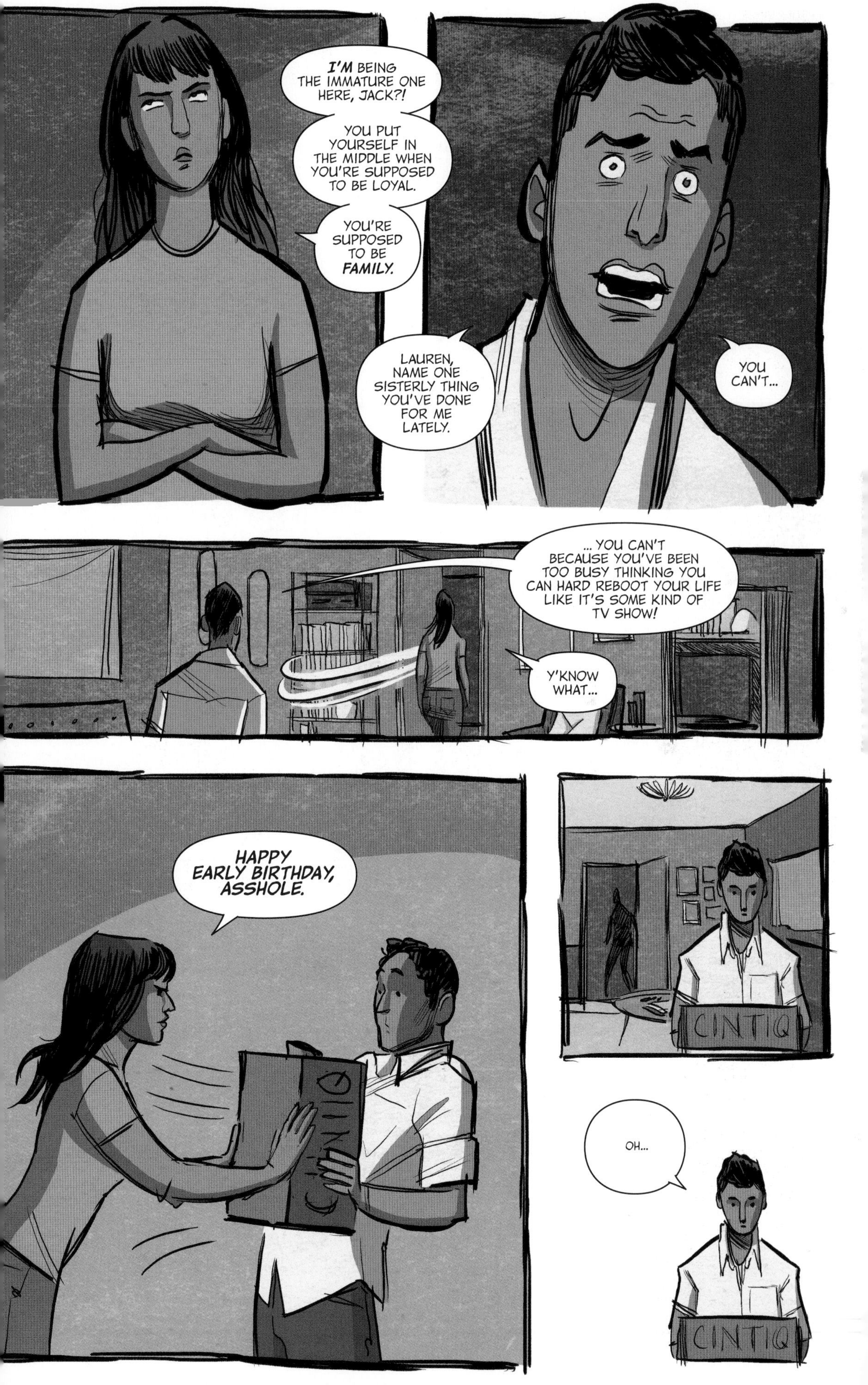

I'M BEING THE IMMATURE ONE HERE, JACK?!
YOU PUT YOURSELF IN THE MIDDLE WHEN YOU'RE SUPPOSED TO BE LOYAL.
YOU'RE SUPPOSED TO BE FAMILY.
LAUREN, NAME ONE SISTERLY THING YOU'VE DONE FOR ME LATELY.
YOU CAN'T...
... YOU CAN'T BECAUSE YOU'VE BEEN TOO BUSY THINKING YOU CAN HARD REBOOT YOUR LIFE LIKE IT'S SOME KIND OF TV SHOW!
Y'KNOW WHAT...
HAPPY EARLY BIRTHDAY, ASSHOLE.
CINTIQ
OH...
CINTIQ

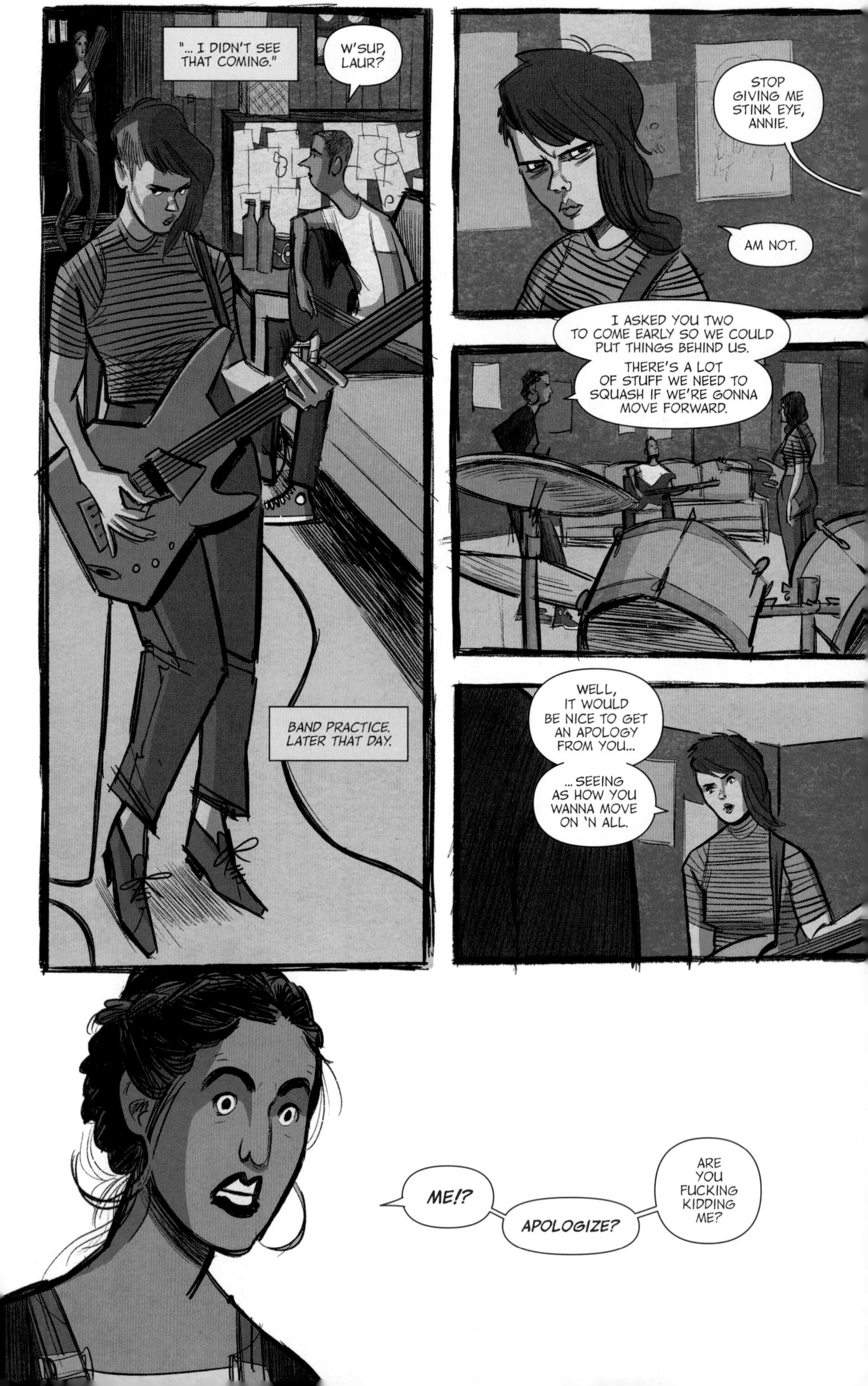
"... I DIDN'T SEE THAT COMING."
W'SUP, LAUR?
BAND PRACTICE. LATER THAT DAY.
STOP GIVING ME STINK EYE, ANNIE.
AM NOT.
I ASKED YOU TWO TO COME EARLY SO WE COULD PUT THINGS BEHIND US.
THERE'S A LOT OF STUFF WE NEED TO SQUASH IF WE'RE GONNA MOVE FORWARD.
WELL, IT WOULD BE NICE TO GET AN APOLOGY FROM YOU...
...SEEING AS HOW YOU WANNA MOVE ON 'N ALL.
ME!?
APOLOGIZE?
ARE YOU FUCKING KIDDING ME?

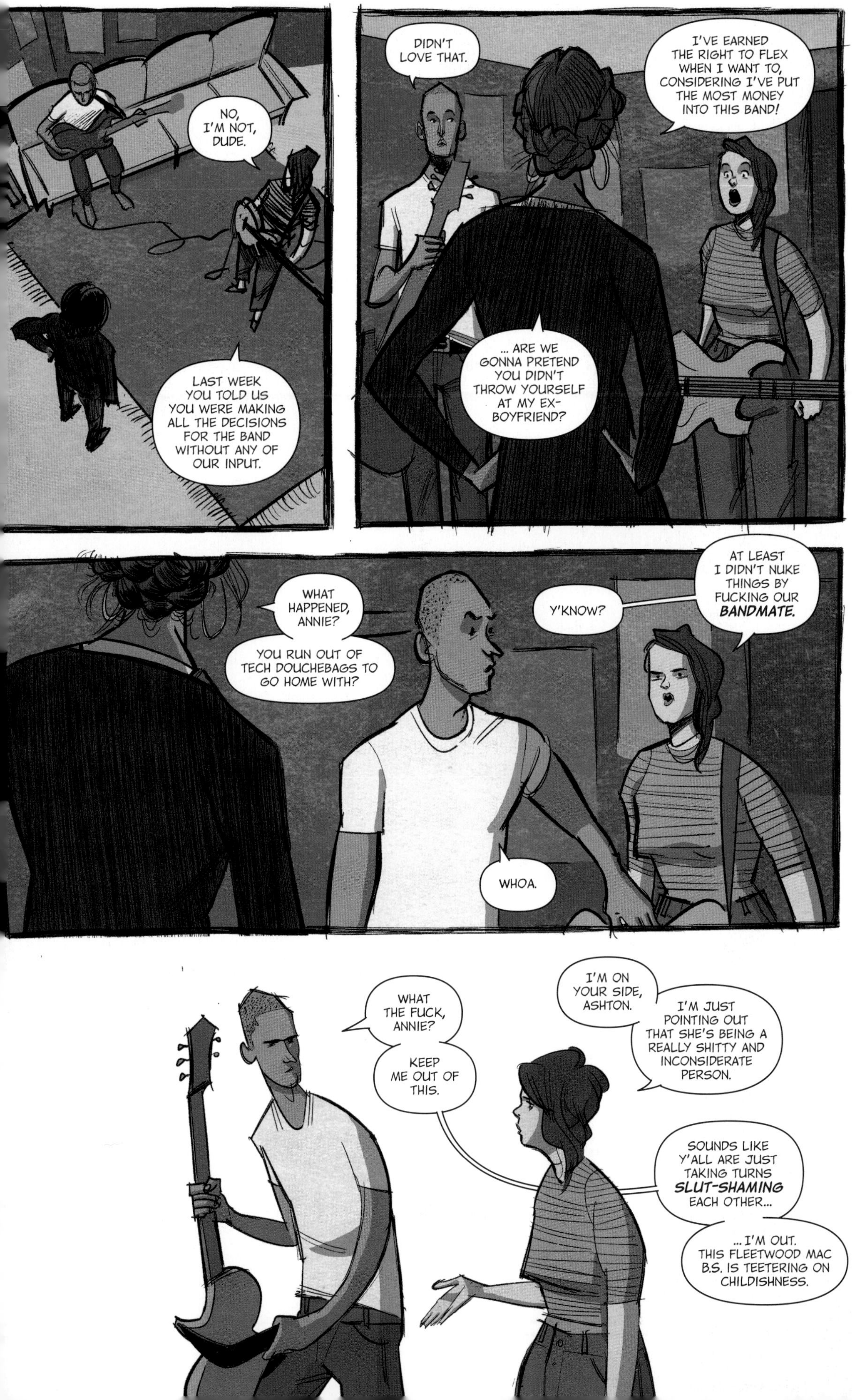
NO, I'M NOT, DUDE.
LAST WEEK YOU TOLD US YOU WERE MAKING ALL THE DECISIONS FOR THE BAND WITHOUT ANY OF OUR INPUT.
DIDN'T LOVE THAT.
I'VE EARNED THE RIGHT TO FLEX WHEN I WANT TO, CONSIDERING I'VE PUT THE MOST MONEY INTO THIS BAND!
... ARE WE GONNA PRETEND YOU DIDN'T THROW YOURSELF AT MY EX-BOYFRIEND?
WHAT HAPPENED, ANNIE?
YOU RUN OUT OF TECH DOUCHEBAGS TO GO HOME WITH?
AT LEAST I DIDN'T NUKE THINGS BY FUCKING OUR **BANDMATE.**
Y'KNOW?
WHOA.
WHAT THE FUCK, ANNIE?
KEEP ME OUT OF THIS.
I'M ON YOUR SIDE, ASHTON.
I'M JUST POINTING OUT THAT SHE'S BEING A REALLY SHITTY AND INCONSIDERATE PERSON.
SOUNDS LIKE Y'ALL ARE JUST TAKING TURNS ***SLUT-SHAMING*** EACH OTHER...
... I'M OUT. THIS FLEETWOOD MAC B.S. IS TEETERING ON CHILDISHNESS.

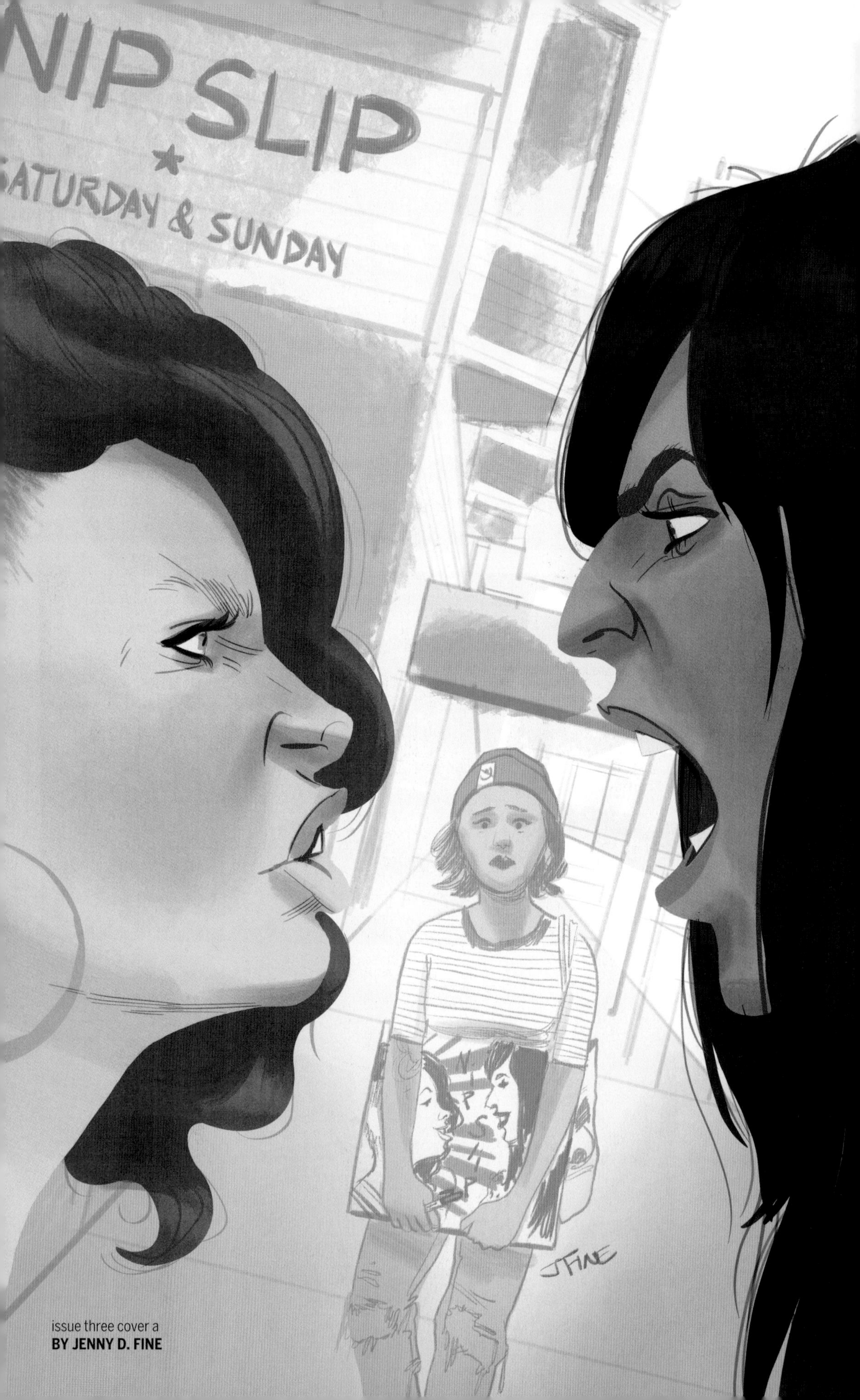
NIP SLIP
SATURDAY & SUNDAY
JFINE

issue three cover a
BY JENNY D. FINE

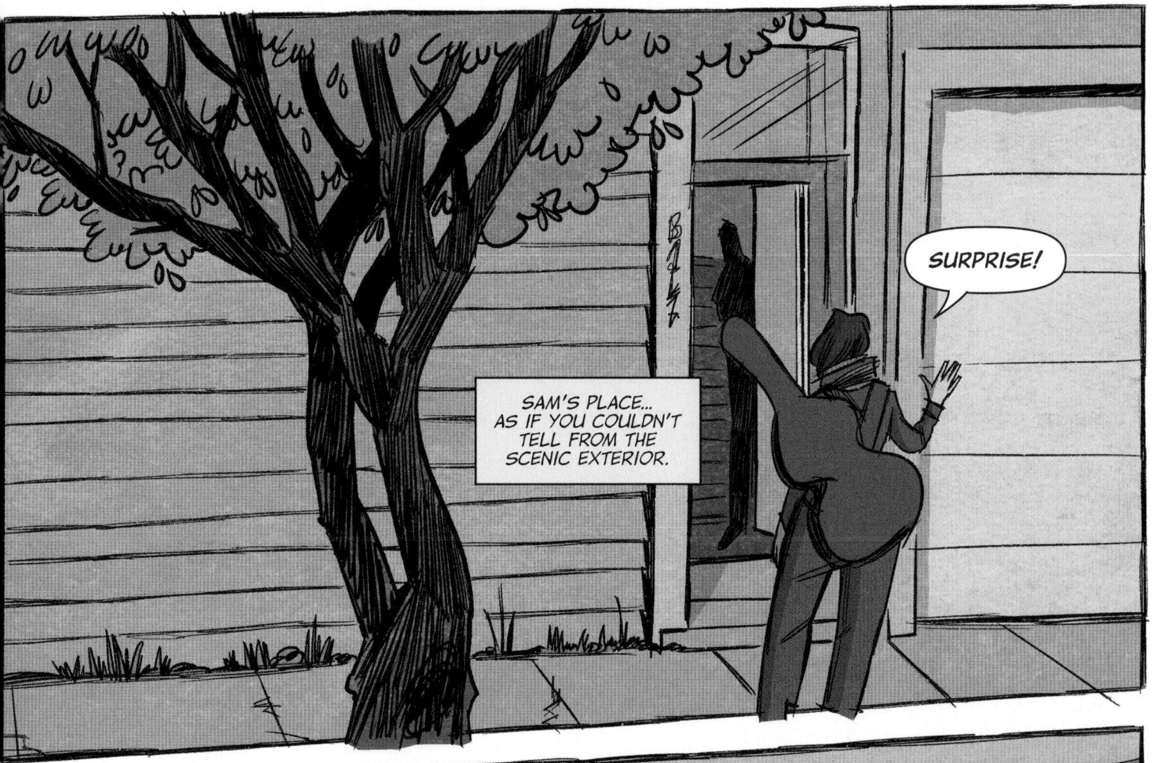
SURPRISE!
SAM'S PLACE... AS IF YOU COULDN'T TELL FROM THE SCENIC EXTERIOR.

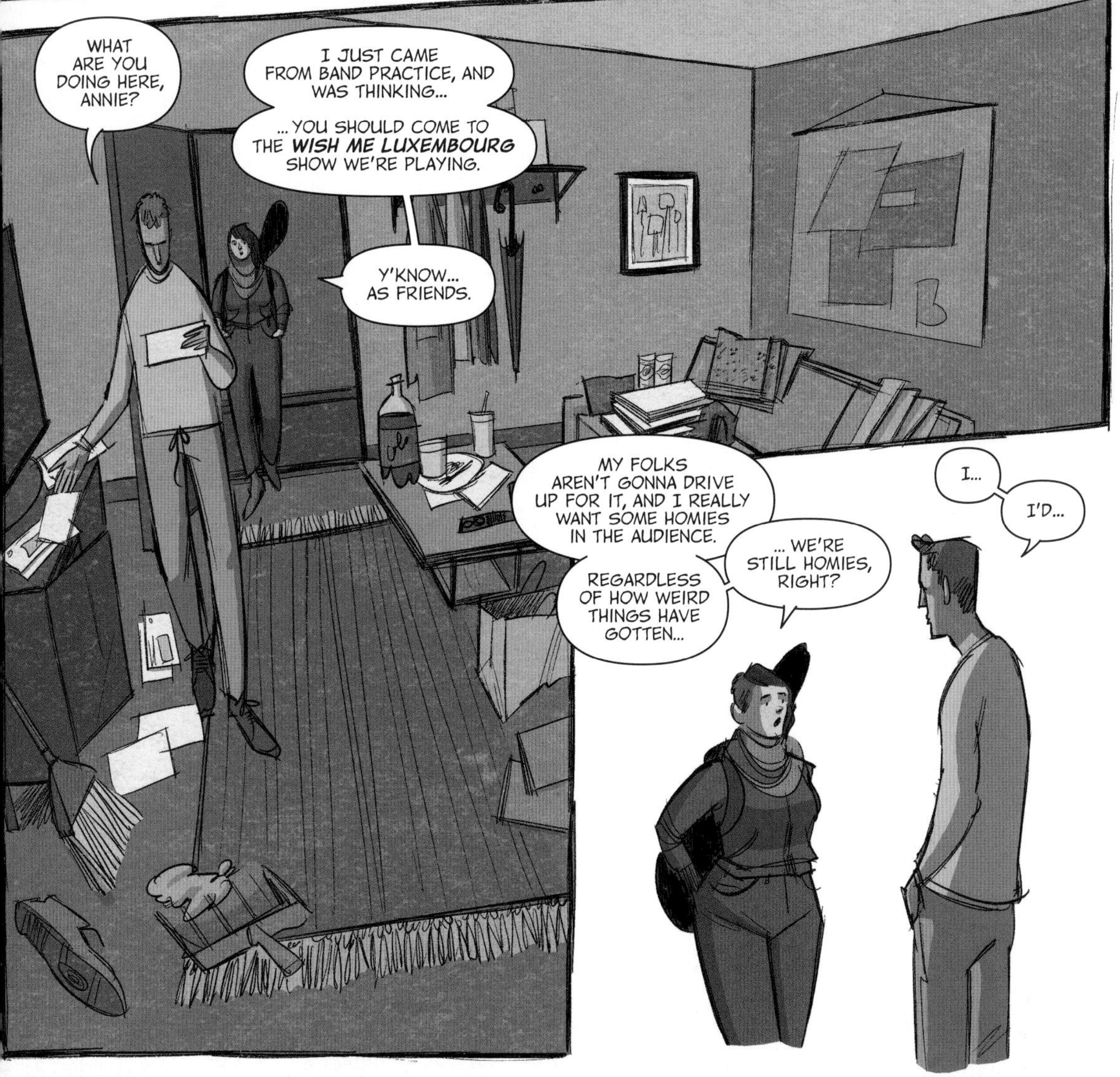
WHAT ARE YOU DOING HERE, ANNIE?
I JUST CAME FROM BAND PRACTICE, AND WAS THINKING...
...YOU SHOULD COME TO THE **WISH ME LUXEMBOURG** SHOW WE'RE PLAYING.
Y'KNOW... AS FRIENDS.
MY FOLKS AREN'T GONNA DRIVE UP FOR IT, AND I REALLY WANT SOME HOMIES IN THE AUDIENCE.
REGARDLESS OF HOW WEIRD THINGS HAVE GOTTEN...
... WE'RE STILL HOMIES, RIGHT?
I...
I'D...

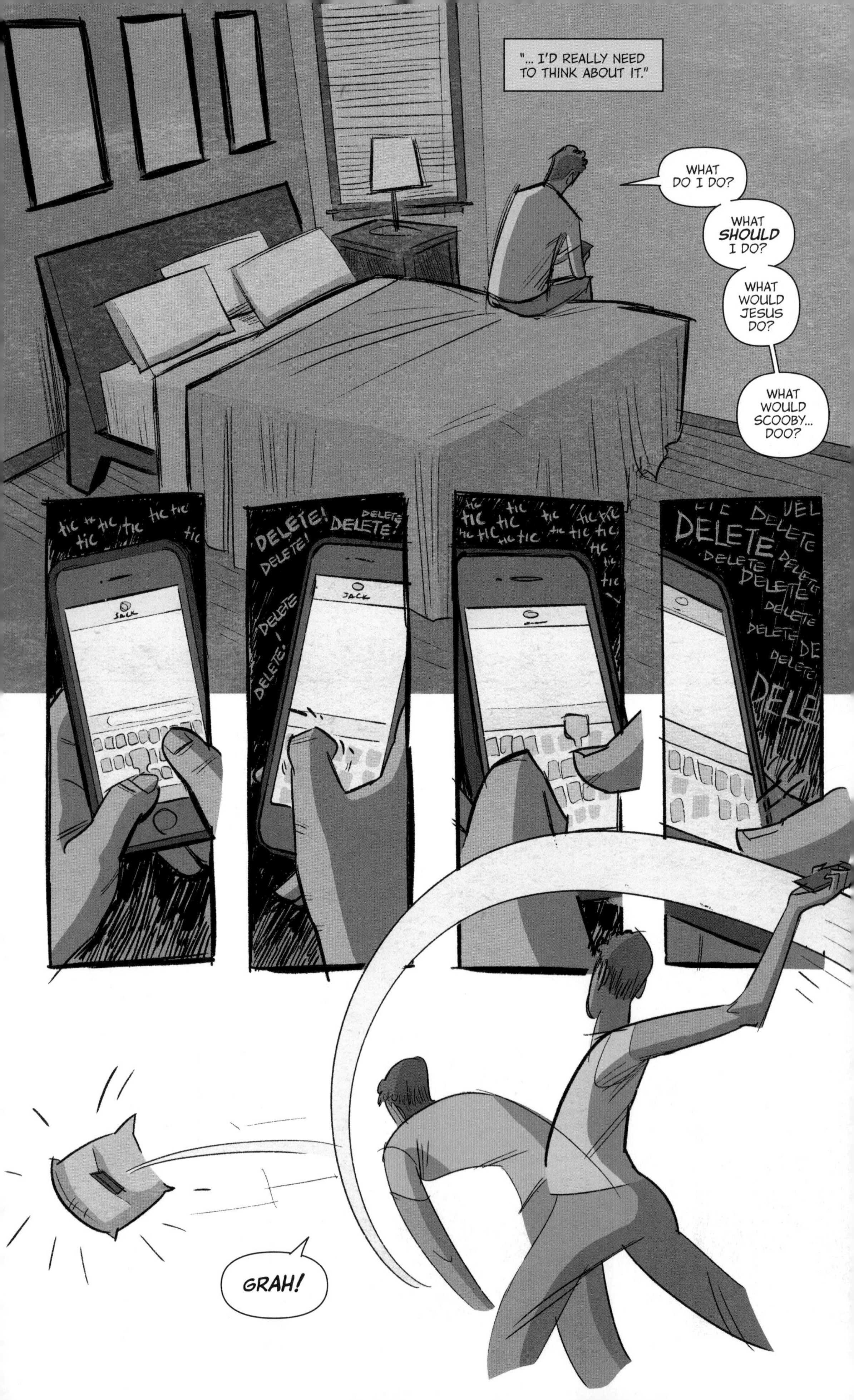
"... I'D REALLY NEED TO THINK ABOUT IT."
WHAT DO I DO?
WHAT SHOULD I DO?
WHAT WOULD JESUS DO?
WHAT WOULD SCOOBY... DOO?
tic tic tic tic tic tic tic
DELETE! DELETE! DELETE! DELETE! DELETE!
tic tic tic tic tic tic tic tic tic tic tic
DELETE DELETE DELETE DELETE DELETE DELETE DELETE
GRAH!

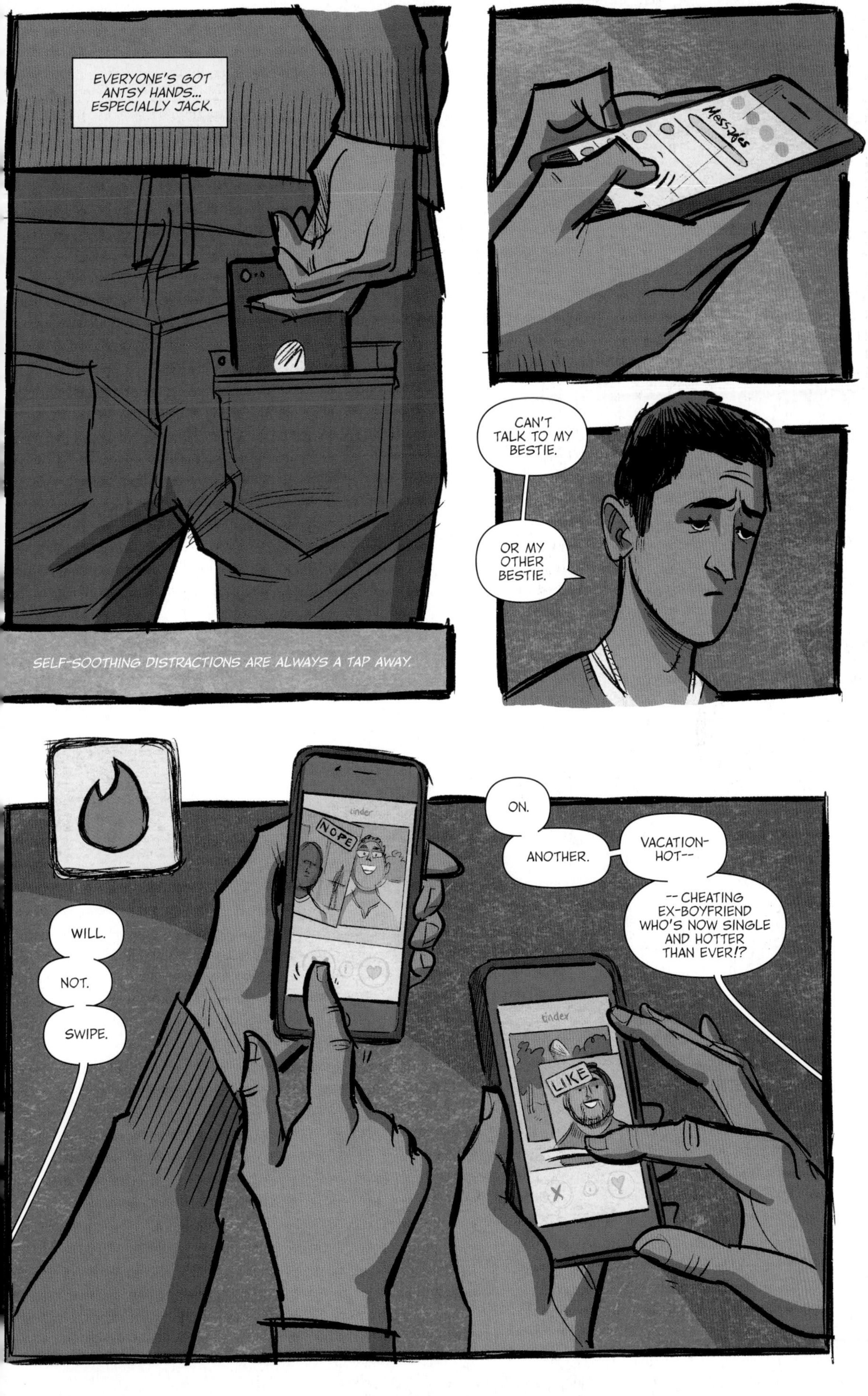
EVERYONE'S GOT ANTSY HANDS... ESPECIALLY JACK.
Messages
SELF-SOOTHING DISTRACTIONS ARE ALWAYS A TAP AWAY.
CAN'T TALK TO MY BESTIE.
OR MY OTHER BESTIE.
WILL.
NOT.
SWIPE.
tinder
NOPE
ON.
ANOTHER.
VACATION-HOT--
--CHEATING EX-BOYFRIEND WHO'S NOW SINGLE AND HOTTER THAN EVER!?
tinder
LIKE

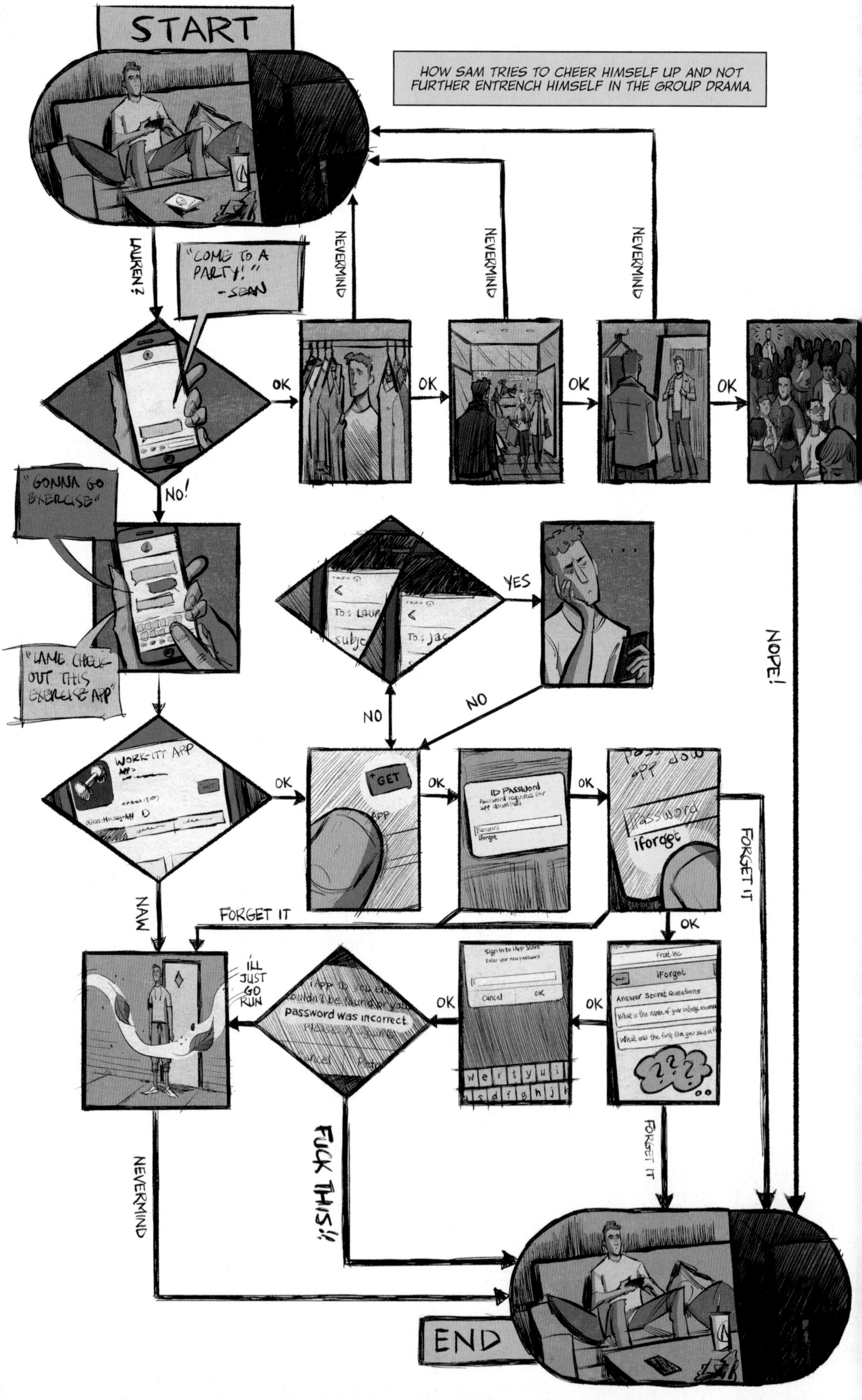

START
HOW SAM TRIES TO CHEER HIMSELF UP AND NOT FURTHER ENTRENCH HIMSELF IN THE GROUP DRAMA.
LAUREN?
"COME TO A PARTY!" -SEAN
OK
NEVERMIND
OK
NEVERMIND
OK
NEVERMIND
OK
NO!
"GONNA GO EXERCISE"
"LAME. CHECK OUT THIS EXERCISE APP"
To: Laur
To: Jac
YES
NO
NO
NOPE!
WORK-ITT APP
OK
GET
OK
ID Password
iforgot
OK
Password
iforget
FORGET IT
NAW
FORGET IT
OK
Sign In to App Store
Cancel
OK
iForgot
Answer Secret Questions
OK
I'LL JUST GO RUN
password was incorrect.
OK
NEVERMIND
FUCK THIS!!
FORGET IT
END

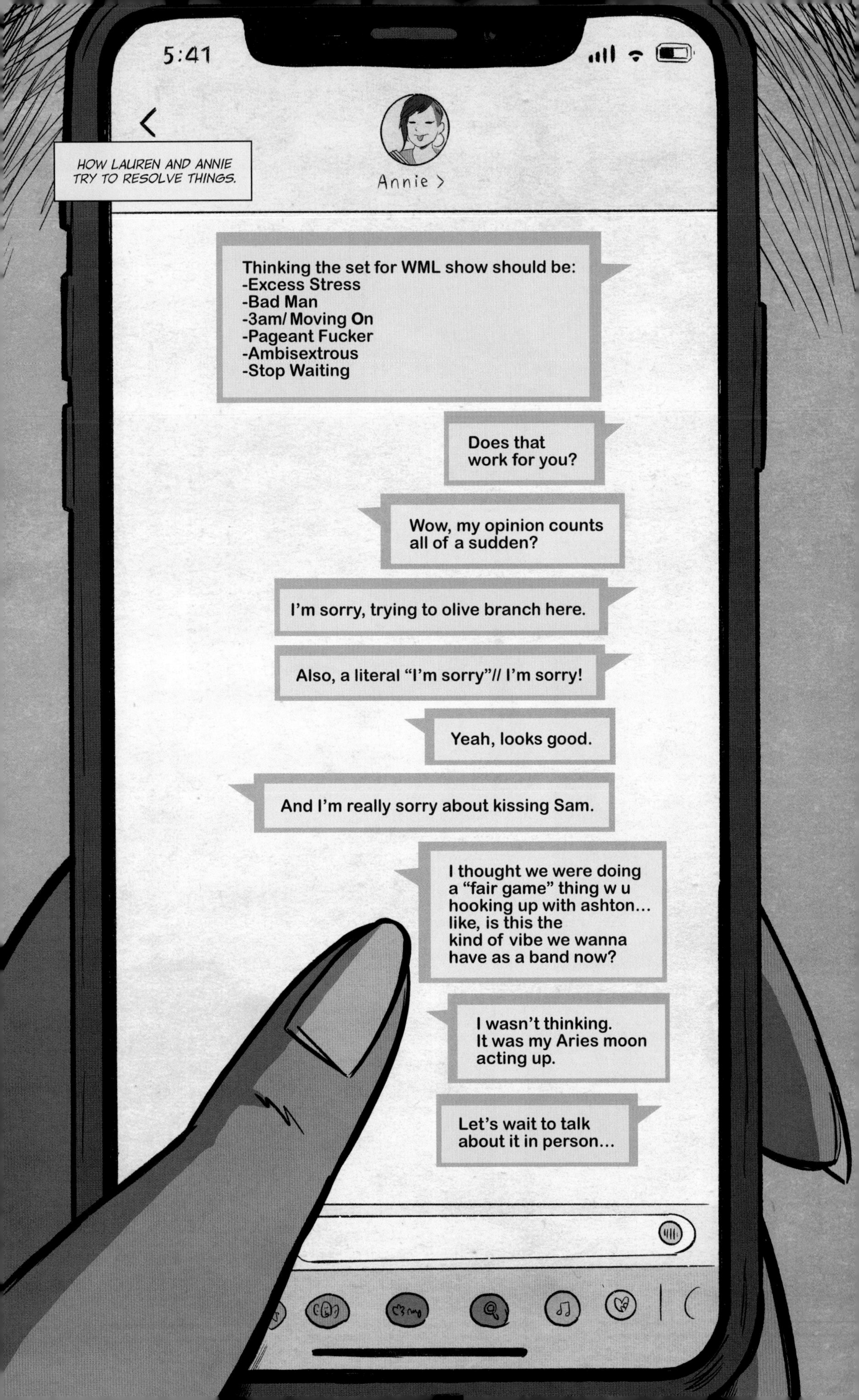
HOW LAUREN AND ANNIE TRY TO RESOLVE THINGS.
5:41
Annie >
Thinking the set for WML show should be:
-Excess Stress
-Bad Man
-3am/ Moving On
-Pageant Fucker
-Ambisextrous
-Stop Waiting
Does that work for you?
Wow, my opinion counts all of a sudden?
I'm sorry, trying to olive branch here.
Also, a literal "I'm sorry"// I'm sorry!
Yeah, looks good.
And I'm really sorry about kissing Sam.
I thought we were doing a "fair game" thing w u hooking up with ashton... like, is this the kind of vibe we wanna have as a band now?
I wasn't thinking. It was my Aries moon acting up.
Let's wait to talk about it in person...

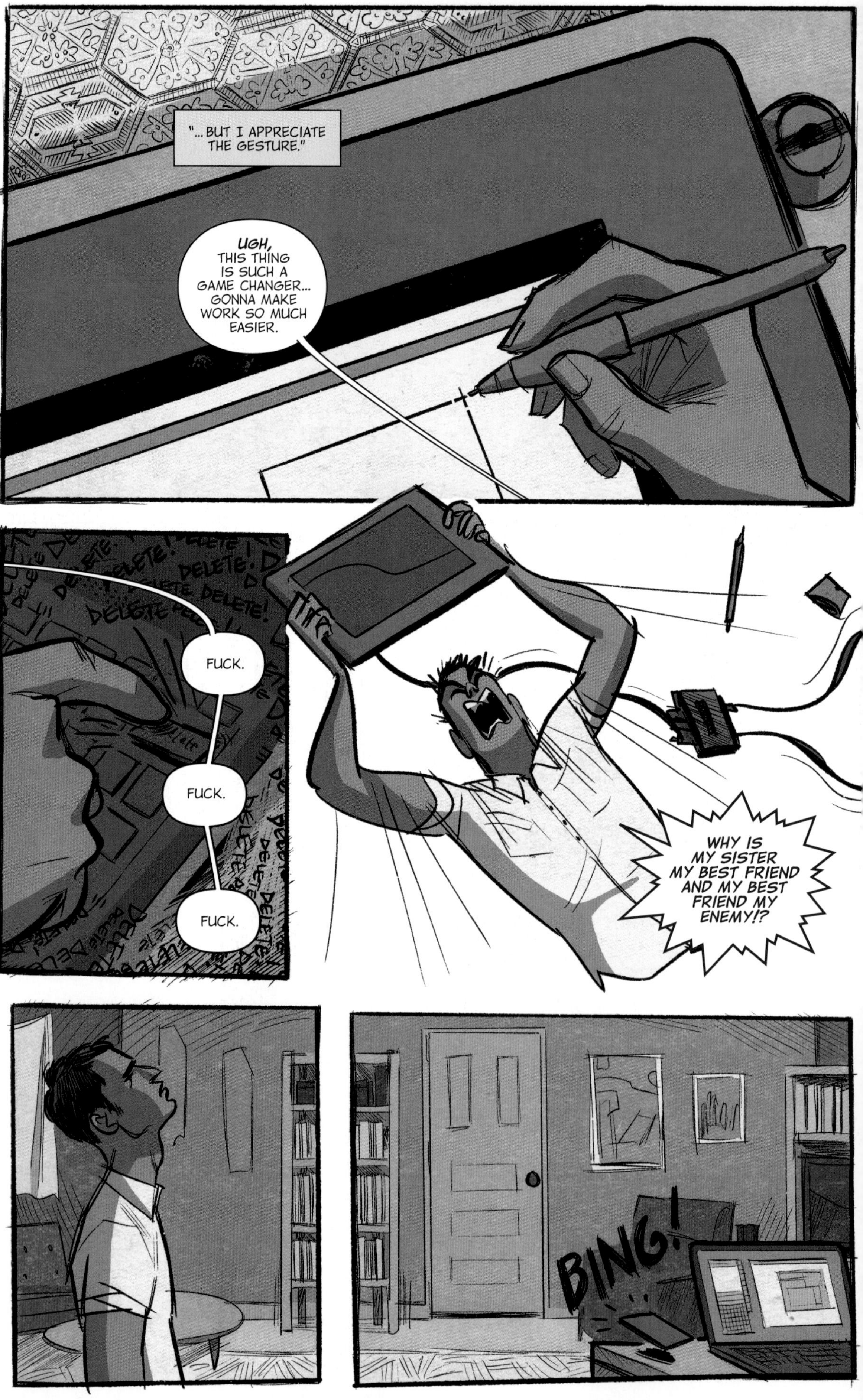
"...BUT I APPRECIATE THE GESTURE."
UGH, THIS THING IS SUCH A GAME CHANGER... GONNA MAKE WORK SO MUCH EASIER.
DELETE! DELETE! DELETE!
FUCK.
FUCK.
FUCK.
WHY IS MY SISTER MY BEST FRIEND AND MY BEST FRIEND MY ENEMY!?
BING!

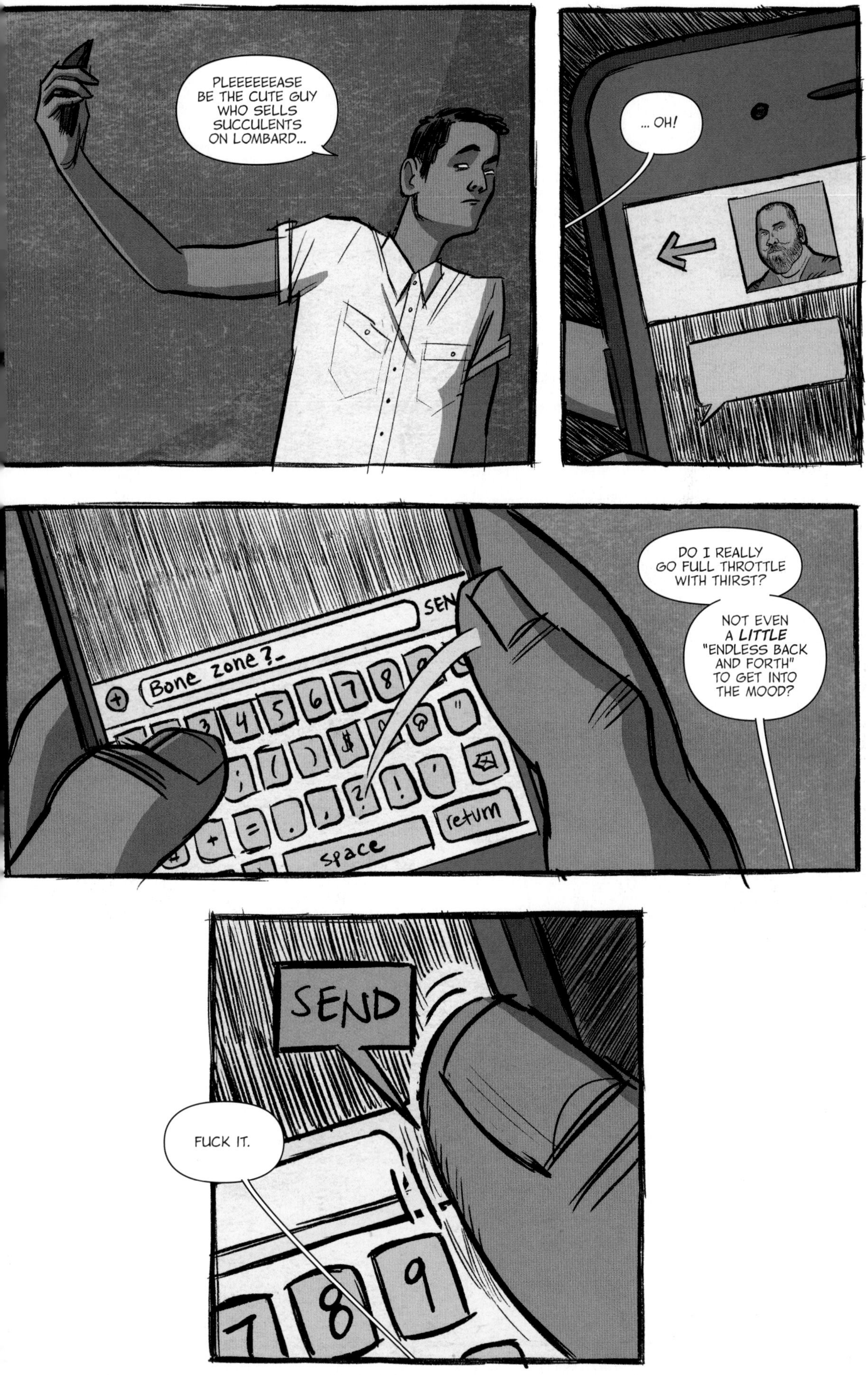
PLEEEEEEASE BE THE CUTE GUY WHO SELLS SUCCULENTS ON LOMBARD...
... OH!
Bone zone?
DO I REALLY GO FULL THROTTLE WITH THIRST?
NOT EVEN A *LITTLE* "ENDLESS BACK AND FORTH" TO GET INTO THE MOOD?
SEND
FUCK IT.

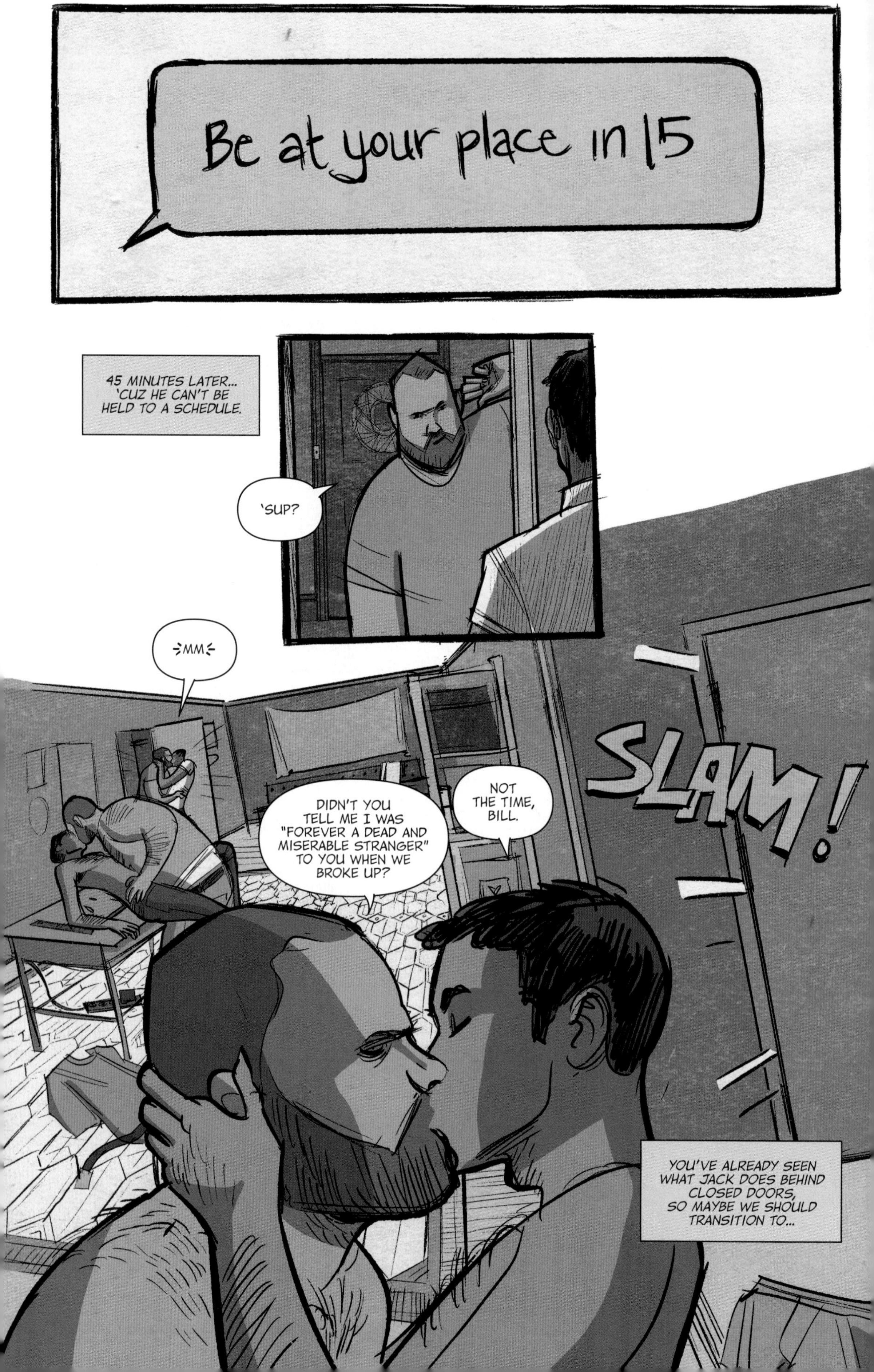
Be at your place in 15
45 MINUTES LATER... 'CUZ HE CAN'T BE HELD TO A SCHEDULE.
'SUP?
MM
DIDN'T YOU TELL ME I WAS "FOREVER A DEAD AND MISERABLE STRANGER" TO YOU WHEN WE BROKE UP?
NOT THE TIME, BILL.
SLAM!
YOU'VE ALREADY SEEN WHAT JACK DOES BEHIND CLOSED DOORS, SO MAYBE WE SHOULD TRANSITION TO...

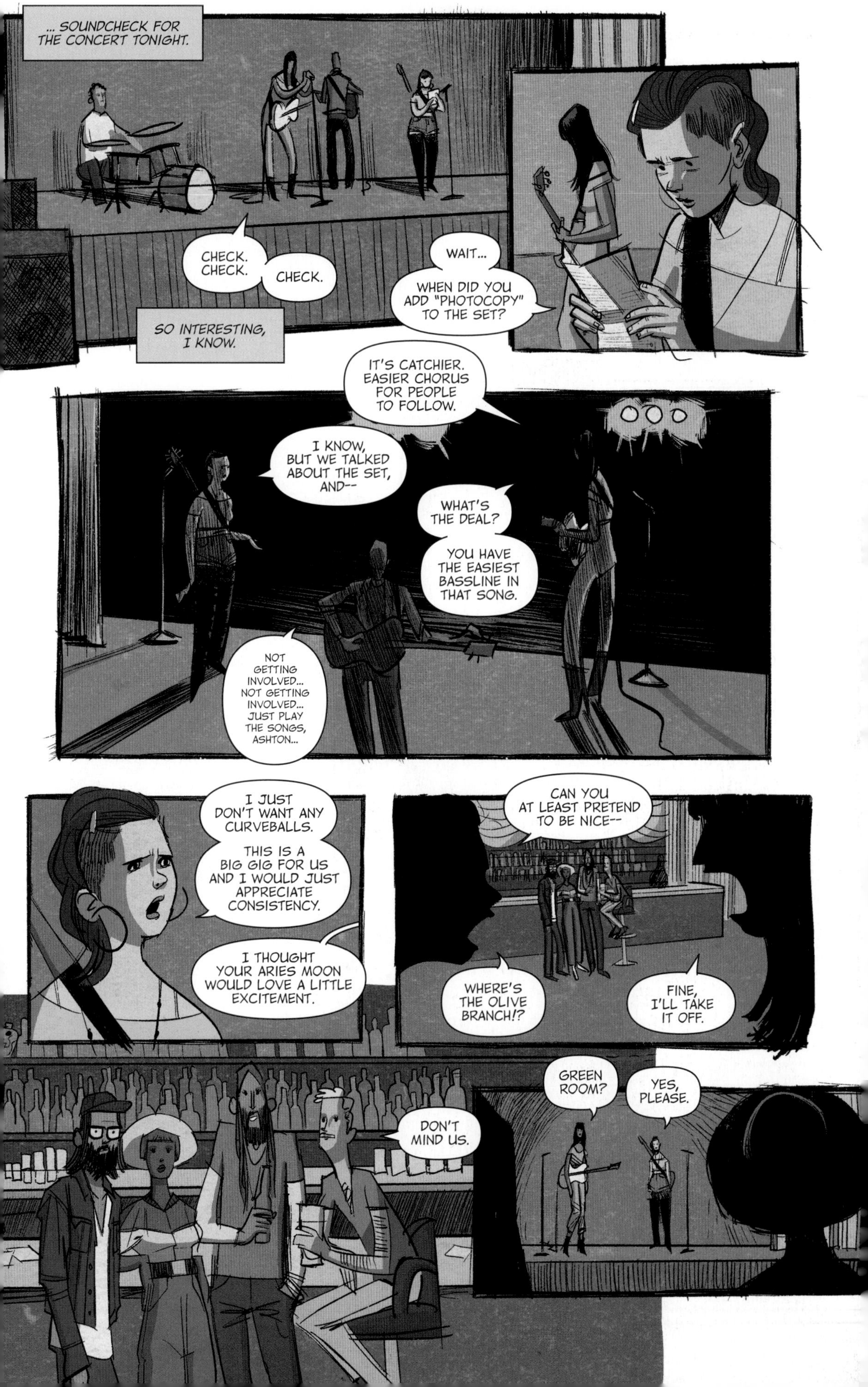
... SOUNDCHECK FOR THE CONCERT TONIGHT.
CHECK. CHECK.
CHECK.
SO INTERESTING, I KNOW.
WAIT...
WHEN DID YOU ADD "PHOTOCOPY" TO THE SET?
IT'S CATCHIER. EASIER CHORUS FOR PEOPLE TO FOLLOW.
I KNOW, BUT WE TALKED ABOUT THE SET, AND--
WHAT'S THE DEAL?
YOU HAVE THE EASIEST BASSLINE IN THAT SONG.
NOT GETTING INVOLVED... NOT GETTING INVOLVED... JUST PLAY THE SONGS, ASHTON...
I JUST DON'T WANT ANY CURVEBALLS.
THIS IS A BIG GIG FOR US AND I WOULD JUST APPRECIATE CONSISTENCY.
I THOUGHT YOUR ARIES MOON WOULD LOVE A LITTLE EXCITEMENT.
CAN YOU AT LEAST PRETEND TO BE NICE--
WHERE'S THE OLIVE BRANCH!?
FINE, I'LL TAKE IT OFF.
GREEN ROOM?
YES, PLEASE.
DON'T MIND US.

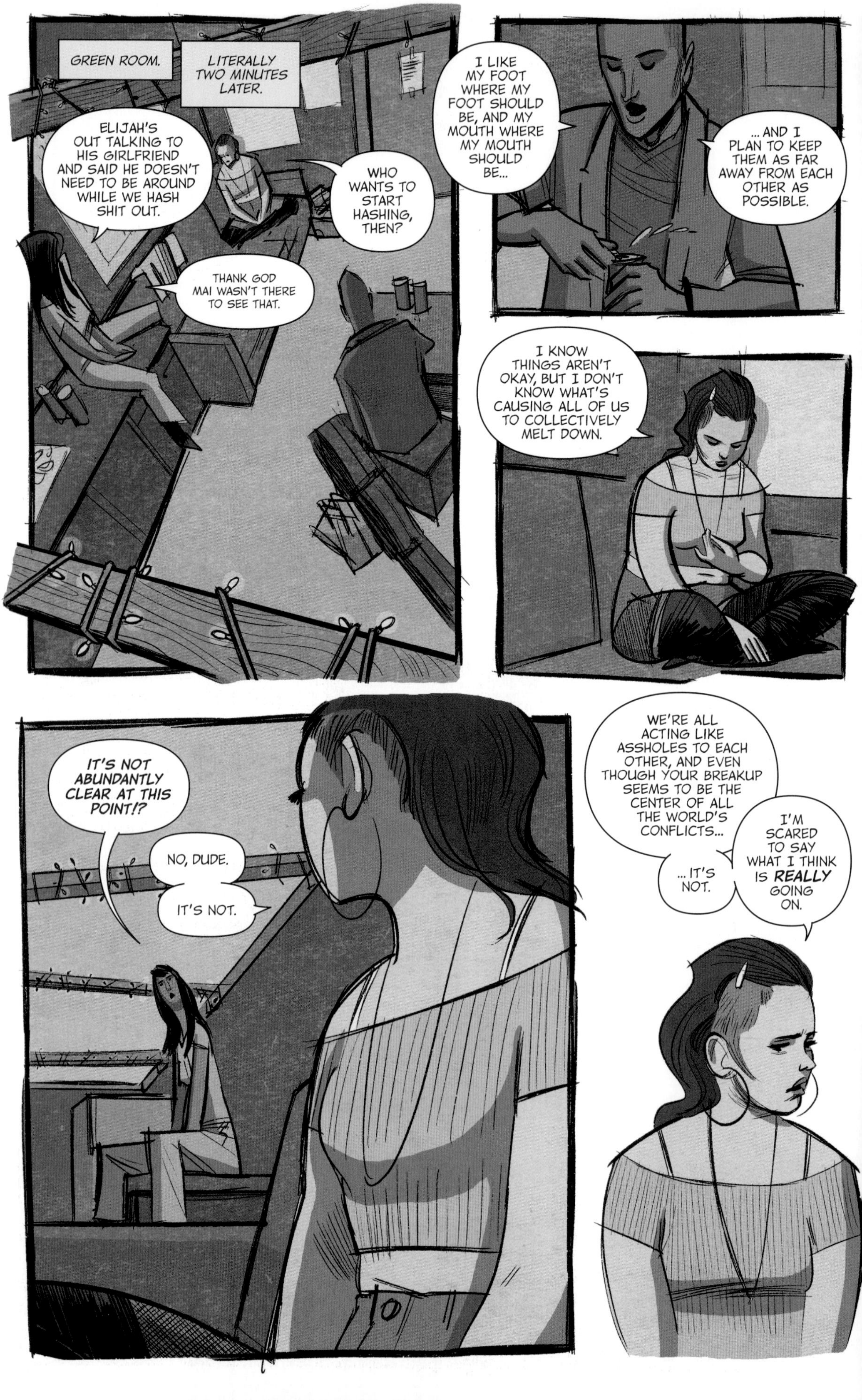
GREEN ROOM.
LITERALLY TWO MINUTES LATER.
ELIJAH'S OUT TALKING TO HIS GIRLFRIEND AND SAID HE DOESN'T NEED TO BE AROUND WHILE WE HASH SHIT OUT.
WHO WANTS TO START HASHING, THEN?
THANK GOD MAI WASN'T THERE TO SEE THAT.
I LIKE MY FOOT WHERE MY FOOT SHOULD BE, AND MY MOUTH WHERE MY MOUTH SHOULD BE...
...AND I PLAN TO KEEP THEM AS FAR AWAY FROM EACH OTHER AS POSSIBLE.
I KNOW THINGS AREN'T OKAY, BUT I DON'T KNOW WHAT'S CAUSING ALL OF US TO COLLECTIVELY MELT DOWN.
IT'S NOT ABUNDANTLY CLEAR AT THIS POINT!?
NO, DUDE.
IT'S NOT.
WE'RE ALL ACTING LIKE ASSHOLES TO EACH OTHER, AND EVEN THOUGH YOUR BREAKUP SEEMS TO BE THE CENTER OF ALL THE WORLD'S CONFLICTS...
...IT'S NOT.
I'M SCARED TO SAY WHAT I THINK IS ***REALLY*** GOING ON.

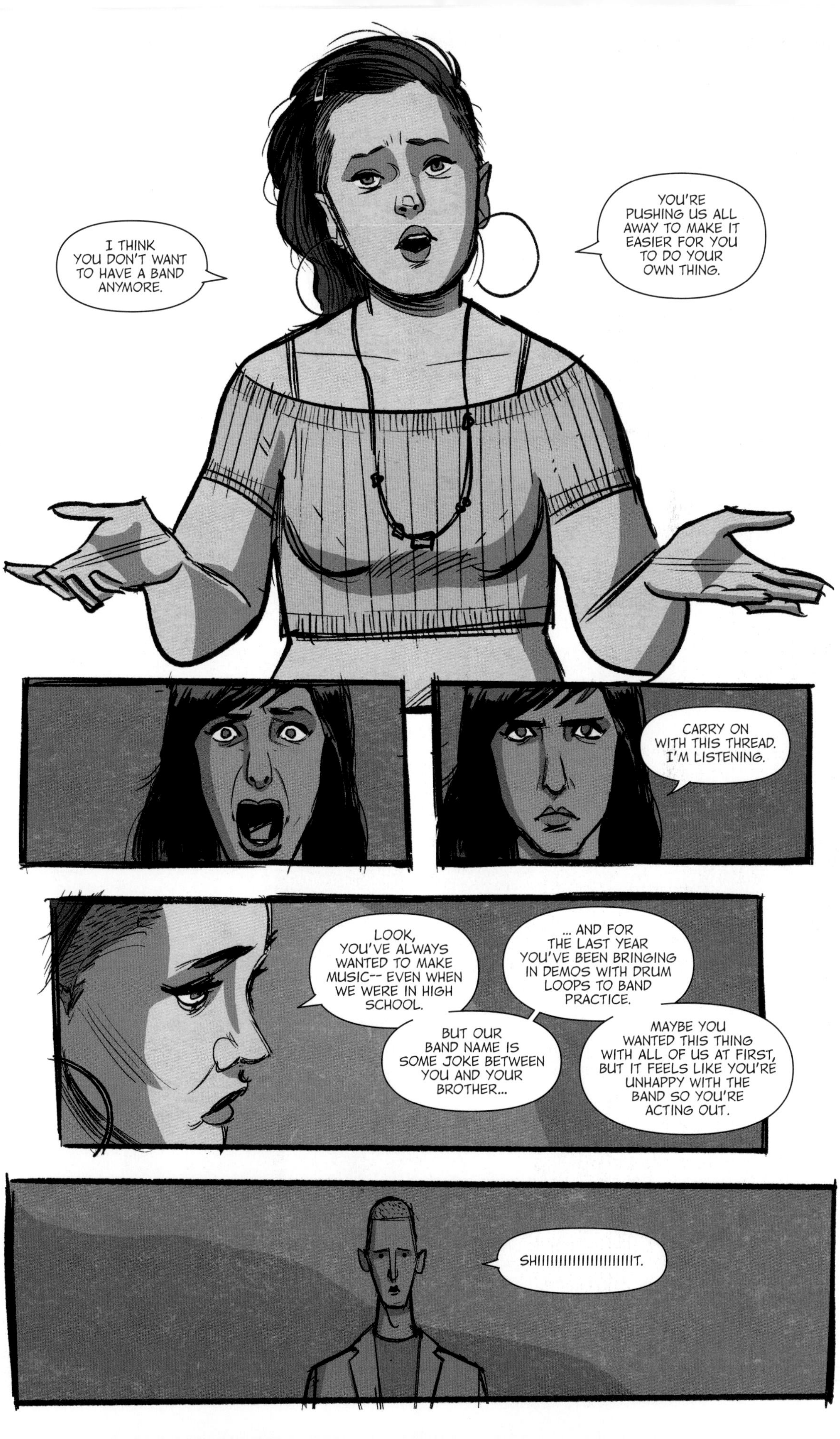
I THINK YOU DON'T WANT TO HAVE A BAND ANYMORE.
YOU'RE PUSHING US ALL AWAY TO MAKE IT EASIER FOR YOU TO DO YOUR OWN THING.
CARRY ON WITH THIS THREAD. I'M LISTENING.
LOOK, YOU'VE ALWAYS WANTED TO MAKE MUSIC-- EVEN WHEN WE WERE IN HIGH SCHOOL.
BUT OUR BAND NAME IS SOME JOKE BETWEEN YOU AND YOUR BROTHER...
... AND FOR THE LAST YEAR YOU'VE BEEN BRINGING IN DEMOS WITH DRUM LOOPS TO BAND PRACTICE.
MAYBE YOU WANTED THIS THING WITH ALL OF US AT FIRST, BUT IT FEELS LIKE YOU'RE UNHAPPY WITH THE BAND SO YOU'RE ACTING OUT.
SHIIIIIIIIIIIIIIIIIIIIIT.

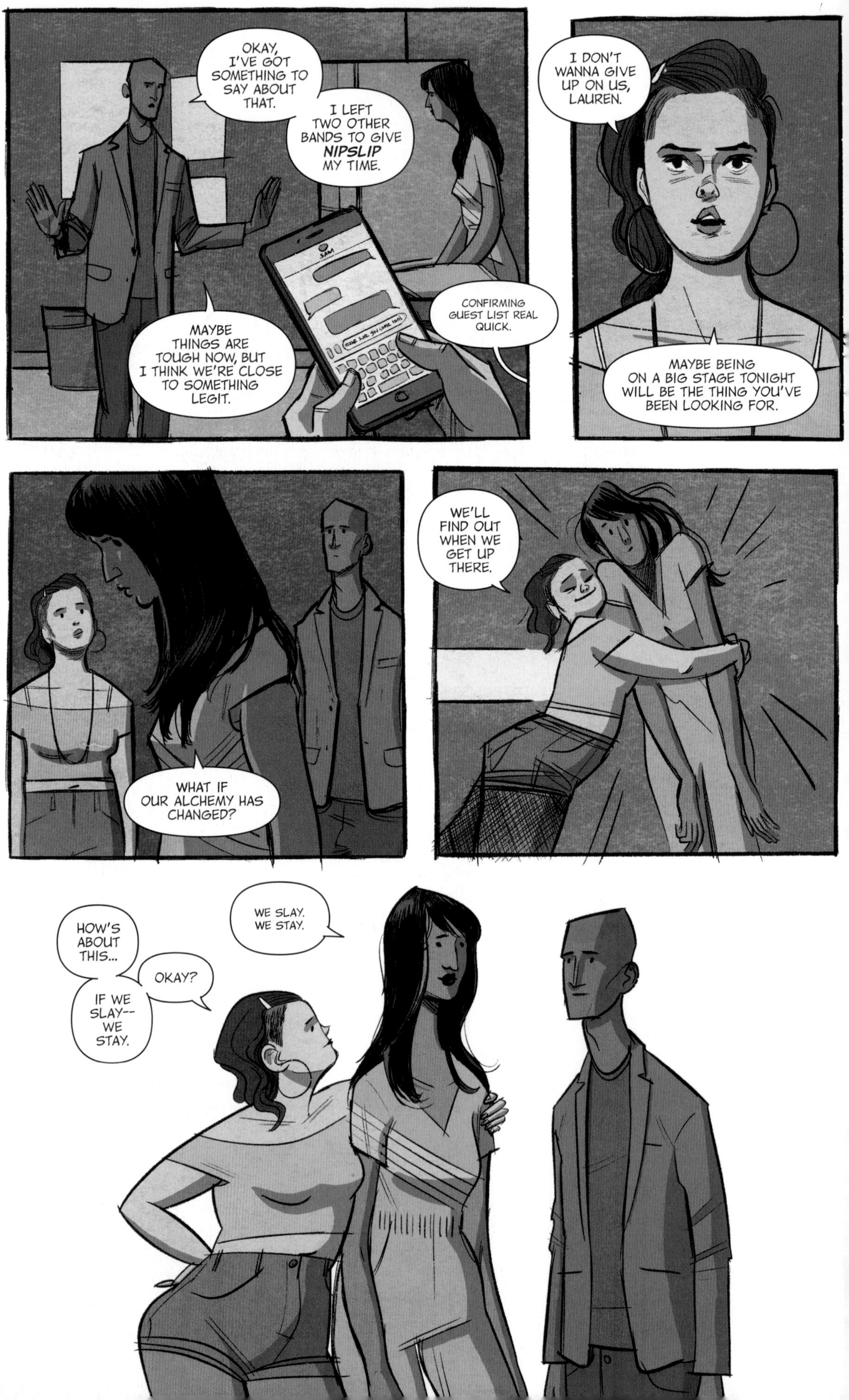
OKAY, I'VE GOT SOMETHING TO SAY ABOUT THAT.
I LEFT TWO OTHER BANDS TO GIVE **NIPSLIP** MY TIME.
MAYBE THINGS ARE TOUGH NOW, BUT I THINK WE'RE CLOSE TO SOMETHING LEGIT.
CONFIRMING GUEST LIST REAL QUICK.
I DON'T WANNA GIVE UP ON US, LAUREN.
MAYBE BEING ON A BIG STAGE TONIGHT WILL BE THE THING YOU'VE BEEN LOOKING FOR.
WHAT IF OUR ALCHEMY HAS CHANGED?
WE'LL FIND OUT WHEN WE GET UP THERE.
HOW'S ABOUT THIS...
OKAY?
IF WE SLAY-- WE STAY.
WE SLAY. WE STAY.

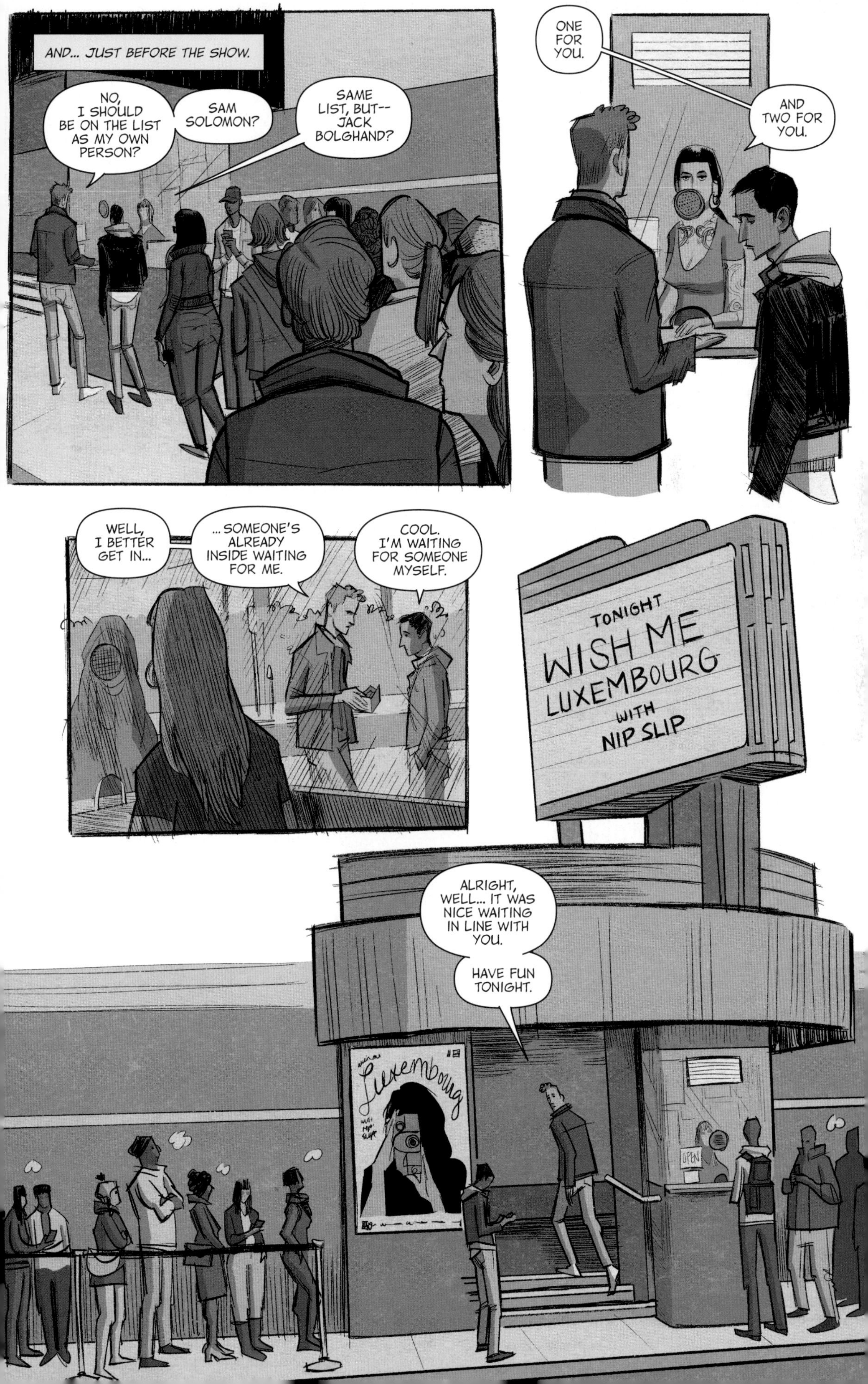
AND... JUST BEFORE THE SHOW.
NO, I SHOULD BE ON THE LIST AS MY OWN PERSON?
SAM SOLOMON?
SAME LIST, BUT-- JACK BOLGHAND?
ONE FOR YOU.
AND TWO FOR YOU.
WELL, I BETTER GET IN...
...SOMEONE'S ALREADY INSIDE WAITING FOR ME.
COOL. I'M WAITING FOR SOMEONE MYSELF.
TONIGHT
WISH ME LUXEMBOURG
WITH
NIP SLIP
ALRIGHT, WELL... IT WAS NICE WAITING IN LINE WITH YOU.
HAVE FUN TONIGHT.
Luxembourg
OPEN

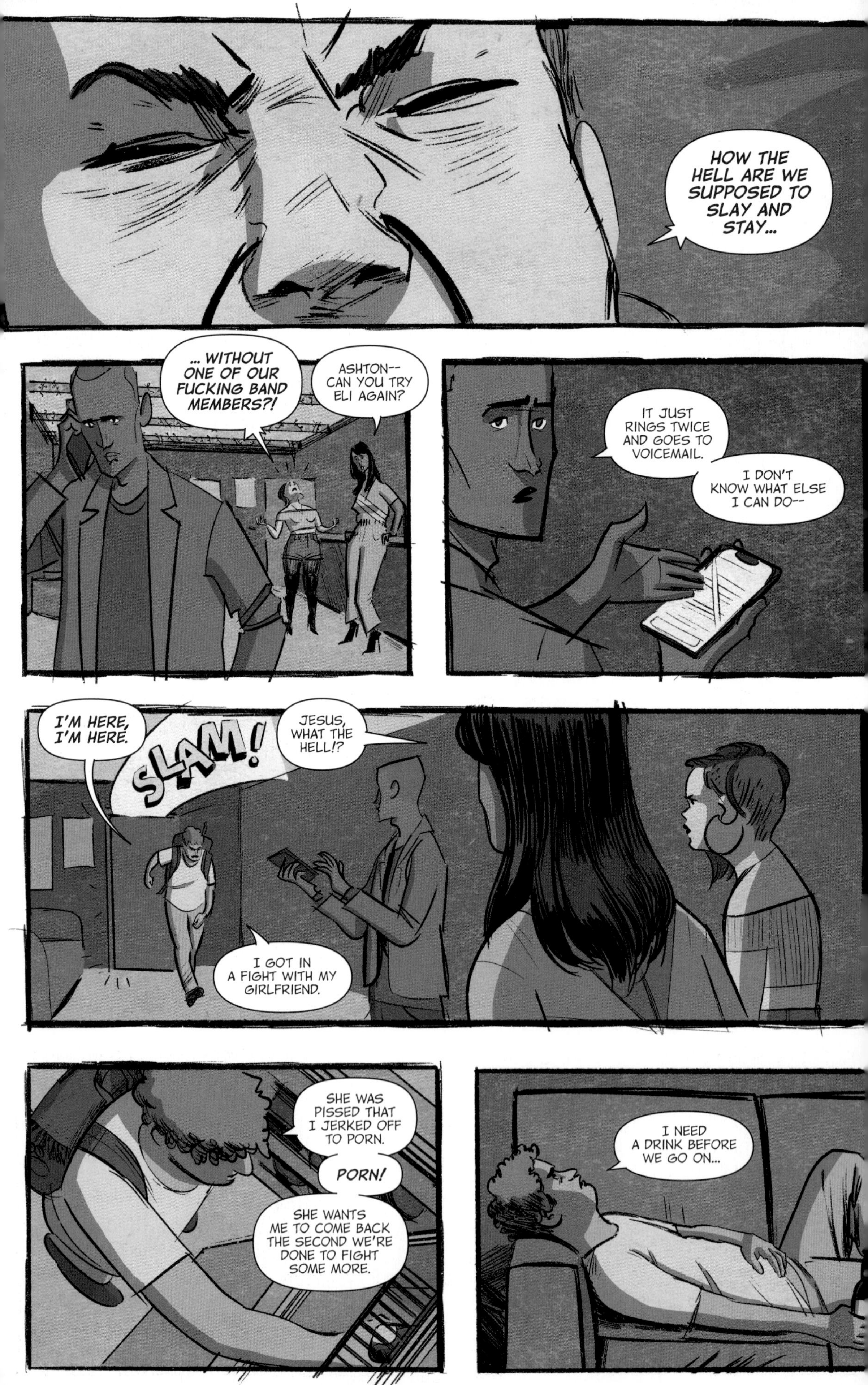
HOW THE HELL ARE WE SUPPOSED TO SLAY AND STAY...
... WITHOUT ONE OF OUR FUCKING BAND MEMBERS?!
ASHTON-- CAN YOU TRY ELI AGAIN?
IT JUST RINGS TWICE AND GOES TO VOICEMAIL.
I DON'T KNOW WHAT ELSE I CAN DO--
I'M HERE, I'M HERE.
SLAM!
JESUS, WHAT THE HELL!?
I GOT IN A FIGHT WITH MY GIRLFRIEND.
SHE WAS PISSED THAT I JERKED OFF TO PORN.
PORN!
SHE WANTS ME TO COME BACK THE SECOND WE'RE DONE TO FIGHT SOME MORE.
I NEED A DRINK BEFORE WE GO ON...

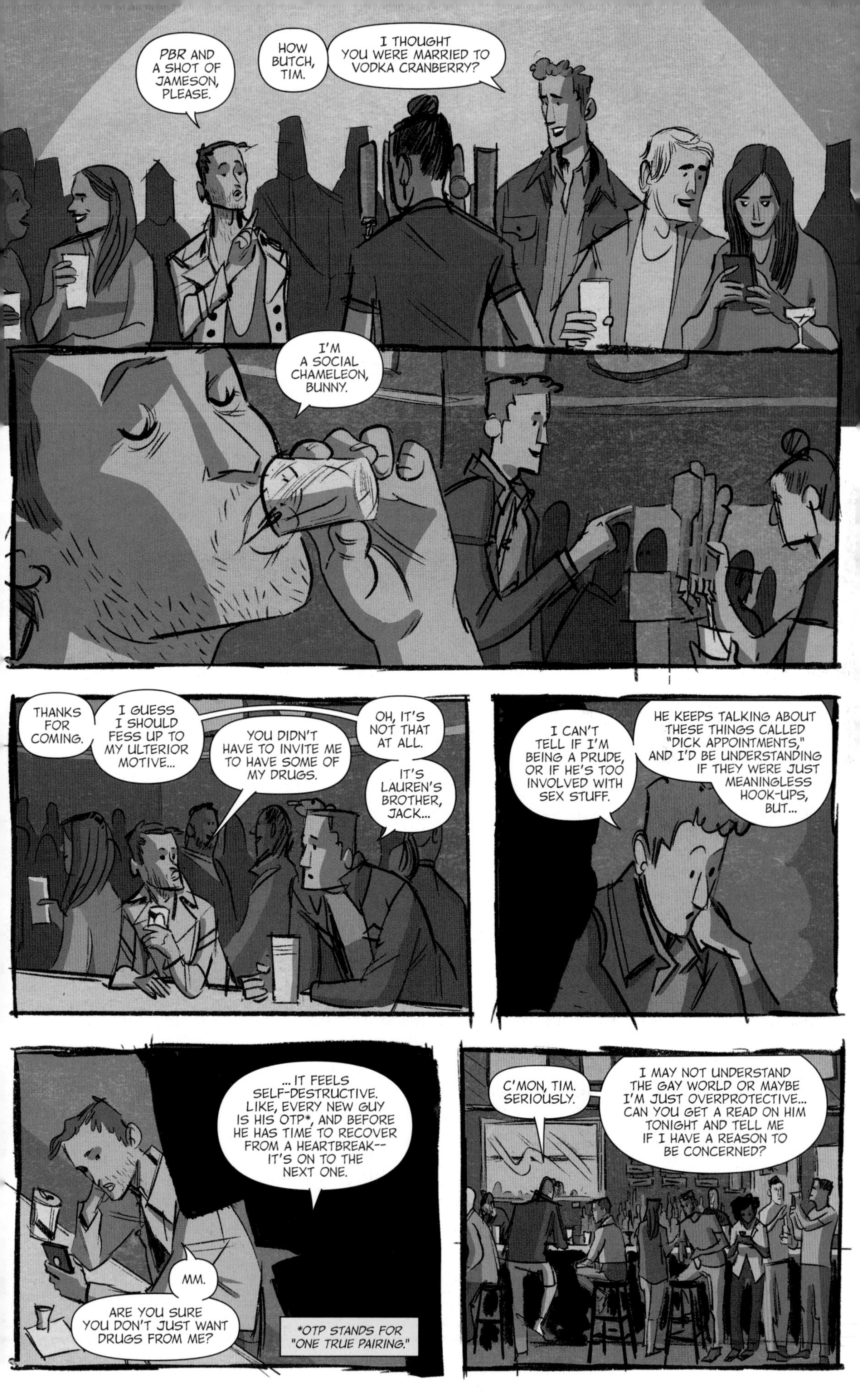
PBR AND A SHOT OF JAMESON, PLEASE.
HOW BUTCH, TIM.
I THOUGHT YOU WERE MARRIED TO VODKA CRANBERRY?
I'M A SOCIAL CHAMELEON, BUNNY.
THANKS FOR COMING.
I GUESS I SHOULD FESS UP TO MY ULTERIOR MOTIVE...
YOU DIDN'T HAVE TO INVITE ME TO HAVE SOME OF MY DRUGS.
OH, IT'S NOT THAT AT ALL.
IT'S LAUREN'S BROTHER, JACK...
I CAN'T TELL IF I'M BEING A PRUDE, OR IF HE'S TOO INVOLVED WITH SEX STUFF.
HE KEEPS TALKING ABOUT THESE THINGS CALLED "DICK APPOINTMENTS," AND I'D BE UNDERSTANDING IF THEY WERE JUST MEANINGLESS HOOK-UPS, BUT...
... IT FEELS SELF-DESTRUCTIVE. LIKE, EVERY NEW GUY IS HIS OTP*, AND BEFORE HE HAS TIME TO RECOVER FROM A HEARTBREAK-- IT'S ON TO THE NEXT ONE.
MM.
ARE YOU SURE YOU DON'T JUST WANT DRUGS FROM ME?
*OTP STANDS FOR "ONE TRUE PAIRING."
C'MON, TIM. SERIOUSLY.
I MAY NOT UNDERSTAND THE GAY WORLD OR MAYBE I'M JUST OVERPROTECTIVE... CAN YOU GET A READ ON HIM TONIGHT AND TELL ME IF I HAVE A REASON TO BE CONCERNED?

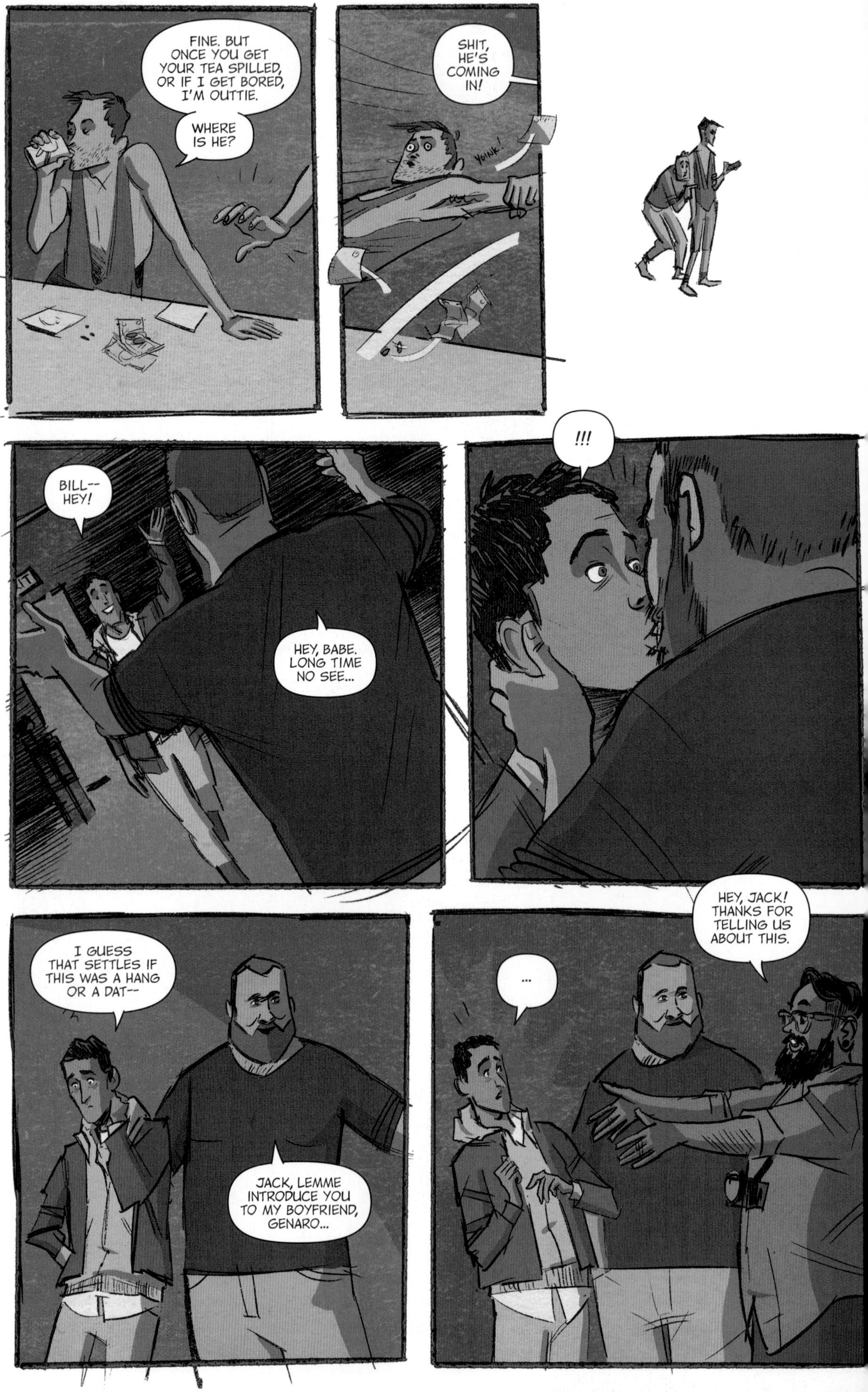
FINE. BUT ONCE YOU GET YOUR TEA SPILLED, OR IF I GET BORED, I'M OUTTIE.
WHERE IS HE?
SHIT, HE'S COMING IN!
YOINK!
BILL-- HEY!
HEY, BABE. LONG TIME NO SEE...
!!!
I GUESS THAT SETTLES IF THIS WAS A HANG OR A DAT--
JACK, LEMME INTRODUCE YOU TO MY BOYFRIEND, GENARO...
...
HEY, JACK! THANKS FOR TELLING US ABOUT THIS.

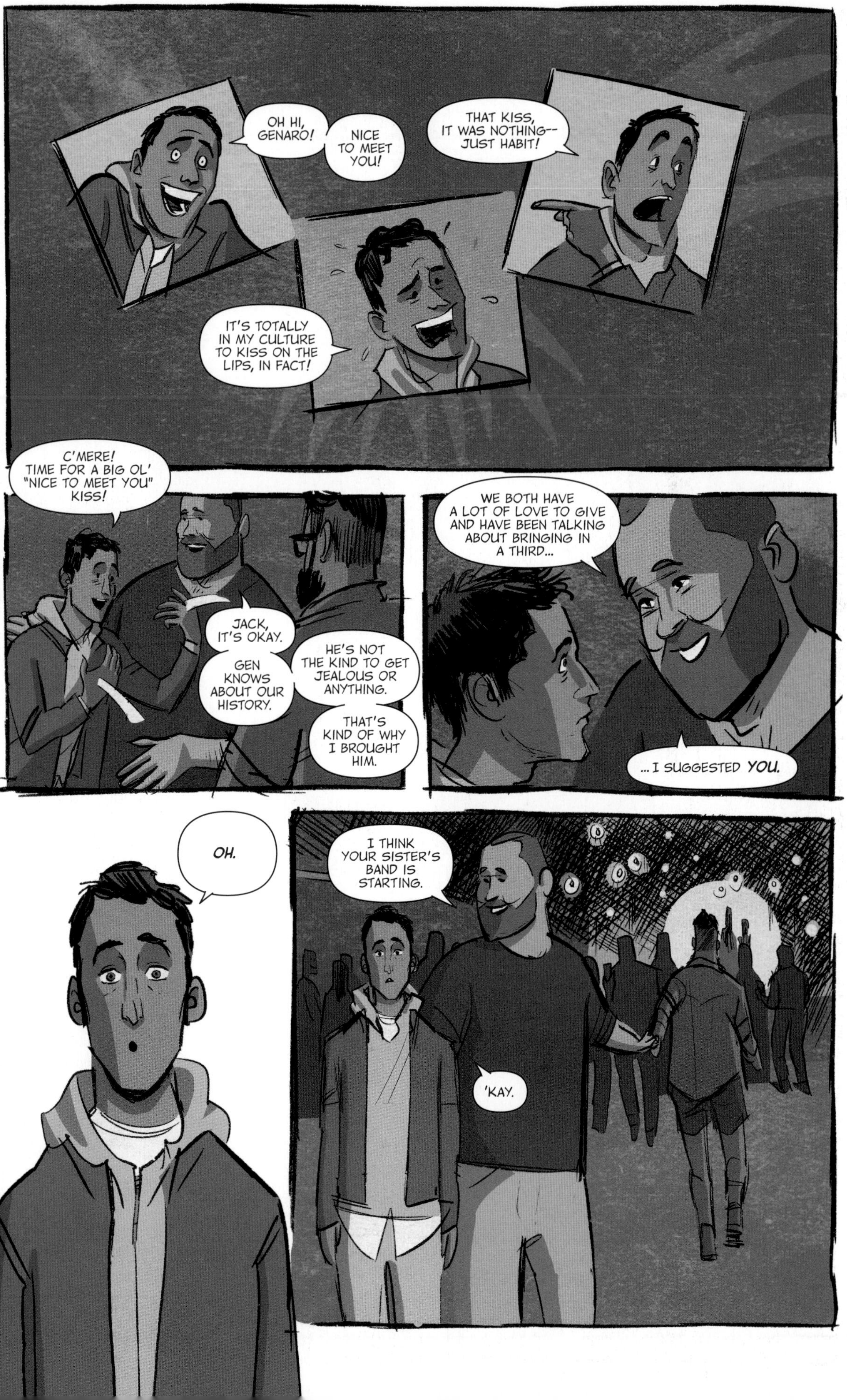
OH HI, GENARO!
NICE TO MEET YOU!
THAT KISS, IT WAS NOTHING-- JUST HABIT!
IT'S TOTALLY IN MY CULTURE TO KISS ON THE LIPS, IN FACT!
C'MERE! TIME FOR A BIG OL' "NICE TO MEET YOU" KISS!
JACK, IT'S OKAY.
GEN KNOWS ABOUT OUR HISTORY.
HE'S NOT THE KIND TO GET JEALOUS OR ANYTHING.
THAT'S KIND OF WHY I BROUGHT HIM.
WE BOTH HAVE A LOT OF LOVE TO GIVE AND HAVE BEEN TALKING ABOUT BRINGING IN A THIRD...
...I SUGGESTED YOU.
OH.
I THINK YOUR SISTER'S BAND IS STARTING.
'KAY.

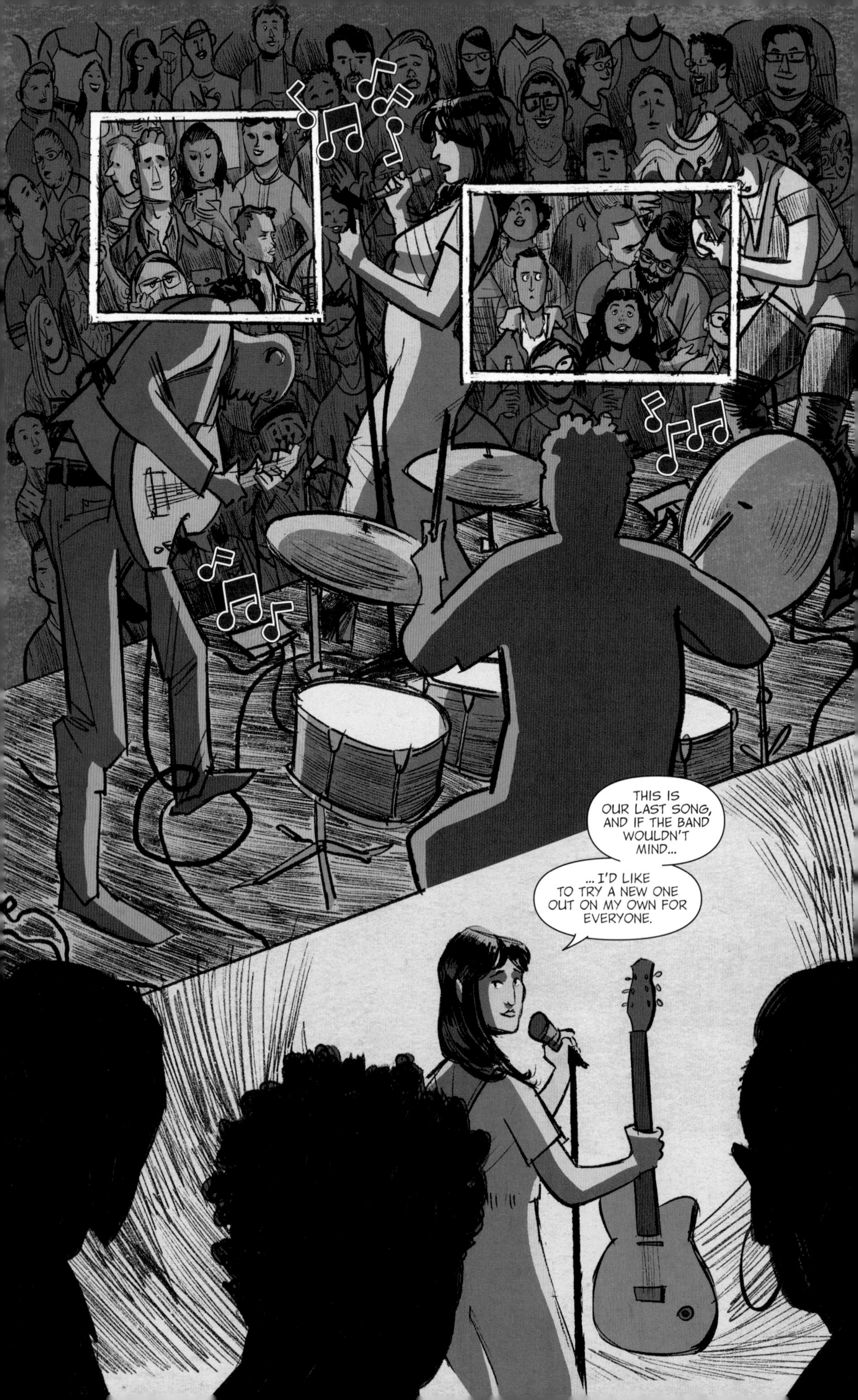
THIS IS OUR LAST SONG, AND IF THE BAND WOULDN'T MIND...
... I'D LIKE TO TRY A NEW ONE OUT ON MY OWN FOR EVERYONE.

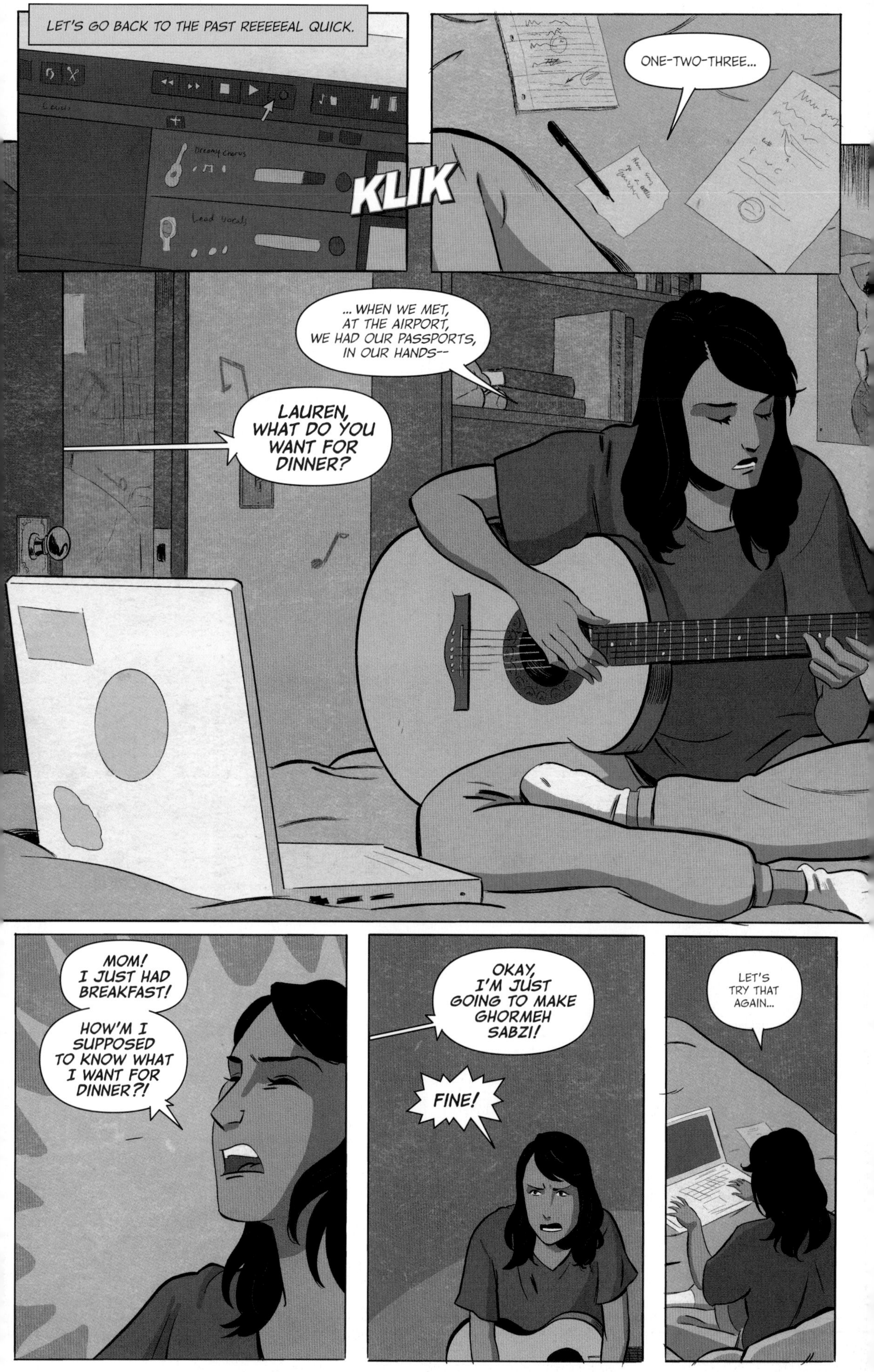
LET'S GO BACK TO THE PAST REEEEEAL QUICK.
ONE-TWO-THREE...
KLIK
... WHEN WE MET, AT THE AIRPORT, WE HAD OUR PASSPORTS, IN OUR HANDS--
LAUREN, WHAT DO YOU WANT FOR DINNER?
MOM! I JUST HAD BREAKFAST!
HOW'M I SUPPOSED TO KNOW WHAT I WANT FOR DINNER?!
OKAY, I'M JUST GOING TO MAKE GHORMEH SABZI!
FINE!
LET'S TRY THAT AGAIN...

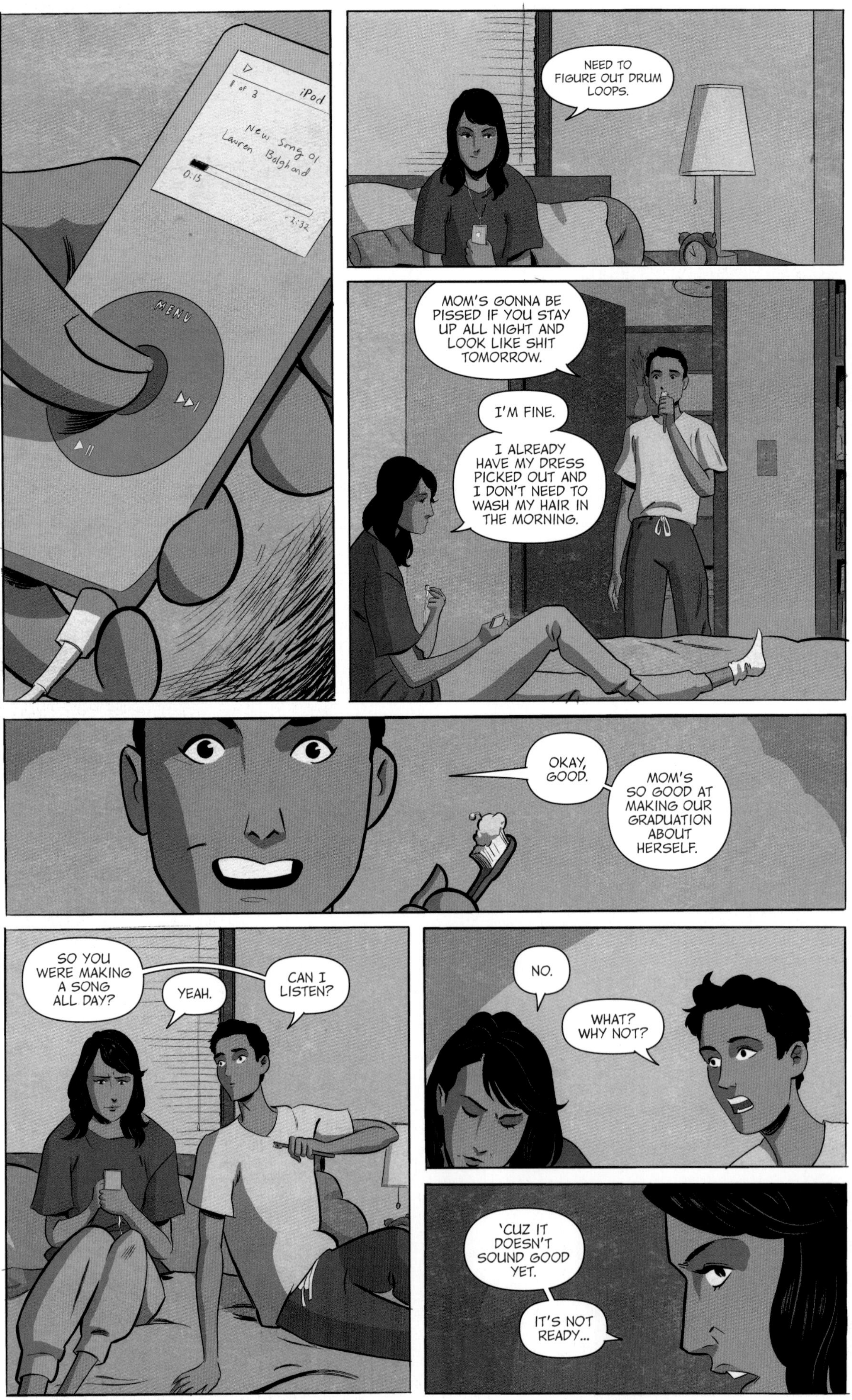

1 of 3
iPod
New Song 01
Lauren Bolghand
0:15
-2:32
MENU
NEED TO FIGURE OUT DRUM LOOPS.
MOM'S GONNA BE PISSED IF YOU STAY UP ALL NIGHT AND LOOK LIKE SHIT TOMORROW.
I'M FINE.
I ALREADY HAVE MY DRESS PICKED OUT AND I DON'T NEED TO WASH MY HAIR IN THE MORNING.
OKAY, GOOD.
MOM'S SO GOOD AT MAKING OUR GRADUATION ABOUT HERSELF.
SO YOU WERE MAKING A SONG ALL DAY?
YEAH.
CAN I LISTEN?
NO.
WHAT? WHY NOT?
'CUZ IT DOESN'T SOUND GOOD YET.
IT'S NOT READY...

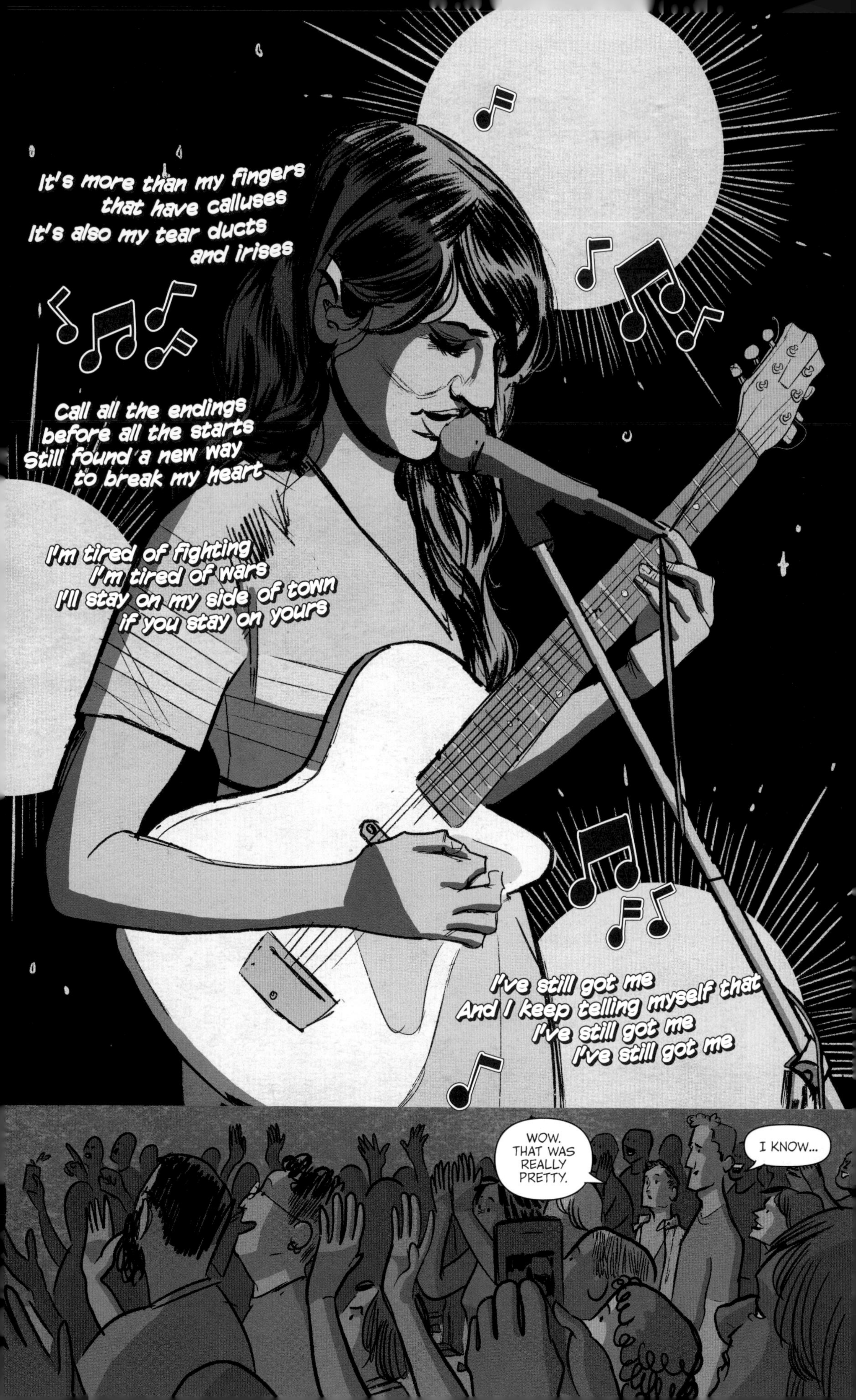
It's more than my fingers
that have calluses
It's also my tear ducts
and irises
Call all the endings
before all the starts
Still found a new way
to break my heart
I'm tired of fighting
I'm tired of wars
I'll stay on my side of town
if you stay on yours
I've still got me
And I keep telling myself that
I've still got me
I've still got me
WOW. THAT WAS REALLY PRETTY.
I KNOW...

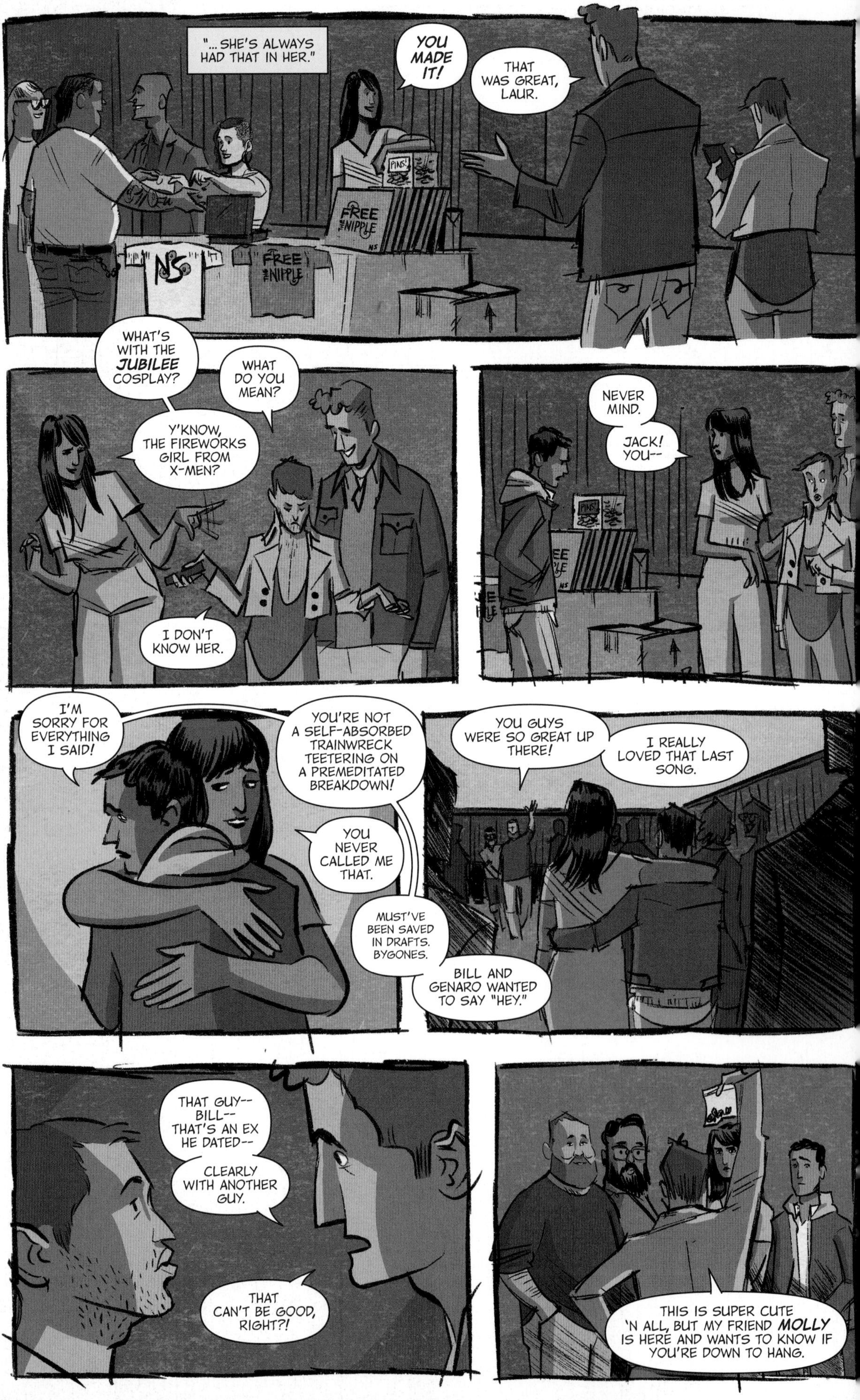
"...SHE'S ALWAYS HAD THAT IN HER."
YOU MADE IT!
THAT WAS GREAT, LAUR.
PINS!
FREE THE NIPPLE
NS
FREE THE NIPPLE
WHAT'S WITH THE JUBILEE COSPLAY?
WHAT DO YOU MEAN?
Y'KNOW, THE FIREWORKS GIRL FROM X-MEN?
I DON'T KNOW HER.
NEVER MIND.
JACK! YOU--
I'M SORRY FOR EVERYTHING I SAID!
YOU'RE NOT A SELF-ABSORBED TRAINWRECK TEETERING ON A PREMEDITATED BREAKDOWN!
YOU NEVER CALLED ME THAT.
MUST'VE BEEN SAVED IN DRAFTS. BYGONES.
YOU GUYS WERE SO GREAT UP THERE!
I REALLY LOVED THAT LAST SONG.
BILL AND GENARO WANTED TO SAY "HEY."
THAT GUY-- BILL-- THAT'S AN EX HE DATED--
CLEARLY WITH ANOTHER GUY.
THAT CAN'T BE GOOD, RIGHT?!
THIS IS SUPER CUTE 'N ALL, BUT MY FRIEND MOLLY IS HERE AND WANTS TO KNOW IF YOU'RE DOWN TO HANG.

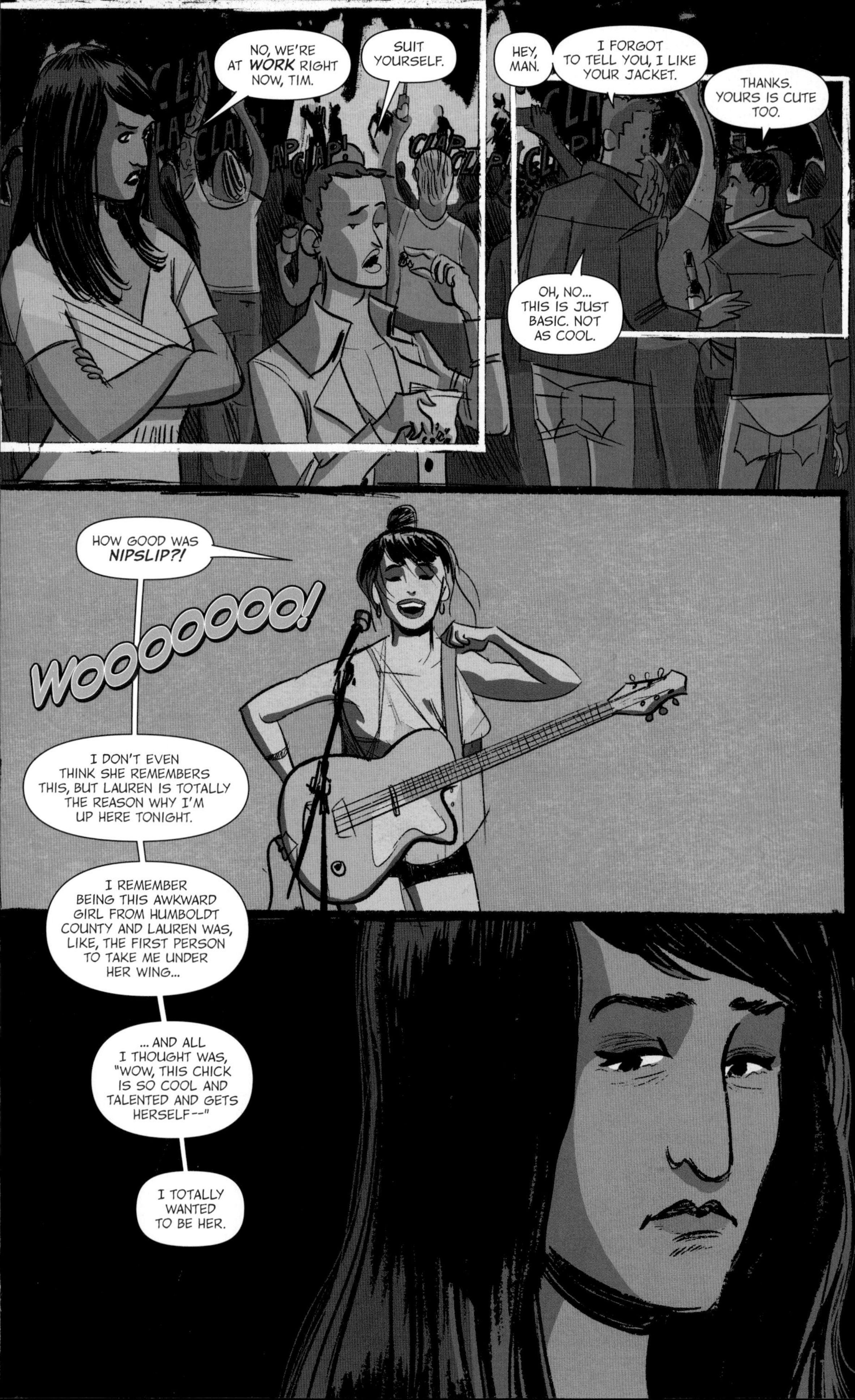
NO, WE'RE AT WORK RIGHT NOW, TIM.
SUIT YOURSELF.
HEY, MAN.
I FORGOT TO TELL YOU, I LIKE YOUR JACKET.
THANKS. YOURS IS CUTE TOO.
OH, NO... THIS IS JUST BASIC. NOT AS COOL.
CLAP CLAP! CLAP CLAP!
HOW GOOD WAS NIPSLIP?!
WOOOOOOOO!
I DON'T EVEN THINK SHE REMEMBERS THIS, BUT LAUREN IS TOTALLY THE REASON WHY I'M UP HERE TONIGHT.
I REMEMBER BEING THIS AWKWARD GIRL FROM HUMBOLDT COUNTY AND LAUREN WAS, LIKE, THE FIRST PERSON TO TAKE ME UNDER HER WING...
... AND ALL I THOUGHT WAS, "WOW, THIS CHICK IS SO COOL AND TALENTED AND GETS HERSELF--"
I TOTALLY WANTED TO BE HER.

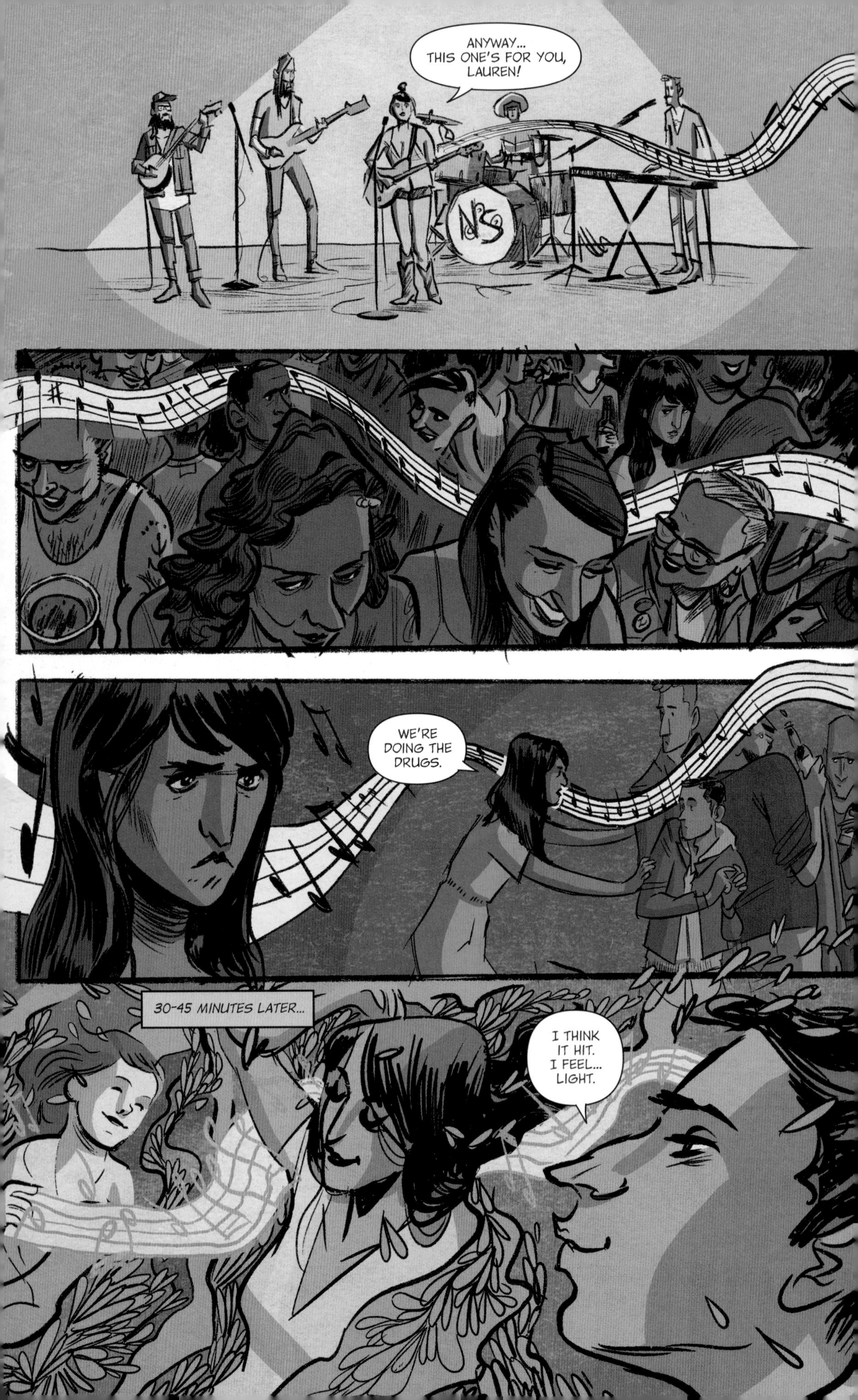
ANYWAY... THIS ONE'S FOR YOU, LAUREN!
WE'RE DOING THE DRUGS.
30-45 MINUTES LATER...
I THINK IT HIT. I FEEL... LIGHT.

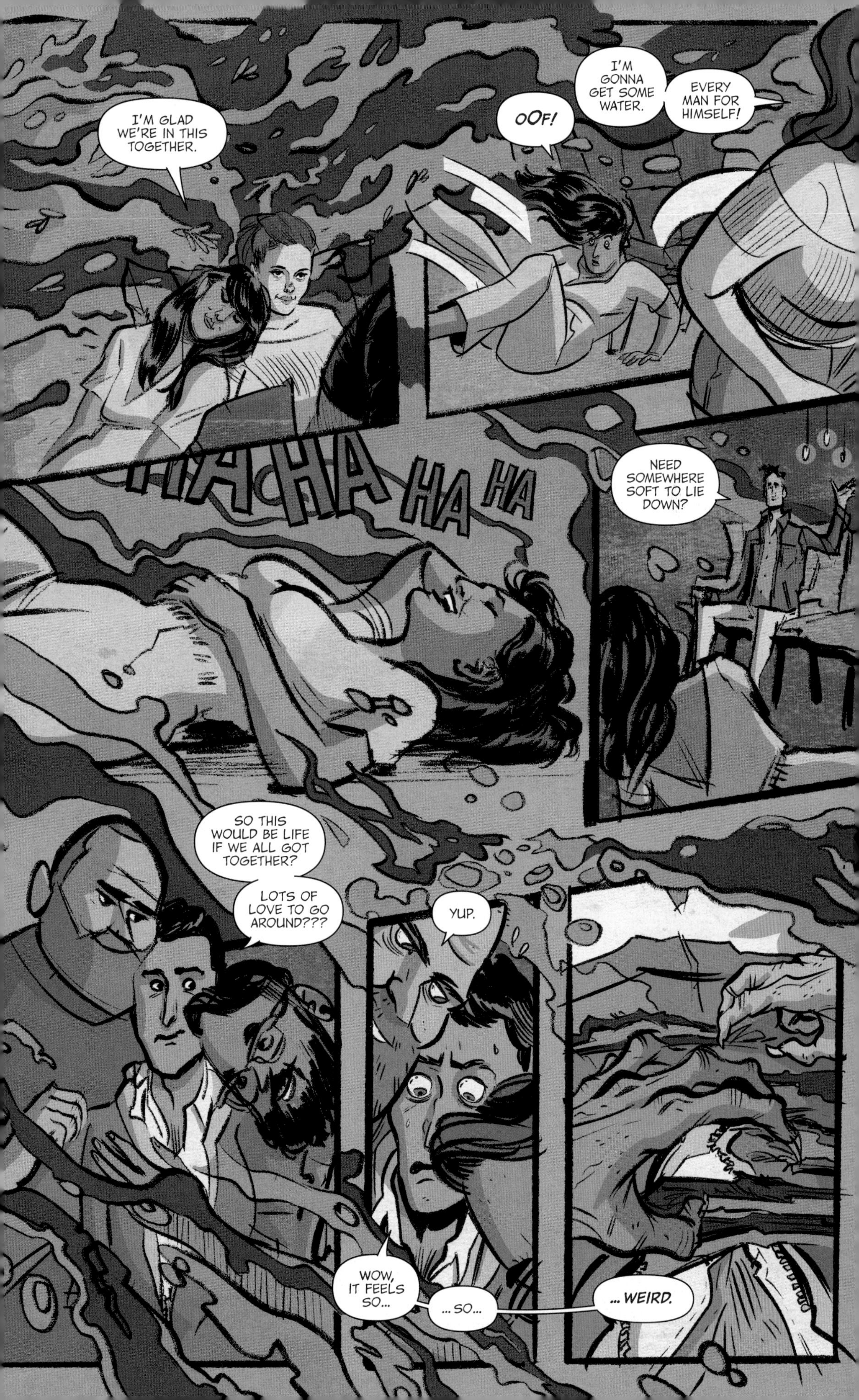
I'M GLAD WE'RE IN THIS TOGETHER.
OOF!
I'M GONNA GET SOME WATER.
EVERY MAN FOR HIMSELF!
HA HA HA HA HA
NEED SOMEWHERE SOFT TO LIE DOWN?
SO THIS WOULD BE LIFE IF WE ALL GOT TOGETHER?
LOTS OF LOVE TO GO AROUND???
YUP.
WOW, IT FEELS SO...
... SO...
... WEIRD.

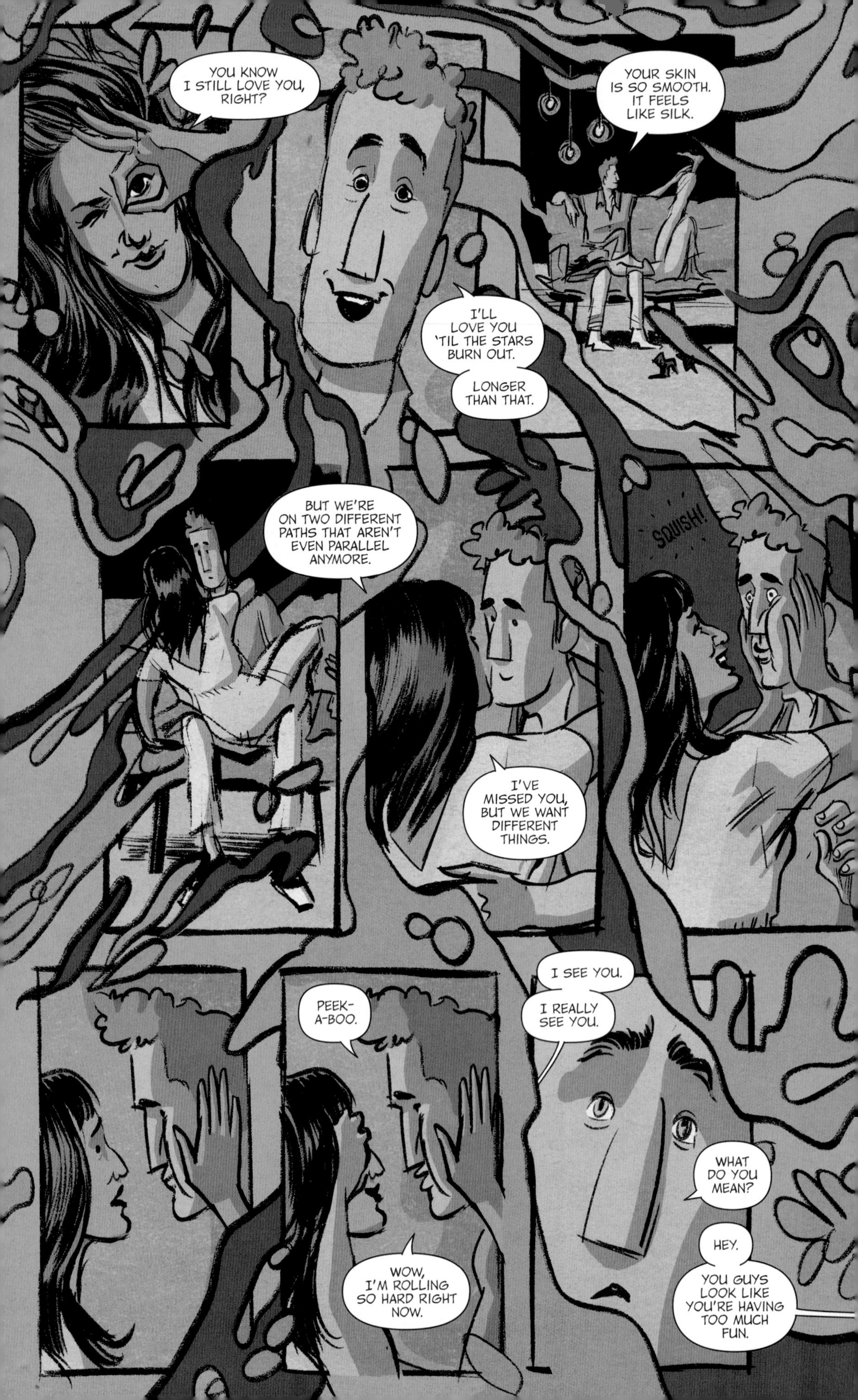
YOU KNOW I STILL LOVE YOU, RIGHT?
YOUR SKIN IS SO SMOOTH. IT FEELS LIKE SILK.
I'LL LOVE YOU 'TIL THE STARS BURN OUT.
LONGER THAN THAT.
BUT WE'RE ON TWO DIFFERENT PATHS THAT AREN'T EVEN PARALLEL ANYMORE.
SQUISH!
I'VE MISSED YOU, BUT WE WANT DIFFERENT THINGS.
PEEK-A-BOO.
WOW, I'M ROLLING SO HARD RIGHT NOW.
I SEE YOU.
I REALLY SEE YOU.
WHAT DO YOU MEAN?
HEY.
YOU GUYS LOOK LIKE YOU'RE HAVING TOO MUCH FUN.

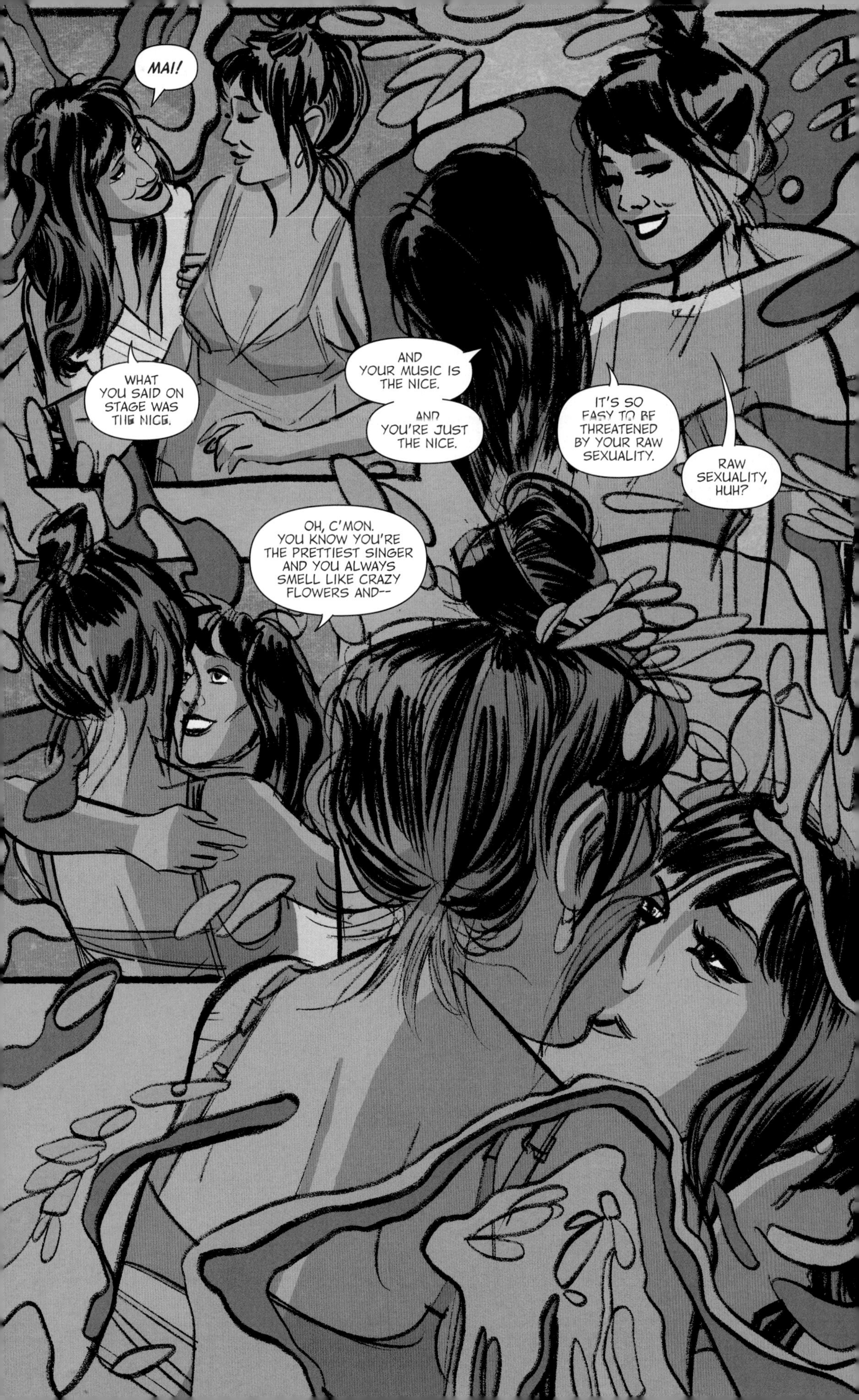
MAI!
WHAT YOU SAID ON STAGE WAS THE NICE.
AND YOUR MUSIC IS THE NICE.
AND YOU'RE JUST THE NICE.
IT'S SO EASY TO BE THREATENED BY YOUR RAW SEXUALITY.
RAW SEXUALITY, HUH?
OH, C'MON. YOU KNOW YOU'RE THE PRETTIEST SINGER AND YOU ALWAYS SMELL LIKE CRAZY FLOWERS AND--

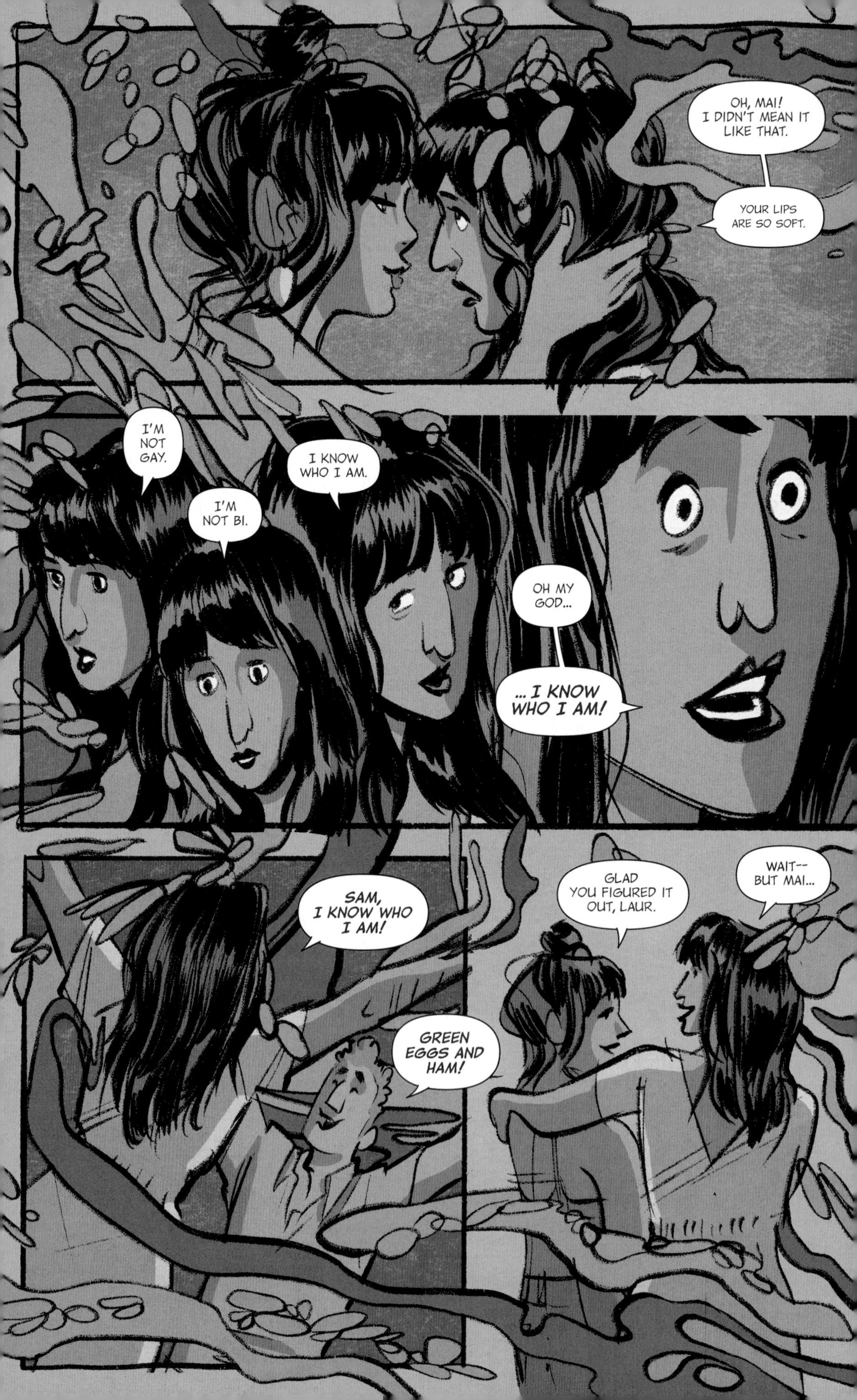
OH, MAI! I DIDN'T MEAN IT LIKE THAT.
YOUR LIPS ARE SO SOFT.
I'M NOT GAY.
I'M NOT BI.
I KNOW WHO I AM.
OH MY GOD...
... I KNOW WHO I AM!
SAM, I KNOW WHO I AM!
GREEN EGGS AND HAM!
GLAD YOU FIGURED IT OUT, LAUR.
WAIT-- BUT MAI...

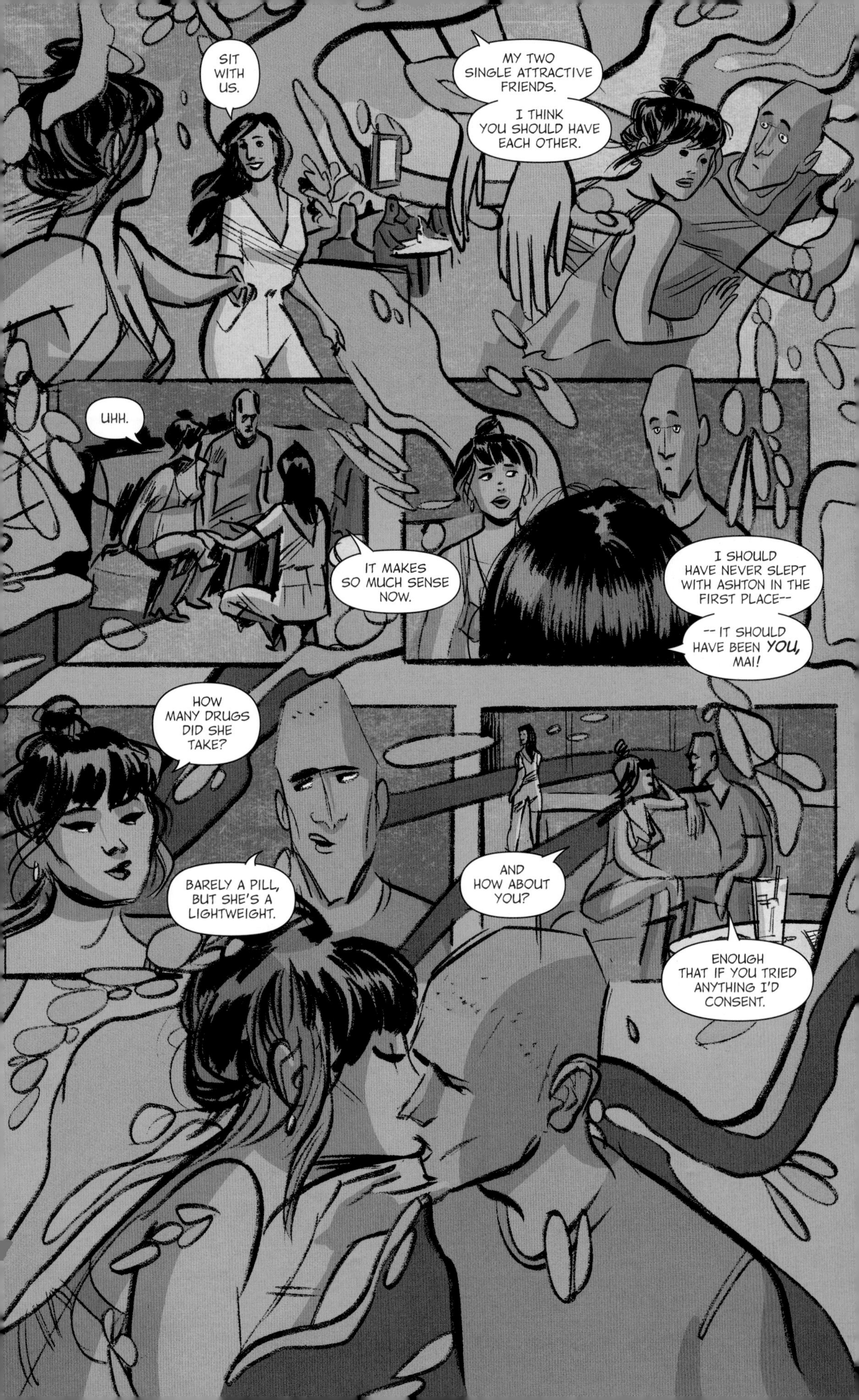
SIT WITH US.
MY TWO SINGLE ATTRACTIVE FRIENDS.
I THINK YOU SHOULD HAVE EACH OTHER.
UHH.
IT MAKES SO MUCH SENSE NOW.
I SHOULD HAVE NEVER SLEPT WITH ASHTON IN THE FIRST PLACE--
-- IT SHOULD HAVE BEEN YOU, MAI!
HOW MANY DRUGS DID SHE TAKE?
BARELY A PILL, BUT SHE'S A LIGHTWEIGHT.
AND HOW ABOUT YOU?
ENOUGH THAT IF YOU TRIED ANYTHING I'D CONSENT.

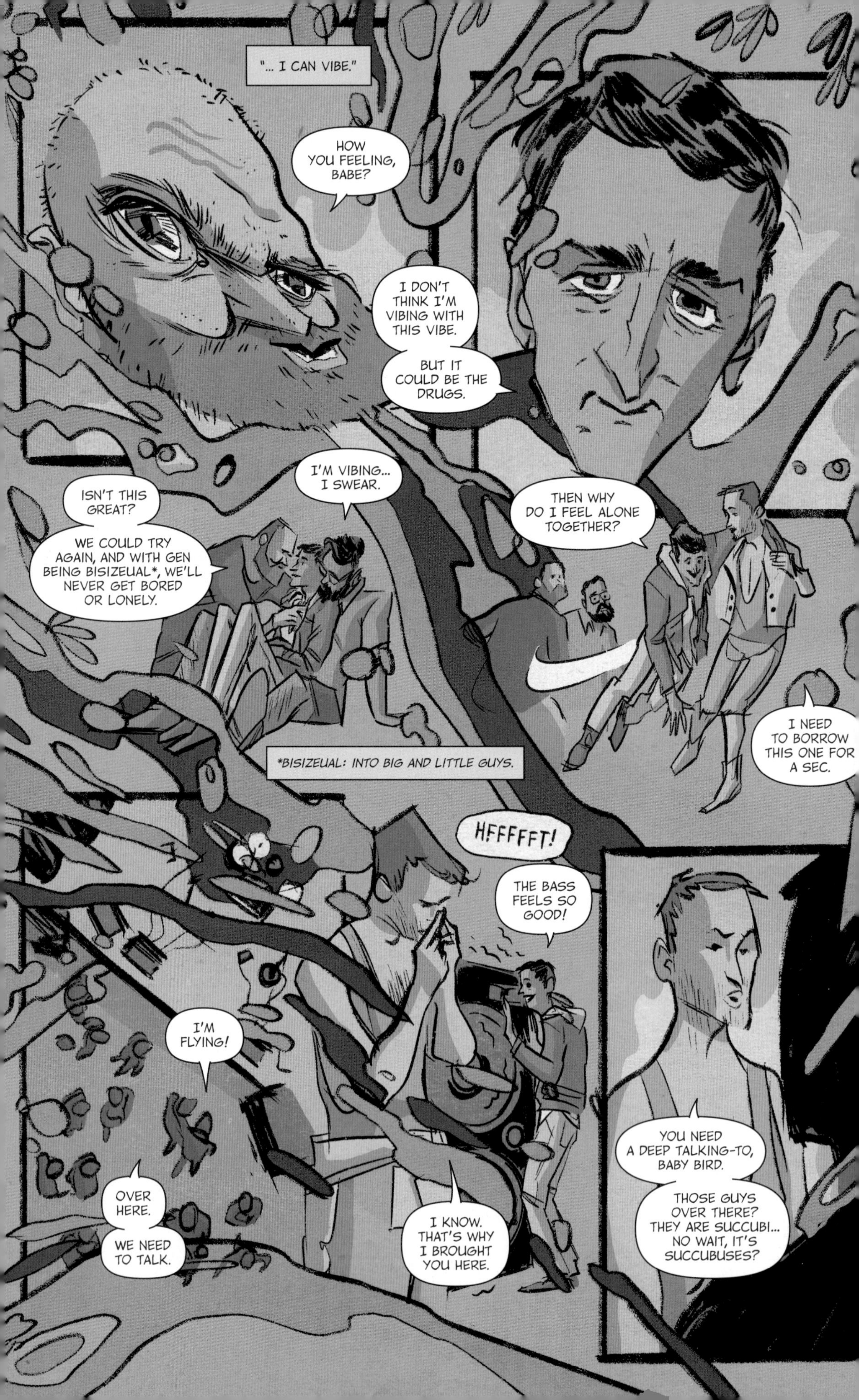
"... I CAN VIBE."
HOW YOU FEELING, BABE?
I DON'T THINK I'M VIBING WITH THIS VIBE.
BUT IT COULD BE THE DRUGS.
ISN'T THIS GREAT?
WE COULD TRY AGAIN, AND WITH GEN BEING BISIZEUAL*, WE'LL NEVER GET BORED OR LONELY.
I'M VIBING... I SWEAR.
THEN WHY DO I FEEL ALONE TOGETHER?
I NEED TO BORROW THIS ONE FOR A SEC.
*BISIZEUAL: INTO BIG AND LITTLE GUYS.
HFFFFFT!
THE BASS FEELS SO GOOD!
I'M FLYING!
OVER HERE.
WE NEED TO TALK.
I KNOW. THAT'S WHY I BROUGHT YOU HERE.
YOU NEED A DEEP TALKING-TO, BABY BIRD.
THOSE GUYS OVER THERE? THEY ARE SUCCUBI... NO WAIT, IT'S SUCCUBUSES?

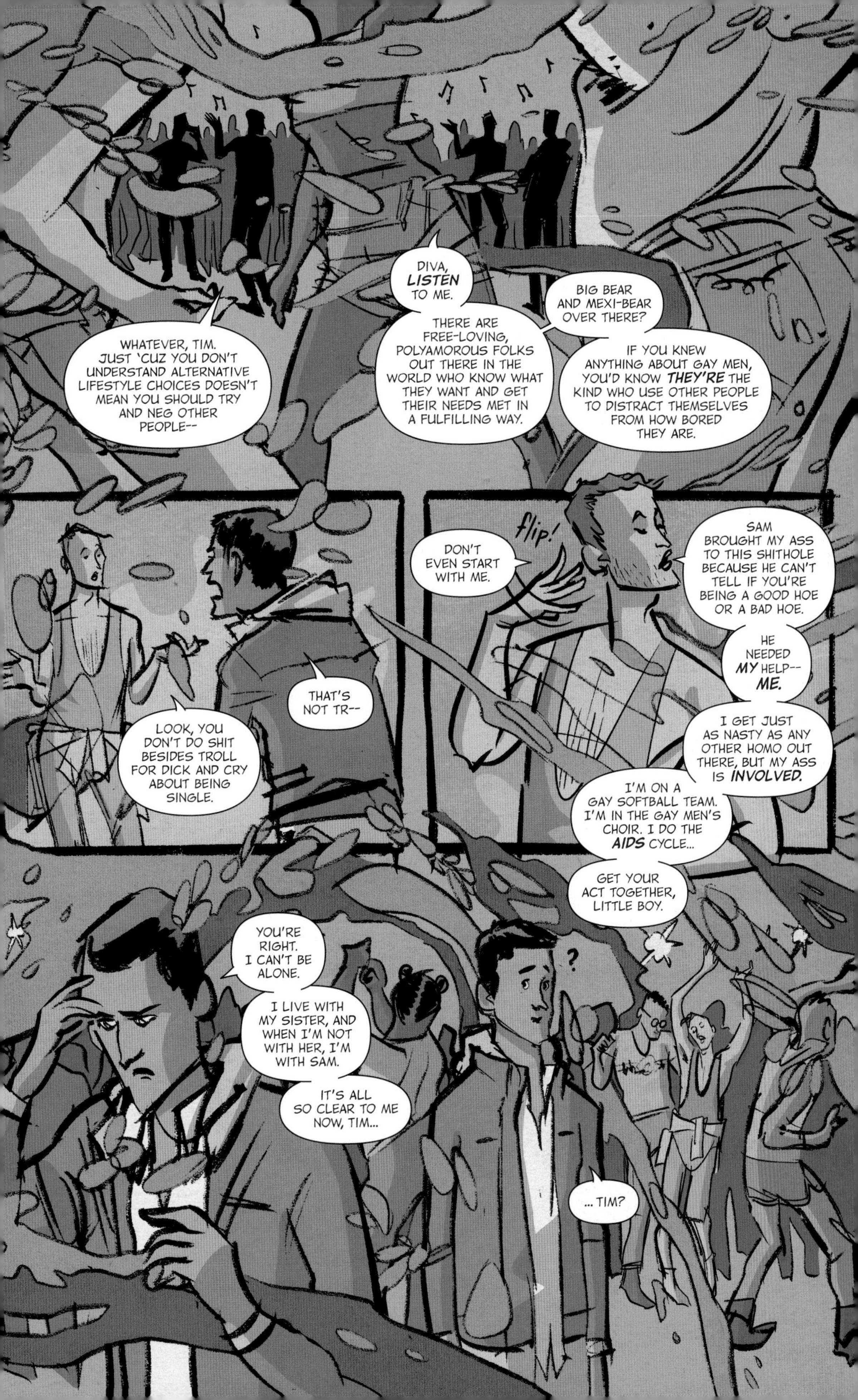
WHATEVER, TIM. JUST 'CUZ YOU DON'T UNDERSTAND ALTERNATIVE LIFESTYLE CHOICES DOESN'T MEAN YOU SHOULD TRY AND NEG OTHER PEOPLE--
DIVA, **LISTEN** TO ME.
THERE ARE FREE-LOVING, POLYAMOROUS FOLKS OUT THERE IN THE WORLD WHO KNOW WHAT THEY WANT AND GET THEIR NEEDS MET IN A FULFILLING WAY.
BIG BEAR AND MEXI-BEAR OVER THERE?
IF YOU KNEW ANYTHING ABOUT GAY MEN, YOU'D KNOW ***THEY'RE*** THE KIND WHO USE OTHER PEOPLE TO DISTRACT THEMSELVES FROM HOW BORED THEY ARE.
THAT'S NOT TR--
LOOK, YOU DON'T DO SHIT BESIDES TROLL FOR DICK AND CRY ABOUT BEING SINGLE.
flip!
DON'T EVEN START WITH ME.
SAM BROUGHT MY ASS TO THIS SHITHOLE BECAUSE HE CAN'T TELL IF YOU'RE BEING A GOOD HOE OR A BAD HOE.
HE NEEDED ***MY*** HELP-- ***ME.***
I GET JUST AS NASTY AS ANY OTHER HOMO OUT THERE, BUT MY ASS IS ***INVOLVED.***
I'M ON A GAY SOFTBALL TEAM. I'M IN THE GAY MEN'S CHOIR. I DO THE ***AIDS*** CYCLE...
GET YOUR ACT TOGETHER, LITTLE BOY.
YOU'RE RIGHT. I CAN'T BE ALONE.
I LIVE WITH MY SISTER, AND WHEN I'M NOT WITH HER, I'M WITH SAM.
IT'S ALL SO CLEAR TO ME NOW, TIM...
?
...TIM?

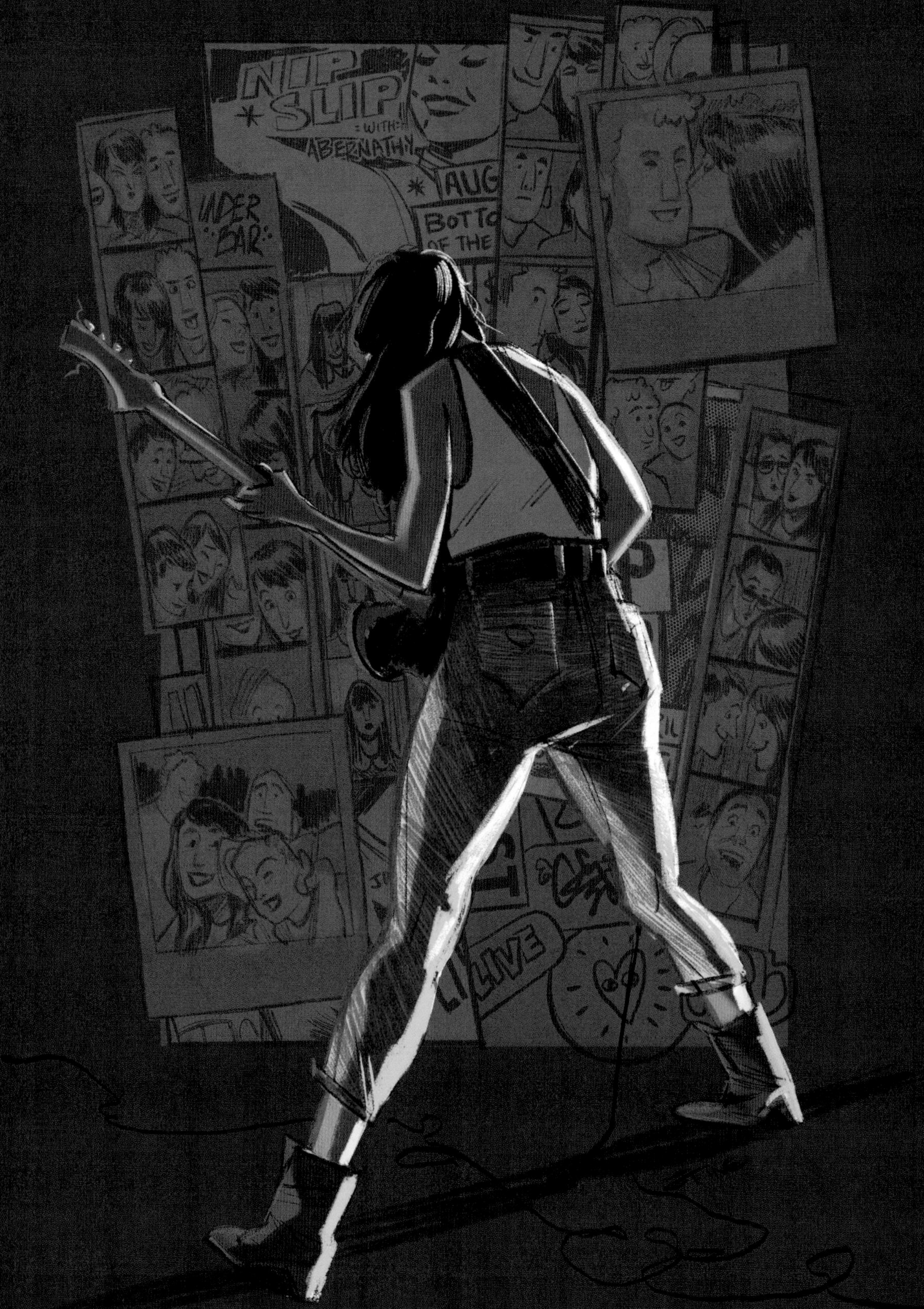
NIP SLIP
WITH
ABERNATHY
UNDER BAR
AUG
BOTTO
OF THE
LIVE

issue four cover a
BY JENNY D. FINE

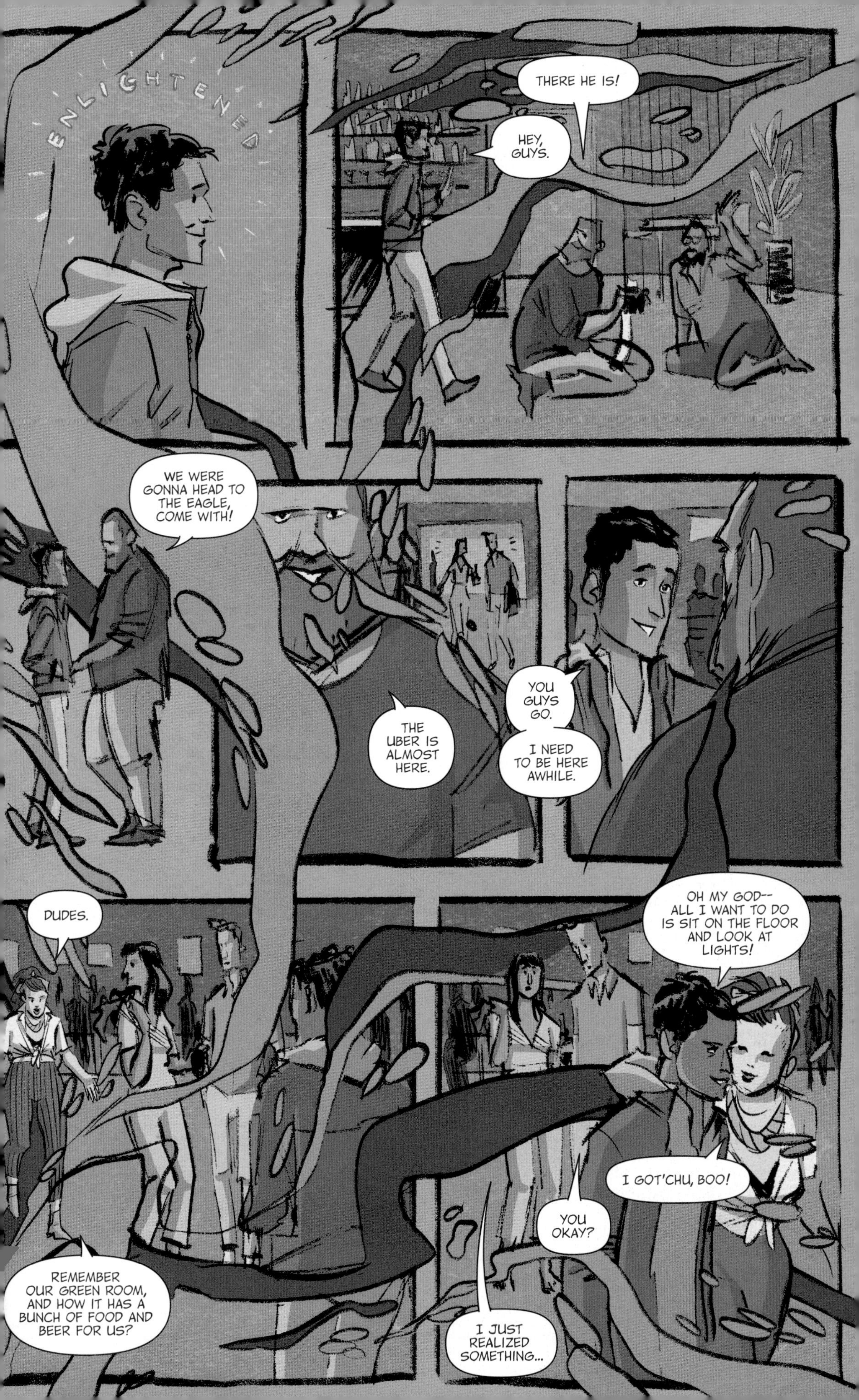
ENLIGHTENED
THERE HE IS!
HEY, GUYS.
WE WERE GONNA HEAD TO THE EAGLE, COME WITH!
THE UBER IS ALMOST HERE.
YOU GUYS GO.
I NEED TO BE HERE AWHILE.
DUDES.
REMEMBER OUR GREEN ROOM, AND HOW IT HAS A BUNCH OF FOOD AND BEER FOR US?
OH MY GOD-- ALL I WANT TO DO IS SIT ON THE FLOOR AND LOOK AT LIGHTS!
I GOT'CHU, BOO!
YOU OKAY?
I JUST REALIZED SOMETHING...

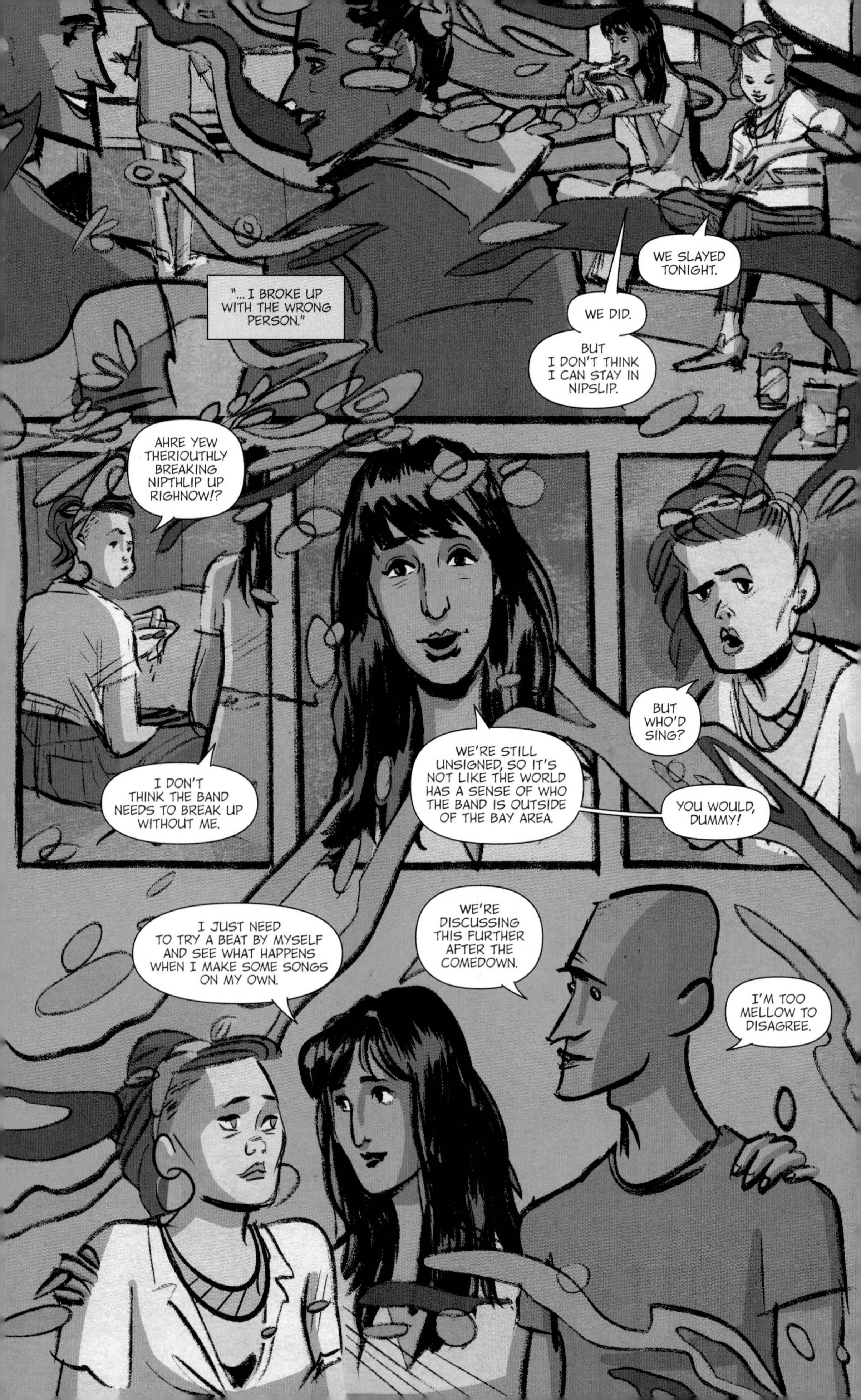
"... I BROKE UP WITH THE WRONG PERSON."
WE SLAYED TONIGHT.
WE DID.
BUT I DON'T THINK I CAN STAY IN NIPSLIP.
AHRE YEW THERIOUTHLY BREAKING NIPTHLIP UP RIGHNOW!?
BUT WHO'D SING?
I DON'T THINK THE BAND NEEDS TO BREAK UP WITHOUT ME.
WE'RE STILL UNSIGNED, SO IT'S NOT LIKE THE WORLD HAS A SENSE OF WHO THE BAND IS OUTSIDE OF THE BAY AREA.
YOU WOULD, DUMMY!
I JUST NEED TO TRY A BEAT BY MYSELF AND SEE WHAT HAPPENS WHEN I MAKE SOME SONGS ON MY OWN.
WE'RE DISCUSSING THIS FURTHER AFTER THE COMEDOWN.
I'M TOO MELLOW TO DISAGREE.

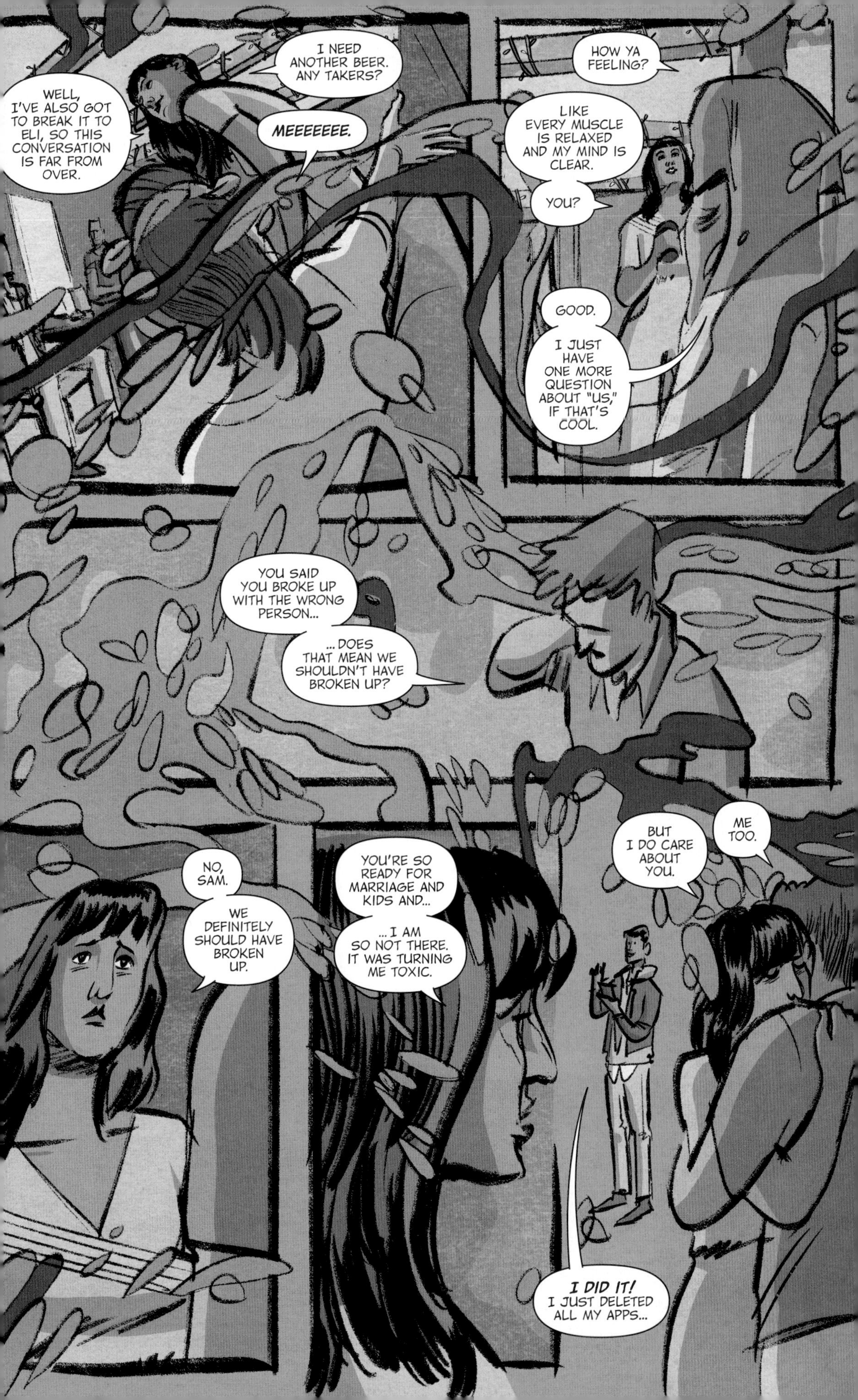
I NEED ANOTHER BEER. ANY TAKERS?
WELL, I'VE ALSO GOT TO BREAK IT TO ELI, SO THIS CONVERSATION IS FAR FROM OVER.
MEEEEEEE.
HOW YA FEELING?
LIKE EVERY MUSCLE IS RELAXED AND MY MIND IS CLEAR.
YOU?
GOOD.
I JUST HAVE ONE MORE QUESTION ABOUT "US," IF THAT'S COOL.
YOU SAID YOU BROKE UP WITH THE WRONG PERSON...
...DOES THAT MEAN WE SHOULDN'T HAVE BROKEN UP?
NO, SAM.
WE DEFINITELY SHOULD HAVE BROKEN UP.
YOU'RE SO READY FOR MARRIAGE AND KIDS AND...
...I AM SO NOT THERE. IT WAS TURNING ME TOXIC.
BUT I DO CARE ABOUT YOU.
ME TOO.
I DID IT! I JUST DELETED ALL MY APPS...

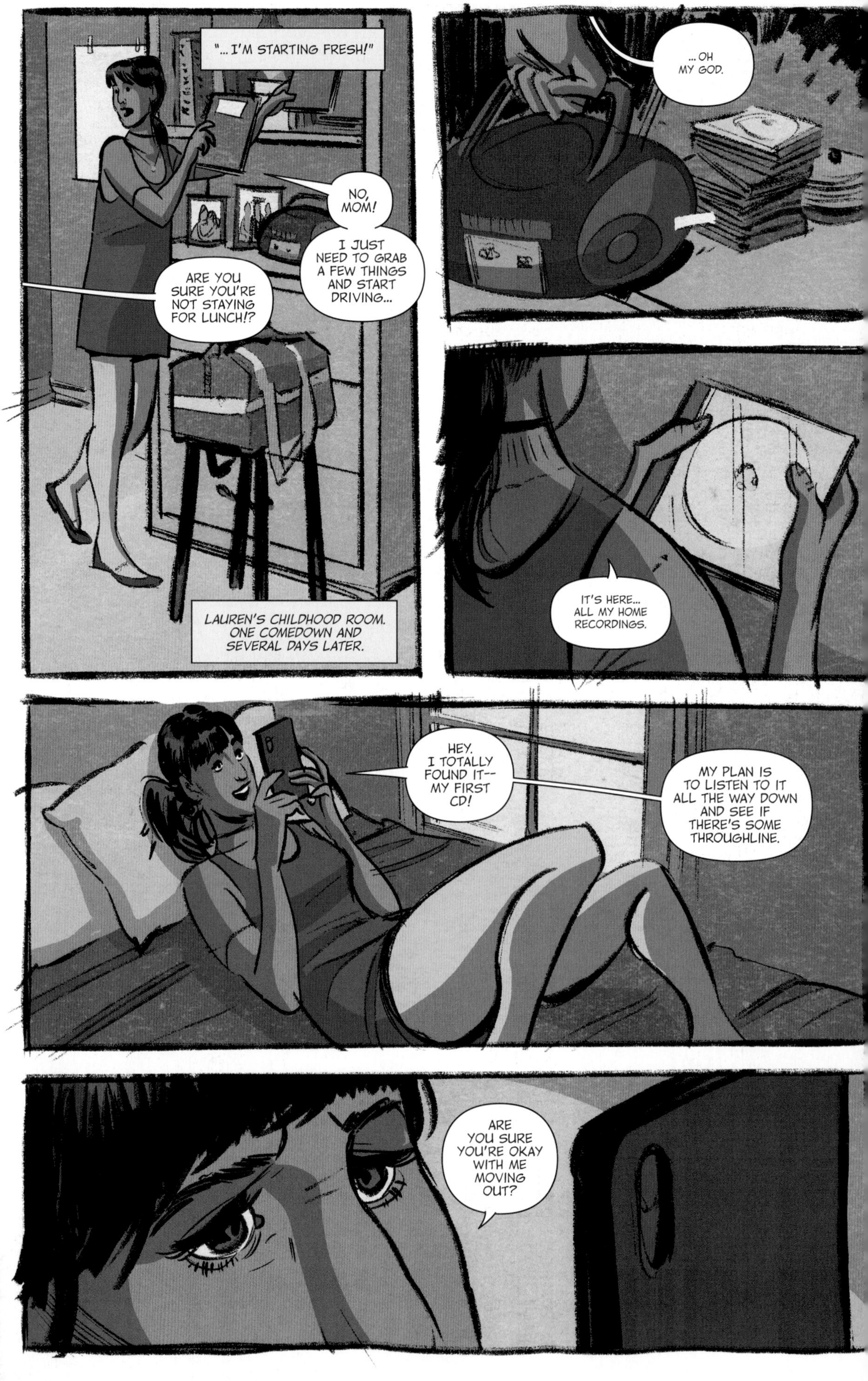
"... I'M STARTING FRESH!"
NO, MOM!
I JUST NEED TO GRAB A FEW THINGS AND START DRIVING...
ARE YOU SURE YOU'RE NOT STAYING FOR LUNCH!?
LAUREN'S CHILDHOOD ROOM. ONE COMEDOWN AND SEVERAL DAYS LATER.
... OH MY GOD.
IT'S HERE... ALL MY HOME RECORDINGS.
HEY. I TOTALLY FOUND IT-- MY FIRST CD!
MY PLAN IS TO LISTEN TO IT ALL THE WAY DOWN AND SEE IF THERE'S SOME THROUGHLINE.
ARE YOU SURE YOU'RE OKAY WITH ME MOVING OUT?

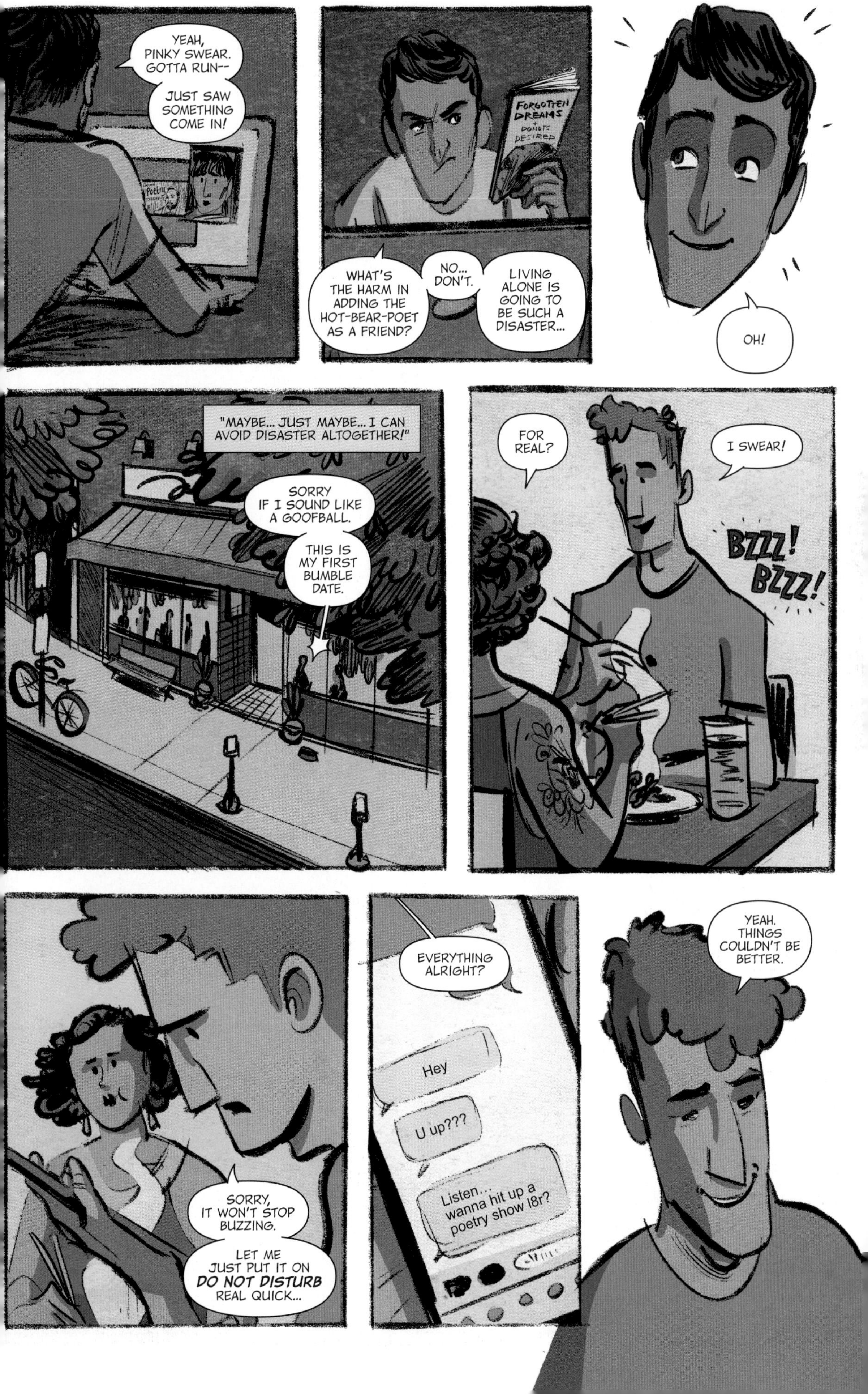
YEAH, PINKY SWEAR. GOTTA RUN--
JUST SAW SOMETHING COME IN!
Poetry
FORGOTTEN DREAMS + DONUTS DESIRED
WHAT'S THE HARM IN ADDING THE HOT-BEAR-POET AS A FRIEND?
NO... DON'T.
LIVING ALONE IS GOING TO BE SUCH A DISASTER...
OH!
"MAYBE... JUST MAYBE... I CAN AVOID DISASTER ALTOGETHER!"
SORRY IF I SOUND LIKE A GOOFBALL.
THIS IS MY FIRST BUMBLE DATE.
FOR REAL?
I SWEAR!
BZZZ! BZZZ!
SORRY, IT WON'T STOP BUZZING.
LET ME JUST PUT IT ON ***DO NOT DISTURB*** REAL QUICK...
EVERYTHING ALRIGHT?
Hey
U up???
Listen... wanna hit up a poetry show l8r?
YEAH. THINGS COULDN'T BE BETTER.

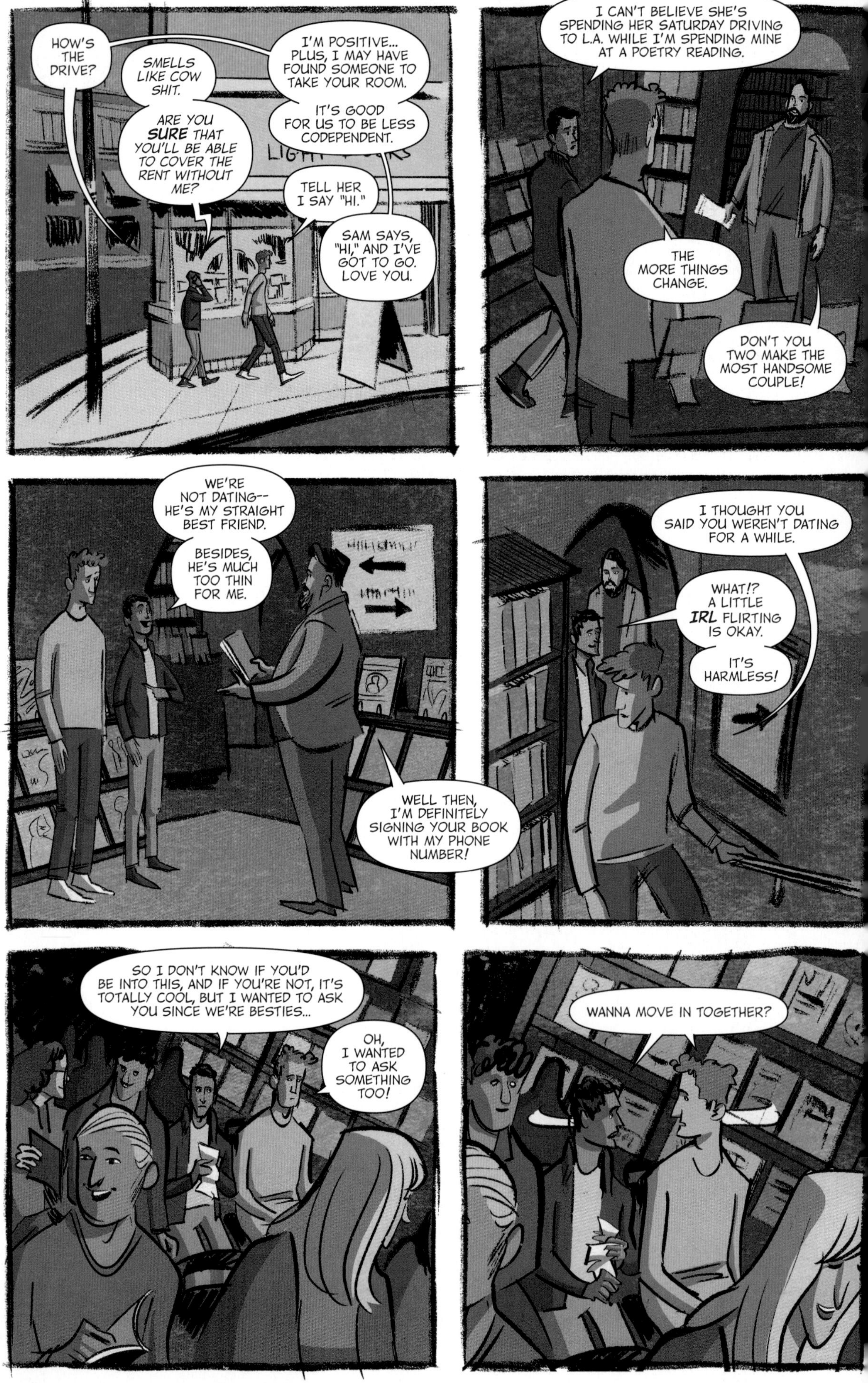
HOW'S THE DRIVE?
SMELLS LIKE COW SHIT.
ARE YOU SURE THAT YOU'LL BE ABLE TO COVER THE RENT WITHOUT ME?
I'M POSITIVE... PLUS, I MAY HAVE FOUND SOMEONE TO TAKE YOUR ROOM.
IT'S GOOD FOR US TO BE LESS CODEPENDENT.
TELL HER I SAY "HI."
SAM SAYS, "HI," AND I'VE GOT TO GO. LOVE YOU.
I CAN'T BELIEVE SHE'S SPENDING HER SATURDAY DRIVING TO L.A. WHILE I'M SPENDING MINE AT A POETRY READING.
THE MORE THINGS CHANGE.
DON'T YOU TWO MAKE THE MOST HANDSOME COUPLE!
WE'RE NOT DATING-- HE'S MY STRAIGHT BEST FRIEND.
BESIDES, HE'S MUCH TOO THIN FOR ME.
WELL THEN, I'M DEFINITELY SIGNING YOUR BOOK WITH MY PHONE NUMBER!
I THOUGHT YOU SAID YOU WEREN'T DATING FOR A WHILE.
WHAT!? A LITTLE IRL FLIRTING IS OKAY.
IT'S HARMLESS!
SO I DON'T KNOW IF YOU'D BE INTO THIS, AND IF YOU'RE NOT, IT'S TOTALLY COOL, BUT I WANTED TO ASK YOU SINCE WE'RE BESTIES...
OH, I WANTED TO ASK SOMETHING TOO!
WANNA MOVE IN TOGETHER?

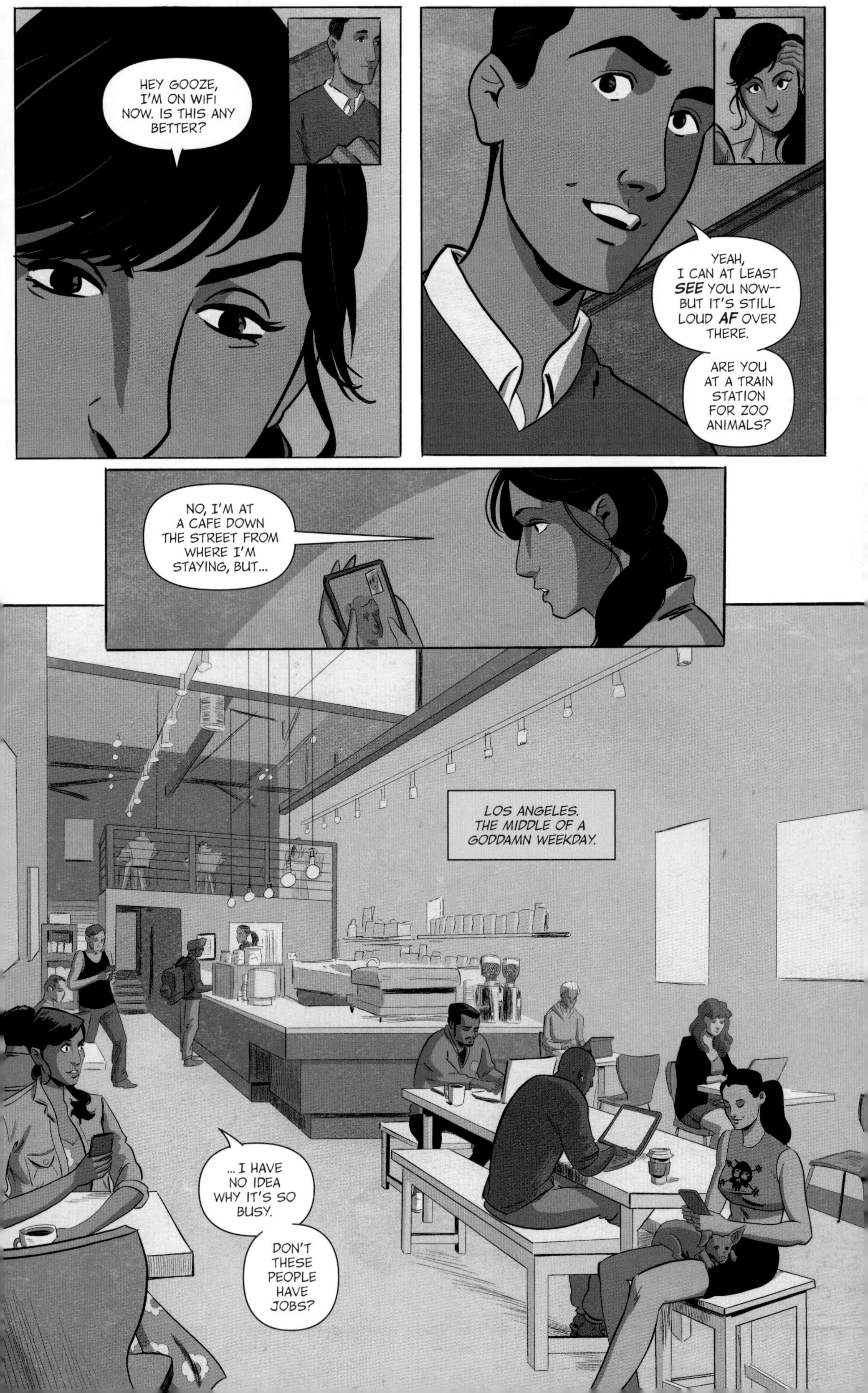
HEY GOOZE, I'M ON WIFI NOW. IS THIS ANY BETTER?
YEAH, I CAN AT LEAST **SEE** YOU NOW-- BUT IT'S STILL LOUD **AF** OVER THERE.
ARE YOU AT A TRAIN STATION FOR ZOO ANIMALS?
NO, I'M AT A CAFE DOWN THE STREET FROM WHERE I'M STAYING, BUT...
LOS ANGELES. THE MIDDLE OF A GODDAMN WEEKDAY.
...I HAVE NO IDEA WHY IT'S SO BUSY.
DON'T THESE PEOPLE HAVE JOBS?

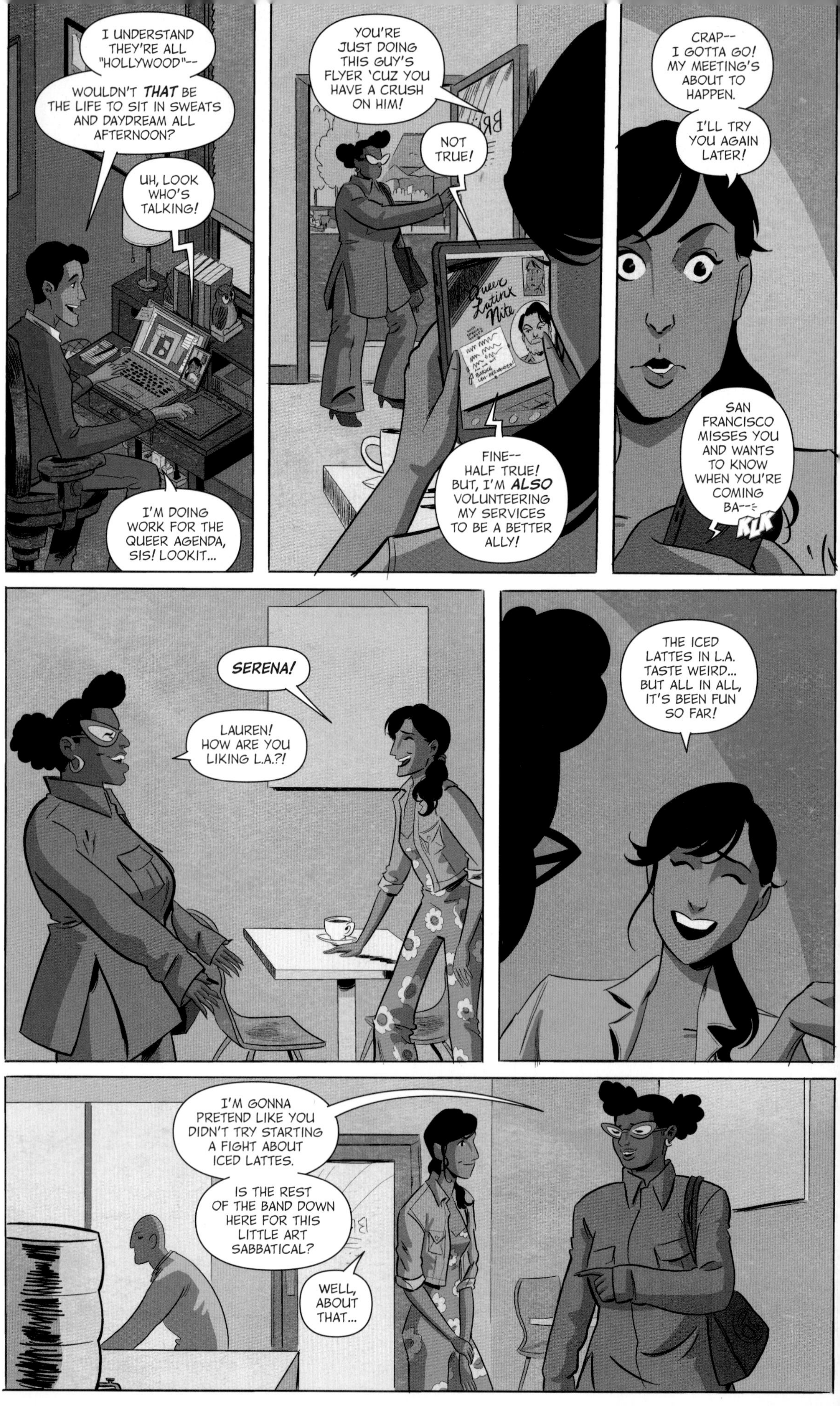
I UNDERSTAND THEY'RE ALL "HOLLYWOOD"--
WOULDN'T *THAT* BE THE LIFE TO SIT IN SWEATS AND DAYDREAM ALL AFTERNOON?
UH, LOOK WHO'S TALKING!
I'M DOING WORK FOR THE QUEER AGENDA, SIS! LOOKIT...
YOU'RE JUST DOING THIS GUY'S FLYER 'CUZ YOU HAVE A CRUSH ON HIM!
NOT TRUE!
Queer Latinx Nite
FINE-- HALF TRUE! BUT, I'M *ALSO* VOLUNTEERING MY SERVICES TO BE A BETTER ALLY!
CRAP-- I GOTTA GO! MY MEETING'S ABOUT TO HAPPEN.
I'LL TRY YOU AGAIN LATER!
SAN FRANCISCO MISSES YOU AND WANTS TO KNOW WHEN YOU'RE COMING BA--
KLK
SERENA!
LAUREN! HOW ARE YOU LIKING L.A.?!
THE ICED LATTES IN L.A. TASTE WEIRD... BUT ALL IN ALL, IT'S BEEN FUN SO FAR!
I'M GONNA PRETEND LIKE YOU DIDN'T TRY STARTING A FIGHT ABOUT ICED LATTES.
IS THE REST OF THE BAND DOWN HERE FOR THIS LITTLE ART SABBATICAL?
WELL, ABOUT THAT...

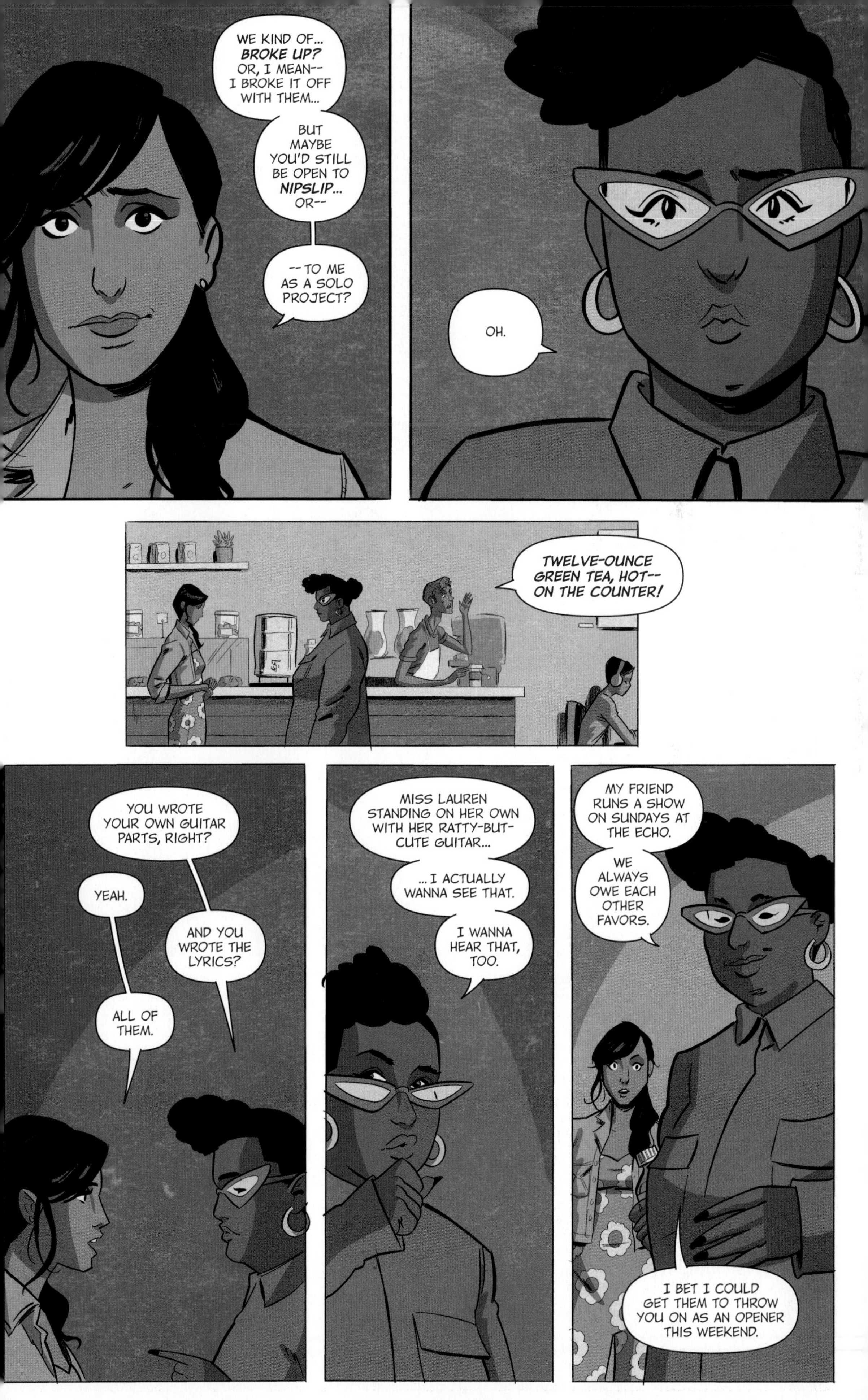
WE KIND OF... **BROKE UP?** OR, I MEAN-- I BROKE IT OFF WITH THEM...
BUT MAYBE YOU'D STILL BE OPEN TO **NIPSLIP...** OR--
--TO ME AS A SOLO PROJECT?
OH.
TWELVE-OUNCE GREEN TEA, HOT-- ON THE COUNTER!
YOU WROTE YOUR OWN GUITAR PARTS, RIGHT?
YEAH.
AND YOU WROTE THE LYRICS?
ALL OF THEM.
MISS LAUREN STANDING ON HER OWN WITH HER RATTY-BUT-CUTE GUITAR...
...I ACTUALLY WANNA SEE THAT.
I WANNA HEAR THAT, TOO.
MY FRIEND RUNS A SHOW ON SUNDAYS AT THE ECHO.
WE ALWAYS OWE EACH OTHER FAVORS.
I BET I COULD GET THEM TO THROW YOU ON AS AN OPENER THIS WEEKEND.

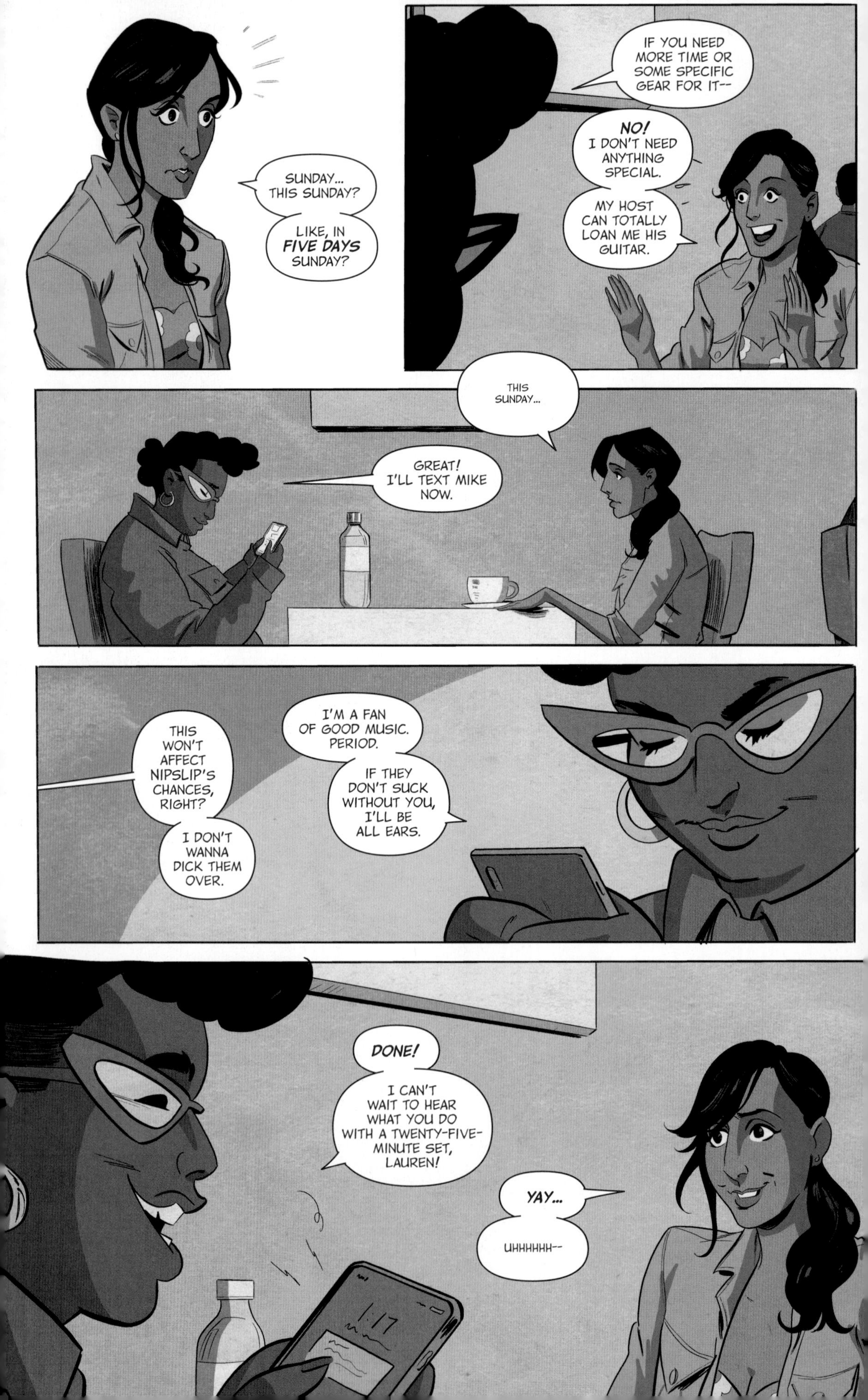
SUNDAY... THIS SUNDAY?
LIKE, IN *FIVE DAYS* SUNDAY?
IF YOU NEED MORE TIME OR SOME SPECIFIC GEAR FOR IT--
NO! I DON'T NEED ANYTHING SPECIAL.
MY HOST CAN TOTALLY LOAN ME HIS GUITAR.
THIS SUNDAY...
GREAT! I'LL TEXT MIKE NOW.
THIS WON'T AFFECT NIPSLIP'S CHANCES, RIGHT?
I DON'T WANNA DICK THEM OVER.
I'M A FAN OF GOOD MUSIC. PERIOD.
IF THEY DON'T SUCK WITHOUT YOU, I'LL BE ALL EARS.
DONE!
I CAN'T WAIT TO HEAR WHAT YOU DO WITH A TWENTY-FIVE-MINUTE SET, LAUREN!
YAY...
UHHHHHH--

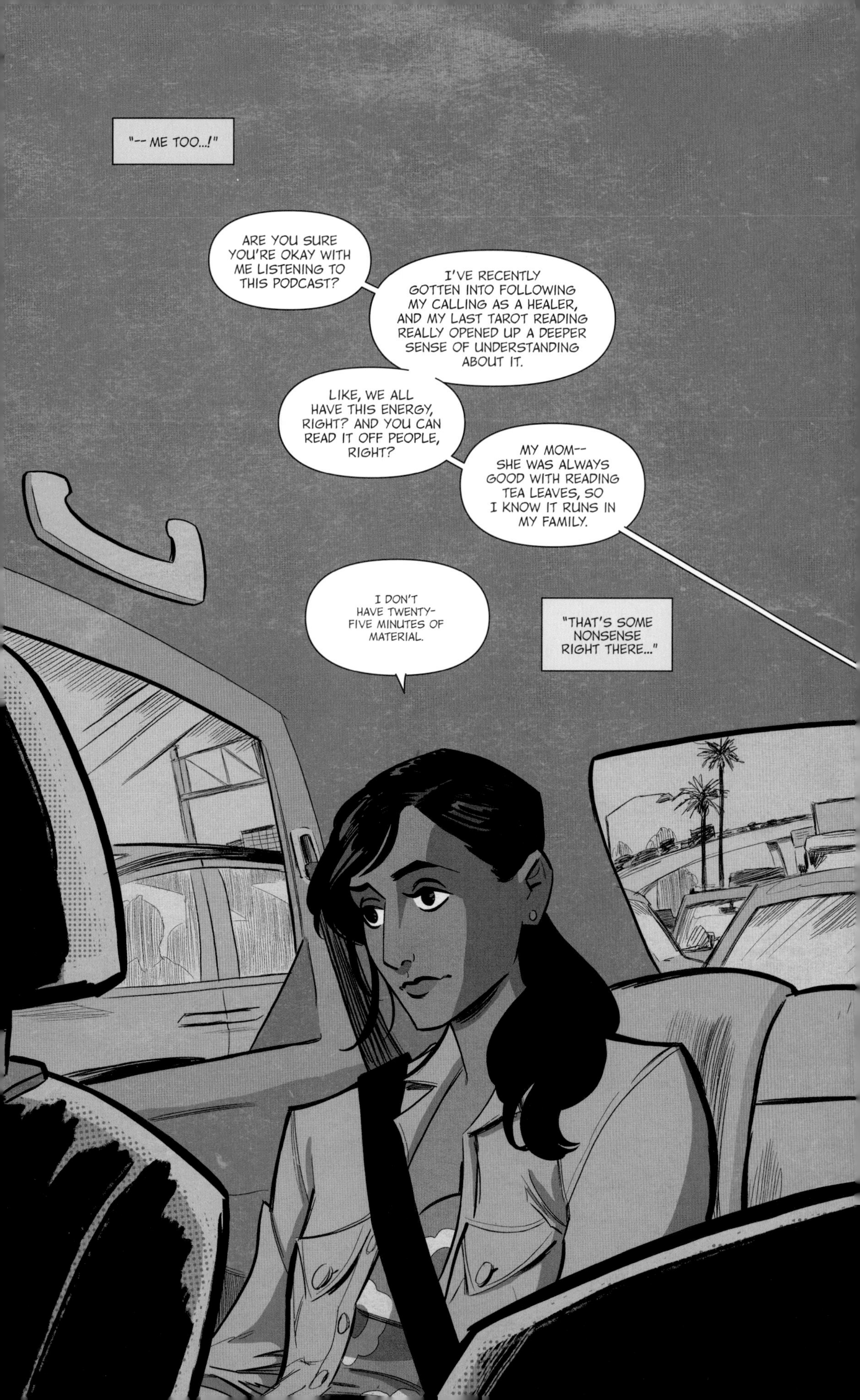
"-- ME TOO...!"
ARE YOU SURE YOU'RE OKAY WITH ME LISTENING TO THIS PODCAST?
I'VE RECENTLY GOTTEN INTO FOLLOWING MY CALLING AS A HEALER, AND MY LAST TAROT READING REALLY OPENED UP A DEEPER SENSE OF UNDERSTANDING ABOUT IT.
LIKE, WE ALL HAVE THIS ENERGY, RIGHT? AND YOU CAN READ IT OFF PEOPLE, RIGHT?
MY MOM-- SHE WAS ALWAYS GOOD WITH READING TEA LEAVES, SO I KNOW IT RUNS IN MY FAMILY.
I DON'T HAVE TWENTY-FIVE MINUTES OF MATERIAL.
"THAT'S SOME NONSENSE RIGHT THERE..."

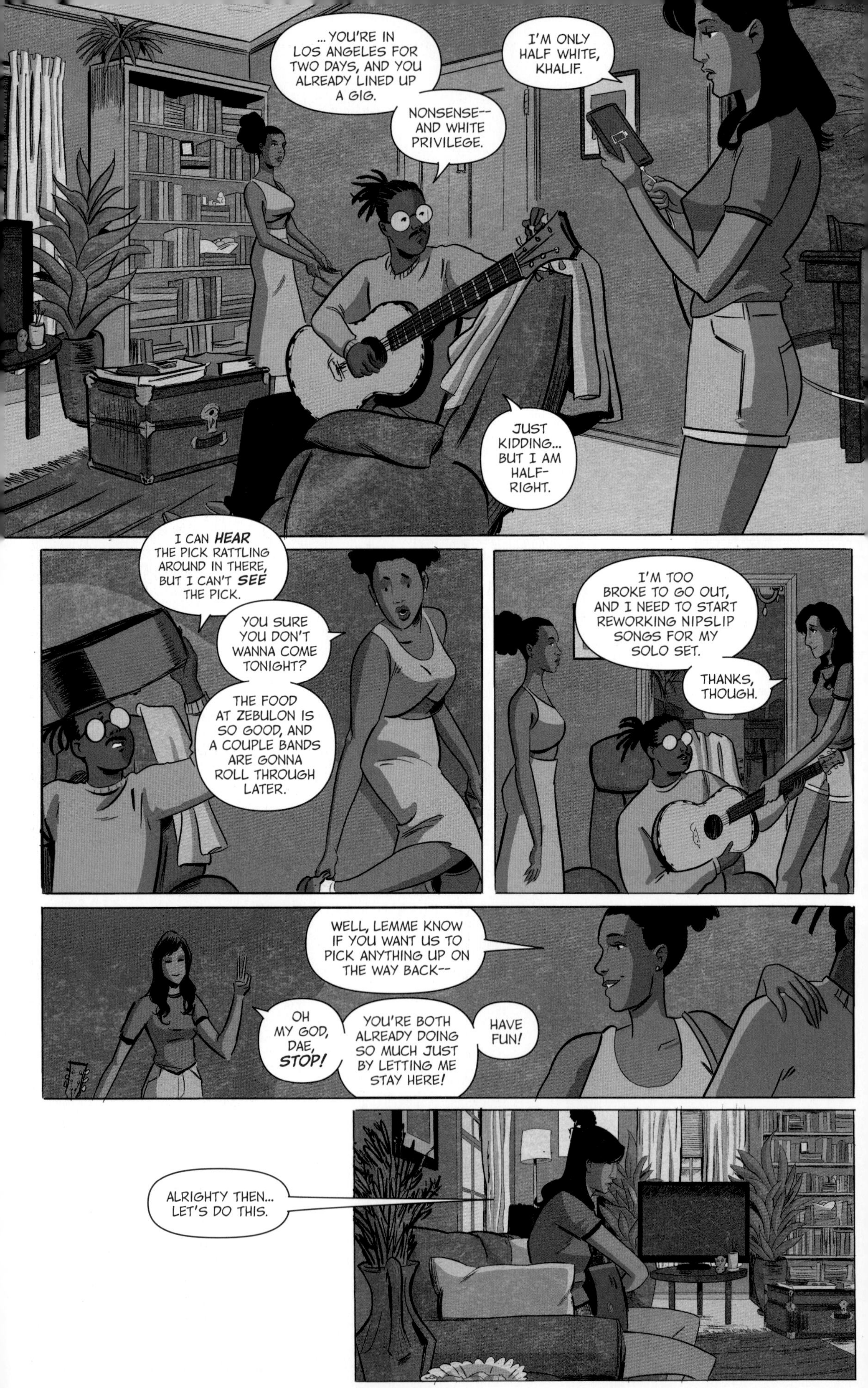
...YOU'RE IN LOS ANGELES FOR TWO DAYS, AND YOU ALREADY LINED UP A GIG.
NONSENSE-- AND WHITE PRIVILEGE.
I'M ONLY HALF WHITE, KHALIF.
JUST KIDDING... BUT I AM HALF-RIGHT.
I CAN HEAR THE PICK RATTLING AROUND IN THERE, BUT I CAN'T SEE THE PICK.
YOU SURE YOU DON'T WANNA COME TONIGHT?
THE FOOD AT ZEBULON IS SO GOOD, AND A COUPLE BANDS ARE GONNA ROLL THROUGH LATER.
I'M TOO BROKE TO GO OUT, AND I NEED TO START REWORKING NIPSLIP SONGS FOR MY SOLO SET.
THANKS, THOUGH.
WELL, LEMME KNOW IF YOU WANT US TO PICK ANYTHING UP ON THE WAY BACK--
OH MY GOD, DAE, STOP!
YOU'RE BOTH ALREADY DOING SO MUCH JUST BY LETTING ME STAY HERE!
HAVE FUN!
ALRIGHTY THEN... LET'S DO THIS.

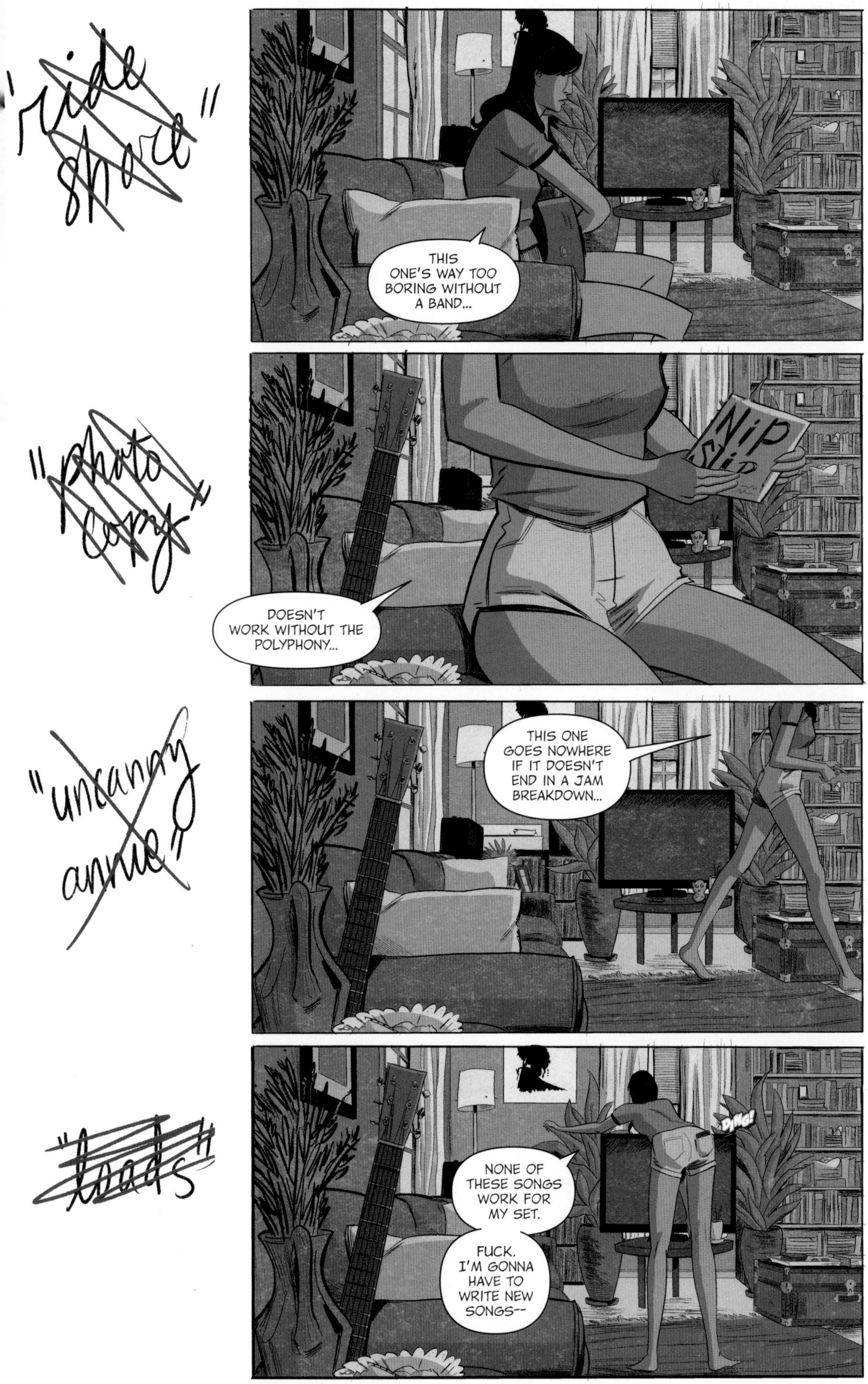
THIS ONE'S WAY TOO BORING WITHOUT A BAND...
DOESN'T WORK WITHOUT THE POLYPHONY...
THIS ONE GOES NOWHERE IF IT DOESN'T END IN A JAM BREAKDOWN...
DING!
NONE OF THESE SONGS WORK FOR MY SET.
FUCK. I'M GONNA HAVE TO WRITE NEW SONGS--

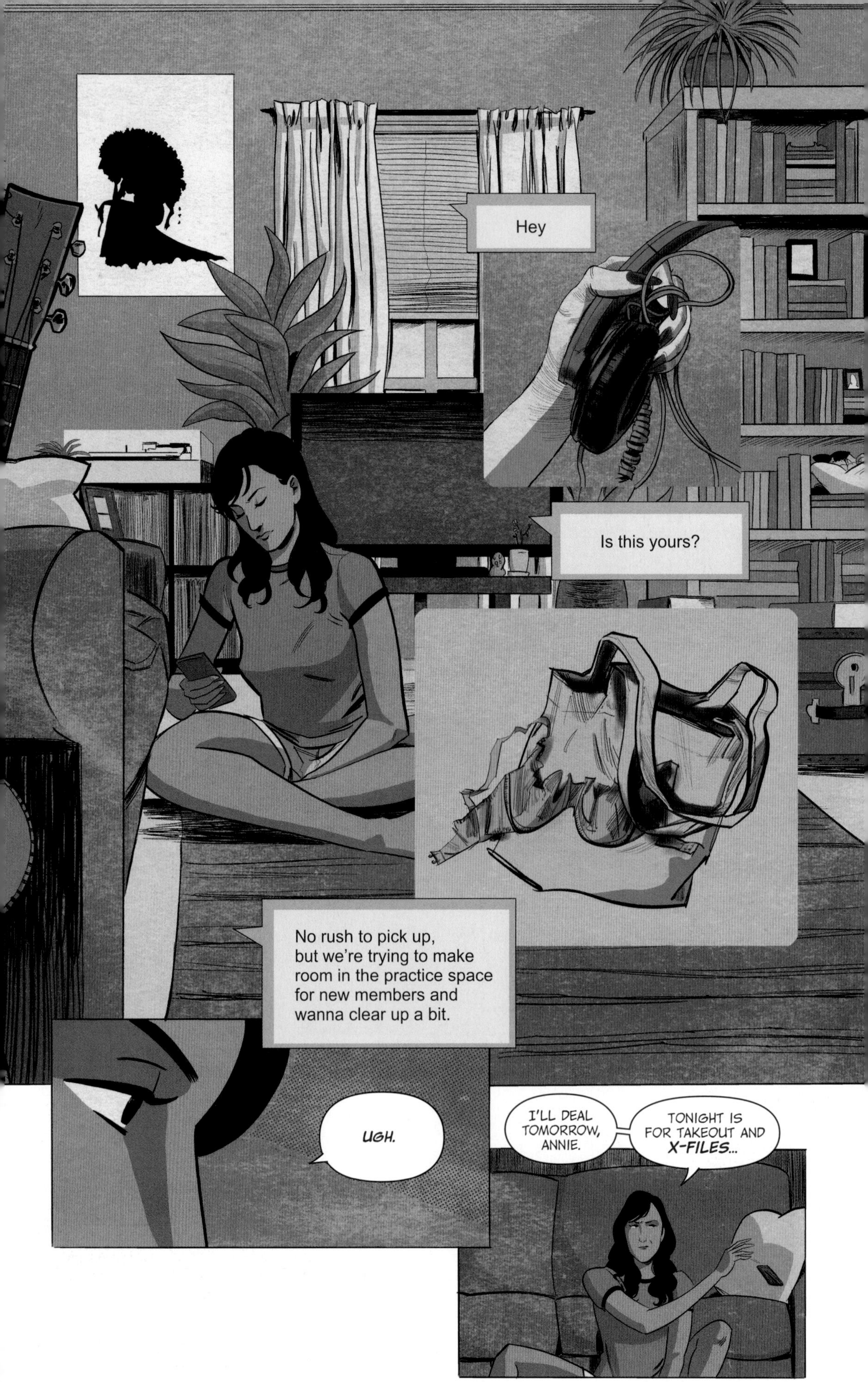
Hey
Is this yours?
No rush to pick up, but we're trying to make room in the practice space for new members and wanna clear up a bit.
UGH.
I'LL DEAL TOMORROW, ANNIE.
TONIGHT IS FOR TAKEOUT AND X-FILES...

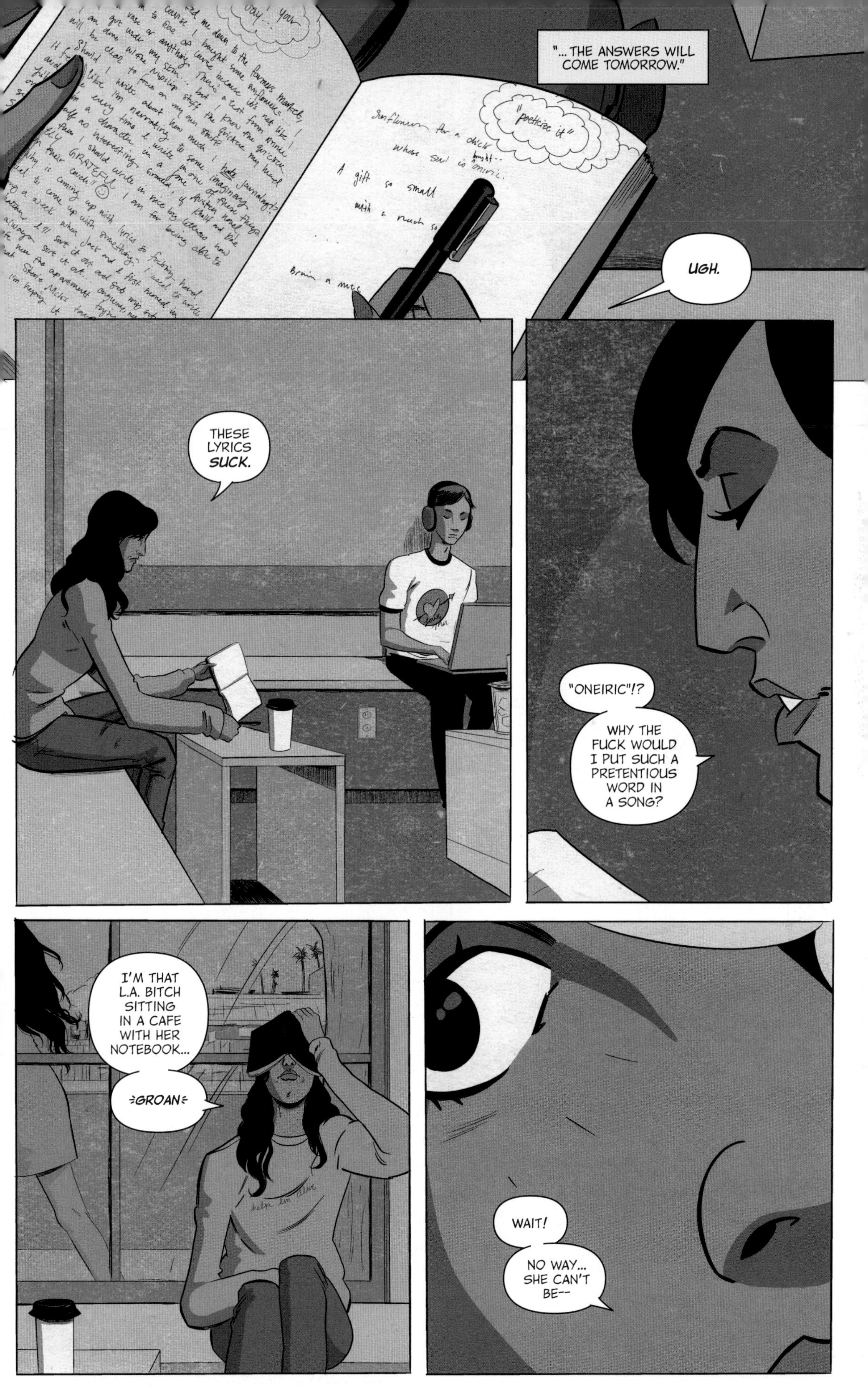
"...THE ANSWERS WILL COME TOMORROW."
"poeticize it"
A gift so small
UGH.
THESE LYRICS SUCK.
"ONEIRIC"!?
WHY THE FUCK WOULD I PUT SUCH A PRETENTIOUS WORD IN A SONG?
I'M THAT L.A. BITCH SITTING IN A CAFE WITH HER NOTEBOOK...
GROAN
WAIT!
NO WAY... SHE CAN'T BE--

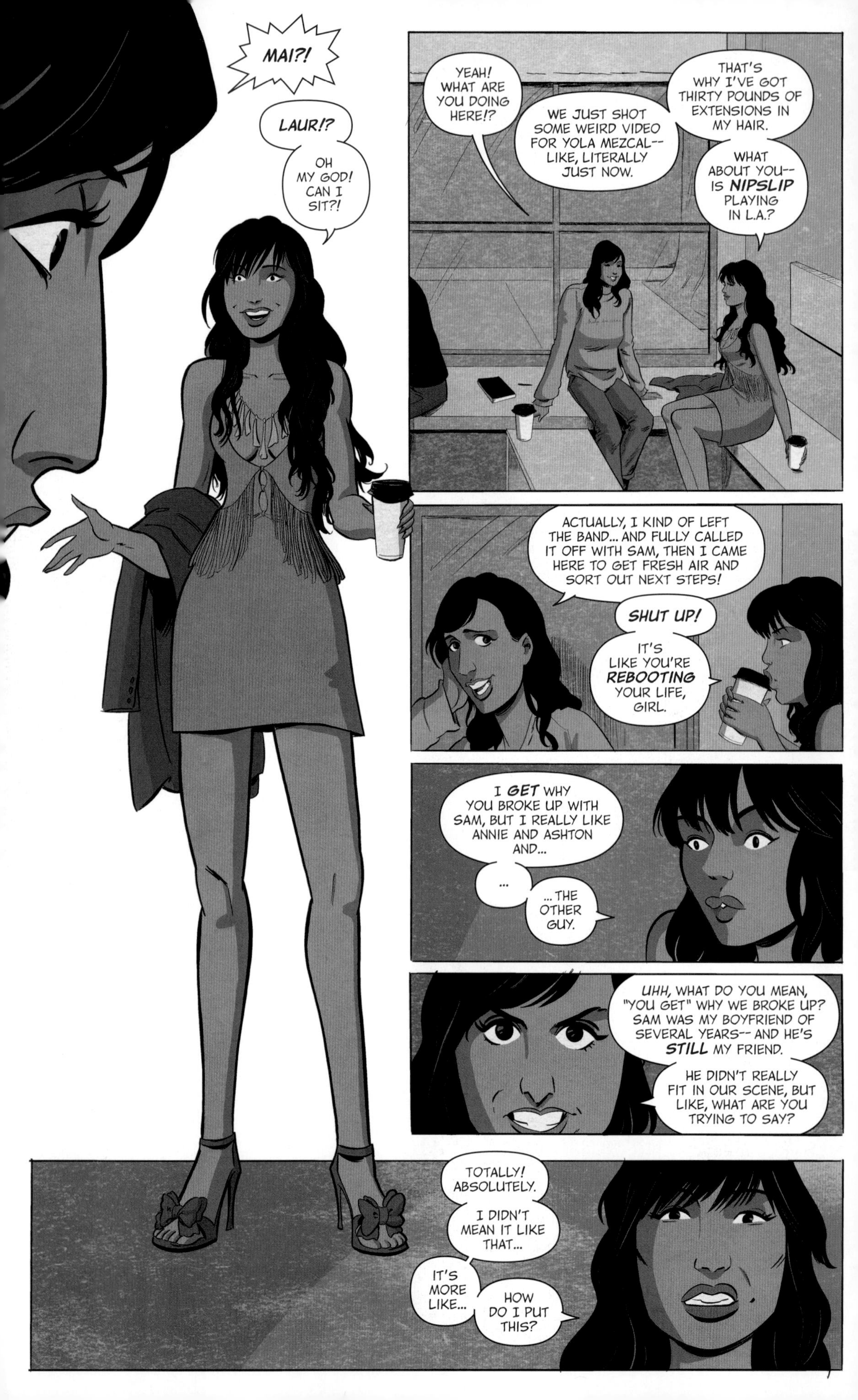
MAI?!
LAUR!?
OH MY GOD! CAN I SIT?!
YEAH! WHAT ARE YOU DOING HERE!?
WE JUST SHOT SOME WEIRD VIDEO FOR YOLA MEZCAL-- LIKE, LITERALLY JUST NOW.
THAT'S WHY I'VE GOT THIRTY POUNDS OF EXTENSIONS IN MY HAIR.
WHAT ABOUT YOU-- IS NIPSLIP PLAYING IN L.A.?
ACTUALLY, I KIND OF LEFT THE BAND... AND FULLY CALLED IT OFF WITH SAM, THEN I CAME HERE TO GET FRESH AIR AND SORT OUT NEXT STEPS!
SHUT UP!
IT'S LIKE YOU'RE REBOOTING YOUR LIFE, GIRL.
I GET WHY YOU BROKE UP WITH SAM, BUT I REALLY LIKE ANNIE AND ASHTON AND...
...
... THE OTHER GUY.
UHH, WHAT DO YOU MEAN, "YOU GET" WHY WE BROKE UP? SAM WAS MY BOYFRIEND OF SEVERAL YEARS-- AND HE'S STILL MY FRIEND.
HE DIDN'T REALLY FIT IN OUR SCENE, BUT LIKE, WHAT ARE YOU TRYING TO SAY?
TOTALLY! ABSOLUTELY.
I DIDN'T MEAN IT LIKE THAT...
IT'S MORE LIKE...
HOW DO I PUT THIS?

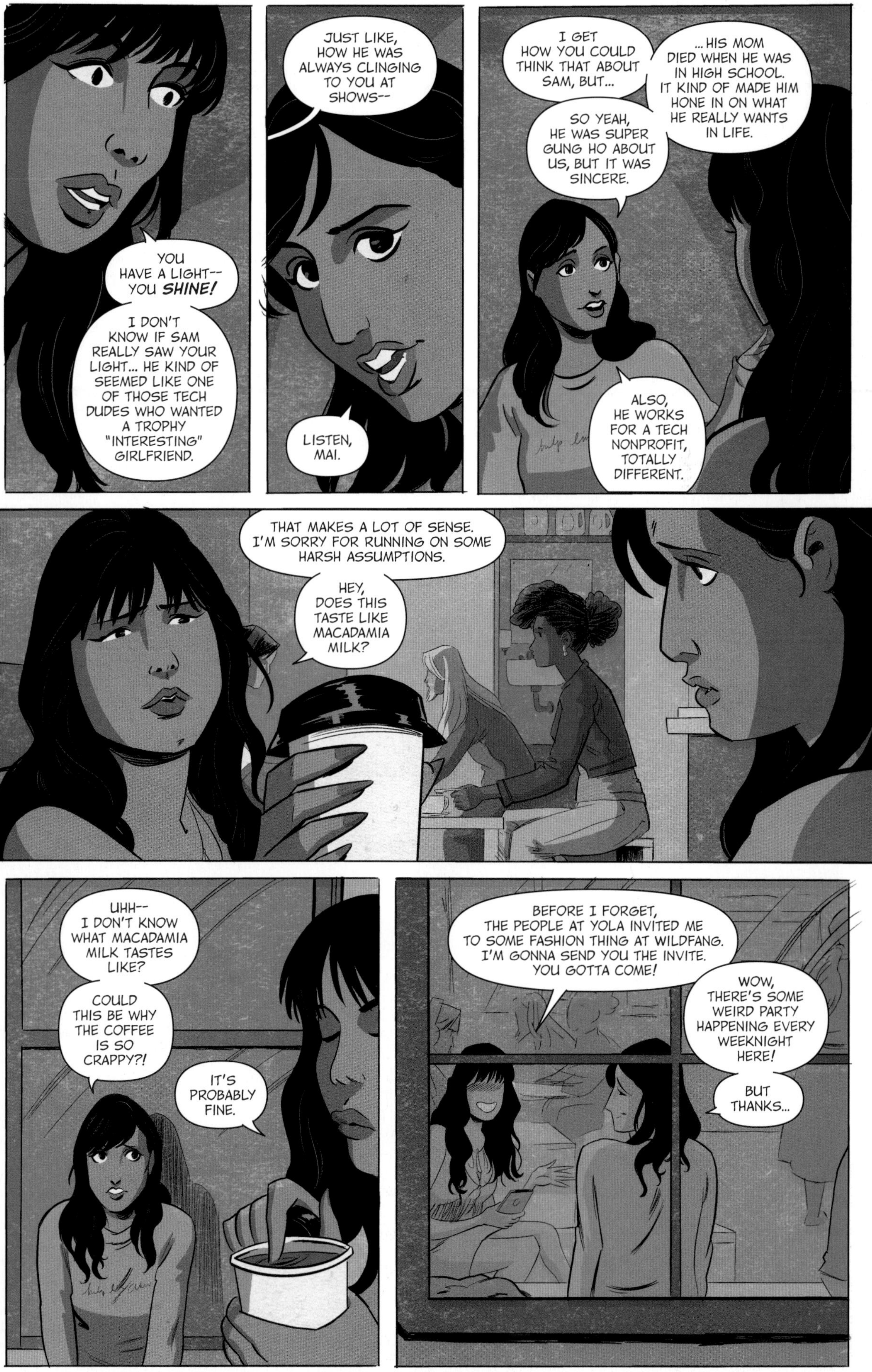
YOU HAVE A LIGHT-- YOU SHINE!
I DON'T KNOW IF SAM REALLY SAW YOUR LIGHT... HE KIND OF SEEMED LIKE ONE OF THOSE TECH DUDES WHO WANTED A TROPHY "INTERESTING" GIRLFRIEND.
JUST LIKE, HOW HE WAS ALWAYS CLINGING TO YOU AT SHOWS--
LISTEN, MAI.
I GET HOW YOU COULD THINK THAT ABOUT SAM, BUT...
...HIS MOM DIED WHEN HE WAS IN HIGH SCHOOL. IT KIND OF MADE HIM HONE IN ON WHAT HE REALLY WANTS IN LIFE.
SO YEAH, HE WAS SUPER GUNG HO ABOUT US, BUT IT WAS SINCERE.
ALSO, HE WORKS FOR A TECH NONPROFIT, TOTALLY DIFFERENT.
THAT MAKES A LOT OF SENSE. I'M SORRY FOR RUNNING ON SOME HARSH ASSUMPTIONS.
HEY, DOES THIS TASTE LIKE MACADAMIA MILK?
UHH-- I DON'T KNOW WHAT MACADAMIA MILK TASTES LIKE?
COULD THIS BE WHY THE COFFEE IS SO CRAPPY?!
IT'S PROBABLY FINE.
BEFORE I FORGET, THE PEOPLE AT YOLA INVITED ME TO SOME FASHION THING AT WILDFANG. I'M GONNA SEND YOU THE INVITE. YOU GOTTA COME!
WOW, THERE'S SOME WEIRD PARTY HAPPENING EVERY WEEKNIGHT HERE!
BUT THANKS...

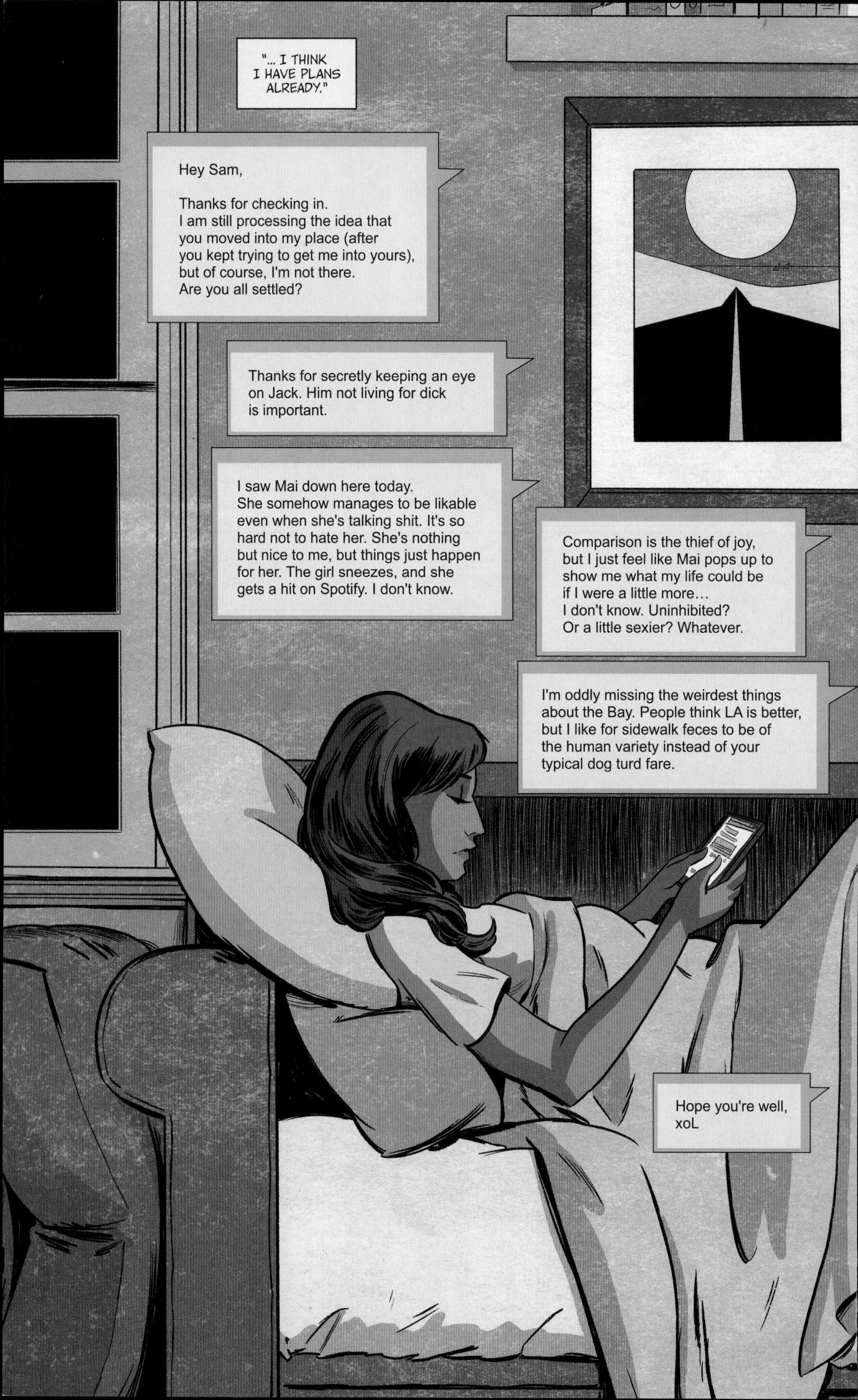
"... I THINK I HAVE PLANS ALREADY."
Hey Sam,
Thanks for checking in.
I am still processing the idea that you moved into my place (after you kept trying to get me into yours), but of course, I'm not there.
Are you all settled?
Thanks for secretly keeping an eye on Jack. Him not living for dick is important.
I saw Mai down here today.
She somehow manages to be likable even when she's talking shit. It's so hard not to hate her. She's nothing but nice to me, but things just happen for her. The girl sneezes, and she gets a hit on Spotify. I don't know.
Comparison is the thief of joy, but I just feel like Mai pops up to show me what my life could be if I were a little more…
I don't know. Uninhibited?
Or a little sexier? Whatever.
I'm oddly missing the weirdest things about the Bay. People think LA is better, but I like for sidewalk feces to be of the human variety instead of your typical dog turd fare.
Hope you're well,
xoL

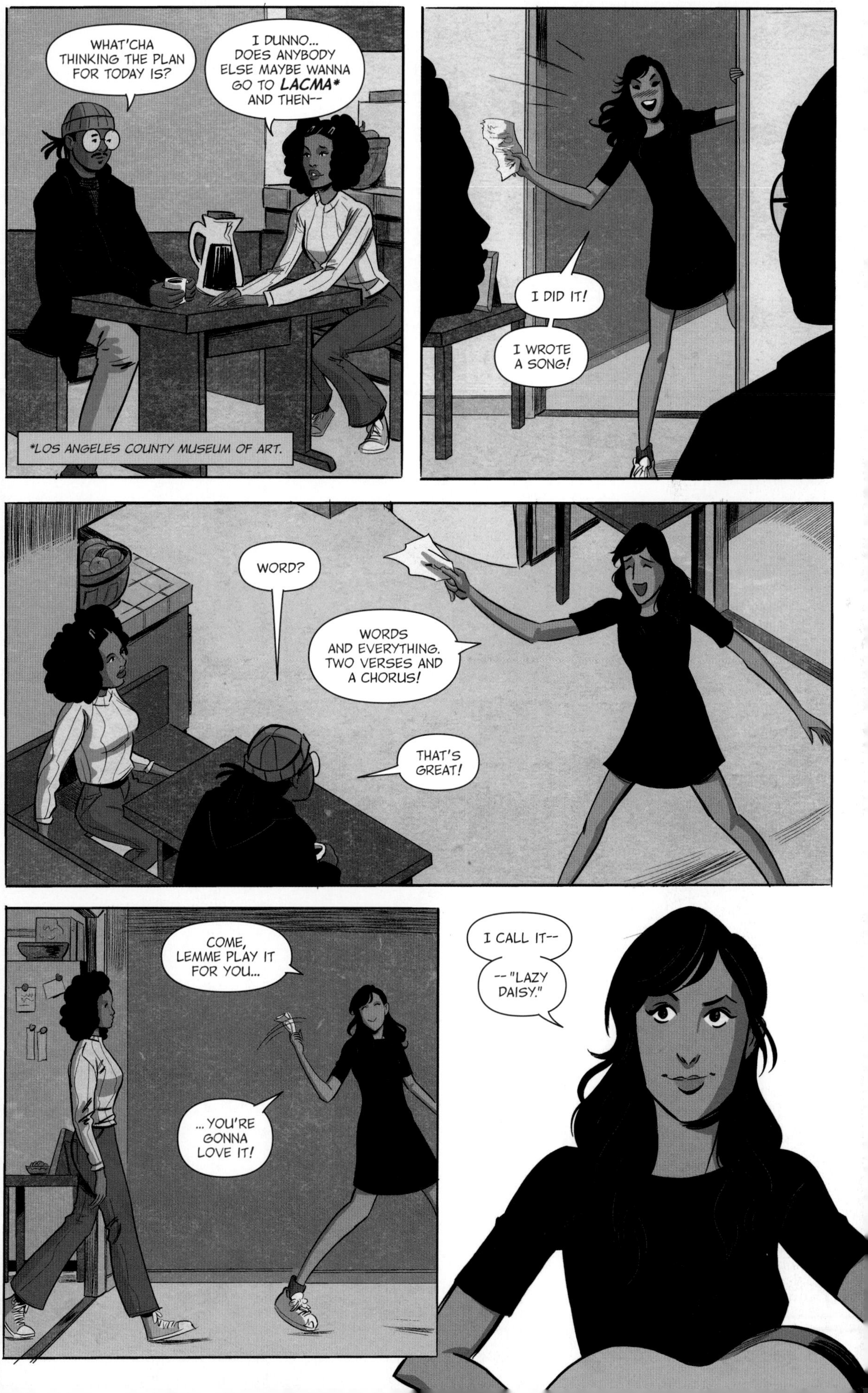
WHAT'CHA THINKING THE PLAN FOR TODAY IS?
I DUNNO... DOES ANYBODY ELSE MAYBE WANNA GO TO **LACMA***
AND THEN--
*LOS ANGELES COUNTY MUSEUM OF ART.
I DID IT!
I WROTE A SONG!
WORD?
WORDS AND EVERYTHING. TWO VERSES AND A CHORUS!
THAT'S GREAT!
COME, LEMME PLAY IT FOR YOU...
...YOU'RE GONNA LOVE IT!
I CALL IT--
--"LAZY DAISY."

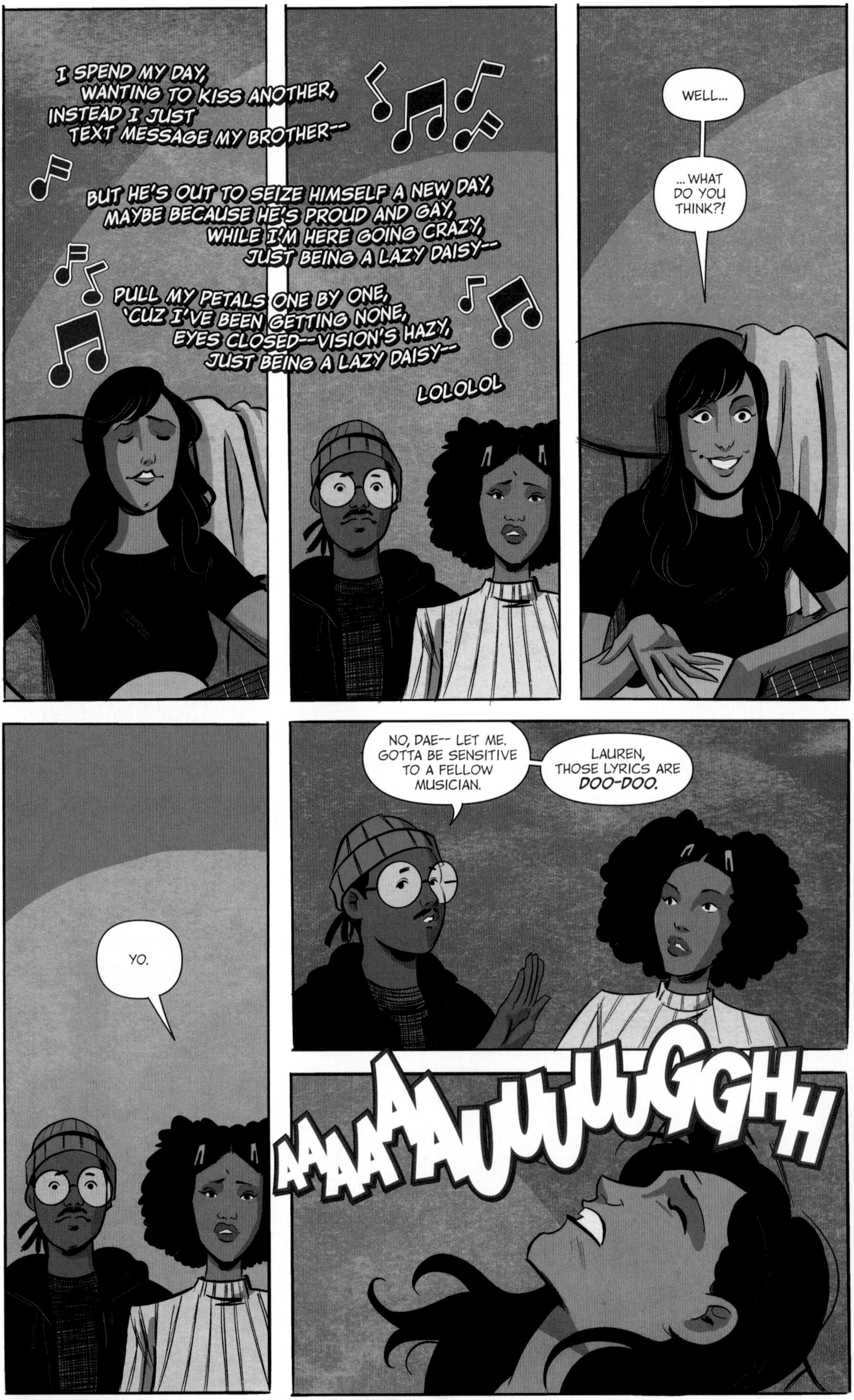
I SPEND MY DAY,
WANTING TO KISS ANOTHER,
INSTEAD I JUST
TEXT MESSAGE MY BROTHER--
BUT HE'S OUT TO SEIZE HIMSELF A NEW DAY,
MAYBE BECAUSE HE'S PROUD AND GAY,
WHILE I'M HERE GOING CRAZY,
JUST BEING A LAZY DAISY--
PULL MY PETALS ONE BY ONE,
'CUZ I'VE BEEN GETTING NONE,
EYES CLOSED--VISION'S HAZY,
JUST BEING A LAZY DAISY--
LOLOLOL
WELL...
...WHAT DO YOU THINK?!
YO.
NO, DAE-- LET ME. GOTTA BE SENSITIVE TO A FELLOW MUSICIAN.
LAUREN, THOSE LYRICS ARE DOO-DOO.
AAAAAAUUUUUGGHH

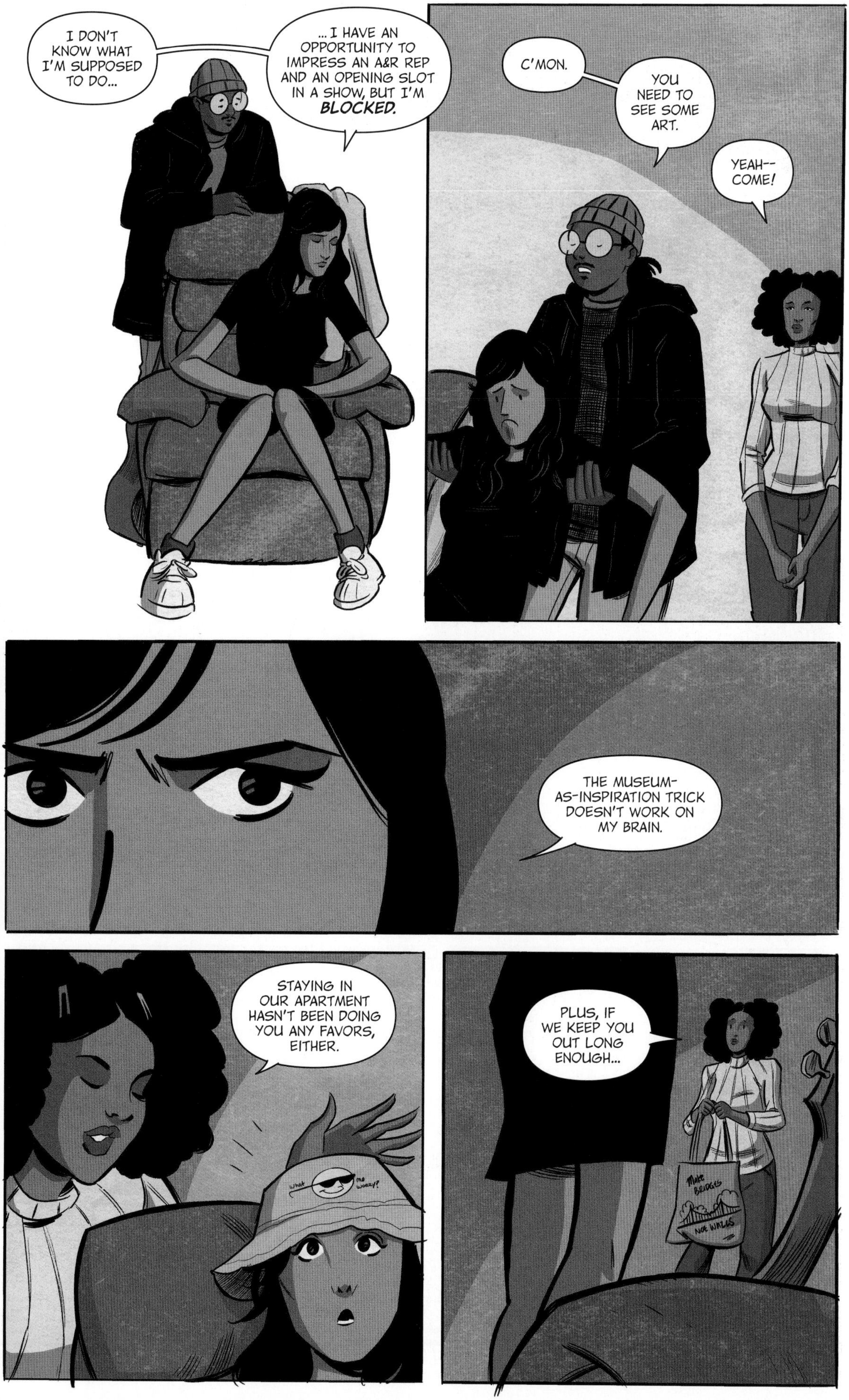
I DON'T KNOW WHAT I'M SUPPOSED TO DO...
... I HAVE AN OPPORTUNITY TO IMPRESS AN A&R REP AND AN OPENING SLOT IN A SHOW, BUT I'M **BLOCKED.**
C'MON.
YOU NEED TO SEE SOME ART.
YEAH-- COME!
THE MUSEUM-AS-INSPIRATION TRICK DOESN'T WORK ON MY BRAIN.
STAYING IN OUR APARTMENT HASN'T BEEN DOING YOU ANY FAVORS, EITHER.
PLUS, IF WE KEEP YOU OUT LONG ENOUGH...

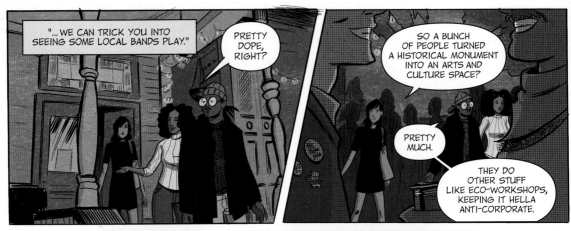

"...WE CAN TRICK YOU INTO SEEING SOME LOCAL BANDS PLAY."

PRETTY DOPE, RIGHT?

SO A BUNCH OF PEOPLE TURNED A HISTORICAL MONUMENT INTO AN ARTS AND CULTURE SPACE?

PRETTY MUCH.

THEY DO OTHER STUFF LIKE ECO-WORKSHOPS, KEEPING IT HELLA ANTI-CORPORATE.

COOL.

I'M GONNA GRAB A DRINK AND EXPLORE A LITTLE.

HAVE FUN! WE'LL BE OVER THERE.

REALLY, JACK? NOT GONNA CHECK ON YOUR SISTER? OR AGREE TO PICK UP HER SHIT FROM ANNIE?

OKAY, SETTLE SOMETHING FOR ME...

BEER
WINE
BOTTLE H₂O
BUBBLY H₂O

DOES THE MACADAMIA MILK AT GORILLA COFFEE IN THE MISSION TASTE LIKE USED SOCKS?

OR IS IT JUST ME?

HOT GUY TALKING TO LAUREN ABOUT COFFEE =

SCHWIING

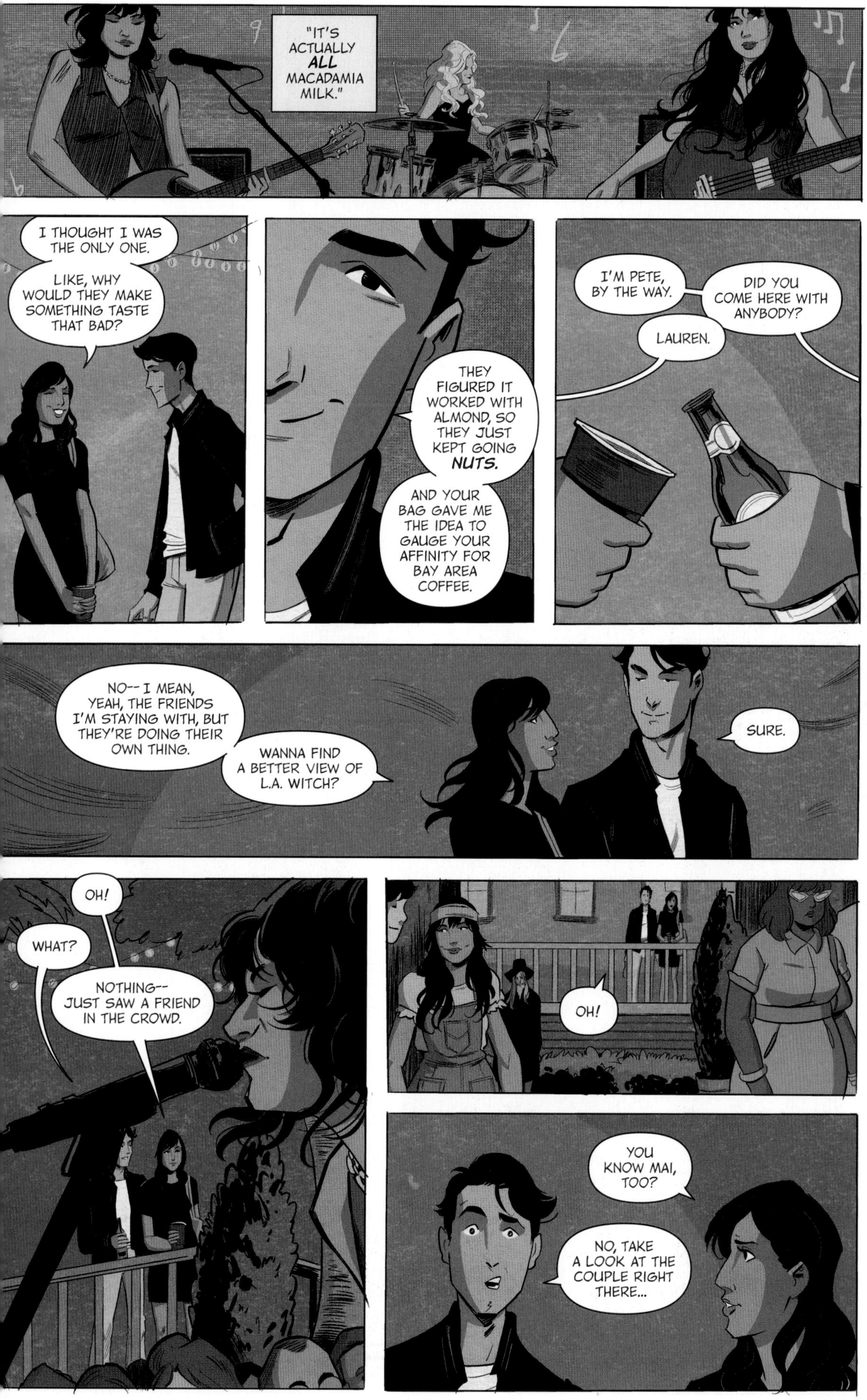
"IT'S ACTUALLY **ALL** MACADAMIA MILK."
I THOUGHT I WAS THE ONLY ONE.
LIKE, WHY WOULD THEY MAKE SOMETHING TASTE THAT BAD?
THEY FIGURED IT WORKED WITH ALMOND, SO THEY JUST KEPT GOING **NUTS.**
AND YOUR BAG GAVE ME THE IDEA TO GAUGE YOUR AFFINITY FOR BAY AREA COFFEE.
I'M PETE, BY THE WAY.
LAUREN.
DID YOU COME HERE WITH ANYBODY?
NO-- I MEAN, YEAH, THE FRIENDS I'M STAYING WITH, BUT THEY'RE DOING THEIR OWN THING.
WANNA FIND A BETTER VIEW OF L.A. WITCH?
SURE.
OH!
WHAT?
NOTHING-- JUST SAW A FRIEND IN THE CROWD.
OH!
YOU KNOW MAI, TOO?
NO, TAKE A LOOK AT THE COUPLE RIGHT THERE...

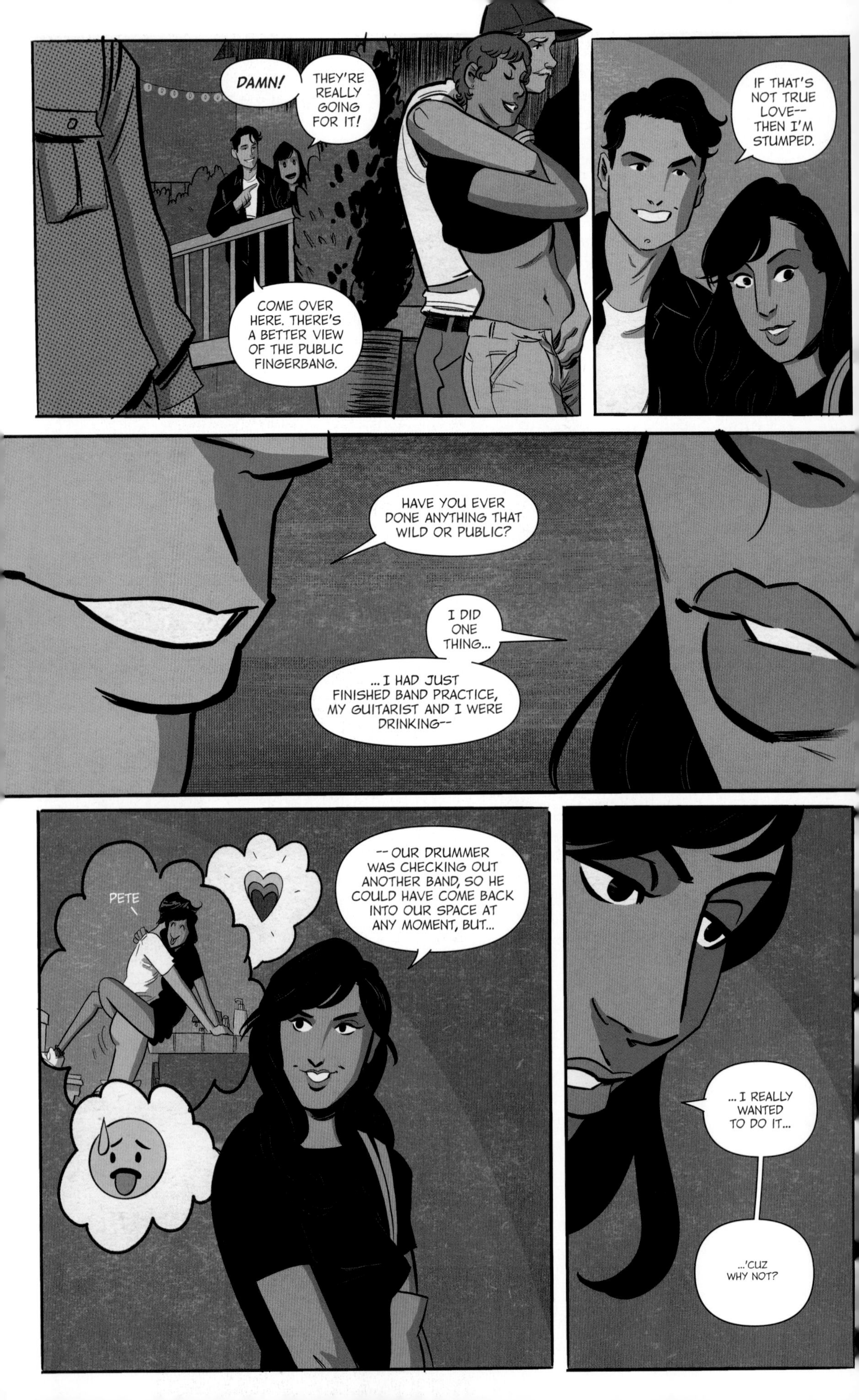
DAMN!
THEY'RE REALLY GOING FOR IT!
COME OVER HERE. THERE'S A BETTER VIEW OF THE PUBLIC FINGERBANG.
IF THAT'S NOT TRUE LOVE-- THEN I'M STUMPED.
HAVE YOU EVER DONE ANYTHING THAT WILD OR PUBLIC?
I DID ONE THING...
... I HAD JUST FINISHED BAND PRACTICE, MY GUITARIST AND I WERE DRINKING--
PETE
-- OUR DRUMMER WAS CHECKING OUT ANOTHER BAND, SO HE COULD HAVE COME BACK INTO OUR SPACE AT ANY MOMENT, BUT...
... I REALLY WANTED TO DO IT...
...'CUZ WHY NOT?

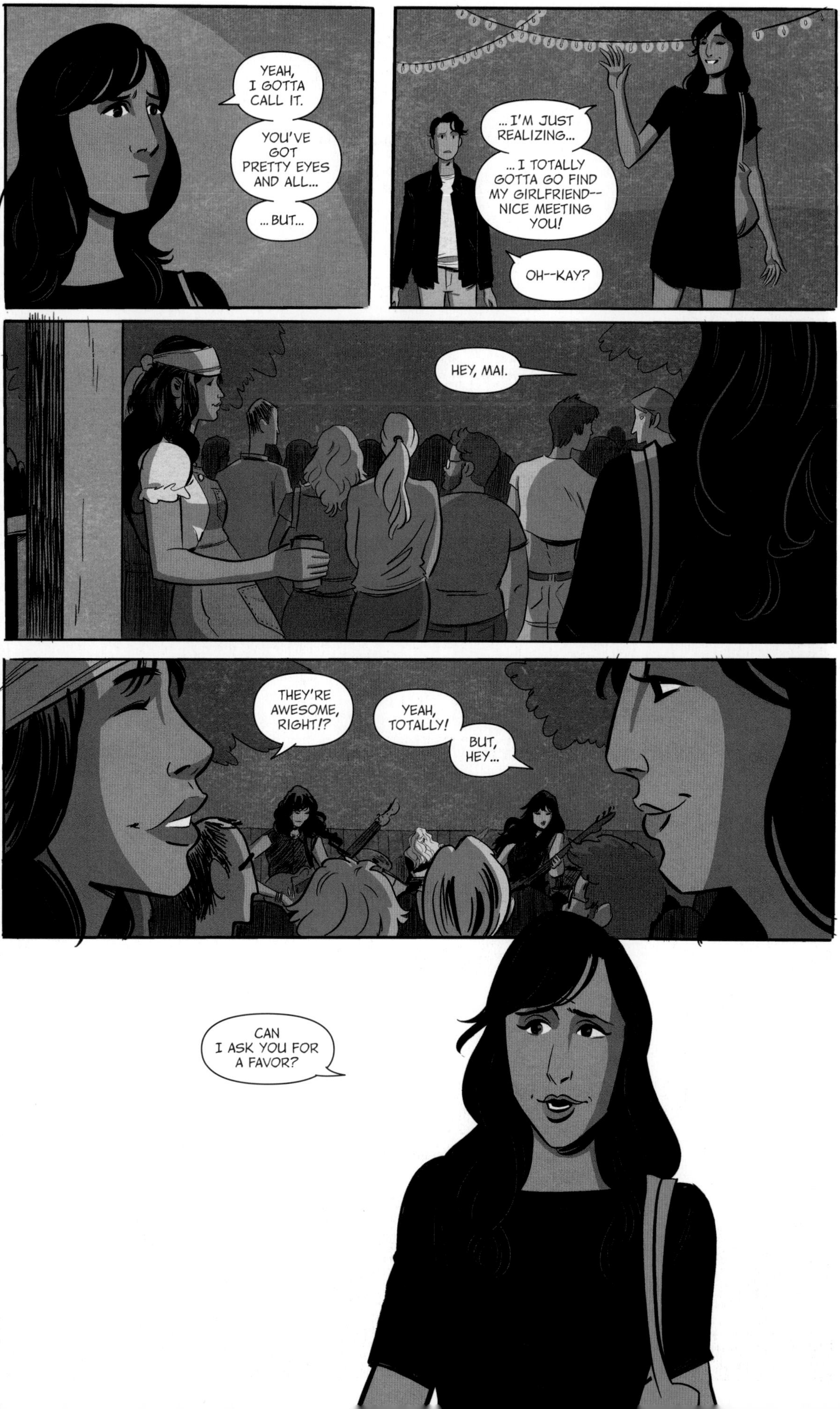
YEAH, I GOTTA CALL IT.
YOU'VE GOT PRETTY EYES AND ALL...
...BUT...
...I'M JUST REALIZING...
...I TOTALLY GOTTA GO FIND MY GIRLFRIEND-- NICE MEETING YOU!
OH--KAY?
HEY, MAI.
THEY'RE AWESOME, RIGHT!?
YEAH, TOTALLY!
BUT, HEY...
CAN I ASK YOU FOR A FAVOR?

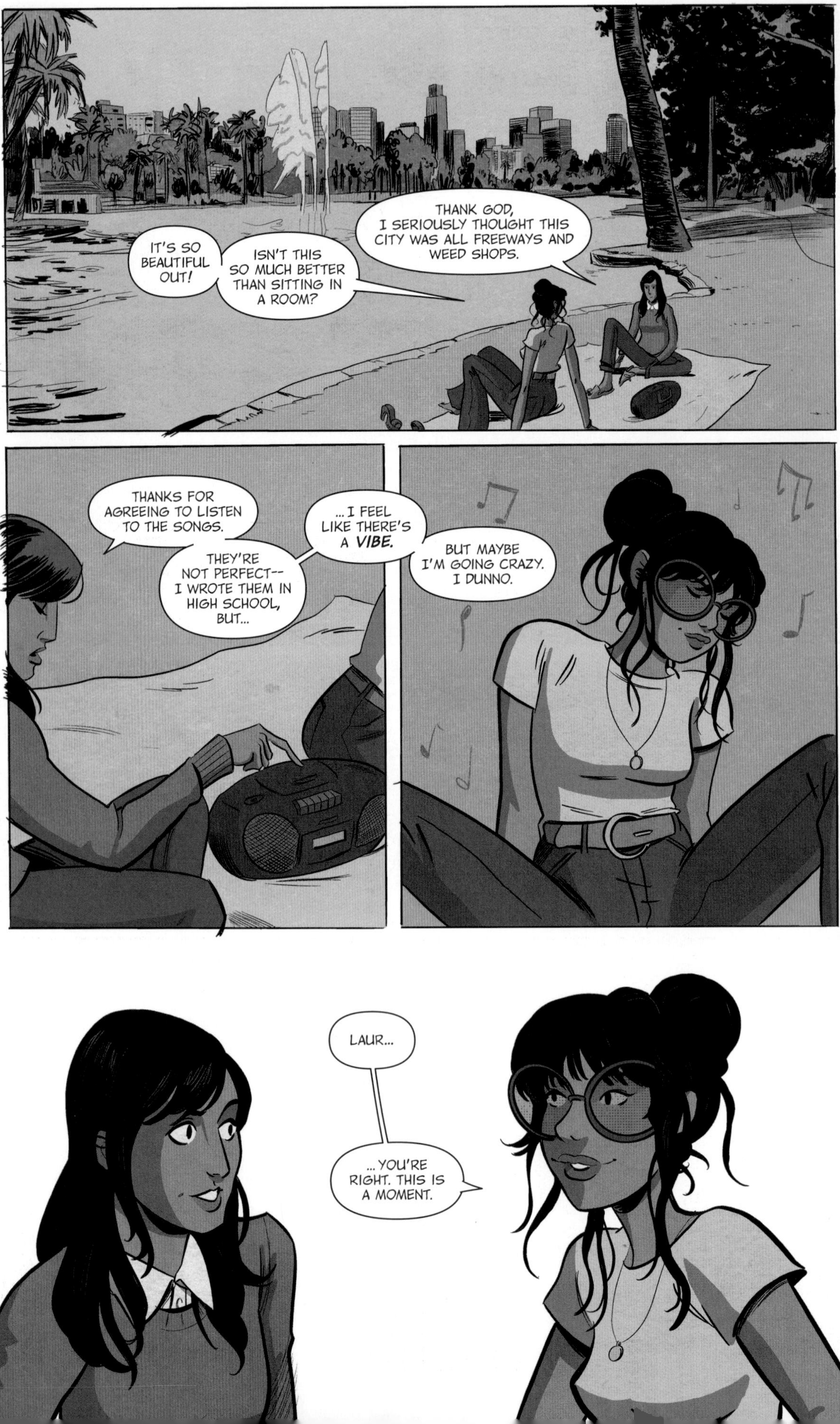
IT'S SO BEAUTIFUL OUT!
ISN'T THIS SO MUCH BETTER THAN SITTING IN A ROOM?
THANK GOD, I SERIOUSLY THOUGHT THIS CITY WAS ALL FREEWAYS AND WEED SHOPS.
THANKS FOR AGREEING TO LISTEN TO THE SONGS.
THEY'RE NOT PERFECT-- I WROTE THEM IN HIGH SCHOOL, BUT...
...I FEEL LIKE THERE'S A *VIBE.*
BUT MAYBE I'M GOING CRAZY. I DUNNO.
LAUR...
...YOU'RE RIGHT. THIS IS A MOMENT.

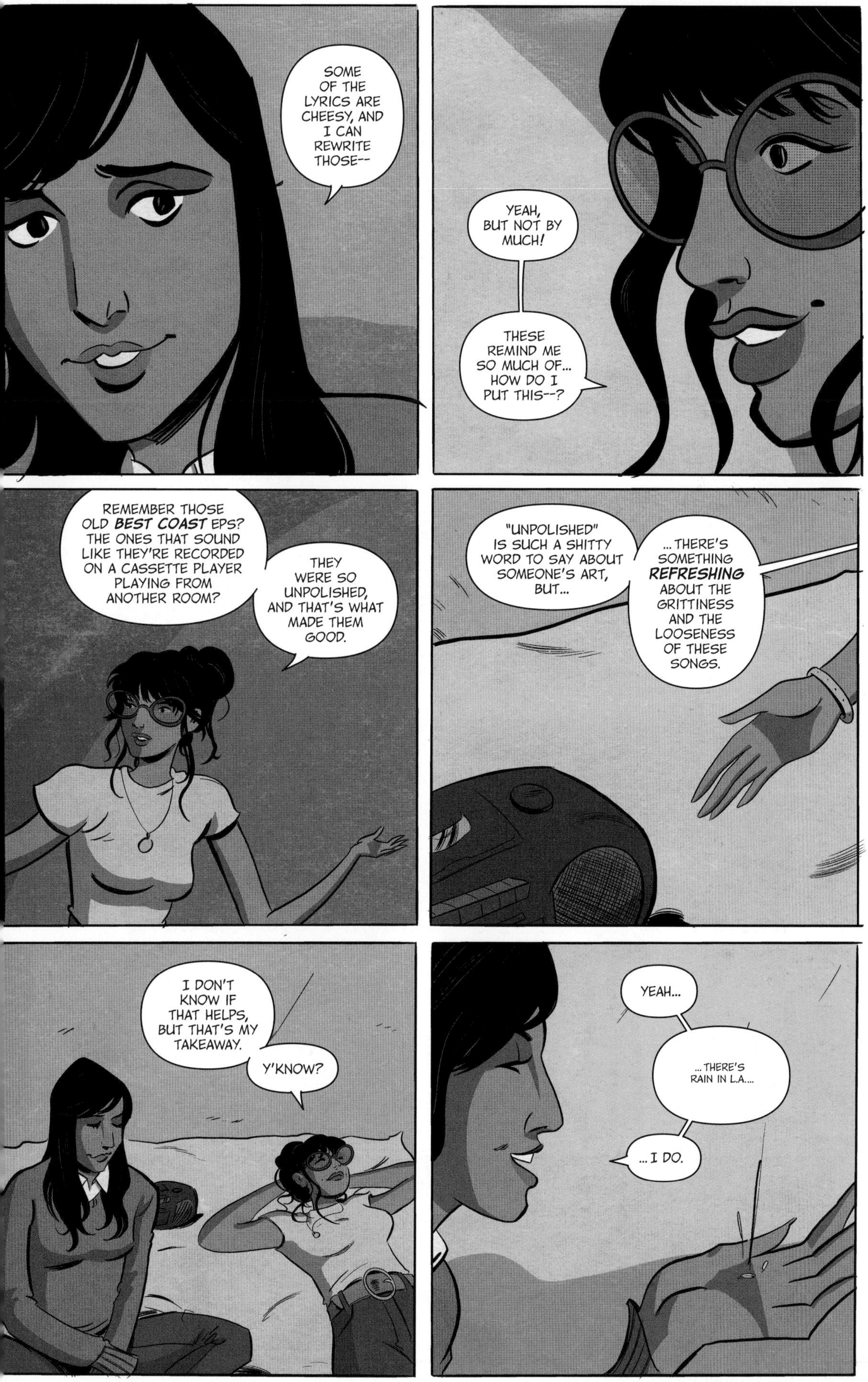
SOME OF THE LYRICS ARE CHEESY, AND I CAN REWRITE THOSE--
YEAH, BUT NOT BY MUCH!
THESE REMIND ME SO MUCH OF... HOW DO I PUT THIS--?
REMEMBER THOSE OLD BEST COAST EPS? THE ONES THAT SOUND LIKE THEY'RE RECORDED ON A CASSETTE PLAYER PLAYING FROM ANOTHER ROOM?
THEY WERE SO UNPOLISHED, AND THAT'S WHAT MADE THEM GOOD.
"UNPOLISHED" IS SUCH A SHITTY WORD TO SAY ABOUT SOMEONE'S ART, BUT...
... THERE'S SOMETHING REFRESHING ABOUT THE GRITTINESS AND THE LOOSENESS OF THESE SONGS.
I DON'T KNOW IF THAT HELPS, BUT THAT'S MY TAKEAWAY.
Y'KNOW?
YEAH...
... THERE'S RAIN IN L.A....
... I DO.

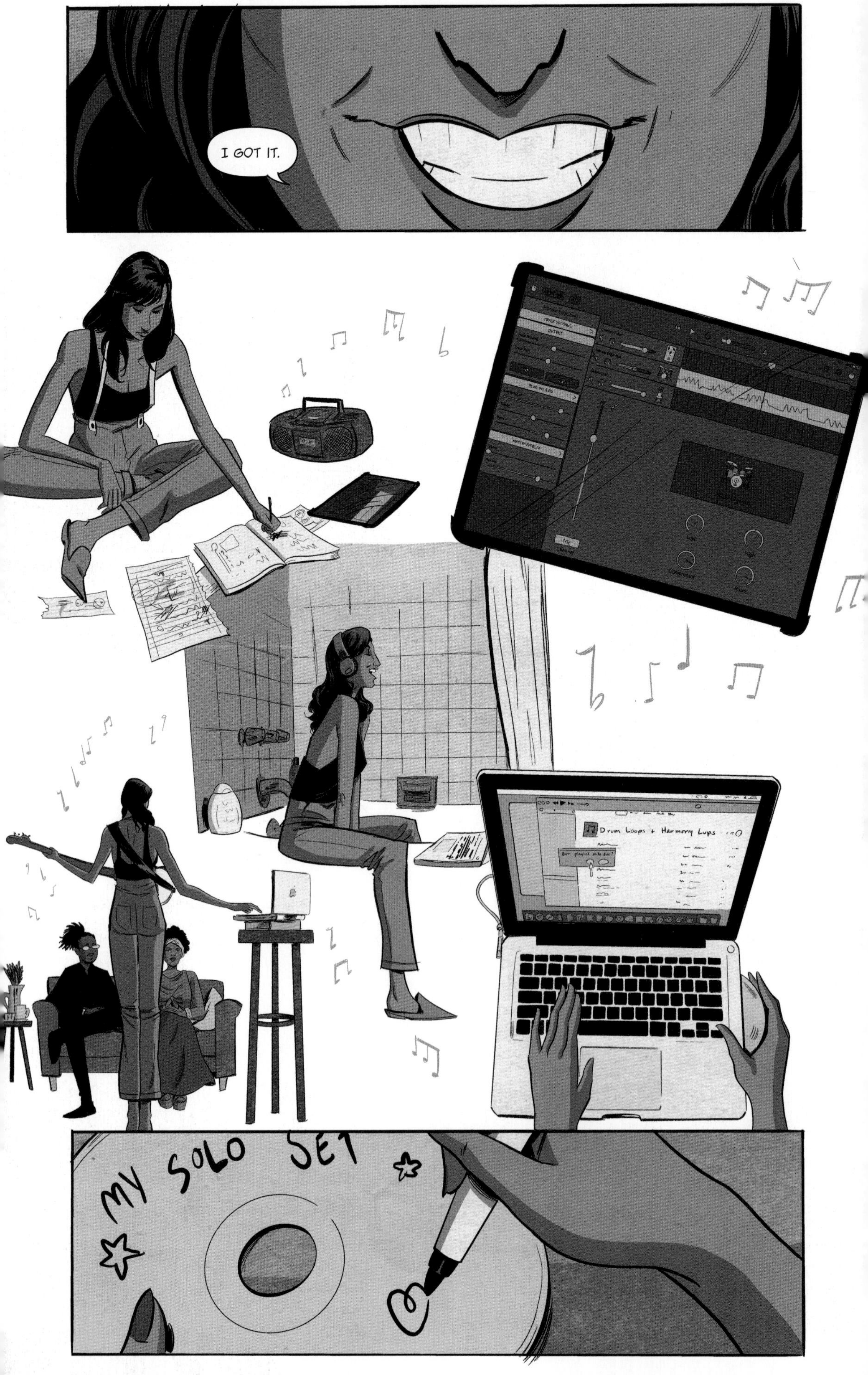
I GOT IT.
Drum Loops + Harmony Lups
Burn playlist onto disc?
MY SOLO SET

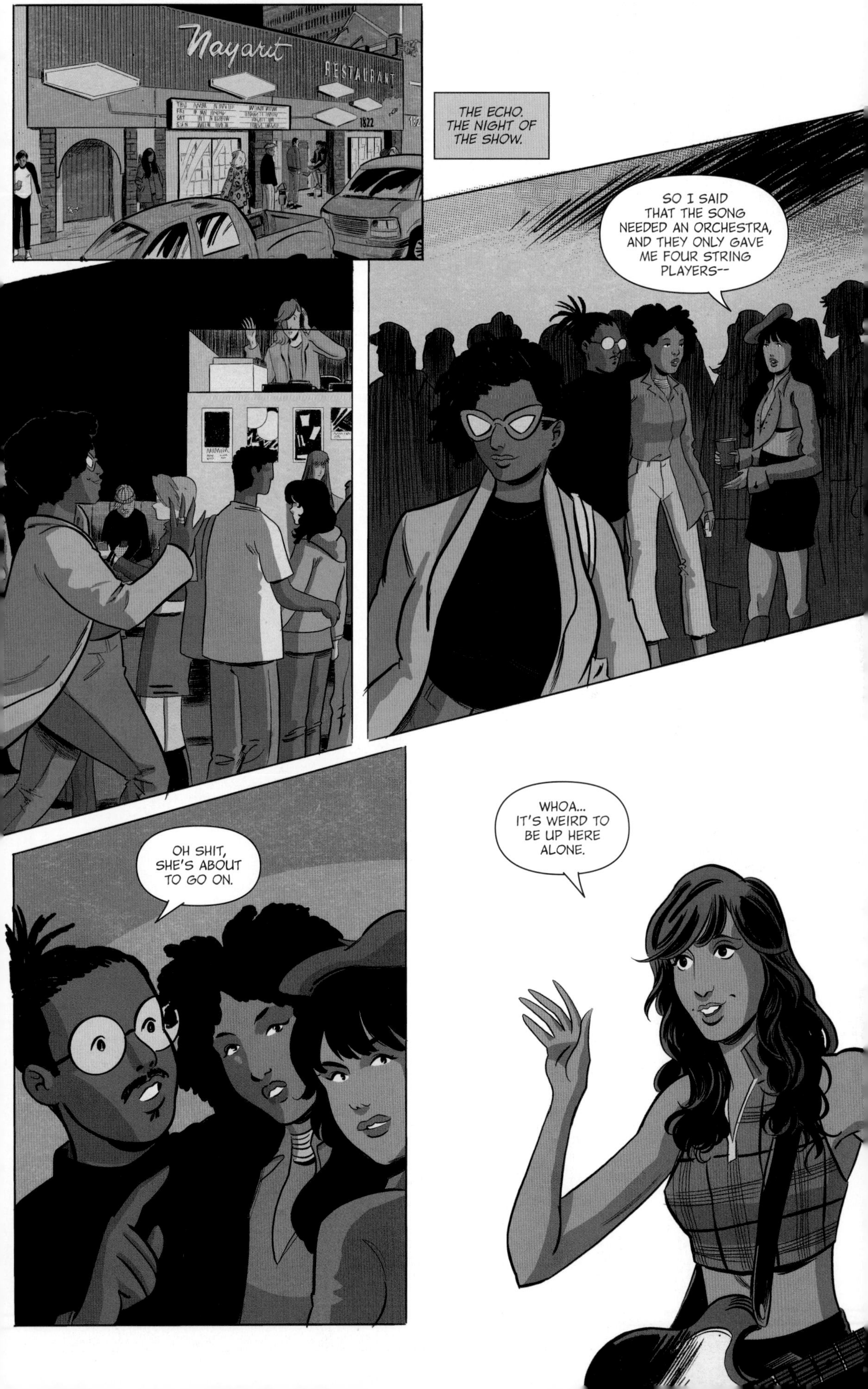
Nayarit
RESTAURANT
1822
THE ECHO. THE NIGHT OF THE SHOW.
SO I SAID THAT THE SONG NEEDED AN ORCHESTRA, AND THEY ONLY GAVE ME FOUR STRING PLAYERS--
OH SHIT, SHE'S ABOUT TO GO ON.
WHOA... IT'S WEIRD TO BE UP HERE ALONE.

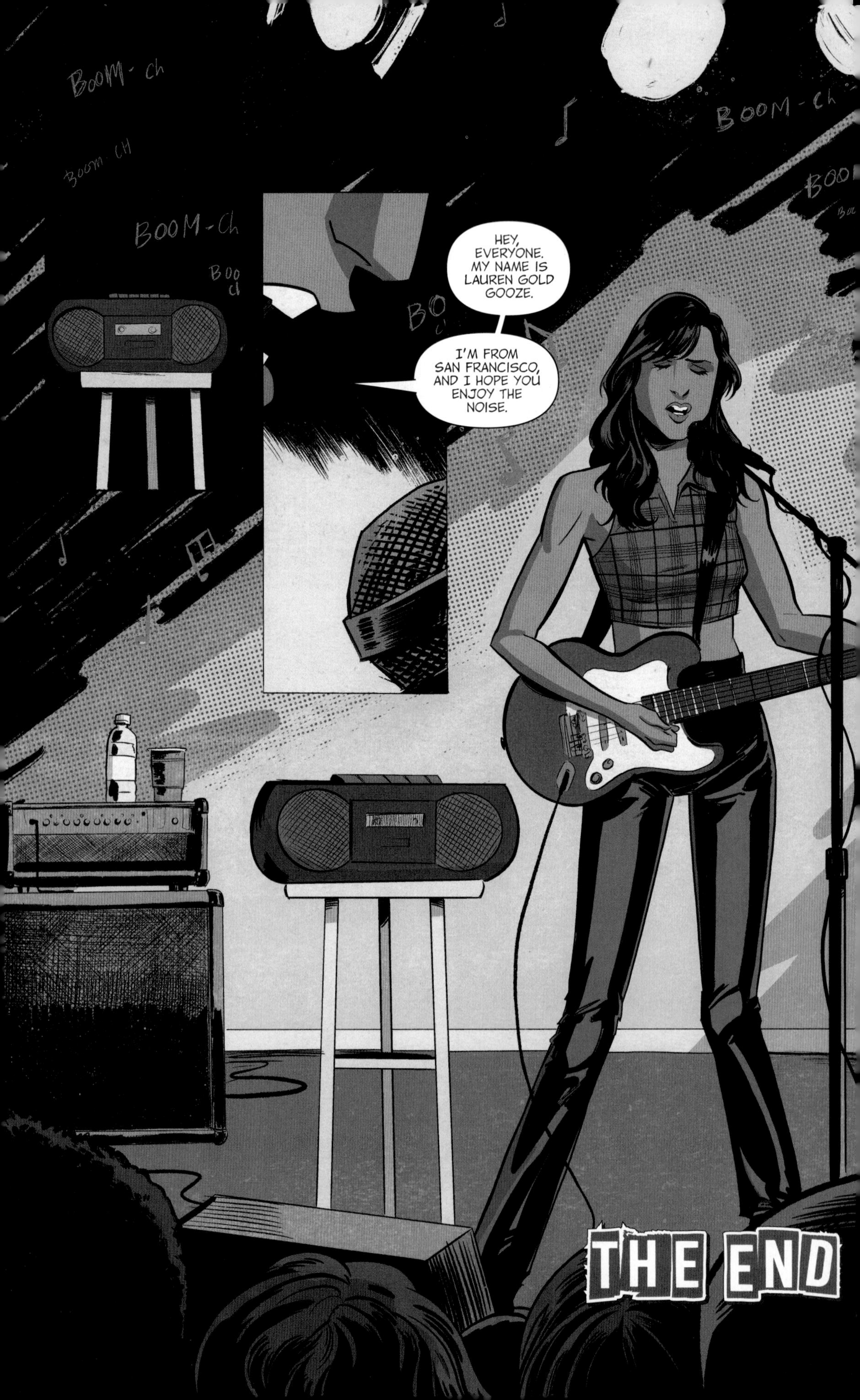
BOOM-Ch
BOOM CH
BOOM-Ch
BOOM-Ch
BOO
HEY, EVERYONE. MY NAME IS LAUREN GOLD GOOZE.
I'M FROM SAN FRANCISCO, AND I HOPE YOU ENJOY THE NOISE.
THE END

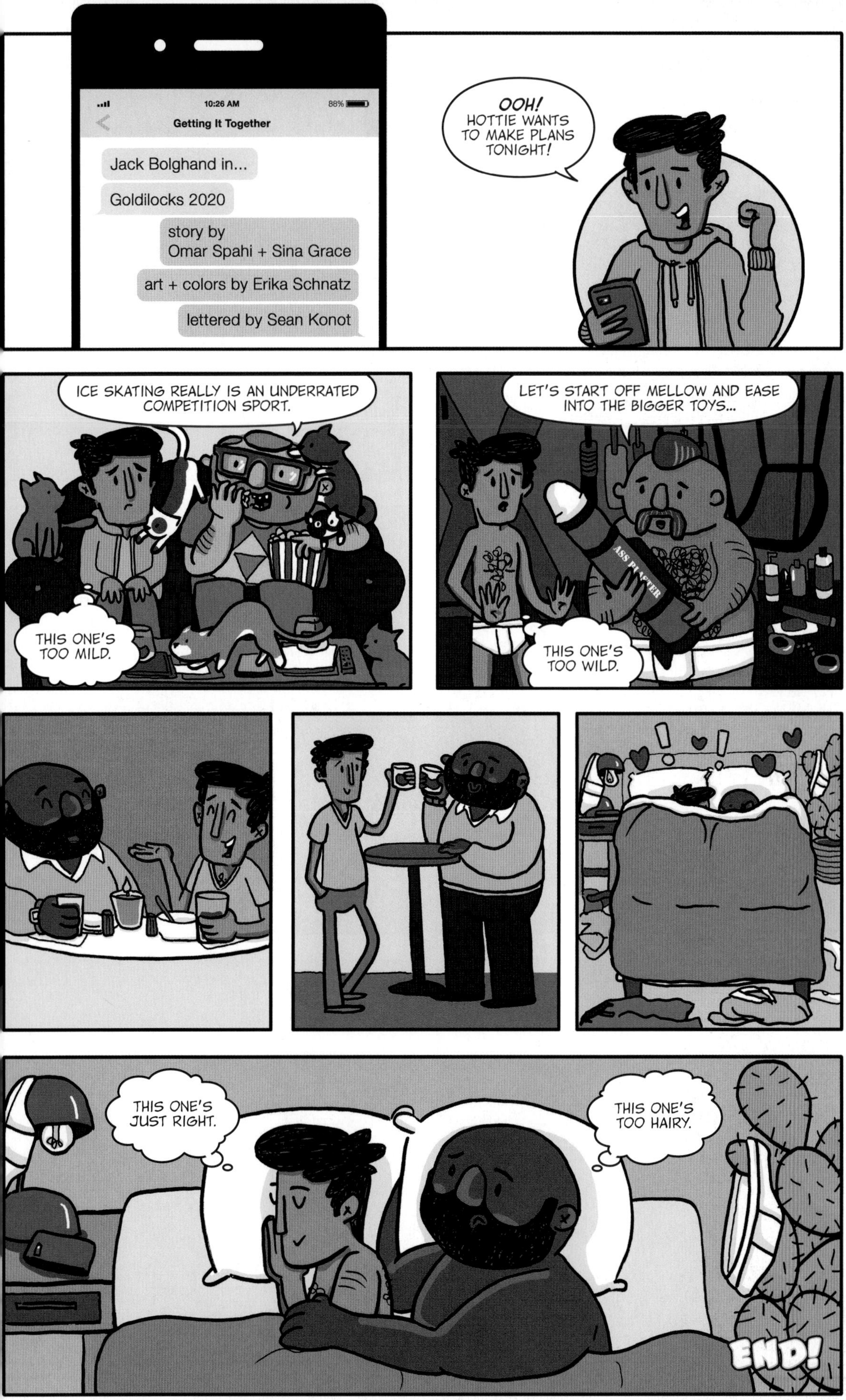
10:26 AM
88%
Getting It Together
Jack Bolghand in...
Goldilocks 2020
story by
Omar Spahi + Sina Grace
art + colors by Erika Schnatz
lettered by Sean Konot
OOH! HOTTIE WANTS TO MAKE PLANS TONIGHT!
ICE SKATING REALLY IS AN UNDERRATED COMPETITION SPORT.
THIS ONE'S TOO MILD.
LET'S START OFF MELLOW AND EASE INTO THE BIGGER TOYS...
ASS BLASTER
THIS ONE'S TOO WILD.
THIS ONE'S JUST RIGHT.
THIS ONE'S TOO HAIRY.
END!

"SAM'S STORY" STORY **SINA GRACE & OMAR SPAHI** ART + COLORS **ERIKA SCHNATZ** LETTERS **SEAN KONOT**

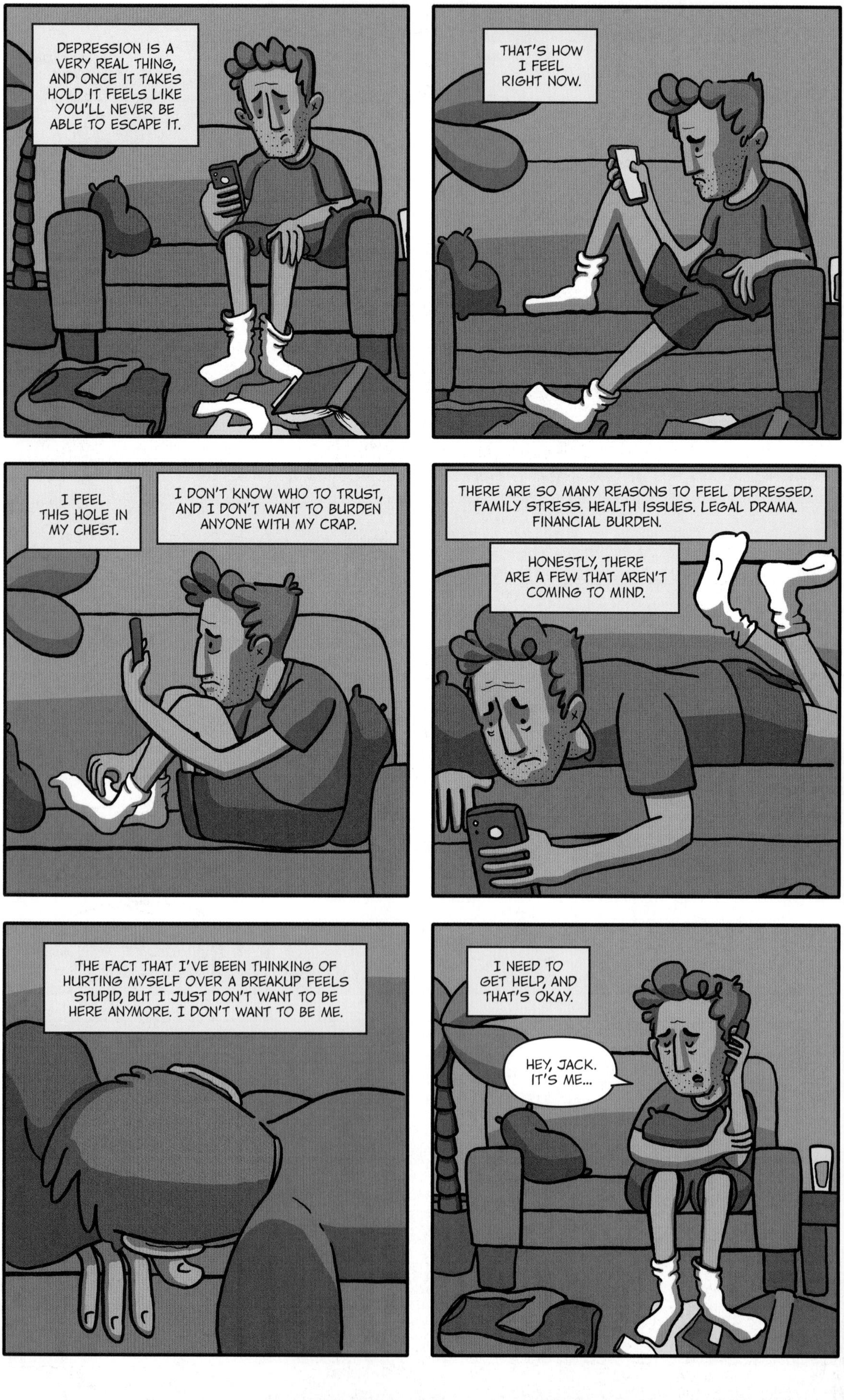
DEPRESSION IS A VERY REAL THING, AND ONCE IT TAKES HOLD IT FEELS LIKE YOU'LL NEVER BE ABLE TO ESCAPE IT.
THAT'S HOW I FEEL RIGHT NOW.
I FEEL THIS HOLE IN MY CHEST.
I DON'T KNOW WHO TO TRUST, AND I DON'T WANT TO BURDEN ANYONE WITH MY CRAP.
THERE ARE SO MANY REASONS TO FEEL DEPRESSED. FAMILY STRESS. HEALTH ISSUES. LEGAL DRAMA. FINANCIAL BURDEN.
HONESTLY, THERE ARE A FEW THAT AREN'T COMING TO MIND.
THE FACT THAT I'VE BEEN THINKING OF HURTING MYSELF OVER A BREAKUP FEELS STUPID, BUT I JUST DON'T WANT TO BE HERE ANYMORE. I DON'T WANT TO BE ME.
I NEED TO GET HELP, AND THAT'S OKAY.
HEY, JACK. IT'S ME...

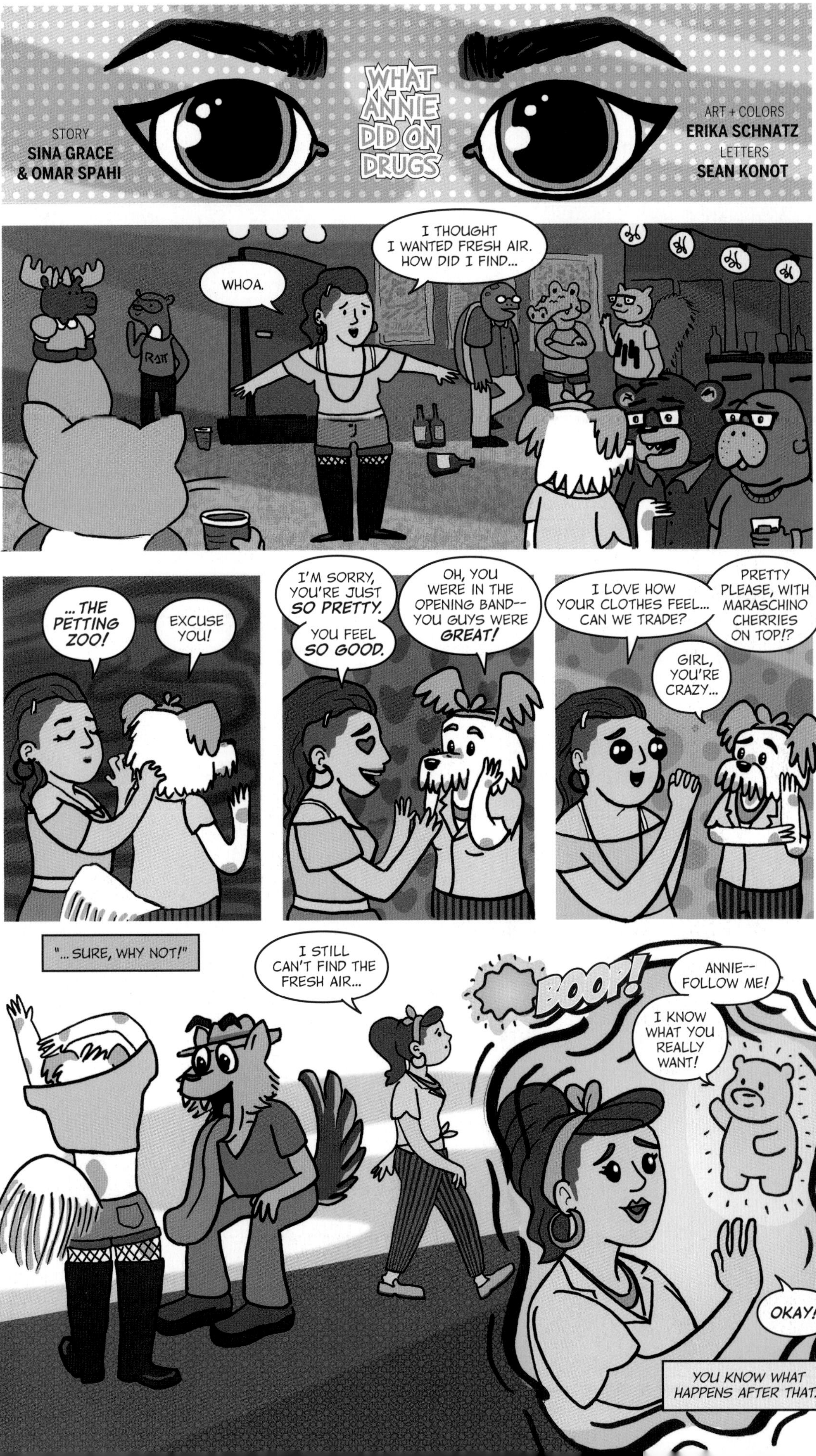
STORY
SINA GRACE
& OMAR SPAHI
WHAT ANNIE DID ON DRUGS
ART + COLORS
ERIKA SCHNATZ
LETTERS
SEAN KONOT
WHOA.
I THOUGHT I WANTED FRESH AIR. HOW DID I FIND...
RATT
...THE PETTING ZOO!
EXCUSE YOU!
I'M SORRY, YOU'RE JUST SO PRETTY.
YOU FEEL SO GOOD.
OH, YOU WERE IN THE OPENING BAND-- YOU GUYS WERE GREAT!
I LOVE HOW YOUR CLOTHES FEEL... CAN WE TRADE?
PRETTY PLEASE, WITH MARASCHINO CHERRIES ON TOP!?
GIRL, YOU'RE CRAZY...
"...SURE, WHY NOT!"
I STILL CAN'T FIND THE FRESH AIR...
BOOP!
ANNIE-- FOLLOW ME!
I KNOW WHAT YOU REALLY WANT!
OKAY!
YOU KNOW WHAT HAPPENS AFTER THAT.

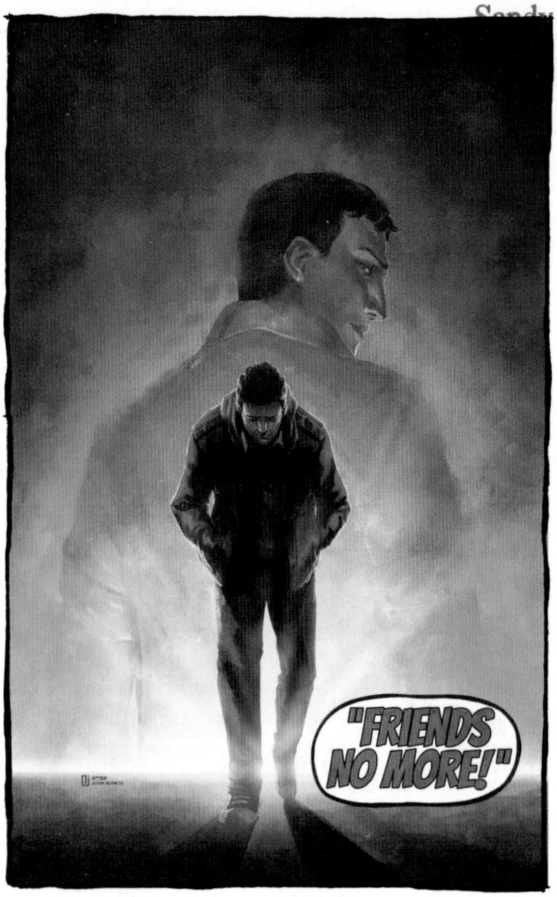
"FRIENDS NO MORE!"

issue three cover b
BY PEEJAY CATACUTAN

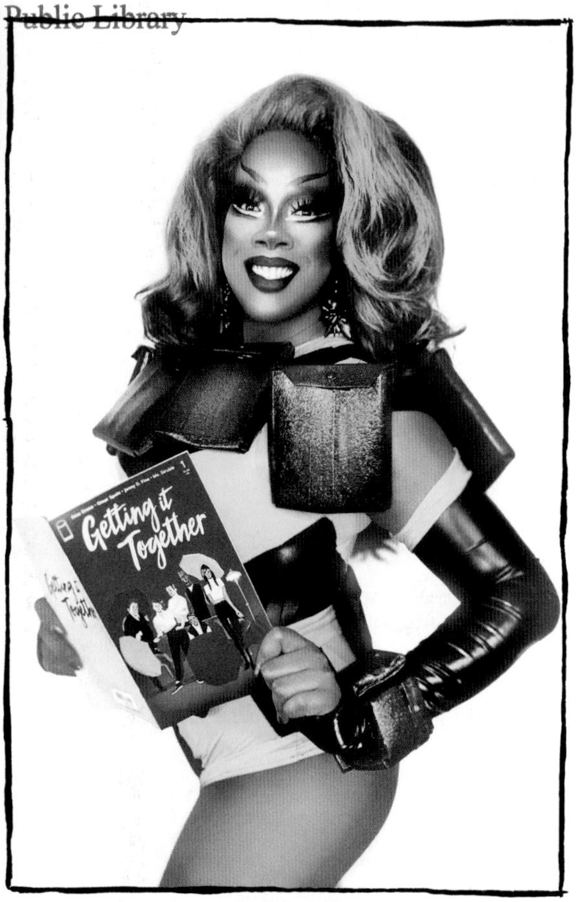
Getting it Together

issue three photo variant
BY DAX EXCLAMATIONPOINT

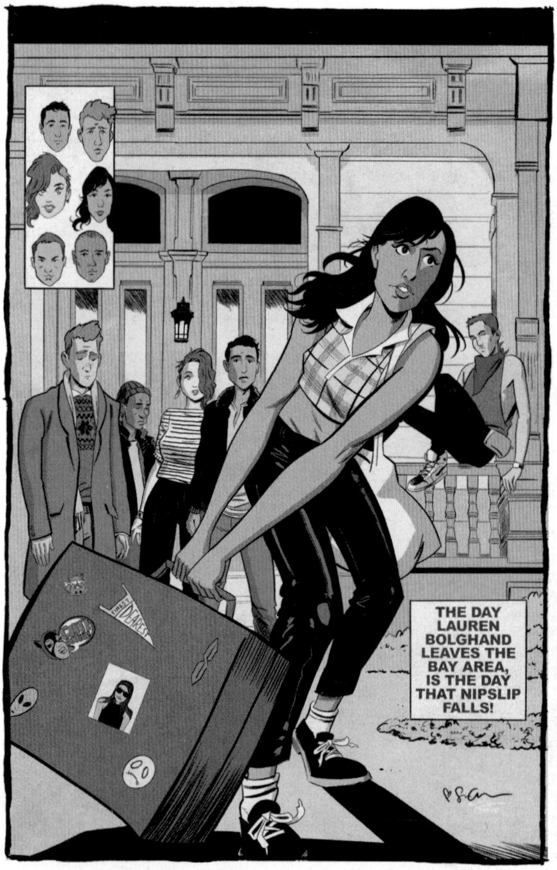
THE DAY LAUREN BOLGHAND LEAVES THE BAY AREA, IS THE DAY THAT NIPSLIP FALLS!

issue four cover b
BY SINA GRACE & MX. STRUBLE

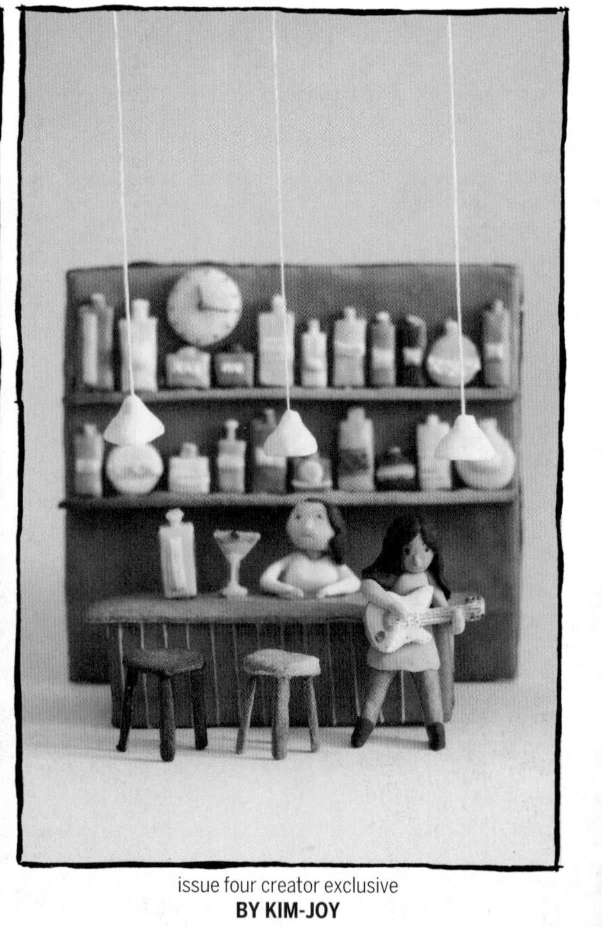

issue four creator exclusive
BY KIM-JOY